A Single Thread

MARIE BOSTWICK

KENSINGTON BOOKS
http://www.kensingtonbooks.com

KENSINGTON BOOKS are published by

Kensington Publishing Corp.
850 Third Avenue
New York, NY 10022

All Kensington titles, imprints, and distributed lines are available at special quantity discounts for bulk purchases for sales promotion, premiums, fund-raising, educational, or institutional use.

Special book excerpts or customized printings can also be created to fit specific needs. For details, write or phone the office of the Kensington Special Sales Manager: Attn. Special Sales Department. Kensington Publishing Corp., 850 Third Avenue, New York, NY 10022. Phone: 1-800-221-2647.

Kensington and the K logo Reg. U.S. Pat. & TM Off.

ISBN-13: 978-0-7582-2257-2
ISBN-10: 0-7582-2257-2

First Printing: November 2008
10   9   8   7

Printed in the United States of America

A Single Thread

Also by Marie Bostwick

ON WINGS OF THE MORNING

RIVER'S EDGE

FIELDS OF GOLD

"A High-Kicking Christmas" in COMFORT AND JOY

Published by Kensington Publishing Corporation

For my sister,
Elizabeth Walsh

With Gratitude

This story was inspired by the real life story of a wonderful and lovely lady, Deb Mella. Until recently, Deb was the owner of my favorite local quilt shop. She has now closed the shop to fully devote herself to her family, friends, and to raising breast cancer awareness. Thank you, Deb, for being so generous with your time and for educating me about this disease as well as the challenges of running a quilt shop. It is my fervent wish that, if only in a small way, this book will be a useful tool to you and others who are leading the charge for breast cancer awareness.

I am also deeply grateful to Joan Berlin for sharing her story with me and for answering my many questions about the diagnosis, treatment, and emotional impact of living with breast cancer. Joan, your open heart and candor made this book better. Thank you.

While A SINGLE THREAD is not an official sponsor of the foundation, I urge readers to join me in supporting the efforts of Susan G. Komen for the Cure® in their promise to end breast cancer. Whether you participate in a Quilt Pink event, run a 5K Race for the Cure, or simply write a check, your help is needed and appreciated. For more information, please visit *www.komen.org*.

Also, many thanks to Chris Boersma Smith, a dear friend and quilter extraordinaire, for taking my vision of the "Broken Hearts Mending" quilt and turning it into an actual design that even we quilters who are somewhat less than extraordinaire can make.

And finally, my thanks to the people I've come to think of as "the team," Brad Skinner, Audrey LaFehr, Jill Grossjean, Nancy Berland, Adam Kortekas, and Sherry Kuehl.

Prologue

Evelyn Dixon

One of my happiest memories is one of my mother's worst.
It was summer. I was five years old and would be starting kindergarten in a few weeks, so Mother decided to take me shopping for school shoes. She got behind the wheel of our Ford Fairlane and cranked down the window so we wouldn't be stifled by heat and the exhaled smoke of her cigarettes. I climbed into the front seat and off we went.

The safety belt, an accessory made mandatory by the enlightened legislators of Wisconsin two years before, was wedged down a narrow crevasse between the seats, forgotten among the gas receipts, discarded gum wrappers, and a grainy mixture of sand and cookie crumbs—the debris of our annual vacation trip to the beaches of Door County. The idea of unearthing the belt and buckling it low and tight across my lap for our trip to the J. C. Penney department store never crossed my mother's mind. It was 1963. There was less to be afraid of then.

Penney's had the only escalator in our town, a distinction it would claim for another eight years. Later, when someone built a big shopping center on the edge of town, J. C. Penney would desert its downtown store and move there, leaving Main Street with a full city block of darkened display windows and empty parking spaces. The new mall would have three escalators, a glass elevator with gold-tone trim and white marquee lights in the middle, and four stores with at least twice the square footage of our old J. C. Penney. But back in 1963, Penney's was the biggest store in town, and I believed they carried at least one of every single thing that was offered for sale on the face of the earth.

After we bought a pair of tan and white saddle shoes exactly like the pair I'd just outgrown, Mother decided she needed one of those new electric coffee percolators, so we rode the escalator upstairs to the housewares department.

Normally, I stuck close to my mother's side, so I don't know what made me do it, but while she was trying to decide between an eight- or ten-cup model, I quietly slipped away to explore the bed and bath department.

Walking between a valley of shelves piled high with sheets, I admired the delicate scallops and embroidery stitching on the edges of pillowcases, poking holes through the cellophane wrappings of the packages so my fingers could stroke the smooth, crisp sheeting inside, marveling as I considered the folded towers surrounding me and realized that white wasn't just white but an enormous spectrum of whiteness from snow and alabaster to marshmallow and pearl. Amazing.

Then I heard my mother's voice calling, beckoning me with the calm, singsong "Eve-lyn" she used to summon me to supper every night, the first syllable accented and extended before dropping into a short, lower-toned chirrup at the end, a secret call between hen and chick. I began walking toward the sound of my mother's voice, but when I turned a corner in the valley of sheets, I stopped, frozen and fascinated.

My eyes rested upon midnight, then rolled skyward to navy, royal, cobalt, progressing to aqua, seafoam, avocado, moss, and forest, and then, reaching the ceiling, floated down a row of yellows, lemon to electric and every sunny tint between, then to the orange shades, peach to rust, before reaching the floor and beginning the journey again. It was an entire wall of towels, a delicious, soft rainbow that, as I drew closer, filled every inch of my field of vision and made me feel, for reasons I still cannot explain, simply and completely happy.

I forgot all about my mother, didn't hear her soft chirp rise in volume and intensity as a minute passed and then two with no answer from me. Wanting to take in the full perspective of what lay before me the way an art lover backs away from a canvas to experience the impact of a painting, I retreated a few steps until I backed into a cabinet holding a pile of shower curtains and sank down to the floor. I wrapped my arms around my knees and pulled them up under my chin, making myself very quiet and very small, hearing nothing, seeing only the colors displayed before me . . . for me.

Until the day she died, whenever Mother told this story, relating her growing panic, the numbers of clerks and customers that combed the aisles, dressing rooms, and interiors of clothing racks searching for me, and the relief that actually made her dizzy when a dishwasher salesman finally found me, she instinctively clutched at her heart as if reliving the palpitations. Then she would shake her head and say, "Evelyn, you were always such a good little girl. Whatever were you thinking of?"

I never did find a way to explain it to her. For my mother, those fifteen minutes when I was "lost" were pure hell. For me, pure bliss.

Those rich, rolling gradations of color spoke to me, like finding the end of the rainbow and walking into it, reaching out with both hands and discovering that which had, from a distance, seemed no more substantial than vapor, refracted light, and hope had heft, and texture, and substance if you drew close. I found comfort in the predictability and measured pace of the spectrum as it progressed from blue to green to yellow to red and back to blue again, excitement and unbounded promise as I considered the infinite number of patterns and expressions that could be achieved simply by lifting one color, or two, or twenty from their natural context and placing them somewhere else in the column. For a five-year-old in 1963, a time when Crayolas came twenty-four to a box, it was an astounding revelation.

I never knew how to explain the importance of that moment to my mother, though later I would come to understand what it meant to her. For Mother, my disappearance was a reminder that in the time it takes to decide between eight cups and ten, or to turn your back, or take a breath, the things you love most can be lost, perhaps forever. Between one breath and the next, your whole world can change.

One morning, you may wake up on a sunny day in early spring, happy, your mind filled with nothing weightier than the thought of what you'll put in your garden this year or what fabrics should go into your next quilt. And then a conversation begins, or the telephone rings, or the lab report arrives, and everything you thought you knew for certain is suddenly called into question.

It's a lesson I've learned from personal experience, and, for a time, the weight of that lesson almost sank me. But then I learned something else: the pendulum swings both ways.

One moment you may be trapped in a maze of despair so thick there seems to be no hope of ever finding your way back to the place where you were happy, or at least happy enough, and then you stumble around a corner and find yourself in a different world. Taking one step down a cobblestone path that looks like a blind alley, and then another, going forward not from any sense of expectation or faith but only because there is nowhere else to go, you suddenly and surprisingly find yourself in a wide, sunny place where potted geraniums bloom in scarlet mounds and dormant dreams lie behind wooden doors with chipped paint and rusting hinges, waiting. From one breath to the next, everything changes.

Life is as terrible and wonderful as all that. I know from experience.

1

Evelyn Dixon

Later I would learn that that particular stretch of Interstate 84, crossing from New York into Connecticut, is usually choked with traffic. But at one in the morning with only fifty miles to my destination, mine was the only car in sight, and I sailed down the empty lanes. It wasn't until he pulled up behind me that I saw the state trooper and looked down at my speedometer.

Ninety. He had me. I called myself a name, shifted my foot from the accelerator to the brake, and started to pull over even before the pulsating strobe of colored lights filled my rearview mirror.

The patrolman was a nice-looking young man. If he had smiled he would have looked a lot like Garrett, but his expression was stony. Strange to be face-to-face with an authority figure young enough to be my son, but when he asked for my license and registration I obediently handed them over.

"Ms. Dixon, do you have any idea how fast you were going?"

"About ninety," I said honestly. There was no point in lying when I already knew he knew the truth; besides, I'm a terrible liar. "I started out in Nashville this morning and decided to drive straight through to New Bern, but I wasn't deliberately speeding.

The road was clear, and I guess I just got lost in my thoughts. I didn't realize how fast I was going until I saw you."

He looked at my license. "You're from Texas? And you're driving all the way to New Bern by yourself?" I nodded.

"What brings you here?" he asked.

"It's kind of a long story."

Three days before, I'd had no more thought of driving to New England than of becoming an astronaut and taking a trip to the International Space Station.

When the doorbell rang at exactly ten-thirty that morning, I knew who it was: Mr. Lindsay from Elite Moving and Storage. Rob's secretary had left a message the day before saying that a Mr. Lindsay would be coming to give me an estimate and a date to pack my furniture and move it out of the house I'd called home for the last twenty years.

Mr. Lindsay was wearing a pair of polished brown Justin cowboy boots just like Rob's. He smiled broadly as he sat at down at my kitchen table, pulled a clipboard out of his briefcase, and started filling out paperwork. I disliked him instantly.

"And what address will we be delivering to?" he asked without looking up.

"I don't know."

He lifted his head, his eyebrows rising to arcs of annoyance. "Mrs. Dixon, I can't very well estimate the price for your move if I don't know how far we're moving you."

"Well, I'm sorry about that, Mr. Lindsay, but I simply don't know yet!" I snapped. "And if that is inconvenient for you, or Elite Moving and Storage, or Rob Dixon . . . well, I frankly don't give a damn. It isn't like *I* invited you to come over here!"

This outburst was so unlike me. For the last several weeks all I'd been able to do was cry; now here I was cursing at a complete stranger. I was shocked, but Mr. Lindsay didn't appear to be.

Putting two and two together, his brows lowered and his face became a mask of practiced, utterly unconvincing sympathy. He had seen this all before.

"I'm sorry, Mrs. Dixon. I wasn't aware of the circumstances of your move. I know how hard this must be for you; divorce always is. But please understand, I'm just trying to help you. Now, it's my understanding that the new owners are planning on moving in on the fifth, so that means you'll need to be out of here by the end of next month. When do you think you'll finalize your plans?" His voice was smooth and unflappable.

I sighed. "I'm looking at several condos in the area, but I haven't made up my mind yet. Not that it really makes much difference. They all look the same—fake granite countertops in tiny kitchens, white paint, four walls, sliding glass doors looking out onto a sad five-by-five square of concrete they call a patio. Each one is just as depressing as the one before."

"You know, there is a complex we've moved several ladies in your situation to, and they've been very happy," he said brightly.

"I see. You mean there's a central depot for storing discarded wives these days? Someplace where they warehouse the women who've passed their sell-by date and been replaced with newer models? How convenient." There was no point in taking my anger out on this man, but I couldn't help myself. It didn't seem to bother him though. He ignored my sarcasm and kept talking.

"My sister-in-law works in the sales office. Have you seen Rolling Hills at River's Edge? If you'd like, I could give Beverly a call and—"

I shook my head. "You mean the place over on Alamo Drive? The place with no hills and no river? No thanks."

"Well," Mr. Lindsay chuckled, "they might have been taking a little bit of literary license with the name, I'll give you that. There aren't any real hills between here and Austin, but there will be a river. Beverly told me that they're starting on the excavation next week."

"A fake river?" I laughed. "Thanks, Mr. Lindsay, but I'm up to here with that sort of thing—plastic flowers, simulated wood-grain cabinets, planned communities, absent friends, false promises, broken homes. I want something real. I've had enough of counterfeits, and, for that matter, I've had enough of this conversation." The legs of the chair made a scraping sound against the laminate wood flooring as I got to my feet. Mr. Lindsay looked surprised and a little confused.

"Mrs. Dixon, I know you're upset, but we really do have to make some decisions here—"

"No." I shook my head. "*We* don't have to do anything. And *I'm* not going to. Not today. I'm sorry that you came out here for nothing, Mr. Lindsay, but this is still my home." I could feel tears pooling in my eyes, but my voice sounded strong in my ears. "You need to leave."

As I walked him to the front door and opened it, it occurred to me that I needed to do the same.

The next thing I knew, I was in the front seat of my car, heading northeast, and my suitcase was in the back. I really didn't know where I was going, only that I was. But by the time I neared the city limits, I decided I'd better tell someone that I was leaving. I called his office in Seattle.

"Claremont Solutions. This is Garrett."

"Hi, honey. It's Mom."

"Hi, Mom. Are you all right?" Garrett is my only child. He's a good son and has always been protective of me, even more so since the divorce.

"I'm fine, sweetheart. I've just decided to go on a trip, and I thought you'd want to know."

"Well, that's great," he said cautiously. "I've been telling you to take a vacation for months now—anything besides sitting around the house and moping—but this is kind of sudden, isn't it? Where are you going?"

And suddenly I knew. "To New England. To see the fall colors. I've wanted to go for years, but your dad never would. His idea of a vacation has always involved sitting on a beach and baking to a golden brown, even if that meant I had to spend the whole time hiding under an umbrella."

My complexion has always been fair. Twenty minutes in strong sun can leave me with a nasty burn. But even after the dermatologist removed a malignant mole from my shoulder a few years ago, Rob continued booking our vacations in tropical locales. I knew I shouldn't subject Garrett to my acrimonious memories of his father, but sometimes it was impossible to swallow back the anger.

When Garrett took a job as a computer programmer all the way in Seattle after college, I was so disappointed. I'd been hoping he'd settle down closer to home, someplace where he could come home for holidays or drop by on weekends. Now I was almost happy that he lived so far away, too far to get caught in the fallout as Rob and I flung accusations at each other across a battlefield barbed with betrayal and lawyers. No matter how bitter I was, I never wanted Garrett to feel like he had to take sides in all this.

"Well, that sounds great, Mom," Garrett replied, ignoring my commentary. "Do you know when you'll be back? Where are you staying?"

"Actually"—I smiled to myself—"I have no idea. I guess I'll stay wherever looks good and come back when I feel like it."

I heard Garrett tap-tapping his finger against the telephone receiver. "Excuse me? Operator? Excuse me? There must be some problem with this connection. I just thought I heard my mother, Evelyn Dixon, President of the Boy's Club Annual Benefit Auction, as well as the Altar Guild, the Children's Library Advisory Committee, the Neighborhood Association, and the foremost list-maker in all of Texas, say that she didn't have a plan. Someone must have crossed our wires." He laughed, and I smiled. Even in my darkest moments, the sound of Garrett laughing has cheered me.

"I know. It isn't like me, but, as you've probably noticed, being myself hasn't been working out too well for me lately. I thought I'd try being someone else, someone spontaneous and unpredictable."

"I see," Garrett said with a television therapist twang. "How's that working for you so far?"

"Well, I haven't even crossed into Rockwall County yet, so it's a little too soon to tell. At the moment, I feel better than I have in quite a while, but it can't last. Right about now, your dad is being told by some moving-company cowboy that I kicked him out and refused to set a date to move, which means it won't be long before Rob will be calling my cell phone to ask if I've lost my mind." I chuckled. "I don't know. Maybe I have, but do you think I should tell him?"

"Don't bother. Bet he already knows. I always did," Garrett teased, and then his voice became more serious.

"Listen, Mom, I've got to get back to work, but I think it's great that you're getting away for a few days. You've got plenty of time before you need to move, so don't worry about it. If it comes down to the wire, I'll jump on a plane and fly out there to help you pack."

"Thanks, honey. You won't need to do that; I'll be back in plenty of time to move, but I appreciate the offer."

I hit the end button on the phone. Glancing into the rearview mirror across the pancake-flat landscape, I could see the downtown skyline marked by air-conditioned temples of commerce shrinking in the distance. I turned up the volume on the radio, drowning out the tinny, computer-generated version of "Your Man" that always played on my cell phone when Rob called, and kept driving northeast.

The young policeman stared, waiting for me to answer the question.

"What brings me to Connecticut? Just a whim." I shrugged. "I've always wanted to see the fall foliage."

He nodded slowly, probably wondering if he should have me take a Breathalyzer test but apparently deciding against it. Maybe I reminded him of his mother.

"Well, I'm sorry your vacation is starting off on a sour note," he said as he wrote, "but as fast as you were going, I really don't have a choice." He tore the ticket off the pad and handed it to me.

"Welcome to New England, Ms. Dixon."

2

Evelyn Dixon

Standing in the middle of downtown that day and turning in a slow circle, I decided that New Bern, Connecticut, looked exactly as a New England village should. I still think so.

The tallest building in town is the Congregational Church. It stands at the narrow, western end of the Green, an imposing façade that dominates the landscape, as if anchoring the town to the Almighty, reminding the residents of the meaning of the word "omnipresent." With its evenly spaced doors and windows aligned beneath the exact center of a white wooden belfry, it is a monument to symmetry. Next to it, and painted in the same simple white clapboard as the church, stands a line of antique homes, probably from the late eighteen hundreds, on smallish lots. They are nearly identical, two-storied and rectangular in shape with wide porches and high-pitched roofs and, at least in comparison to the grand mansions that line the village's main east/west residential street, Elm, rather modest.

The lots on Elm are large, some measured in acres instead of feet, and the homes sitting on them represent a variety of architectural styles—Colonials, Federals, Greek Revivals, and Victorians.

Historic plaques on the homes list dates of construction stretching from pre-Revolutionary times to post–Civil War, the most recent having been built in 1902. Walking down the sidewalk on an autumn afternoon, under a canopy of red gold maple leaves shot through with shafting sunbeams, you half expect a man in a tall beaver top hat and morning coat, or a woman wearing hoopskirts and pulling on hand-tatted lace gloves, to open the gate in one of the white picket fences and wish you good-day. New Bern is a town with an active and powerful historic preservation society, and it shows.

There is little distance or demarcation here between residential and commercial; people who live in town are within easy walking distance of New Bern's businesses, a small but diverse collection of restaurants, galleries, antique shops, and boutiques housed in two-story brick storefronts with hand-painted signs. There isn't an inch of neon on New Bern's main commercial street, aptly called Commerce. And even though the village shops clearly cater to the tourist trade (you'd be hard-pressed to buy a quart of milk or packet of shoelaces in the village; all those mundane but necessary transactions take place in charmless cinderblock buildings along the state route leading out of town), there is a feeling of authenticity to the place.

Taking a quick walk around, perusing the village before deciding how to spend the rest of my day, I was pleased to see there was nothing too precious or souvenirlike for sale in the store windows, no T-shirts claiming that the wearer's girlfriend, husband, or grandma went to New Bern and all they got was a lousy T-shirt, and none of the merchants had dubbed their boutiques a "shoppe." I was looking forward to poking through the stores, but my rumbling stomach insisted that lunch come first.

There were three or four restaurants to choose from, and all of them looked nice, but I settled on a place called the Grill on the Green. Though it was still early, the restaurant was packed, and I had to wait for a few minutes to be seated. Waiting for my table, I noticed that while many of the customers were obviously tourists (the shopping bags and cameras gave them away), the handsome, gray-haired gentleman who was seating diners greeted many by their first names, kissing the ladies on the cheek and exchanging hearty handshakes and laughter with the men. Clearly, the restaurant was a favorite of locals as well as visitors. It was easy to see why; the atmosphere was elegant but relaxed, with brick red wainscoting running beneath walls painted a warm yellow. The simple black Windsor chairs looked cozy around the white-clothed tables. And the food? To die for! The chicken and endive salad I ordered was one of the best things I've ever eaten. Normally, I hate eating alone; it always makes me feel so conspicuous. But with the French patio doors at the front of the restaurant open to catch a warm, fall breeze, a pleasant buzz of conversation in the background, and a great glass of pinot grigio to sip, I found myself smiling for the first time in a long time.

The waitress brought me a cappuccino to finish my meal. "So, are you up from New York for the day?"

"Texas, actually. I took a room at the Inn for a few days. I've always wanted to see the fall colors."

"Texas?" she commented, looking at me with interest before placing the cup on the table. "That's a long way. Well, you picked the perfect time for it. The weather's beautiful. We'll be packed this weekend, that's for sure."

"I noticed. Do you always have so many tourists?"

She shook her head and put a ceramic container filled with pink, blue, and white sugar packets down near my cup. "We've always got a steady stream of weekenders from New York, but we're too far from the city to be a big tourist destination—not like the Hamptons or anything. Which is fine with me." She grinned. "I went to East Hampton for the weekend once and I couldn't wait to get home—too many people! Here, we're busy in the summer, and, of course, we get a lot of visitors now, during leaf season, but that only lasts a few weeks. Most businesses make seventy percent of their income in about three months' time. Things get pretty quiet after that."

"Doesn't that make it hard to make a living?" I asked.

The waitress shrugged. "In a way, I guess. If we run into a summer with bad weather, and the tourists stay home, it can be tough, but I've lived here all my life and always managed. Probably I'd make more money if I lived somewhere else, but New Bern is a good place to raise my kids. Can't see that making more money would make me any happier, so I guess I'm here to stay."

We had been talking for quite a while. Standing near the bar, the maitre d' shot the waitress a look that reminded her she had other tables.

"Is there anything else I can get for you?" she asked quickly.

"No, thank you. Just a check."

She pulled the already-prepared bill out of her black apron pocket and placed it on the table. "It was nice talking to you," she said. "I hope you enjoy your trip. If you get a chance, drive over to the nature preserve and walk the trails. They're real pretty this time of year."

"Thanks. I'll do that."

I'd planned to do some window-shopping after lunch, but changed my mind when a motor coach pulled up and disgorged a swarm of camera-wielding senior citizens onto the sidewalk. Instead, I crossed the street and took a walk on the Green, hoping the crowd of seniors would disperse by the time I returned.

The Green, I soon learned, is just a quaint word for a municipal park that marks the center of town and is a fixture in most New England villages. In New Bern, the Green is a block wide and three blocks long. Commerce and Elm Streets run on its long, east/west edges; Maple and Church streets bound the shorter sides. Those four are the most important thoroughfares in town, though I would later learn that Proctor Street, which parallels the back side of Elm, is where the real mansions are. Those homes, owned by old Yankees with old money, with layers of trees and hedges to camouflage them from prying eyes, don't look like much from the road. But once you get past the overgrown shrubbery you'll discover grounds dotted with tennis courts, swimming pools, and carriage houses surrounding stately, enormous homes that rarely change hands. The owners' last names match those of the oldest headstones in the cemetery. In this part of the world, amassing a great fortune is considered admirable; flaunting it is not.

I took my time strolling through the Green, gazing up at the tapestry of brilliant-leaved trees. Some, towering overhead like massive columns, had obviously been there for decades if not centuries. Others, more recently planted, with slender, pliable trunks, were scattered haphazardly on the carpet of grass. Hardy yellow and orange mums mounded in indiscriminately placed flowerbeds near bushes of purplish hydrangeas at their peak and leggy geraniums that were far past it. But for the sidewalks cutting through the park at tidy right angles until they met at the granite memorial to the Civil War dead, the Green would have given the impression of nature run amok. Instead, the feeling was one of humanity imposing order upon nature, but lightly, respectfully, recognizing that, while they might adapt and make use of the natural world, the people of New Bern weren't so arrogant as to suppose they could control it.

It's like a quilt, I thought to myself as I approached the war memorial. *All the different patches of green coming together to make a whole. That's why I feel so comfortable here.*

I'd made my first quilt twenty-five years before, when I was expecting Garrett. From that moment on, I was hooked. I love quilting, the sheer geometry of it, the endless patterns and combinations that can be achieved by the arrangement and rearrangement of something as simple as a straight line. The order and precision of quilting appeals to that part of me that wants a refuge from life's chaos, while the unbounded possibilities of color, fabric, and finishing speak to the part of me that wants to live life surprised. The most wonderful thing about quilting is that if a whole stadium full of people were to make a quilt in the exact same pattern, no two of those quilts would be alike. No matter how untutored or timid she may be, when it comes to quilting, everyone is an artist. Expertly, or innocently, or inadvertently, the quilter cannot help but reveal something true.

That's what I was feeling as I left the Green and joined the dwindling groups of shoppers enjoying the last lazy rays of sunlight on that fall afternoon: that I had stumbled upon something true, a town completely and unapologetically itself. No one here would think of digging a river where nature hadn't seen fit to put one in the first place, trying to impose some counterfeit, saccharine-quaint overlay of what someone in Corporate thought the landscape should look like based on the most recent polling numbers and focus groups. Here, the sidewalks were uneven in spots, and tufts of grass sprouted insistently between the cracks. Walking past the Grill on the Green, where clutches of diners lingered over coffee and dessert, I looked up and saw that the hand-painted wooden sign suspended overhead had spots of chipped paint, scars from a hailstorm. No one had thought to touch it up after the ravages of winter, trying to restore it to some ideal of pristine perfection. The residents and merchants of New Bern weren't striving to achieve perfection, because they understood it was the *imperfections* that made their village perfect, because that was what made it real.

One of the first bits of wisdom imparted to a novice quilter is that the Amish, who make some of the most simple but exquisite quilts in the world, purposely plan a mistake into each of their projects because they believe attempts at human perfection mock God. Of course, any quilter knows that you don't have to plan for imperfections in your work; they come quite naturally on their own, so I don't know if this bit of Amish folklore rings true or not, but the idea does.

If there were such a thing as human perfection, it would mean that there was one ideal; one standard for beauty, one right answer to every question. And maybe, for the Mr. Lindsays of the world, the people who can't see any difference between a real river and a freshly dug one, who can't understand why someone would go to all the trouble of stitching a quilt by hand when you could make one faster on a machine, or better yet, buy one cheap from the discount store for $49.95, which is less than you'd pay for the fabric; maybe for those people there is some universal ideal. Maybe they simply can't recognize the sublime splendor of imperfection. But I bet the Amish do, and the young waitress who thinks a smaller paycheck is a fair trade for happiness, and whoever owns the sign over the restaurant and lets the chipped paint stay chipped because they realize that tradition and endurance are what ultimately bring us to perfection. They understand. So do I.

Maybe that's why, after only a few hours in this little village, I felt more at ease here than I did after twenty years of living in a suburban planned development.

How odd, I thought as I opened the door of the antique store I'd been browsing in and waved in response to the owner's farewell, *to be surrounded by strangers and feel so at home. If I believed in past lives, I might think I'd spent one in New Bern. Of course, that couldn't be. There's no quilt shop here, and even in reincarnation I can't see me spending a whole lifetime without a place to buy fabric. If not for that, I'd never want to leave.*

It was nearing five o'clock, and some of the shopkeepers were locking up. I was almost at the end of Commerce Street and had investigated every shop. Tomorrow I planned to take the young waitress's advice and spend the day hiking through the nature preserve, so I knew I should go back to the Inn and turn in early, but I really didn't want to. I wanted to make the day last. There was a bakery on the corner with a sign that promised fresh cookies and strong coffee. People were still coming in and out the door. I wasn't really hungry, but lingering over a cup of coffee seemed a good way to prolong the afternoon.

The sun was beginning to dip lower in the sky, and it was getting chilly. I shoved my hands in my coat pockets as I hurried toward the bakery. I'd almost reached the door when I heard a bird chirrup that sounded surprisingly close and loud.

If the bird hadn't called at the moment it did, I'd have missed it entirely, but when I turned my head to see where the noise came from I noticed an opening between the two buildings I'd just passed. It was an alley paved with old-fashioned cobblestones, wide enough to allow people to pass on foot but too narrow for a car. A faded sign posted on a brick wall announced that this was Cobbled Court, and an arrow beneath pointed the way in.

There weren't any lights in the alley. Even if there were any shops down the passageway, they were surely closed by now, but curiosity got the best of me. Ignoring the damage that the uneven cobbles were inflicting on my high heels, I set out to investigate the passage that, in all probability, led to nothing more interesting than back doors where shopkeepers piled their empty shipping crates and trash cans. But that's why you mustn't bet the bank on probability; sometimes it's better to follow your instincts.

The dark, narrow passageway ended abruptly, opening onto a generous, cobbled square large enough to let a wide column of light stream into the center. When I stepped out of the dim alleyway and into the light-filled courtyard, it felt like I was passing into a secret world, a place that didn't exist before I discovered it.

At a right angle to the alley I'd just exited, I saw another passage that I thought might lead to Maple Street, which meant the courtyard could be accessed from two of New Bern's most important streets. There were a few small storefronts opening onto the courtyard—a gift shop, an art gallery, and an attorney's office—but, as I had anticipated, they were all closed.

One store, much larger than all the others combined, took up an entire brick building. It was empty. Judging from its appearance, it had been for a long time. The red paint on the wooden door was peeling, and the big bowfront display window with dozens of panes of glass was clouded with dirt and cobwebs. I moved closer and spied a faded For Rent sign taped to the window.

Using my sleeve to wipe some of the grime from the glass, I peered inside and saw that the interior of the shop was even bigger than it appeared from the street. I could make out stone floors and scarred wooden counters topped with an old-fashioned black cash register that probably hadn't rung up a sale in decades.

The place was in terrible shape. Water stains on the walls testified to the existence of bad plumbing or a leaky roof, probably both. Several of the windowpanes were cracked, and one was completely missing, allowing me to get a strong whiff of wet and mildew when I leaned closer. The window frames were soft in spots where termites had been feasting. In spite of all this, I could see that, once upon a time, it had been charming. Closing my eyes, I could envision how the dozens of tiny windows would have gleamed when they were clean and new and how inviting the red wooden door must have looked when the paint was fresh. In my mind, the sour odor of mold was banished by the perfume of scented geraniums growing in pots under the window, and I could hear a cheery, frequent jingling as the door swung open and the bells alerted the shopkeeper to the arrival of yet another customer. I could see it all, but only with my eyes closed. Opening them again, I stood face-to-face with a ruin of a building, an abandoned memory.

It must have been lovely, but that was a long time ago. It would take pots of money and a mountain of work to make it look that way again.

I didn't care.

I backed away from the broken window and started rummaging through my purse for a pen and scrap of paper so I could write down the name and number of the realtor. This was it. What I had been looking for without even knowing it. My place, my town, my shop. The dream I'd nearly forgotten had been waiting for me at the end of a blind alley.

I closed my eyes again, and the vision came back to me, the shining windows, the gleaming red door, this time with a hand-painted sign overhead that read:

COBBLED COURT QUILTS

I was in luck. Though it was after hours when I called the real estate office, someone answered the phone. Wendy Perkins said she'd just been getting ready to leave, but, seeing as I was only a couple of blocks away, she'd be willing to wait if I came right over.

"But," she asked doubtfully, "are you sure we're talking about the same building? That great big space in Cobbled Court? The one with the broken windows?"

"Yes," I assured her. "I'm standing in front of it right now. Red door and a bowfront window. How much does it rent for?"

"Honestly, I don't remember. It's been so long since anyone inquired that I'll have to look up the information in my files, but I'll have it by the time you get here."

When I walked through the door of the office I was enthusiastically greeted by an older woman with a white beehive hairdo. She wore a big pair of rhinestone-encrusted sunglasses on a rhinestone-encrusted chain around her neck and pants that were a size too small. She snorted whenever she laughed, which was often, wrinkling her nose, folding her tongue into a little U shape when she did and involuntarily thrusting it through the O of her lips. She reminded me of that Lily Tomlin character, Ernestine, the wickedly funny telephone operator whose weekly appearances on *Laugh-In*, back when I was a teenager, always had me rolling. I liked her instantly.

"It's in here somewhere, Evelyn," she said, frowning and pushing her glasses up on her nose while she dug through the file drawer. "It'll just take me a minute or two to find it. The paperwork on that building must be older than me." Snort! Snort!

She laughed, and I joined in. It was impossible not to.

"What's the history of the building?"

"Well, it was originally a drugstore, way back at the turn of the century. Fielding Drug Emporium. It was family run all the way up until the sixties, but then Jim Fielding died of a heart attack real sudden, and the place closed down. After that, there were a couple of boutiques that tried their luck, but, you know, it's such a big space and not an ideal location. People don't know it's there unless they walk down that passage. It'd be fine if you were catering to a clientele of alley cats and rats." Snort! Snort! "You're not looking to open a pet-supply store, are you?" Snort!

I smiled. "No, I'm afraid not. I'm a quilter. Years ago, when I was first married, I dreamed of opening a quilt shop of my own back in Wisconsin. That's where my husband and I grew up. At one point, I actually inquired about getting a loan and started working on a business plan, thinking I'd do it as soon as my son was in school and I had a little more time. But you know how things go. My husband got a job offer in Texas for a lot more money. It was too good an opportunity to pass up. At the time, I thought I'd just open my store in Texas, but the town we moved to didn't support small businesses. Two quilt shops opened while I was there. They asked me to teach some classes, which I loved, and sometimes I'd help out in the store too. Just part-time work, you know. But in the end they couldn't compete against the big fabric stores, so they closed. Then, too, I was very involved with my son, his school, and I volunteered for all kinds of community things." I shrugged.

"It's no one's fault but mine, but I eventually kind of gave up on my dream and, in a way, on myself. I don't know when it happened, but it did. Now I find myself nearing fifty and newly single, and when I saw that empty storefront today, I knew . . . I just knew . . ." Wendy's eyes were fixed on me as I spoke. Suddenly I felt very foolish, telling my life story to a stranger.

"Well, you know what they say—'Better late than never'!" I laughed, but this time Wendy didn't join in. Instead, she leaned forward, making the springs on the desk chair squeak, and placed her hand on my knee.

"Evelyn, believe me, I'm happy to make this deal, but you seem like a nice lady. You need to think this through. You've just gone through a divorce. Maybe this isn't the time for you to be making such a big decision or moving to a town where you don't know anyone. At a time like this, you need friends around, old friends who know you and what you've been through. People who can support you.

"This is a huge change you're contemplating, and an expensive one. I don't know what your financial situation is, but if you're like most recent divorcees, then this is the worst possible time for you to be taking a big financial risk. I know what I'm talking about. You think I'd be sitting in an office trying to sell real estate at six-thirty on a Thursday night if I didn't? At my age, I should be sitting on a beach in Florida, calling my children and nagging them because they never come see me." She snorted, but halfheartedly. Her eyes became serious again.

"And even if you weren't reeling from the effects of your divorce, be practical. New Bern isn't big enough to support a quilt shop. You won't last six months."

❧ 3 ❧

Abigail Burgess Wynne

People like me.

I'm aware that some might consider this a less-than-humble statement, perhaps even arrogant. But really, humility is an over-rated quality, don't you think? Besides, in my case, it's true. People *do* like me. They always have, and if I'd ever harbored any doubts on the subject (though I never really did), they were assuaged last night.

Yesterday, March 14, was my sixty-second birthday. Franklin Spaulding, who has been my attorney for decades, hosted a party in my honor at the Grill on the Green. Positively everyone I knew attended, plus a few people I didn't: the pastor and deacons of the Congregational Church (whose new fellowship hall I financed and whose services I attend on major holidays), the directors of the Wynne Memorial Library, the County Women's Shelter, the New Bern Historic Preservation Society, the Nature Preserve Foundation, the Concert Association, and assorted other community organizations that count on me for advice and contributions, as well as the various board members of those organizations, not to mention the many merchants who own the antique shops, art galleries, design studios, clothing boutiques, jewelers, restaurants, and bookstores that I frequent, plus all the people I know through my memberships in the tennis, golf, and equestrian clubs, and, of course, the spouses, partners, and significant others of all the aforementioned.

There were so many guests that the party completely took over the restaurant, which might have proved frustrating to other prospective diners, but I don't think so. It's still too chilly for tourists, especially on a Thursday before the weekenders are due, so the only people who would have been planning to eat at the Grill were locals, and, as I say, nearly all the locals were at the party.

Of course, I'm aware that all the party guests I've listed had a vested interest, if not an obligation, in making an appearance at the celebration. I'm the wealthiest woman in New Bern, possibly the wealthiest woman in this part of the state, though I don't know that for certain. Franklin, my attorney, keeps track of my investments and financial dealings. I'm not much interested in the actual figures or details of my portfolio, but Franklin says I have plenty of money to live well and to be a generous benefactor in my community, so I do and I am. Certainly that generosity could lead you to believe that many of those who came to celebrate my natal day did so because they felt they had to—not that I'd have faulted them if they did; there's nothing wrong with filling one's community and social obligations—but that wasn't the case. I have proof.

During the course of the evening, I had to visit the ladies' room. When I went in, both stalls were occupied, so I was obliged to wait my turn. While doing so, I inadvertently heard an interesting exchange between two of the partygoers. It's so strange, isn't it? The way women have long, in-depth conversations while in the toilet? I don't think men do that, do you? And I certainly never would, but all the same, if you're careful about where you stand and keep quiet, you can learn a lot in the ladies' room. Not that I'd want anyone to think I'm an eavesdropper, but really, who isn't interested in hearing how people honestly feel about them? It isn't my fault that women insist on talking in semipublic places.

One of the speakers was Grace Kahn. I've known Grace for years. She volunteers three days a week at the library and sits on the board too. For the previous twenty-four years, until her knee surgery a few months ago, we played doubles tennis every Wednesday.

The other voice belonged to a woman I'd met for the first time that night, Margot Matthews. She owns a little two-bedroom carriage house on Marsh Lane that, until recently, she only occupied on weekends. We have a few of those in New Bern, New Yorkers mostly, who keep a house in the country for weekends and summers. Some of the locals grumble about them, but not me. They're nice enough people for the most part, and they certainly help out the local economy, so what's to complain about? I go to Manhattan to enjoy the delights of the city; why shouldn't urbanites feel free to enjoy the delights of the country? Everyone needs a change of scenery now and then.

But I digress. I was speaking of Margot Matthews.

Until recently, she worked in Manhattan, in the marketing department of some large firm that sells semiconductors or some such thing; I wasn't paying that much attention when she told me about her former business. Dull stuff, business. But once I found out that Miss Matthews studied ballet as a child, the conversation became much more interesting. People's hobbies tend to be so much more intriguing than their professions, don't you agree? Grace whispered in my ear that the poor thing had been downsized—that is to say, fired—and was living in New Bern full-time because finances had forced her to sublet her apartment in the city until she could find a new job.

Grace had noticed Margot sitting at the same computer workstation in the library, day after day, searching the Internet for job postings.

"She seemed so forlorn. She doesn't know anyone," Grace whispered to me as she beckoned to the young woman, who was just getting a glass of wine at the bar, "so I invited her to come along tonight. I hope you don't mind, Abigail."

And, of course, I didn't. Why should I? It wasn't as if I had to take on Margot Matthews as my new best friend; besides, I enjoy meeting new people. And they enjoy meeting me, as evidenced by the cross-stall conversation that took place between Margot and Grace in the restaurant ladies' room.

"Thank you for bringing me along tonight, Grace. I can't tell you how ready I was for a night out! After all those hours I've spent sending out e-mails to human resources departments and getting no response, it's lovely just to talk with some real human beings—especially Abigail. She's fascinating! I can't believe she actually knows Mikhail Baryshnikov. It was awfully nice of her to let me crash the party."

"I knew she wouldn't mind. Abigail likes meeting new people. She loves drawing them out, finding some common ground for conversation." Grace laughed. "I think she enjoys the challenge, as if she was out to solve some sort of mystery. She looks straight at you with those intense brown eyes as if every word you were saying was completely and utterly absorbing, and, of course, you end up falling in love with her. It's impossible not to. In some way or another, everyone in that room owes Abigail something, but that's not why they're here tonight. Even if Abigail wasn't a benefactress to half the town, no one would dream of missing her birthday party. People like her."

See? What did I tell you?

"How did the two of you meet?" Margot inquired.

"Playing tennis. I was her doubles partner for years. She used to play singles *and* doubles until last year. Abigail has ten years on me, but she can still run me off the court. She's very athletic. Hiking, riding, sailing—name a sport and Abigail excels at it."

"Well, I'd never have guessed she was sixty-two if you hadn't told me."

"She is amazing looking, isn't she? Her skin positively glows. And it's all natural. At least, I think it is."

It is. I don't put much faith in cosmetic surgeons, or cosmetics, for that matter. Everyone ages; I don't understand why people spend so much time and money trying to avoid the inevitable. At my age, beauty is a ship that has sailed; the best one can hope for is to be thought of as handsome, and while I try my best to keep myself up, a little face powder and lipstick is as far as I go. When it comes to makeup and fashion, simplicity is best. My closet is filled with classic clothing of excellent quality—well-cut wool slacks, silk blouses, an array of cashmere sweaters, and, for more formal occasions like this evening, an assortment of black cocktail dresses. Oh, and shoes. Good shoes are a must. My preference is for Stuart Weitzman; classic designs that are just different enough to be interesting and have heels you can actually walk in—not far, mind you, but far enough. If you carry yourself well, that is really all you need in the way of fashion. That and a few pieces of well-chosen jewelry: pearls, matching earrings, a good diamond tennis bracelet, and, perhaps, one simply spectacular ring, like the enormous yellow diamond Woolley Wynne gave me when he proposed.

"Well, she's certainly a handsome woman," Margot commented.

Thank you, Margot.

"You should have seen her when she was younger. She was stunning! She looked like Katharine Hepburn. In fact, she still reminds me of Hepburn. She has those same amazing cheekbones, that confident spring in her step. You get the sense that she enjoys life fully. And well . . . I don't mean that she's conceited necessarily, but she's just entirely pleased to be Abigail. If she wasn't so clearly interested in others, she'd probably come off as arrogant, but she's not. She's just supremely confident, and I think people find that attractive. And, of course, she's very well educated. She can talk intelligently on almost any subject . . ."

Well, that isn't so very difficult. If people would just read more instead of spending so much time in front of the television, the world would be a much more interesting place. I think we owe it to other people to be interesting, or at least not to be dull.

". . . so she is very much in demand when it comes to parties. Do you know that there are people in New Bern who have actually canceled their parties or changed the date when they heard that Abigail couldn't come?"

"Really? You're kidding!"

Margot laughed at this, and I could understand why. It really is ridiculous, canceling an entire party just because one person can't come, but it has been known to happen.

"It's true," Grace confirmed. "I know it sounds silly, but I don't half blame them. If Abigail shows up, the party is bound to be a success. She flits from group to group like a bumblebee among the flowers, touching down here and there and kind of pollinating the conversation before she moves on. Next thing you know, everyone is talking and laughing and having a marvelous time."

There was a rustle of tissue from inside one of the stalls. I took a silent step backward and put my hand on the door, just in case.

"Well, she seems really lovely," Margot said. "You're lucky to have someone like that for a friend."

"A friend? I've known Abigail for decades, but I don't think you could say we're friends."

"No? Then who are her friends?"

Grace was quiet for a moment, considering. "I don't think she has any, really. Not the way most people think of friendship. I adore Abigail, of course—everyone does, and she likes us—but I don't think she thinks of any of us as friends. She doesn't let anyone get that close."

The sound of rushing water told me that it was time to leave, so I slipped out of the room undetected. It might have been interesting to hear more, but I didn't really need to. Grace's revelation to Margot was no surprise to me. She was quite right.

I like people. They like me. And I like me too. But I don't have close friendships, and I see no need to develop any.

Friends, in my opinion, are supremely inconvenient; they are people who have a grasp on one's affections and therefore have the right to call upon one for financial or emotional support, usually at the most inopportune moments. I suppose that's why I've always avoided them.

The first prospect doesn't distress me too much. I'm certainly in a position to be generous. But the second? That is a different matter. Emotions are sticky things, and even more inconvenient than friendships. I don't trust them.

Truthfully, I don't trust in much of anything except my own ability to handle whatever life sends my way. If I am proud of anything, it is that. I can take care of myself, and I always have.

My father used to say, "Never complain and never explain." Which I took to mean that the only person you can or should depend upon is yourself, so it's best to keep yourself to yourself.

It was advice I took to heart, and, until my phone rang at nine forty-five on the day after my birthday party, it was advice that served me well.

4

Abigail Burgess Wynne

I don't have e-mail or, for that matter, a computer. I don't trust machines. When I want cash, I walk into the bank and let the teller know how much I need. And I'd open a vein before I'd ring up my own groceries on one of those automated check-out lines. But caller identification? The ability to see who is ringing and decide if it's someone you want to talk to or to avoid? That's one innovation I've embraced wholeheartedly.

Of course, technology does have its limitations. Even when the caller is someone you do wish to speak with, you can't guarantee that the subject they're calling to discuss is a welcome one. If such a thing were possible, I doubt I'd have picked up the phone that morning. But as soon as I looked at the screen and saw that Franklin was phoning, I picked up the receiver. I assumed he was calling to talk about the party.

"Franklin, you're a darling! Thank you so much! You shouldn't have gone to all that trouble, but it was a wonderful birthday. I had such a lovely time. Everyone else did too, don't you think?"

"Yes, Abbie. They did. It was a great party." His voice sounded distracted, but I didn't think anything of it. Franklin is a founding partner of Spaulding, Ketchum, and Ryan, the largest law firm in the county. He was calling during business hours, so I assumed he was just thinking about business, as usual. He's a very conscientious attorney, and a very good one. Part of the reason I never have to worry about my business is because I know I can count on Franklin to do it for me.

"It was, thanks to you. I was planning on phoning you a little later, but you beat me to it. Can you join me at the club for dinner tonight?" After he organized that entire soiree, treating Franklin to dinner was the least I could do; and besides, I always enjoy dining with Franklin. He makes me laugh.

"Yes, yes. Fine," he said, but he sounded so preoccupied that I wondered if he'd really heard me. "Listen, Abbie. I'm downtown. . . . Actually, I'm at the city jail, and I need you to come down here. We've got a problem."

I was shocked. "Franklin! Are you in jail?"

"No, no, Abbie. Not me. It's Liza."

I didn't respond.

"Liza Burgess," he repeated, questioning my memory.

"I know who she is, Franklin."

He cleared his throat, treading lightly. "Sorry. I just didn't . . . I know you've never actually met, so I—"

"Franklin," I interrupted. "You said we have a problem. What is it?"

"Like I said, Liza's in jail. She's been arrested for shoplifting and will be appearing in front of a judge at ten-thirty."

"And that would be a problem for me? Why?"

"For God's sake, Abigail!" Apparently he was done treading lightly. "She's your niece, your only living relative! Her mother is dead. She's got nobody in the world besides you, Abbie. You've got to help her."

Now it was my turn to be direct. "Actually, I have to do no such thing, Franklin. The girl may be my niece, but that's simply an accident of biology. I've had nothing to do with her before, and I don't see why her arrest changes that. It's not my responsibility. After all, *I* didn't steal anything. So I don't see how any of this involves me."

"You don't? Well, how about this? In about forty-one minutes, your niece, Liza Burgess, is going to appear in front of a judge for shoplifting a sweater from a local boutique—a sweater, by the way, that she had more than enough money in her purse to pay for—and about five minutes after she walks into the courtroom, whatever bright, eager cub reporter is covering the crime beat in New Bern is going to figure out that the two of you are related. Then he's going to race back to his desk and pound out a story, something about how the poor, orphaned daughter of Abigail Burgess Wynne's estranged, deceased sister, Susan, has resorted to shoplifting for clothes while her aunt, the sixth wealthiest woman in the state, lives a life of luxury in her Proctor Street mansion. And there will be pictures. One of you, probably the portrait they have on file from the library dedication, and another of Liza, being led away in handcuffs. It will be front-page news, Abbie, and everyone in town will read it, but that will be just the beginning.

"Some other reporter, someone much more talented than our New Bern cub, someone from the *Times* or, worse yet, *the Daily News*, will spot the story and say to themselves, 'Abigail Burgess Wynne? Wasn't her name on the list of major donors to the Opera Ball?' And then he'll start digging. He'll rent a car in the city and take a ride out to New Bern and start asking questions, questions about you, and Liza, and Susan. And the answers he'll get will make him smile and think about putting in for a promotion, because he'll know what he's stumbled upon, Abigail. Stories like yours can run for months on end, because these are the ones the public just can't get enough of—stories of the misery of the rich and famous or, if they are juicy enough, and this one is, stories of the misery of the merely rich. These are the stories that the tabloids love, the ones that feed their bottom line.

"So it doesn't matter if you were the one who stuffed the sweater under your coat and walked out without paying or not, Abbie. This *is* your problem. And if you don't get down to the courthouse in the next fifteen minutes, it's going to be a much bigger one."

Oh my God, I thought, *he's right. One way or another, I'm in this. Damn that stupid girl! And damn Franklin! What am I going to do?* My mind was racing.

"Abbie?" he asked. "Did you hear me?"

"I did. Meet me at the courthouse in seven minutes. At the side entrance. I don't want anyone to see us come in. Find out who the judge will be."

I was in luck. The judge was Harry Gulden. He and my late husband, Woolly, were college roommates. I've known Harry and his wife, Judy, for years. He agreed to hear Liza's case in his chambers.

This is one of the advantages of living in a small town. When people know you personally, they're more willing to put aside strict formalities and procedures that could serve no purpose but causing you embarrassment. Not bending the law, of course. I'd never ask Harry to do that. But as long as justice was served, Harry didn't see what harm there would be in conducting private matters in private, especially since this was a first offense.

I sat perched on the edge of a chair in front of Harry's desk while he went over the arrest report. Franklin was standing behind me along with a young attorney who introduced himself as Scott Corey; he was from the district attorney's office.

It was everything I could do to sit still and keep quiet, as Franklin had said I must. A thousand questions ran through my mind. What in the world had possessed the girl to shoplift a sweater, especially when she had the money to pay for it? How did Franklin manage to get himself mixed up in this? And what was the girl doing in New Bern anyway? When Susan was alive, she and Liza lived in the opposite corner of the state in a townhouse in Stamford, where it was easy for Susan to commute to her job in New York. The last I'd heard, Liza was at college in Rhode Island, getting a degree in studio art, or design, or some such thing. I didn't know much about my sister's child, but I was aware of the basics of her living situation. I'd asked Franklin to keep an eye on them. Whatever was Liza doing in New Bern? And the biggest question of all, what was I, who'd never gotten so much as a speeding ticket, doing at the courthouse on what should have been a perfectly normal Friday morning?

I twisted in my chair and looked a question at Franklin, who was standing behind me, but he shook his head and frowned, silently warning me that I mustn't risk saying anything in front of the judge or Mr. Corey that might hurt Liza's case. I frowned back, impatient but grudgingly compliant. The door opened, and Liza was escorted into the room by a bailiff.

Judge Gulden looked over the tops of his glasses. "Thank you, Carolyn. You can leave this young lady with us," he said, dismissing the bailiff.

Franklin was wrong. I had seen her before, but only once, when she was a baby. I'd never imagined her growing up to be so tall. But truth to tell, I'd never really imagined her at all. For the last nineteen years, I'd done my best to forget that she existed, and at my best I am very good indeed. Now there was no getting around it. The tall, slim young woman with the torn jean jacket, too-bleached blond hair, and brown eyes scowling from a face that looked disconcertingly like my own, did exist, and, like it or not, her life was now entangled with mine. Just how entangled was something I did not yet fully realize.

She looked quickly at me and then at Franklin. "What is she doing here?" she asked him. The directness of her inquiry and familiarity of her tone turned on the lights for me. She and Franklin knew each other—well. Before Franklin could respond, Judge Gulden motioned to the empty chair next to mine, indicating that Liza should take a seat. We both stared straight ahead, avoiding eye contact with each other.

"Your aunt came here to see if she could help you." He slid his glasses back up his nose and looked at her case file.

"It seems you've gotten yourself into quite a predicament, Miss Burgess. The arrest report says that yesterday evening you strolled into the Kaplan's Clothes Closet on Commerce Street and, after browsing around in a manner that made a store employee suspicious, stuffed this green sweater, valued at two hundred and seventynine dollars . . ."

Cashmere. Very nice. She might be a thief, but at least she was a thief with good taste.

". . . under your coat and then left the store without paying. Is that what happened?" The judge looked at her pointedly, and Liza blushed. At least she had the good sense to be embarrassed by her behavior. Heaven knew I was.

"I . . . I guess I forgot to pay for it," she mumbled, her soft, almost childish voice strangely at odds with her torn, tough-girl clothing and rock-and-roll hairstyle.

"Hmmm," the judge replied, clearly unconvinced. "I suppose that's why you started running down the street when the store clerk called for you to come back and pay, not stopping until you were apprehended by a police officer who was writing out a parking ticket. So, are you still saying it was all a big mistake?" Liza blushed even deeper, but she didn't respond.

"I thought so." Judge Gulden sighed and removed his glasses completely. "How do you plead?"

"Guilty," she whispered.

"Miss Burgess, you have no prior record, and, in spite of yesterday's events, you don't seem like someone who is looking to lead a life of crime. I don't wish to start you off on that road, nor do I wish to add to our already overcrowded prison population. However, this is a serious matter. I cannot simply let you leave here with a slap on the wrist.

"Because of your clean record and," he said glancing at me, "because I know you come from a fine family with deep roots and a sterling reputation in the community, I am inclined to be lenient in this case. I'm sure the district attorney agrees with me."

Behind me, Mr. Corey cleared his throat and shifted his feet, but didn't say anything, which made me wonder how strong his agreement was. But I didn't wonder much. I didn't care how this might look to some junior lawyer in the D.A.'s office. I just wanted this whole sordid affair to be done with so Liza could go back to Rhode Island and I could get back to living my life. If that meant I needed to pay off whatever fine Harry was about to pronounce upon this black sheep of the family, so be it. No matter how much it cost me, it would be worth it ten times over to see the back of her.

Franklin cleared his throat. "Your Honor, given the circumstances, I'd like to suggest Accelerated Rehabilitation for Miss Burgess."

"I agree," said the judge.

"What's Accelerated Rehabilitation?" Liza asked.

"It means that we can drop the charges," Harry said. I felt my shoulders relax and out of the corner of my eye, I saw Liza's do the same. "However," he raised a warning finger, "we will only do so under the following conditions.

"First of all, you must pay a five hundred dollar fine. Also, you will be put on probation and must check in with your assigned probation officer according to the schedule he or she suggests. Finally, you must appear before me again in thirteen months. If, in that time, you have gotten into any trouble at all, even so much as having an overdue book at the library, then the charges against you will be reinstated. If that happens, then I assure you, you will be charged with fifth degree larceny, and you will go to jail. However, if you have stayed out of trouble, then the charges will be dropped and you will leave my courtroom with a completely clean record. Do you understand?"

"Yes," Liza said quietly. "Thanks."

"Thank you, Harry." I said at almost the same time. What a relief!

"Wait a minute!" Judge Gulden interrupted. "I'm not finished. Miss Burgess, I understand you are a student, is that right?"

I could feel Liza flinch next to me.

"I am . . . I mean . . . I was . . ."

I frowned. What was this? Had she dropped out of school?

Franklin answered for her. "Your Honor, until recently, Miss Burgess was working toward her degree in art. However, her circumstances have changed."

"Meaning?"

"Meaning, I left school," Liza said. "I flunked out, your Honor. That's why I'm here. Yesterday I had to move off campus and . . ." Her voice began to quaver, threatening to give way to tears but she choked them back. In spite of my irritation at being forced to play a role in this family drama, I felt a grudging respect for the way in which my niece refused to get carried away by emotion. She was definitely a Burgess.

"I didn't know what I should do, so I caught a bus to New Bern," she said in a more composed voice. "Mr. Spaulding was my mother's attorney and is in charge of her estate."

He was? He is? I shot Franklin a look, but he ignored me.

"There wasn't much left after all her medical expenses, but he made sure my school bills got paid and, after she died, he helped me with the funeral and everything." She shrugged. "He was nice to me.

"I don't know why," she continued, "but I just wanted to talk to him about what he thought I should do. I didn't have anywhere else to go, so I caught a bus to New Bern. When I got to Mr. Spaulding's office his secretary said he'd left early, to go to my aunt's birthday party. The secretary knew my last name was Burgess; I guess she assumed I was in town for the party. She told me to go downtown to the restaurant and I'd find Mr. Spaulding there. So I did, even though I wasn't invited to the party. There were a lot of people inside. I could see them through the front window, laughing and talking.

"The stores are open late on Thursday, so I decided to check them out while I waited for Mr. Spaulding. That's when I went into Kaplan's and . . ." she hesitated and then, for the first time, turned to look at me.

"I didn't plan on this," she said in a defiant tone, "and I wasn't trying to get your attention. No matter what you might think, I'm not a thief."

That's funny, I thought, tossing an arch look in her direction. *How is it you happen to have stolen goods in your possession?*

Judge Gulden groaned and rubbed his face with his hands. "So, Miss Burgess, are you saying that, as of yesterday, you are no longer a college student? That you have no permanent home or address?" Still scowling, Liza nodded.

"Well, this presents something of a problem. I can't just let you walk out of here and hope that you'll come back when you're supposed to. It was already complicated enough since you were going to school out of state. However, I had planned on making contact with someone at your college and asking them to be responsible for you . . ."

"I can be responsible for myself!" Liza snapped.

"Yes, we can all see that," I mumbled under my breath.

"Hey!" Liza shouted. "Who asked you? I never asked you to come down here! You can just keep out of this!"

"That is perfectly fine with me. I never wanted any part of this to begin with."

I rose from my chair and was getting ready to walk out the door when Harry pointed a finger at me and said in a commanding tone, "Abigail! Sit down!"

I hesitated, but the look on his face told me I'd better comply.

Smoldering, I slowly lowered myself back into the chair while the judge started speaking to Liza.

"Miss Burgess, you may think you are capable of being responsible for yourself, but in the eyes of this court, that is clearly not the case. And Abigail," he continued, turning to me, "you may not want any part of your niece's life, but given her current living situation, there really isn't another choice."

"Excuse me," I interrupted, the gist of Harry's meaning beginning to dawn on me. "Are you saying that . . ."

He nodded to me and then spoke to Liza and me in turn. "Miss Burgess, I am releasing you to the custody and recognizance of your Aunt Abigail. Abigail, from this moment forward, you are responsible for your niece—for her care, her conduct, and for making sure she returns to my court in thirteen months' time."

It wasn't possible! He couldn't mean it! I started to tell him exactly that and Liza was doing the same thing, but he wasn't listening.

"Ladies!" he bellowed, stunning us into silence. "Enough! That is how I have ruled and that is how it will be. Unless, of course, you'd rather we explore some other options, trials, jail-time, that sort of thing?" He paused as if waiting for us to respond before getting to his feet. No one said a word.

"In that case, I'll be going. I'm already thirty minutes behind schedule," he muttered to himself, walking out without even saying goodbye.

I couldn't believe what had just happened.

"He can't be serious," I said, turning around and looking at Franklin, who was looking at me with an expression that, had I not been certain that he had to realize the disastrous nature of the situation, might have passed for amusement. "This will never work! Not in a million years.

Franklin didn't say anything, just stood there with that odd look on his face.

Mr. Corey picked up his briefcase. "Well, it looks like we're all finished here. Mrs. Burgess-Wynne," he said breezily, nodding to me before walking out the door, "you're certainly fortunate to number someone as prominent and wise as Judge Gulden among your friends. I'd say you got very lucky today." He grinned in a manner that told me how he really felt, that far from being "let off the hook," I, the innocent bystander to this whole affair, had just been handed a thirteen-month sentence.

Turning to look at my scowling, belligerent, delinquent niece, I couldn't have agreed more.

5

Evelyn Dixon

Standing in a puddle of not-quite-subsided water, the plumber shook his head.

"A quilt shop? In New Bern? Lady, you must be crazy. You won't last six months."

"So I've been told"—I yawned, weary from a night of bailing—"about six hundred times. Just figure out how to fix the pipe and give me the estimate, would you please? I'll be upstairs, making coffee. Would you like a cup?"

"Oh yeah. That'd be great. Thanks. With cream if you've got it."

"I do."

I trudged up the wooden staircase at the back of the shop that led to my small apartment and plugged in the coffeemaker before flopping onto the sofa. When I'd peered through the dirty window of the shop, more than six months before, and decided that this filthy, decrepit ruin of a building was the stuff dreams were made of, I didn't realize that there was an apartment above the store. But then again, there were a lot of things I hadn't realized six months ago. And it was probably just as well. If I'd completely understood what I getting into, I might have changed my mind.

When I went back to Texas to pack up the house and have my things shipped to Connecticut, almost everyone thought I'd lost my mind. When I asked my neighor, Maureen Stimmons, to check the mailbox for a day or two after the moving truck left, just to make sure the mail was being forwarded properly, she was quite vocal in her disapproval.

"A quilt shop? You've never even held a full-time job! Evelyn, if you ask me, I think you're a few sandwiches short of a picnic," she declared, which was her way of saying she thought I was crazy. It's more colorful and maybe a teeny bit more polite than just coming out and telling someone they're nuts, but it means the same thing. There's a lot of that in Texas.

But I hadn't asked her, so I just smiled and said good-bye. My mother had an old saying too; not as colorful, but it had always stood me in good stead: If you don't have anything nice to say, then don't say anything at all. And I definitely didn't have anything nice to say to Maureen or, for that matter, to most any of my former friends—if you could call them that.

For the previous couple of decades, we'd lived in the same neighborhood, wheeled our babies and walked our dogs together, been in each other's babysitting co-ops, belonged to each other's book clubs, served on the same PTAs and high school booster clubs and church committees, gone to each other's Mary Kay Cosmetics parties, and yet, when it came to my divorce, most of those women dropped me like a hot potato, as if I suddenly carried a contagion that threatened to infect their own marriages.

When I saw them in the grocery store, they would ask how I was holding up, their faces a picture of sympathy. Initially, I'd told them the truth, how devastated I felt, how betrayed, how foolish, how lost. For a minute or so they'd keep their eyes fixed to mine, clucking sympathy, and nodding in all the right places, but then they'd look at their watches, suddenly recalling an appointment and scurrying off, promising we'd have lunch real soon, but we never did. It didn't take me long to realize that when someone asks you how you are, "Fine" is really all they want to hear. So the fact that my former friends disapproved of my plans didn't bother me a whit; I'd written them off months before.

There was one person, however, who thought my move to Connecticut was a good one—Mary Dell Templeton. I'd met her only a few months before Rob came home and announced that he wanted a divorce, but I don't know how I'd have gotten through it without her. She was a gift from God. Isn't that strange? Here I was, surrounded by people who'd known me for years, and in the end a woman whom I'd just met turned out to be the best friend I had.

Mary Dell is a native Texan, the real deal. She has a voice like praline syrup, dark and honeyed, and I never saw her without a Dr. Pepper close at hand. We met at the fabric store, where we were both taking an appliqué class. She had recently moved from Waco and was a first-rate quilter. Later, when I went to her home, I saw that the wall of her sewing studio was studded with ribbons she'd won for her original quilt designs, but her skill was obvious from the start. When I expressed surprise that she was bothering to take a class, she said, "Baby Girl, there's always more to learn, you know what I mean? Ripe fruit rots. Isn't that right, Howard?"

Howard was Mary Dell's son. He was about Garrett's age and had Down's syndrome. He accompanied his mother to every quilting class because, as Mary Dell said, "Howard's got a gift for picking out just the right fabrics. Me? I can sew, but I got no more color sense than I got fashion sense, do I, Howard?"

"No, Mama," Howard said with a regretful shake of his head. "None at all."

Which would cause Mary Dell to laugh and me to join in because it was so true. With Howard's help, Mary Dell's quilts radiated a subtle vibrancy that set them apart from the ordinary, but when it came to her wardrobe, subtlety went out the window. She liked to mix bright colors and bold patterns, usually several within the same outfit, as if she were a walking, talking crazy quilt. And topping it all off were her astounding earrings: enormous hoops, dangly beaded chandeliers that nearly brushed her shoulders, and huge clip-ons studded with geegaws and rhinestones that would have come in real useful if she'd ever been stranded on a desert island and needed to signal a passing ship.

"I don't care what anyone else thinks, I like them and I'm the only one I'm looking to please. The way I see it, little earrings are for little girls, and I'm a woman. W-O-M-A-N!" she declared, and then she said it again, just for good measure.

Though we'd only known each other for a couple of months, on the day I showed up at class with bags under my red-rimmed eyes, Mary Dell quickly assessed the situation. She insisted on taking me out to lunch after class and listened while I sobbed out my heartache over a pile of extra-spicy buffalo chicken wings. It was the longest I'd ever seen her sit without saying anything.

"I'm sorry," I sniffed, blowing my nose into a paper napkin then adding it to the tear-soaked pile next to my plate. "People are going to think I've lost my mind, crying in public like this."

"No such thing," Mary Dell assured me. "It's just the wings—all that hot sauce is making your eyes tear up. Here, drink some more Dr. Pepper. The sugar'll do you good."

From that day forward, Mary Dell was by my side. She called me every day and made up all kinds of excuses to get me out of the house, insisting that she and Howard needed dates for lunch, fabric shopping, shoe shopping, and quilt shows. And when I came back from Connecticut and announced my plans, Mary Dell was my cheerleader, telling me that I was absolutely up to it, helping me begin working on my business plan, brainstorming and daydreaming about the kinds of fabric I should stock, even helping load the boxes into my car for my trip north.

I was excited and nervous when we said good-bye in the driveway, but Mary Dell gave me confidence, saying, "You're going to be a real big success! This is going to be your lucky year. I'm sure of it!"

"Really? Why?"

"Because you're due, Baby Girl!"

At the time, I'd found some logic in her argument, so I drove to Connecticut and a new life, certain that my fortunes were about to change. But that was six months before. Recently, my confidence had begun to wane. Waking up in the middle of the night to the sound of running water and stumbling downstairs to discover four inches of wet ruining the freshly painted walls and the carpeting that had been installed just the day before hadn't helped matters.

The night before, I'd been so busy running around trying to find the water shut-off valve and bailing that I really didn't stop and consider the magnitude of this setback. But now, lying back on the sofa with my eyes closed, listening to the steady drip of the coffeemaker, I realized that leak was going to seriously delay my opening.

"Again!" I groaned aloud and clutched a sofa pillow to my stomach, then called out to the ceiling, "Why? Why does everything have to happen to me? Couldn't you cut me some slack, just this once?"

"Sorry? Are you talking to me?" the plumber asked, standing with one foot in the door, not quite committed to entering my apartment. I sat up and tossed the pillow aside.

"No, I was talking to God. Actually, I was just complaining to God, but don't worry about it. He's used to it."

The plumber nodded slowly and stared at me, trying to decide if I was joking or not.

"So," I asked, "what's the damage?"

He smiled, clearly relieved to be on more familiar ground. "Well, it could be worse—a lot worse. There's only one leak. It's a big one, but it won't be that hard to fix. I can get started on it today, probably finish tomorrow or the day after. Considering the age of the building, the pipes are in pretty good shape. You shouldn't have any more trouble once this is fixed."

"How much is it going to cost?"

"Not too bad. Maybe fifteen hundred depending on time and materials. Definitely no more than seventeen fifty," he declared and then, seeing the look on my face, quickly added, "but don't worry! I'm sure you can bill the landlord for it. You don't own the building, do you?"

"No, I'm leasing. I signed a two-year lease with the stipulation that I wouldn't have to pay anything for the first six months while I did the remodeling. At the time, I thought I was so clever. I was sure I'd have my doors open in three months." I rolled my eyes at the memory of my own naïveté.

"But first there was a holdup on the closing of my house in Texas, so I didn't have the money to start remodeling, then I unknowingly hired an architect who was the estranged ex-husband of the woman who issues building permits, then my sheetrocker decided to go to Florida to pick up some work after hurricane season, then I managed to order the only carpet in the store that was backordered for a month, not that anyone thought to tell me this at the time! And then, just as a little extra bonus, my painter won sixty-three thousand dollars in the lottery and decided to give up painting and go to law school!"

"Oh, you know Tommy?" the plumber asked brightly. "Yeah, wasn't that something? First time he ever bought a lottery ticket, and it turns out to be a winner. You know, I said to him . . ." He stopped and looked at me. "Oh. Sorry. Yeah, you've had a run of bad luck, that's for sure."

I nodded grimly. "If it weren't for bad luck, I'd have no luck at all."

He grinned. "Is that one of those Texas sayings? My cousin's wife is from there, and she's always saying stuff like that. Like when

Tommy won the lottery, she said he was so lucky he could sit on a fence and the birds would feed *him*." He laughed.

"Of course, it wasn't true. Tommy was real sick with Lyme disease year before last, and then, when he finally got well, a guy ran into him and totaled his truck. The insurance company didn't want to pay but half of what it was worth. That's why Tommy decided he wanted to go to law school, so I was real happy for him when he won that money, you know? He was due."

I bit my lip and decided not to comment.

"What it all comes down to," I continued, "is that, as of last week, I had to start paying rent on a shop I've spent twenty thousand dollars fixing up but has yet to make its first dollar or welcome its first customer."

"Well," the plumber observed, "at least you've been able to live rent free for six months. That's worth something. And it's a nice place you've got here. Small. But nice."

I looked around at the apartment and sighed. "Small" was the word, all right—just one bedroom and bath with a tiny closet, and this room, the living-sewing-dining-kitchen area. But it had a real wood-burning fireplace, which I'd always wanted but never had, exposed brick walls, the perfect backdrop to display my favorite quilts, and two tall windows that let in plenty of sunlight and looked out onto the cobbled courtyard. There was just enough room for everything I needed: my sofa, the easy chair with my standing quilt hoop, a scarred oak table and four chairs I'd found in one of the antique stores, and, most importantly, my sewing machine and cutting table, tucked neatly into a well-lit corner. He was right. It was a nice apartment, and, up until last week, it hadn't cost me a thing to live here.

"Thanks. I like it, too," I said, standing up and taking three strides to get from living-sewing to dining-kitchen. "Coffee's ready. Would you still like a cup?"

"Sure. That'd be great."

I opened the cupboard and took out two coffee mugs. "You said cream and sugar?"

"No. Just cream. If you've got it. Otherwise black is fine."

"No problem," I assured him as I opened the refrigerator door, "I just bought some yesterday, and—oh no!" I cried and then turned my face to the ceiling again. "I suppose you think this is funny!" I called out, my voice cracking.

Concern creased the plumber's brow, and he stepped up behind me, gingerly.

"Lady, you okay? What is it? Oh jeez. That's a shame," he said as he peered into the open refrigerator. "All your food is spoiled. The leak must have shorted out the power to your fridge. Well, at least you still got power everywhere else. But it don't smell too good, that's for sure."

"No," I echoed softly, "it sure don't."

"Hey, lady. Cheer up. It's not that bad. You're not going to cry or anything are you?" I shook my head silently. The plumber looked relieved. He pulled on his nose, thinking.

"I've got a friend who's an electrician. If you want, I can give him a call. He's usually pretty busy, but if I asked him, I'm sure he'd come right away. He owes me a favor. Would you like me to ask him?"

"Would you, please?" I swallowed hard and grabbed my purse. "Sorry about the cream, but you and your friend can help yourselves to coffee."

"Sure thing, but . . . ," he said, his eyes narrowing as he watched me head for the stairs. "Lady, where are you going?"

"To lunch. I need some buffalo chicken wings and Dr. Pepper. And I need them now."

6

Evelyn Dixon

The server, a handsome, tall man with gray hair and blue eyes who might have been a few years younger or older than myself, and whose brogue brought forth visions of green hills in the old country, wore a disdainful expression.

"Madam," he said, "I may be an Irish restaurateur, but this is a fine dining establishment, not a pub. We do not serve bar food here. I can offer you a very fine duck confit, a dish that recently caused the food critic from the *Globe* to lay her head on the table and weep for joy, but chicken wings never have and never will appear on the menu of Grill on the Green. And there isn't a restaurant within five hundred miles that serves Dr. Pepper. This is New England, not the Alamo."

There was something in his eye, just the barest glimmer of a twinkle, that indicated he might be teasing me, but I wasn't sure, so I dutifully ordered a ginger ale and the duck and made no more mention of chicken wings.

"So you're the owner?" I asked as he wrote down the order. "I saw you seating people on my first visit to New Bern."

"I am. Today I'm also the waiter. One of my servers called in sick. Other days I'm the maitre d', the chef, the head dishwasher, bartender, and bouncer—whatever is needed. That's the nature of owning your own business. You've got to be a jack of all trades, able to step in and do anyone's job at a moment's notice—and do it well."

"Yes. I'm beginning to understand that myself. I'm Evelyn Dixon," I said, smiling. "I've taken out a lease on the old Fielding Drug building, in Cobbled Court."

His eyes grew wide, and he started to say something, but suddenly flinched and turned around just in time to see one of his servers nearly drop a tray; it was like he had eyes in the back of his head. "For heaven's sake, Jason!" he exclaimed, grabbing the edge of the tray a split second before it would have clattered to the floor, taking two entrées with it. "Watch what you're doing!"

"Sorry, Charlie," the young server said. "I lost my balance. I'll be more careful."

"You certainly will," he retorted, the threat of the waiter's imminent unemployment clear in his tone. He glared at the young man and then looked down at the tray. "Is this order for table twenty-four? The salmon is for Mrs. Wynne?" The server nodded. "Take it back! Don't even think of serving it like that. Abigail likes her salmon well done, charred on the outside. Black! I've told you that a million times."

"I know." Jason nodded earnestly. "I told Maurice that it was for Mrs. Wynne. I told him what you said, but he said he wouldn't do it. He threw a spatula at me and said it was a crime to serve it like that."

Charlie rubbed his face with his hands. "Well, that is as may be, but Abigail Burgess Wynne is the customer, and one of my best, so Maurice is going to have to put principle aside and cook her salmon the way she wants it. You go back there and tell him I said that, and if he doesn't like it, he can just . . ." Jason, who couldn't have been more than twenty, faced with the prospect of delivering this message from his irate, temperamental boss to the equally irate and temperamental chef, had a look of terror on his face. Charlie sighed, his anger deflating.

"Never mind. I'll deal with Maurice. But if you're ever going to make anything of yourself in the restaurant business, Jason, you've got to grow a spine. Get this lady a ginger ale. And a glass of chardonnay while you're at it, on the house. She's going to need it. She's about to open her own business."

He marched off, jaw set and eyes steely, ready to do battle with the kitchen king.

Within a minute, Jason was back, carefully balancing two glasses on his serving tray. "Oh," I said, gesturing toward the wine glass, "I don't need this. I think he was just kidding."

"Maybe," he said, putting both glasses on the table, "but you can't always tell if Charlie is joking or not. He's not in a good mood, and I'm not taking any chances."

"So he's hard to work for?"

"Not exactly. He's demanding, that's for sure, but he's not any harder on us than he is on himself. When I first started working here, he scared me, but I've learned a lot from him. His family back in Ireland owned restaurants for generations. Charlie knows everything about food. Maurice does the cooking, but if he wasn't so busy running the restaurant, Charlie could do the job himself. He and Maurice plan all the menus together."

Jason grinned as he continued. "Someday, I'd like to have my own restaurant, you know. Nothing as fancy as this. Maybe just a nice diner or something. I figure that by working for Charlie, in a couple of years I'll know enough to make a go of it."

"Does he know that's what you want to do?" I asked, sipping at my ginger ale. "A lot of entrepreneurs might not hire someone who could become the competition in a year or two."

Jason laughed at the idea. "Me? Competition for the Grill? I don't see that happening, but Charlie knows about my plans. I told him during the interview, and he hired me anyway. Ever since then he's been helping me, pulling me aside, explaining the business side of things to me, having me work in different parts of the restaurant so I'll know what it really takes to run one of my own. Charlie's really a good guy deep down; he just comes off a little hard-nosed at first."

"Jason!"

The young waiter jumped, and so did I; Charlie seemed to appear out of nowhere. "Have you been standing here talking all this time?"

"No, Charlie. . . . I got the drinks, just like you said to."

"Well, good for you! And did I then say you could stand here sucking up oxygen while the people at table twenty-six die from thirst because you've neglected to fill the water glasses? Get on with you, boy!"

Jason scuttled away.

"You haven't touched your wine," Charlie said with a frown. "Go on then. Try it," he commanded.

I did. It was delicious, a flavor like oak and black currants and age, an aroma like secret underground caverns.

"Wonderful! It must be expensive."

Charlie shook his head. "Not at all. This is our house chardonnay. It's French and very affordable for the quality. Most people think domestic wines are cheaper, but lately the California vintages have gotten ridiculously overpriced. Many of the European wines are a much better value, if you know what to look for. Of course, we carry wines that cost as much as two or three hundred dollars a bottle for those who want it, but, by and large, our wine list is very accessible. You've got to know what your customers want," he said. "That's true for any business."

"You're right," I sighed. "I know what quilters want in Texas, but I'm a little less sure about the trends in New England. I hope I don't fill my store with Dr. Pepper when what folks are really interested in is ginger ale."

"Yes, I heard about you. News travels fast in New Bern. Everyone says you won't last six months."

"That's me. Evelyn Dixon—insane entrepreneur."

"Well," he shrugged, "aren't we all? Insane, I mean. Charlie Donnelly." He reached out his hand, and I shook it.

"Nice to meet you, Charlie."

"So you're from Texas, are you?" he asked suspiciously. "Where's your accent?"

"Don't have one. I was born in Wisconsin and moved to Texas as an adult."

"Oh, that's too bad," he said, smiling slightly, the hint of a twinkle returning to his eye. "Nothing like an accent to charm the customers."

Just then, a waitress, the same young woman I remembered from my previous visit, approached carrying two steaming plates.

"Thank you, Gina. You can put them right there." Charlie nodded his head in my direction. The waitress put both plates down on the table and left to tend to other customers.

The platters were loaded with a dozen different miniature entrées and appetizers, all beautifully presented. There was a piece of fish cut into a diamond shape, with golden grill marks crisscrossing the tender white flesh swimming in a brilliant green sauce, a miniature crab cake sitting on top of a single leaf of bright red radicchio, a slice of sizzling steak with a pink center that smelled of ginger and garlic and spices I couldn't name, and several other dishes, including a small duck leg placed artfully on top of a mound of ruby-colored chutney—the confit that made food critics cry.

"I didn't order all this," I said helplessly.

"No, of course you didn't. I did. Some of those things aren't even on the menu."

"It looks delicious, but this . . . Well, it's too much. I'll never be able to finish it all. At least sit down and help me eat some of it."

Charlie frowned and shook his head. "Can't do that. I've got a restaurant to run. Every table is full. I never sit down to eat until at least nine o'clock, after the rush is over."

"But I . . ." I really didn't know what to say. The food smelled delicious, and I was starving, but the Grill was not an inexpensive place and I was worried about how I'd pay for all this.

"Try it," Charlie said. Clearly, he was not going to budge until I'd tasted the food. "The confit first. Make sure you eat it with the chutney. It's delicious. My mother's recipe. Well, go on," he said impatiently.

"Charlie . . . I . . . Well, it's just that . . . a pipe burst at the shop this morning, and it's going to cost fifteen hundred dollars to fix it, and now I'll have to delay my opening again. I haven't had any income for months, just money going out for remodeling and buying stock. I've been watching every penny, haven't even gone to the movies in three months. But today was such an awful day that I decided I just had to have a little treat, but I was only thinking of getting a soda and an appetizer, not all this. . . ."

I looked up, trying to read his face, hoping for some sign that he understood my predicament, but it was impossible. Embarrassing as it was, I was just going to have to say it. "Charlie, I can't afford this."

Charlie looked at me blankly for a moment. Then one corner of his mouth twitched, and the other followed, and he smiled. "Well, of course you can't, you silly woman. You're about to open your own business; you don't have two nickels to rub together. You think I don't know that? This is on me, a sort of welcome-to-the-neighborhood dinner. I reckoned I'd better do it while you're still here, because, as everyone says, you won't last six months."

There was the sound of a woman's voice, raised and clearly irritated, coming from the back of the restaurant, and Charlie turned.

"Then again," he said over his shoulder as he walked off to see what the commotion was, "everyone might be wrong. Eat your duck."

I smiled, picked up my knife and fork, cut off a small piece of the bird, and put it into my mouth.

Charlie was right. Tears came into my eyes. I had made a friend.

7

Abigail Burgess Wynne

Jason, one of the newer waiters at the Grill, finally brought our entrées.

"Asian shrimp salad for Mr. Spaulding," he said, putting down the plates, "and the salmon for you, Mrs. Wynne. Sorry for the delay." The poor boy looked frazzled.

"That's fine, Jason. We weren't waiting long." I smiled conspiratorially and rested my hand on his arm for a moment. "I saw Charlie charge back to the kitchen looking ready to explode. Let me guess—Maurice didn't want to burn my salmon?"

Jason smiled but didn't say anything. I laughed.

"A very diplomatic response. Well, you tell Maurice that I said my fish was delicious, absolute perfection, that I think he's a genius and I'm going to tell all my friends to order it just this way. That should really irritate him, don't you think?"

Again, the young server declined comment, but he sounded sincere when he said he hoped we enjoyed our meal before walking toward the kitchen.

"See, Abigail? That's what I'm talking about," Franklin said as he took up his fork and began carefully picking scallions out of his salad. I've never understood why he just doesn't order the salad without the scallions, but that's Franklin. He never wants to be a bother to anyone; and besides, he says that picking out the onions makes him eat more slowly.

"You have such a way with people, even young people like our waiter. He came to the table, completely petrified that we were going to be angry after waiting so long, yet with a few kind words you put him completely at ease. When you want to, you can win anyone over. Now, why can't you do the same thing with Liza?"

"There is a big difference between being pleasant to a waiter, or a bank teller, or even a tennis partner—someone you have to see only occasionally—and dealing with an uninvited guest, or rather a criminal, who is serving out their sentence in your guest room." I picked up my knife and sliced into the crisp, black skin of the salmon. It broke under the blade with a satisfying crunch.

"Abigail, be fair. Liza isn't exactly a criminal." Franklin raised his hand to interrupt a forthcoming protest on my part. "I know. I know. She took a sweater without paying for it, but it isn't like you're harboring a hardened felon under your roof—just a sad, lonely, confused girl who is crying out for help."

I rolled my eyes. "Franklin, please. Don't give me any of that psychological mumbo jumbo. She's a grown woman. She's nineteen years old, not some pitiable, misunderstood child, and she should be responsible for her own actions." He started to say something, but this time it was my turn to cut him off.

"You're too softhearted, Franklin. You see her as this vulnerable little orphan, but you're wrong. I'm telling you, the girl is anything but vulnerable. Pigheaded, that's what she is!"

"Oh, come on, Abigail. She can't be all that bad."

"No? She's impossible, Franklin. Impossible! She's gloomy, rude, and self-centered. She doesn't get up until noon, doesn't go to bed until three, and hides out in her room all day either listening to that cacophony of tin cans and catgut she calls music or working on her so-called 'art.' From what I can see, her three semesters at art school were a complete waste of time and money. All her canvasses are covered with globs of paint, bits of twine, or wire, and who knows what else. 'Found objects' she calls them, which is apparently the art world's new word for trash. Ridiculous! I'm a well-known patron of the arts! True, I've never been enthused about modern art, but I can appreciate it. No one can say I don't. How much did I give to her Geltzmer Museum last year? Ten thousand?"

"Fifteen," Franklin answered without looking up from his plate. The offending onions now pushed to one side, he was concentrated on finishing his salad. I, on the other hand, hadn't eaten more than two or three bites of my salmon. Franklin was right; he did eat too fast.

"There, you see? That's my point exactly. I appreciate modern art more than most people, but this! Do you know, she's just completed a so-called self-portrait—entirely out of bottle caps—and had the audacity to ask if she could hang it up in the foyer! And then, when I suggested it might be more appropriate to hang it in her room, an offer which, frankly, I considered generous, she slammed her door and didn't come out for an entire day!"

"You know what they say, Abbie—beauty is in the eye of the beholder. Maybe she was trying to communicate with you, trying to help you understand where she's coming from. Legally, you're right, Liza is an adult, but she's still very young, a teenager, and she's lost her mother to boot. Heaven knows, I wasn't the best father in the world, but my Janice and Caitlin turned out all right in the end. The real key to dealing with teenagers is trying to see things from their point of view and being willing to negotiate a little."

"I do not negotiate with terrorists," I declared, only half joking.

Franklin ignored my comment. "Really, Abbie, would it have killed you to hang her picture where people could see it?"

"That's not the point!" I was growing increasingly annoyed with Franklin's lack of sympathy for my situation. Whose side was he on anyway? "I don't see why I should have to negotiate a thing. It's my house, and I like it the way it is. My foyer has appeared in the pages of *Architectural Digest.* I'm certainly not going to take down my own carefully arranged artwork to be replaced by a collage of Liza's face composed entirely of filthy, rusting bottle caps. That's not art, Franklin; it's self-indulgence, and it seems to me that Liza Burgess has been indulged quite enough already!"

Just remembering the episode got my blood boiling again, and by the time I'd finished my speech, my voice was raised and I could feel the heat on my face. Charlie Donnelly appeared at the table.

"Everything fine here? Franklin? Abigail, how is your salmon? Black enough for you?"

I took a deep breath and forced a smile to my lips. "Just right. If you were to believe my niece, it's almost as black as my heart." I laughed, trying to sound lighthearted, but knew I wasn't convincing. Because I eat at the Grill several times a week, Charlie knew all about the situation with Liza.

"Forgive me. I didn't mean to raise my voice, Charlie. It's just that I'm finding the rigors of surrogate motherhood rather challenging."

Charlie smiled winningly, turning the full beam of his Irish charm upon me. "Nothing to forgive, Abigail. We understand each other. You're just my kind of woman—difficult!" He winked, and I couldn't help but laugh, meaning it this time.

"I'm going to run back into the kitchen and order you up your usual decaf cappuccino. That'll set you right. Anything for you, Franklin? Maybe a piece of chocolate bread pudding? You can't expect to do a good afternoon's work on just a salad."

Franklin shook his head. "No. Thanks, Charlie. I'm trying to lose a few pounds."

Charlie picked up Franklin's empty plate, brushed a few imaginary crumbs off the tablecloth, and went back to the pantry to make my cappuccino.

Calmer, in a more modulated tone, I picked up where I'd left off. "Either my sister was the worst mother on earth, raising her daughter to behave like this, or she must have found the child abandoned under a cabbage leaf somewhere. It must be the latter. Though Susan's faults were many and well documented, even she couldn't have raised such a monstrous child. Clearly, the girl was a foundling, or there was some mix-up in the maternity ward. I refuse to believe that Liza and I share even a drop of DNA from a common gene pool!"

"DNA comes in strands, not drops," Franklin pointed out as he reached into the bread basket and broke off a crust. His unruffled demeanor was irritating.

"Don't be so pedantic. You know what I mean. I cannot go on like this. She's been in my house barely a month, and I'm already about to tear out my hair! I'll never survive a year of this!"

"Abigail," he said, "do you think you might be overdramatizing this just a bit?"

"No, I don't. She is simply impossible. She barely speaks to me, and when she does, her tone is terribly rude. You'd think she'd be the tiniest bit grateful to me. After all, if it weren't for me she'd be rotting in a jail cell somewhere!"

"It sounds like she's angry."

"Really, Franklin?" I said, arching my eyebrows to their highest point. "How very insightful of you. Of course, she's angry. But she has no right to take her anger out on me. It isn't like I got her into this. Until Harry Gulden foisted her off on me, I'd barely laid eyes on her."

"That's true. She is your niece, but it's not like you've had anything to do with her. What could she possibly have against you? After all, you've done nothing, just left her to her own devices for the last nineteen years—and her mother too."

I looked up. The accusation in his eyes was plain. "That's not fair, Franklin. You of all people should know that. You know what Susan did to me."

"I do, but that was years ago. Couldn't you at least have gone to see her at the end? She was dying."

"And was my going to her bedside, pretending everything was so much water under the bridge, going to change that?" I snapped. "You make me sound utterly heartless, and it's not fair! You know I did what I could. I made sure there was money enough for Susan's doctors, and for Liza's education after. I told you to make sure they had whatever they needed."

Franklin looked at me and said in a cold voice, "What you said was to make sure they had whatever they needed as long as you never had to deal with them personally. You were willing to be generous with your wallet, Abigail, just not with your forgiveness."

"I was protecting them," I hissed. "I didn't want them to be embarrassed about taking money from me. That's why I had you make up that story about Uncle Dwight dying and leaving Susan a legacy. So they wouldn't have to feel beholden to me."

"Abbie, I'm not sure even you believe that speech. Maybe you'd better rehearse it a few more times."

"Franklin Spaulding! How dare you!" This was too much. I was furious, but he didn't seem to care.

"Abbie, I've always thought you were a simply marvelous woman—difficult, as Charlie so aptly observed, though worth the effort. But you've always held everyone at arm's length. Even me, and I've known you, known your secrets, taken care of every detail of your personal affairs, for the last thirty years. It was the same with Susan, though once upon a time she was closer to you than anyone in the world. I know she hurt you terribly, but if you couldn't bring yourself to forgive Susan, or even see her, you might at least have reached out to Liza. After Susan died, she had no one to turn to."

"No one but you! I heard the way she talked to you in the judge's chambers. Clearly, you decided to be the person she could turn to, and look what came from it. She came here, looking for you, but somehow I'm the one who's left to clean up the mess that you, with all your meddling in private affairs that don't concern you, have created. Who asked you to do that? All you were supposed to do was make sure she had enough money. That's all!" In spite of my earlier resolve, my voice was raised. A few people in the restaurant were craning their necks to look at us; many more were pretending not to look. I was mortified. I took a deep breath, touched my napkin to my lips, and laid it on the table.

I got up to leave just as Charlie returned carrying a cup of steaming cappuccino. His eyes moved quickly from my face to Franklin's, assessing the situation. "Abigail," he said soothingly, "sit down and have your coffee. It's got a lovely big cap of foam. I made it myself."

"Thank you, Charlie, but I have to go. I'm not feeling well. Please just add the bill to my tab and leave twenty percent for Jason." I gave him a quick peck on the cheek and picked up my handbag, then leaned down to speak to Franklin.

"Franklin," I said quietly but through clenched teeth, "you're my lawyer. You're not my lover, or my minister, or my therapist. You're my lawyer. That's all. From here on out, I want you to do what I ask you to do, the job I pay you to do, and nothing else. These are family matters, Franklin. I'll thank you to stay out of them."

I stood erect, and Franklin said, "You're right. It is a family matter, Abigail. Your family. Why don't you start acting like it?"

I didn't respond, just squared my shoulders and walked out of the restaurant.

8

Evelyn Dixon

It was a Saturday in midsummer, which meant that even at seven-twelve in the morning, the Blue Bean Coffee and Baking Company was crowded. The bells above the door jingled cheerily as I walked inside, and the line of customers waiting for their morning fix of java turned to look at me.

After only a few months in New Bern, it was easy for me to distinguish the tourists from the locals; it was all about the clothes.

The tourists—or the NFH, as Charlie called them, which stood for Not-From-Here—fell into two fashion categories: those who were from New York and owned only black clothing, and those who were also from New York and tried to fit into the New England landscape but didn't. The latter sported a kind of Ralph Lauren country-preppy-chic with fabrics so crisp and bright you knew they'd been purchased at Saks the day before—a dead giveaway.

The locals were the ones wearing the authentic version of New England style that designers romanticized—run-over loafers worn with no socks, faded cotton button-downs, slightly wrinkled chinos, and, because a summer rain had chilled the air, pilled, shapeless sweaters with varying degrees of wear at the elbows. New Englanders believe in getting value for their money, and as long as the yarn stayed more or less knit together, they kept wearing the same sweaters they did every year. Fashion trends don't enter into it at all. I know a man well into his fifties who proudly wears the same blue cashmere his mother bought for his freshman year at Yale. It's stretched so tight over his post-freshman stomach that you can see pinpoints of his undershirt peeking through the weave, but he insists that it still has plenty of wear in it. He's a true-blue Yankee.

All of them, locals and NFH alike, looked grumpy. The NFH because they couldn't understand why these yokels didn't take a tip from Starbucks and hire enough people for an assembly line instead of relying on one seventeen-year-old girl to take orders, ring them up, and then, one at a time, and taking her time, brew, steam, ice, blend, or foam each individual drink.

Likewise, the locals were irritated because they knew if these people who were Not-From-Here were somewhere else, they'd have had their coffee twenty minutes ago. And though my livelihood depended on the patronage of both groups, at the moment I stood firmly on the side of the locals. I needed my coffee, and I needed it now.

Sitting at one of the Blue Bean's only two tables, a man rattled a newspaper as he turned the page and cleared his throat. It was Charlie. He lowered the paper and peered over the top.

"You're late," he said, holding out a cardboard cup. "I was thirty seconds from drinking your coffee."

"Sorry." I stepped out of the line and pulled up a chair. The other customers, still caffeine deficient, glared at me, jealous of my good fortune.

"Thanks for ordering for me. I thought you'd already come and gone." Several months before, I'd run into Charlie at the Blue Bean and it had become our habit to have our morning coffee together. I dug three dollars out of my purse to pay him back. He put the money in his pocket and then folded up his paper.

"How can you possibly be late? You only live half a block and one flight of stairs from here. Looking at the state of your hair, I know it wasn't because you were up there primping in front of your mirror."

"Thanks very much. It's not like you're so much to look at in the morning yourself."

"True, but Irishmen are known more for wit and our words than looks. Rakish and frumpy—it's part of my charm."

"Seems to me that you rack up a lot of things to your Irish charm."

"Well, I'm a charming man." He shrugged.

"So you are. At times." I took a first sip of coffee, closing my eyes and savoring the moment.

"Mmmm! I needed that. I didn't get to bed until two."

"Out salsa dancing, were you? Having yourself a little TGIF party?"

"Not quite. More like trying to balance my books and then doing it again, hoping to come up with some different figures." I yawned.

"And did you?" Charlie asked.

I shook my head. "Sadly, no. If something doesn't change, drastically, and soon, the naysayers of New Bern might turn out to be right in their predictions; Cobbled Court may not live to celebrate its six-month anniversary."

Charlie looked at me, his blue eyes concerned. "Oh, come now. It can't be as bad as all that. The grand opening was just two months ago. You started out so well."

He was right. I had.

In spite of the flood caused by the broken pipe and some delay in receiving my first shipments of fabric, Cobbled Court Quilts opened its doors for business right after Memorial Day, just in time for the tourist season. It was a huge relief. A good summer season was crucial to my survival; I could expect to make as much as sixty percent of my annual income between Memorial and Labor days.

To attract customers on my first day of business, a beautiful Saturday, I took out an ad in the local newspaper and hung banners saying Grand Opening at both entrances to Cobbled Court. I even hired one of Charlie's off-duty dishwashers to hand out flyers to people on Commerce Street advertising the grand-opening sale offering ten fat quarters for the price of seven and fifteen percent off all bolt fabrics and classes, plus refreshments and a drawing for a mariner's compass quilt I'd made as a class sample. That was Mary Dell's idea. When I'd phoned with the big news that, at long last, I was ready for business, she suggested the raffle as a good way to build a customer mailing list.

"Plus, if folks come in and take a look at the quilt, they'll be more likely to sign up for the class," she said.

"Great idea! And even if they aren't interested in that particular pattern, I'll have their names and addresses so I can send them a flyer whenever I have a sale or a new class brochure. Thanks for the idea, Mary Dell. After all this time, I almost can't believe that this is actually happening—I'm about to open my own quilt shop! It's just so exciting!"

"Well, I'm excited for you, darlin'," Mary Dell drawled. "And I've got some news myself. I hadn't wanted to tell you before 'cause I wasn't sure it was really going to happen, but I got the call yesterday . . ." She paused just long enough to give me a chance to guess her news.

"Don't tell me!" I squealed. "Your book! They're going to publish it!"

When we'd met, Mary Dell told me she'd written a quilting book that she'd titled *Family Ties*. It gave advice on quilting with children and featured a variety of unique patterns, from the simple to the complex, that families could do together. She'd written it when

Howard was little and sent it out to publishers, but none of them had been interested. Recently, noting the increased interest in all kinds of crafts, she'd decided to try again, obviously with more success than she'd had on the first go-round. "Oh, Mary Dell, that is amazing news! I'm just so happy for you!"

I could practically hear her grinning through the phone line. "Yeah, I'm pretty happy myself. In fact, if I was any happier I'd drop my harp plumb through the cloud!"

"This is fabulous! You're an author!"

"Not yet, but soon. Sometime next year, so they tell me. 'Course," she said modestly, "I don't expect they'll sell more than about forty copies—and me and Howard'll probably buy thirty-eight of them."

"What are you talking about? I'm going to order some for the shop today, just so I make sure to get mine before they run out. And when you're a big, famous quilting writer, you've got to promise to come teach a class at Cobbled Court. I'll probably have to rent chairs just to make room for everybody."

Mary Dell laughed aloud at the audacity of my vision. "Sure thing, darlin'! If I'm ever a big, famous quilting writer, I'll come teach at your shop. That'll probably happen about the time that pigs fly, but if you look up in the clouds some morning and see porkers on parade, then go ahead and rent those chairs, Baby Girl; I'll be there. In the meantime, I'll be praying that your grand opening is a real big success!"

And it was. On that first weekend, I was swamped with customers. Well, really there were more browsers than customers, but by the end of the first day I'd signed up four people for the Mariner's Compass class, seven for the beginner's class, added ninety-eight names to my mailing list, and rung up nearly two thousand dollars in sales. At the time, it seemed like a fortune. I went to bed that night exhausted but encouraged that I was off to a great start. Really, I was. And though I soon discovered that exhaustion is the permanent condition of a quilt-shop owner, I loved what I was doing.

Not surprisingly, my favorite part of running the shop was the creative side: teaching classes, sewing samples, helping customers pick out fabrics, answering questions about difficult projects, and, of course, poring over catalogs and samples trying to decide which fabrics, books, and notions I should stock. I'd opened my doors with two thousand bolts of fabric, five hundred more than I'd planned on at first, but I knew that the bigger the fabric inventory, the more likely I'd be to attract quilters from places other than New Bern. If Cobbled Court Quilts was going to survive, it had to be a shop that quilters would drive out of their way to visit. There just weren't enough quilters in New Bern to support it. I had to draw a regional audience.

It was a surprise to discover that I also enjoyed the business side of the shop—not that doing accounting, keeping up with inventories, or managing invoices was exactly a thrill, but it worked a part of my brain that I'd let lie dormant for many years. Sure, I made plenty of mistakes, but I was managing the whole operation on my own. I couldn't help but feel proud of my accomplishment, more confident than I had in years.

You know, it's so odd, but on the day when Rob walked into our kitchen—the kitchen we'd remodeled the year previously and with the granite counters Rob had said that I'd better make sure I liked because we were going to have to live with them until we died or moved into the old folks' home—when he walked into the kitchen that day, stood next to the island where I was chopping green peppers, and said that he wanted a divorce, I felt so stupid.

Yes, I also felt betrayed, bereft, heartbroken, abandoned, all those emotions I'd imagined women must feel when their husbands walked out on them—women whose number I was certain I would never, ever be among—but I'd never once thought to add stupidity to that list. But when the unthinkable happened, there it was.

How could I have been so stupid? How could I have believed that buying granite countertops with a lifetime warranty meant that my marriage was similarly guaranteed against chips, scrapes, younger women, and midlife crisis? It was such a cliché. And I'd never seen it coming. How could I have given my trust to this man who proved so untrustworthy? I felt like a fool.

For a long time after that I didn't trust my own judgment about anything. The thought of having to make a decision simply paralyzed me. Once, when a harried grocery clerk with a long line of customers asked if I wanted paper or plastic, I stood there stammering and unable to decide for what seemed like an eternity. Finally the clerk lost patience and angrily stuffed my bread into a plastic bag, then piled two cans of diced tomatoes and a box of dishwasher detergent on top of the loaves, squashing them flat. I was so embarrassed that I didn't say anything, just handed her a fifty-dollar bill for forty-two dollars' worth of groceries and left without waiting for my change.

But somehow, making that one decision, the decision to drive north to see the fall colors in New England, gave me courage to make the next decision and the next and the next: what display shelving to order, how much money to borrow from the bank, which classes to offer, whether or not to order that extra five hundred bolts of fabric. Every decision was mine alone, which meant that the shop's success or failure was a reflection of me. So when customers said they thought Cobbled Court was the best quilt store around and then confirmed this by making second and third purchases, it was as if they were affirming me personally. I began to have faith in myself again, to believe that, though where my marriage was concerned I might have been foolish, I wasn't a fool. I was capable. I had something to offer.

The growing number of repeat customers may have filled my heart with pride, but, unfortunately, it didn't fill my register with cash—at least not enough of it. Like so many novice entrepreneurs, I had underestimated my expenses and overestimated my income.

The grand-opening weekend had been an anomaly. After that, my receipts shrank. Not to say that the shop was empty, far from it. My sales were growing, slowly, but even so my cash reserves (my half of the proceeds from the sale of the house plus my divorce settlement) were dwindling much more quickly than I could ever have imagined.

"I'm losing money," I admitted to Charlie. "Every week I lose a little less than the one before, but the deficit isn't shrinking quickly enough. Come the end of the tourist season, business will slack off. Unless I get some miraculous inflow of cash, I won't have enough in reserve to last until next summer."

There. I'd said it. The night before, as I'd added up rows and rows of receipts, subtracted my expenses, then redone the calculations over again, hoping against hope that I'd find a mistake in the figures, I'd known the outcome of the equation, but I hadn't wanted to acknowledge the truth. Now I had, and the truth gave me a headache.

Groaning, I rubbed my face with my hands. "Oh, Charlie. What am I going to do?" I didn't expect an answer, just sympathy, but that wasn't Charlie's style.

"Arrange for one," he said.

"Arrange for what?"

"A miracle. As my sainted mother used to say, 'You can accomplish more with a kind word and shillelagh than you can with just a kind word.'"

"A shillelagh? What's that? I don't understand."

Charlie rolled his eyes. "A shillelagh is a kind of stick, made of very hard wood, generally used for walking, but, when the occasion calls for it, it makes a fine club. So what my mother was saying, in her inimitable way, was that talk is cheap. If you want something to happen, it's up to you to make it happen. Do whatever it takes. At least, that's what I always thought she was saying. I've got my own version of her proverb that's a little more to the point: When God closes a door, start running full speed, ram into it, and bash the damned thing down."

My head still hurt. "Well, that's all very poetic, but it isn't exactly like I've been sitting behind my counter and just waiting for the customers to start pouring in. I've taken out ads in the paper. I had that big grand-opening event—raffle, sale, handed out flyers—"

Charlie snorted. "So you took out an ad and had a party. Big deal. Every new business does that. You've got to do more. Think out of the box, Evelyn."

"Okay," I agreed. "How?"

"Well, I don't know. You're the quilter, not me. You've got to figure out what it is that makes your shop unique, what your mission is. And then you've got to find a way to tell people about it. How can you do that?"

Tired and discouraged as I was, I couldn't quite see where he was going. I shrugged. "I don't know. I've got a pretty big inventory, and I offer a good selection of classes for all skill levels, but so do a lot of stores. I think it's a lovely shop, but I don't know if you could call it unique. And as far as my mission . . . Well, I don't know that I have one exactly. I just want to run a good quilt shop and be able to make a living doing it."

"No," Charlie said firmly, almost impatiently. "That's not all there is to it. Sure, you want to be able to support yourself, but there are about two hundred easier ways to do that than owning a quilt shop, and you know it. Think. When you first walked down that alley and peered into that dirty window, what was it you saw? What was in front of you was a run-down wreck of a storefront that no one had thought to rent in years, but that's not what *you* saw. You had a vision, a dream of something special, something that gave you the courage to pull up stakes, empty your bank account, and put everything on the line." His voice was urgent. "What was it?"

I closed my eyes, conjuring the image in my mind.

"I saw women sitting together, sewing, laughing. Friends and strangers walking between rows and rows of fabric bolts, fingering cloth, considering colors, helping each other choose the combination of fabrics that would make the quilt they saw in their mind's eye more beautiful than they could have imagined. I saw ordinary women, women who've never so much as touched a paintbrush, picking up a number ten between needle instead and discovering the artist inside themselves. A place where they could take their love, or memories, or celebrations, or dreams, even their fears and disappointments, and turn them into something they could share with someone else."

I thought back to all the quilts I'd made over the years, each one a mile marker on the road of my life. The blue and yellow crib quilt I'd made by hand when I was pregnant with Garrett. And the second one, a hopeful pink and white, that was only three quarters done when I'd miscarried a baby girl, Julia Margaret, and how my mother and Aunt Lydia cried with me as we quilted little hearts onto the center of each block, creating a memorial to my stillborn daughter. I remembered the brilliant card-tricks quilt I'd designed when I taught my first class, in vibrant batiks that sparkled against the black background like diamonds on dark velvet, and the faces of my students, all beginners, glowing with pride as they showed off their finished projects during our final class. I thought of the dozens of quilts I'd given and received through the years: quilts to applaud, to thank, to comfort, to commemorate. I thought of Mary Dell and the Drunkard's Path quilt we'd made together after Rob left, when I didn't know where to turn and every path led nowhere, and how her encouragement helped me move down a new path. I thought of all the women I'd sat shoulder to shoulder with as we'd cut, and sewn, and quilted. I knew them. I knew their stories. And they knew mine.

I opened my eyes and saw Charlie looking at me, waiting for me to speak.

"I saw a community," I said.

He nodded. "All right. That's it, then. Your mission. That's what you must create—a community. Don't ask me how, but now you have the picture clear in your mind. Now that you do, you'll find a way. I know it."

❧ 9 ❧

Evelyn Dixon

I closed the cover of the magazine I'd been flipping through, a worn copy of *People* that was two years out of date, checked my watch, and sighed impatiently. Twenty minutes past my scheduled appointment time. I didn't have time for this—not today.

Approaching the desk, I tapped on the glass partition that separated me from the receptionist, a young woman named Donna, who was also one of my customers. Donna came in because she'd wanted to make a baby quilt for her sister Cathy's new baby, a little girl named Liesel Christine, who, after Cathy's eight-year struggle with infertility, was a precious gift to the whole family. It was just another example of why I loved owning Cobbled Court Quilts. I got to hear all about the projects my customers were working on and learned a little about their lives in the process. You'd never get that kind of interaction working in a grocery store or a clothing boutique. Buying broccoli or a blouse is just a transaction, but buying fabric for a quilt involves much more than just an exchange of money for goods; it is a commitment of time, an act of love, the opening paragraph of a story.

"Yes, Evelyn?" Donna asked as she slid the glass panel open.

"I don't want to be a pain, but I've been waiting nearly half an hour for my appointment," I said, stretching the truth a little. "Maybe I should reschedule. I've got so much to do yet this afternoon."

Donna nodded sympathetically. "I know. I'm sorry. Dr. Thayer had a delivery this morning, and it's thrown off the whole day. He shouldn't be much longer, but I know you've got your Quilt Pink event tomorrow. By the way, that was a great article in the paper, and a great picture of you, too! I bet you'll have a big turnout."

I nodded. "My phone has been ringing off the hook ever since the story ran. Some of the people coming are experienced quilters, but quite a few are novices. They're coming because they see it as a good way to support a friend or relative with breast cancer."

"One of my neighbors was diagnosed last year," Donna nodded. "She's had a rough time of it. I can't come to the shop tomorrow, but could you make up a kit for me anyway? I can work on it at home. I asked her to let me know if I can do anything to help, but I'm sure everyone says that. This seems like a nice way to let her know that I'm rooting for her."

"Sure. I'll make up an extra kit, and you can come pick it up whenever you like. I'm sure your neighbor will appreciate the thought."

"Thanks." Donna glanced up at the clock and frowned. "Let me run back and ask Dr. Thayer if it would be all right to reschedule you for later in the week."

She was back in a minute, shaking her head. "He'd really prefer to see you today, but promises he won't be much longer. He's just finishing up with another patient."

Reluctantly, I reclaimed my seat. I pulled my to-do list out of my jacket pocket and read it again.

I had to run by the grocery store and pick up trays of fruit and cheese and some pretty paper plates and napkins. Then I needed to stop by the printer's and run off twenty extra patterns. Maybe I should make that thirty, in case there were walk-ins? I scribbled that in the margin. And I'd need another fifty copies of the fall class brochure. After that, I had to run by the bank before it closed to make my deposit and get change for the cash drawer. And then, finally, after I'd finished all my other errands, I would go back to the shop and cut fabric for sixty-seven quilt block kits. Sixty-seven! I'd be lucky to be in bed before midnight. Who would ever have imagined it? Certainly not me and probably not Charlie, though the whole idea had begun with him, at least indirectly.

After our conversation at the Blue Bean, I'd begun racking my brain, trying to imagine what kind of promotion, or event, or class might make my vision a reality and transform Cobbled Court Quilts into a community for quilters. I'd toyed with several ideas, some more promising than others, but none seemed quite right. Then, on one of the rare occasions when I was actually caught up on my work, I'd sat down to enjoy a few moments with a cup of tea and read the latest copy of *American Patchwork and Quilting Magazine,* and there it was—an article about the upcoming Quilt Pink event.

The idea was simple. During one weekend in September, quilters from all over the country would go to their local quilt shops and piece a quilt block that would become part of a donated quilt. Each sponsoring quilt shop would decide on its own design, so no two quilts would be alike. In the spring, the quilts would be auctioned online and the proceeds donated to breast-cancer research.

Before I'd even finished reading the article, I knew this was the event I'd been looking for. One that would bring quilters together to do something good for others, just as they had been since the first group of quilters gathered around a wooden frame to exchange gossip and laughter, plying their needles to create something practical and beautiful to benefit someone else.

That's how I'd decided on the name for our quilt—Basket of

Blessings—a simple, classic design with pink baskets set on the diagonal on a background of assorted shades of brown, from light tan to chocolate. The design would be fairly simple, even for a beginner. The basket part was pieced, and only the handle would have to be appliquéd. And, for the more experienced quilters, I'd have an option to add a few appliquéd flowers in varying shades of pink. I smiled, thinking how pretty it would be to have a handful of blooming baskets sprinkled among the empty ones, all in different tones of pinks and browns, giving each quilter an opportunity to express her individuality while creating a block that would complement the whole quilt. When it was done, I would look at the different blocks, find a pleasing arrangement, and decide what kind of sashing and borders would show the blocks off to their best advantage.

I was so excited! I called Charlie right away to tell him about my idea.

"I'll make up kits for each quilter beforehand with the proper size of fabric squares and patterns. I'll put the different squares out on a big table, and they can choose whatever colors they want, so every block will be different. Then they can sit down, cut out the pattern, hand stitch the blocks right there, and, hopefully, by the end of the day we'll have enough blocks to make a whole quilt. What do you think?"

"What are you going to serve?" he asked.

"Serve?" I was a little taken aback, annoyed that he was asking questions instead of simply applauding my wonderful idea. "I don't know. Maybe some fruit and cheese?"

"And a cake," he mused. "I'll make one for you. Something big and chocolate. With all those women, it'll have to be chocolate." I started to say he didn't have to do that, that I could order one from the bakery, but he interrupted before I could get a word in. "And some punch. I've got a big punchbowl I use for catering that you can borrow. The whole thing should feel like a party."

Beneath Charlie's gruff exterior there beat a heart of gold. He wasn't questioning my idea; he was helping me expand it. And he was right on the money. We'd throw a party.

"Great idea! I'll even come up with some kind of little favor for everyone who comes, maybe a bag with a little marking pencil and a ruler. And I can have a few door prizes too."

"Good," he agreed. "Now, what are you going to charge for each kit?"

"Well, it's for a good cause. I was only planning on charging what I paid for the fabric and pattern copies. I'll donate the refreshments and prizes. Since the women will be donating their time to make the blocks, I want to give something too."

Charlie was quiet for a moment, thinking. "Evelyn, are you sure? You said your books aren't looking good. This will be a lot of work. Seems a shame not to see a little profit for your efforts."

I laughed. "I appreciate your optimism, Charlie, but I don't know if anyone will even show up yet. Besides, a couple of dollars tacked onto each kit isn't going to stave off bankruptcy. If I could see twenty women in my shop all working together on a quilt that might be even a tiny part of helping someone else, that's profit enough for me. And think of it this way: if Cobbled Court doesn't last out the year, at least I'll have the satisfaction of knowing that while it was open, I was able to do a little good."

"You're a good woman, Evelyn. Do you know that?"

I was about to make a joke, tell him to save the blarney for his customers, when my front doorbell rang to signal the arrival of a customer.

"Hey, Charlie. I've got to run. See you at the Bean tomorrow?"

"Bright and early," he confirmed. "You'll recognize me. I'll be the one that's on time."

"Very funny." I smiled as I hung up the phone and greeted my customer. In fact, I smiled for the rest of the afternoon, excited about my plans for the event and grateful to have found a friend as good as Charlie in such a short time.

Before the day was over, I had even more reason to be grateful for that friendship. Near closing time, the shop bell rang again, this time to announce the arrival of a reporter from the *New Bern Herald* who wanted to do a story about me, the shop, and the Quilt Pink event.

"You do?" I asked. "Really?"

"Yeah. Somebody called the news desk and told him about your event. My editor thought it was a good human-interest story for the weekend section, so here I am."

The reporter reached into his black shoulder bag, pulled out a camera that he hung around his neck by a strap, then took out a lined notepad and laid it on the checkout counter. He looked around the shop, squinting, and scratched his chin.

"Let's try a couple of shots in here first. Over there, by those bolts of fabric with that big green quilt behind. Then we can go outside and get a couple of you standing in front of the shop while we've still got enough light. We can do the interview after." He fiddled with the camera lens and then looked up expectantly.

"Ready?"

He took about a dozen photographs, but the shot that appeared on the front page of the Living section showed me standing in front of the red front door, under the black and gold Cobbled Court Quilts sign. Seeing the picture the following Sunday, I was reminded that it had been a long time since I'd darkened the door of a gym, but that picture did the trick.

When I went to church that day (sitting in the last pew as I always did so I could slip out quickly during the recessional hymn and jog across the Green in time to open the shop at noon), I was waylaid by four women who wanted to tell me their, or their sister's, or friend's breast-cancer story and ask how they could sign up for the Quilt Pink event.

I was touched by their willingness to open up to me and ignored the time. Opening up the shop fifteen minutes late, I saw a green light blinking on my answering machine. There were twelve messages from women wanting more information about Quilt Pink. And the calls just kept coming in. Not only that, my walk-in traffic doubled. And with every call and every new customer, there came a story—a memory, or loss, or victory they were compelled to share with someone else. The most passionate ones were the survivors, those who had beaten the disease and were determined to do everything they could to make sure other women didn't have to go through what they had.

They were the reason I was sitting in Dr. Thayer's waiting room, the ones who, once they'd told their stories, immediately asked when I'd had my last mammogram. I told them I was a few months late for my checkup, that I'd been too busy, that my new, cheaper insurance only covered mammograms every two years, that I hated going because every time I did, cysts showed up on the film, benign cysts that had been there since I was twenty-five, and set off all kinds of alarm bells and sent me back to the lab and doctor's office for all kinds of extra tests (just as they had this time) that always turned out to be nothing, but they weren't impressed. They shut their ears to my list of excuses and my promise to go in for a checkup as soon as the event was over and things calmed down. They scolded and hounded me until I made an appointment, not because I was convinced of the urgency of doing so, but because not to do so would have been to tear down the very thing I was trying to build. Busy as I was, helping these women validate their own experience by sharing their warnings and wisdom with others was surely worth the price of a few hours in the doctor's office.

They came through my door by the dozens, looking for a place to share their lives, just as I'd imagined they would. It was my dream, and it was beginning to come true.

And it all started with one little call to the newspaper office, I thought as I tossed the ancient copy of *People* onto the waiting-room coffee table. *Good old Charlie.*

The sound of the glass reception window sliding open startled me from my reverie. "Evelyn?" Donna said. "Come on back. The doctor can see you now."

I had not been worried when, after my mammogram, the technician said that there was a spot that looked a little unusual and the radiologist wanted to do an ultrasound in that area. I was not concerned when Dr. Thayer called and said he wanted to do a needle biopsy on my left breast. I had been through all that before, more than once.

Years before, when Garrett was still little, my doctor had felt something unusual in my breasts and ordered a baseline mammogram. Then, I was only twenty-five years old and terrified. I woke up in the middle of the night, crying, and Rob held me in his arms until morning, assuring me that everything was going to be all right, and it was. I had a number of harmless fibroids in my breasts. But year after year, every time we moved, or my doctor retired or a new physician came to work at the clinic, I was subjected to annoying rounds of post-mammogram testing. Of course, the other tests had been to extract and test fluids from the cysts; they weren't tissue biopsies like this. But because my test results had always come back negative before, I was sure it would be the same this time. Busy as I was, it hadn't crossed my mind to be worried.

But when I stepped through the door from the waiting room and Dr. Thayer himself was there to greet me, my heart started to beat a little faster. Something in his greeting, his solicitous tone as he asked how I was feeling today, and the weight of his arm across my shoulders as he escorted me into his private office rather than the examining room made a sick anticipation rise from the center of my stomach.

But it wasn't until I was sitting in his office and Dr. Thayer folded his hands together, rested them on his desk, and said, "I'm sorry, Evelyn. The biopsy was positive. You have cancer," that I understood what was happening.

He said those three words—You Have Cancer. And for a moment, everything stopped. My heart. My mind. My breath. Everything.

And when I took my next breath, everything had changed.

❦ 10 ❦

Abigail Burgess Wynne

"Excuse me?" I asked, certain that I must have heard her wrong. "You're going to get a what?"

Liza, who had broken with tradition by actually joining me at the breakfast table instead of pouring herself a cup of black coffee and going back to her room to drink it, stared at me over the edge of her cup.

"A tattoo," she said. An inky ribbon of black eyeliner made her large brown eyes look even larger. She blinked them innocently but was unable to completely conceal her pleasure at my horrified reaction. The corner of her mouth twitched, threatening to split her lips into a smile as she went on.

"Nothing too elaborate. Not a drawing or anything, just two words. Lady Burgess. Right here," she said, taking one finger and tracing an imaginary line from her jawline to her collarbone to indicate the proposed tattoo's placement, "in black, gothic lettering. I spoke with a tattoo artist and picked out the design yesterday. My appointment is next week. It's my birthday present to myself. It's going to be incredible. *Very* striking."

My stomach felt queasy, like I'd been poised at the top of a gigantic roller coaster that had suddenly taken a precipitous drop. "You can't be serious."

Liza was grinning openly now, not even trying to disguise her delight over my distress. "Of course I am. It's no big deal, Aunt Abigail. Everyone gets tattoos these days; and besides, it's my body," she declared. "I'm an adult. I can do whatever I want with it, and there really isn't anything you can do about it."

She was right. For the hundredth time, I mentally cursed Harry Gulden. He'd foisted the responsibility for this delinquent monster of a girl onto me, and then he failed to provide me with any effective means of controlling her out-of-control behavior! If she'd been my daughter I'd have threatened to ground her, or eject her from my house, or my will, or something! But she wasn't. And what's more, no matter how immature her behavior was, she was right. She was of age. If she was determined to get a tattoo (and the steely glint in her eye told me she was), there was very little I could do to stop her—even if the tattoo she was determined to get was purposely designed to besmirch our family name and heap as much personal humiliation upon me as possible.

I remembered what I'd said to Franklin that day in the restaurant, my not-quite-joking declaration that I would not negotiate with a terrorist. Today it was even less funny than it had been at the time, because, as far as I was concerned, that's what I was dealing with—a terrorist, or at least a blackmailer. If I didn't negotiate with her, there was no question in my mind that she would do exactly as she threatened. She'd parade up and down the streets of New Bern in her horrible ripped jeans and tight black T-shirts with an enormous, hideously lettered tattoo that shouted our kinship emblazoned on her neck—her neck!

Liza stared at me, and I stared back. I blinked first.

"That's right. It's your birthday next week." I tried to keep my tone casual. "Of course, you can get a tattoo . . . if that's what you really want. You've such a pretty neck, Liza." It was true.

Her neck was thin and elegant, a long, slender arc of white flesh that bowed gracefully from her jawline to her collarbone—a ballerina's neck.

"Those tatoos are permanent, aren't they? What if the design doesn't turn out as well as you'd hoped? Or if the . . . the . . . artist"—it nearly choked me to apply that word to this situation, but if I had a chance of preventing this disaster, I knew I had to deal with Liza on her terms—"makes some kind of mistake?"

"Delilah is a famous tattoo artist. She doesn't make mistakes." That echo of a smile returned to Liza's lips, but she still didn't blink. She knew the game we were playing—and she knew that she was winning.

"Still. It would be a shame if it didn't turn out as you've imagined. And there it would be. On your neck. Forever." I paused. Liza said nothing. "Maybe there's something you'd like more than a tattoo?"

A cashmere sweater? Legally obtained this time? A car? The Hope Diamond? She only had to name her price, and I'd pay it. Anything to keep my name—our name—from being immortalized in ink by a tattoo artist named Delilah.

"If you can think of another birthday gift you'd like in exchange for the tattoo, I'd be happy to get it for you. I was planning on getting you a present." A lie, and we both knew it.

Liza's eyes were triumphant. She had me where she wanted me—up against the ropes of social conformity.

"As a matter of fact, I did have something in mind."

Of course she did. I'd known it from the beginning.

She reached into the back pocket of her jeans and pulled out a folded-up piece of newsprint. At first I was sure it was an advertisement, maybe for a computer, or the latest cell phone, or even a car, but when she unfolded the paper and handed it to me, all I saw was a picture of a middle-aged woman, slender with blue eyes and straight, sandy hair cut in an angled bob that mirrored the slant of her jaw. She wore a black sweater and trim blue jeans with chunky silver and turquoise earrings. A black, purple, and teal paisley shawl was draped over her shoulder, giving her a vaguely bohemian look, as if she'd once taught high-school art classes.

Now the woman obviously was involved in some sort of retail venture. She was standing in front of the old Fielding Drugstore. Dolly Chesterton had said that some woman from Texas had taken out a lease on the place, but I couldn't recall the details. This must be her. Well, she'd certainly done a good job with remodeling the shop. The panes on the bowfront window were new and shining, but she'd been smart enough to retain the old woodwork, so the storefront kept the look and feel of an antique apothecary shop. She'd added another layer of crown molding around the doorframe to give it a more elegant appearance. The frame was painted black, and the sheen of it told me that she'd used an oil-based paint, certainly an extra expense, but the smooth, shining finish was worth it. The door itself was painted a vivid red that exactly matched the color of the potted geraniums on either side of the door. It was a charming effect. The door of the shop couldn't have looked more welcoming.

Clearly, the owner of New Bern's newest boutique had style, taste, and an eye for color. Either that or she knew enough to hire someone with those qualities.

What was this place, I wondered. A clothing store? In such an off-the-beaten-path location? Surely not. Perhaps an interior-design studio? I wasn't exactly keen on the idea of Liza redecorating my guest room. Heaven knew what the girl would want, black wallpaper with white skulls, probably, but if the tasteful woman in the newspaper photograph was the one in charge of the design, it couldn't be that bad. And even if it was, better skulls and crossbones in a back bedroom hidden from the eyes of my neighbors than "Lady Burgess" on Liza's neck where everyone in New Bern would see it.

"It looks like a very nice shop. I'd been thinking myself that your

room could do with a bit of updating," I lied again. It was starting
to become a habit. "New paint, wallpaper, drapes . . . whatever
you'd like to make it reflect your own personality. How much do you
think you'll need?" I pushed the newspaper across the table and
started to get up so I could go retrieve my pocketbook from the antique sideboard, but Liza interrupted.

"The story," she said flatly. "You have to read it."

The smile on her face faded as she handed the paper back to me.
I felt a strange prickling on the back of my head, as if a migraine
were about to come on. I retrieved my reading glasses that always
hung on the chain around my neck, put them on, and began reading.

NEW BERN'S NEWEST ENTREPRENEUR IS FIGHTING THE ODDS

Evelyn Dixon, the owner of New Bern's newest business, Cobbled
Court Quilts, isn't one to shy away from a challenge.

When she first saw the long-abandoned Fielding Drug Emporium during a vacation to New England last year, she knew it
would take time, money, and vision to renovate the old building
and turn it into a sustainable retail venture. And while she had
plenty of vision, time and money were in shorter supply. Plenty of
people, from friends and family to financiers and fabric vendors,
doubted that Cobbled Court Quilts would ever open its doors.
Dixon admits that they had reason to doubt.

"Looking back," the Wisconsin native says with the tiniest trace
of a twang picked up during twenty years of residence in Texas,
"it's probably a good thing that I underestimated just what it
would take to get my business under way. If I hadn't, I'm not sure
I'd have taken the risk. But now that we're open, I'm glad I did. I
love New Bern, and I love running this shop."

And it's clear that the quilters love Cobbled Court Quilts and its spunky owner. One of Cobbled Court's customers, Dominique Martin, who dropped by to ask Evelyn to guide her through the delicate process of joining the points of an eight-pointed star, said, "There are so many beautiful fabrics to choose from. It really gets my creative juices flowing. And Evelyn is a wonderful teacher. When she first suggested this pattern, I thought she was crazy! Now that it's almost done, I have to admit I feel really proud of myself, but I could never have done it without Evelyn. She's an inspiration."

Dixon waves off such effusive praise, noting that collaboration and cooperation have always been part of the quilting tradition. "Quilting is more than just sewing and even more than just creating a piece of beautiful, usable art. Since our great-great-grandmothers' time, quilters have always created community. Quilting is about getting together and helping each other, sharing life, cheering one another on through good times and bad."

And it's that desire to encourage others that is leading Evelyn Dixon to pick up her sewing needle and get into another tough fight: the fight against breast cancer.

On Saturday, September 20, Cobbled Court Quilts will host a "Quilt Pink" event, joining with hundreds of other quilt shops and thousands of quilters around the country as they quilt for a cure, each participant sewing individual quilt blocks that will be joined into a larger quilt. When completed, each quilt will be auctioned off and the money donated . . ."

Quilt Pink. September 20. Breast cancer. I didn't have to read more. I knew what Liza wanted.

When I looked up from the paper, Liza's eyes were dry, but there was a rippling movement under the perfect, unblemished skin of her throat that showed she was swallowing back tears.

"What do you think? Does it ring any bells for you?" she asked. "When I read it, I figured it had to be some kind of omen. So that's it. That's what I want. On September twentieth, the anniversary of the day my mother died from breast cancer, you come to the quilt shop with me and make one of those blocks."

I opened my mouth to speak, but Liza interrupted me.

"And don't even bother to suggest that you make some big donation instead. You have to go yourself, in person, and I'm coming to watch you do it. It's time you actually *did* something. Something besides writing a check." Finally, she blinked, as if waiting for me to say something, but there was nothing to say.

"That's the deal," she said. "Otherwise, I'm getting that tattoo."

"All right. I'll go."

"Good," Liza said, but not convincingly. I got the feeling that she'd have preferred it if I'd argued, giving her an excuse to fight with me, but I wasn't about to do so.

Liza took a final drink of the now-cold coffee, pushed back her chair, and headed toward the back door. "By the way, the quilting thing is for my mother. You still owe me a birthday present. I want three hundred and fifty dollars. You were right. My room needs redecorating."

She let the screen door slam behind her as she stomped down the back porch steps and walked around the side of the house, not bothering to say where she was going or when she'd be back.

I dropped my head into my hands and rubbed my eyes. I'd been right. It was a migraine.

11

Evelyn Dixon

When I was nine years old, my family got our first color television set—a twenty-three-inch Motorola encased in a French Provincial wood cabinet. Never mind that the rest of our furniture was Early American, the French Provincial model was on sale, and we were thrilled to have that giant screen dominating our living room. The first program we watched on it was the Rose Parade, live from Pasadena.

When it was over, I nagged my poor mother until she drove me to Miss Yolanda's School of Baton and enrolled me as a member of the American Sweethearts Twirling Team. For four years, Mother and Dad plunked down twelve dollars a month for twirling lessons and more for the star-spangled swimsuit and white go-go boots that were our uniforms for parades and competitions. I never won a trophy, and I never marched in the Rose Parade, but I did learn to smile.

Miss Yolanda was a stickler for smiling. No matter what happened, you had to keep smiling. If you dropped your baton—smile. If another girl dropped her baton and it hit you on the head—smile. If the Sweetheart's parade placement was right behind the Happy

Hooves Riding Club and you stepped in horse dung up to the top of your white go-go boots—smile.

"The instant you pick up that baton," Miss Yolanda would say, addressing rows of Sweethearts with the gravity of a military commander giving a final briefing to troops headed into battle, "I want to see a smile on your face. Just like your fingers and your baton are two ends of a live wire, and the second they meet—zap! Your face lights up! Like flipping a switch. Don't think. Just smile."

I hadn't thought about Miss Yolanda in years, but for some reason, upon waking from the fitful three hours of sleep that was all I'd been able to manage after my appointment at Dr. Thayer's, her voice was loud and clear in my head.

"Smile!" she commanded. And I did.

As I unlocked the door and greeted the group of quilters already clustered in the courtyard, as I served coffee and Charlie's cake and handed out goody bags tied with pink ribbons, as I pulled the names for door-prize winners out of a basket, as I moved from table to table to table of novice quilters, showing them how to trace quarter-inch stitching lines with marking pencils and secure a seam without using knots, as I discussed color choice and appliqué placement, as I signed up women for new classes, as I rang up sales of fabric, notions, patterns, and quilting books, bagged each purchase, as I thanked customers for coming and waved good-bye when they left, I smiled. I didn't think. I just smiled, going through the motions—breathing, walking, talking, but numb.

My emotions and actions didn't connect with my mind or heart. I'd been that way ever since Dr. Thayer pronounced my sentence—cancer. After that, I'd ceased to hear what he was saying, unable to connect the information to myself. He looked at me sympathetically while speaking of options, treatment plans, disease stages, and next steps. I'd nodded at all the correct intervals and declined his invitation to ask more questions.

By the time I got up from my chair and left the office, I couldn't remember what any of his words meant, or maybe I just didn't want to. Work was the perfect distraction, the antidote to all the fears that plagued me, the truths I didn't want to acknowledge.

By ten o'clock the shop was packed. Thank heaven I'd enlisted the help of a half dozen of my regular customers, including Wendy Perkins, who wore her biggest rhinestone glasses for the occasion. Wendy and the others greeted customers, passed out quilt-block kits, helped refill the refreshment table, and taught novices the basics of hand quilting. Without them, I'd never have survived the day.

At one point, we were so crowded that there were no more available spaces at the sewing tables. I was busy ringing up sales, so Wendy ran around the corner to her real estate office and brought back a couple of folding tables and chairs while some of the others cleared out space in the storeroom and a back corner where I kept refurbished sewing machines for sale.

The day was a blur, but somehow, finally, five o'clock came. I thanked Wendy and the other volunteers for their help, giving them each a tote bag filled with charm packs, a pair of new scissors, and a gift certificate for a free class.

"Evelyn, how sweet!" Gwen Talvert exclaimed. "But you don't have to give us anything. We all had fun, and it was for such a good cause."

"Yes, I do. You worked your tails off today."

Wendy craned her neck to take a peek at her behind, her panty line prominent through her too-tight stretch slacks. "Looks like I still got mine." She snorted a laugh, and the others joined in.

"Well, thank you all so much. You were just great. Wendy, do you want me to bring those tables and chairs back to your office tonight?"

"No. Let it wait until Monday. I'll come over with the truck and get them."

I walked them to the door and said good-bye. Finally, the shop was empty, and, smiling still, my lips frozen, stretched tight across my mouth, I locked the front door, threw away the crumpled napkins and half-empty punch cups from the refreshment table, and walked through the shop, turning out the lights. As I approached the back storage room, the one Wendy had outfitted with one of the folding tables and extra chairs, I heard voices.

Oh no, I thought, and my smile faded. *I was sure they'd all gone.*

I closed my eyes for a moment before taking a deep breath and entering the room, smiling again. There were three women sitting at the table, a teenage girl with bleached blond hair wearing all black clothing and an angry expression, a tall blond with her hair swept back into a ponytail who wore a simple pink button-down blouse under a cream-colored sweater, and an older woman with silver white hair in a French twist who was dressed in a tan cashmere sweater and light woolen skirt, very simple and clearly very expensive. A Dolce & Gabbana handbag, obviously new, lay carelessly at her feet. I recognized her as a customer from the Grill, one of the regulars. Charlie had told me her name, but I couldn't remember it now. She had a long, elegant neck and a surprisingly taut jawline for a woman of her age, or what I supposed was her age. She might have been fifty or seventy; it was hard to tell. She had been a beauty in her youth, and she still was, but I wondered what she was doing in my shop.

Over the years, I have met all manner of quilters. It is the kind of hobby that attracts all kinds of different people. But in my experience, women who could clearly afford to purchase anything their hearts desired seldom felt the need to make anything themselves, and, if they did, they generally went in for painting or sculpting, things that were considered more art than craft, though I consider quilting both. But that's a subject for another time.

What was she doing here? I couldn't quite figure it out. When she looked up from her work, appraising me as I entered the room, I was sure of one thing: she and the teenager were somehow related. They had the same long neck, the same sharp jaw, and the same large brown eyes that held the same expression: a look of loss. They tried to conceal it, the older woman with distance and impeccable manners, the teenager with anger and a mutinous stare, but neither mask was entirely convincing.

"Hi," I said, trying to keep my voice cheerful as I spied pieces of fabric lying all over the table. They hadn't even finished cutting out the pieces of their blocks, which meant it would be at least an hour and more like two before they were finished and I could finally lock the doors of the shop and be alone.

"I'm Evelyn Dixon, the owner. Forgive me for not coming back to say hello before. It's been an awfully busy day. How are you all doing here? Do you need any help?"

"Oh, I think you could say that," the tall brunette said with a self-deprecating giggle. "At least, I know I do. I haven't touched a needle since I made an A-line skirt in my eighth-grade Home Ec class. The teacher gave me a C minus." She smiled as she rose from the table and extended her hand. "I'm Margot Matthews."

The older woman smiled as well, lowering her reading glasses before reaching out to take my hand. "I'm Abigail Burgess Wynne," she said in a voice that sounded like good wine and old money, bright and light but with a smooth finish. It was a voice that revealed nothing.

Wynne. That's who she was. Wynne Memorial Library. Wynne Museum. I remembered now. Charlie said she was one of the wealthiest women in the state.

"And this is Liza Burgess—my niece." She hesitated just a moment before declaring this last, as if reluctant to acknowledge their shared bloodline.

"Nice to meet you."

Abigail peered past me. "Has everyone else gone? I'm afraid we arrived late."

"Yes, sorry about that," Margot said. "I'm between jobs and had a three o'clock phone interview that was supposed to take fifteen minutes but went on for almost an hour."

"*I* wasn't late." Liza growled to her aunt. "I stood outside the shop for two hours waiting for you to show up."

Abigail went on, ignoring the girl. "You're probably exhausted after such a long day. Perhaps we should just leave this for now and come back another time."

I was about to gratefully agree with her when Liza, whose single utterance up until now had been delivered in a mumble, shouted, "No! We have to finish today! That was the deal we made! If you don't do this today, then it doesn't count. The deal will be off! I mean it!" She glowered at her aunt, who glowered right back. Margot, clearly as stunned by the girl's outburst as I was, just stood there.

"That's no problem," I said, trying to get us past the moment. "I don't have any plans for the evening. So you're all new to quilting?" They nodded. "Well, I'll give you your first lesson. It's easier than it looks. All you're doing is sewing straight lines. But first, I'll give you a few tips on cutting your patterns. A nice-looking block begins with an accurately cut pattern."

I showed them how to use a see-through ruler to measure out precisely sized squares and triangles for the main part of the basket, then how to use a sharp pencil held at a sideways angle to trace carefully around the template for the appliquéd basket handle. It was a lesson I had given a dozen times already that day, and I could have delivered it while sleepwalking, which, in a way, was exactly what I was doing. As in any group of quilters, all of the women had different styles, but thankfully, all three caught onto the basic ideas quickly.

Liza, the younger woman, said very little but seemed to have a real feel for color and a willingness to take risks. She quietly asked if it would be all right to make her block in a color scheme that was the opposite of everyone else's, using the brown and mocha shades for her basket and doing the background in pink. I said that would be a good idea, thinking it might be interesting to place that one contrasting block in the center of the quilt as an anchor for the rest.

Margot approached her task with a businesslike attitude, making quick, confident decisions about her color choices and not getting flustered by little errors. I suspected that, as time went on, she would be a good all-around quilter, able to master a variety of techniques quickly and always ready to try more challenging pieces, confident in her ability to puzzle out any problems that might arise.

Abigail, in spite of giving the impression that she'd rather be anywhere but where she was, was a stickler for precision. It was a quality I would normally have applauded, but it was definitely causing her to lag behind the other two. I was so tired, and my head was pounding. All I wanted was for them to finish their blocks and leave so I could fall into bed and a dreamless sleep.

Once the patterns were cut, I showed them how to mark a stitching line with a pencil, so they would understand how that was done, but gave them quarter-inch masking tape to mark their seams so they would finish more quickly. Margot was first to finish piecing her block. I asked if I could borrow it to demonstrate how to appliqué on the handle.

By then, it was nearly dark outside, and I had to turn on the overhead lamps so there would be enough light to work by. My eyes were almost as tired as my body, and I rubbed them and blinked a few times before taking my first stitch, trying to regain my focus.

"All right. Are you all watching?" They were.

"The stitch I'm going to teach you is called the blind stitch, because, if you do it properly, you should barely be able to see the stitches. Now, in appliqué, unlike the running stitch we used to piece our block, we're going to use a knot, but we'll hide it here in the fold of the fabric." I held the folded fabric strip out so they could see where to place the first stitch. Then I pierced the fabric with the needle while they watched.

I don't know how I did it. I've shown that stitch to hundreds of beginners without incident, but somehow or other when I pushed the needle through the fabric, I ended up driving it deep into the flesh of my finger.

"Ouch! Dammit!" I dropped the block and instinctively put my finger into my mouth. I tasted blood on my tongue, sharp and metallic, like sucking on an old penny. It hurt, but it was far from agony and it certainly wasn't the first time I'd pricked my finger while sewing. Still, tears pooled in my eyes. Margot saw them.

"Evelyn, are you all right?" When I didn't answer, she jumped to her feet. "Here. Give me your hand. Let me see." She took my hand and unfolded my fingers. A bright, ruby drop of blood pearled on the end of my fingertip.

"That really must have smarted," she said sympathetically. She reached for a scrap of cast-off fabric and pressed it against my finger to stop the blood. "Don't worry. It'll be all right in a minute."

But it wasn't all right. It wouldn't be all right in a minute, or a month, or maybe ever. The words I'd been trying so hard to smother in my mind—cancer, chemo, radiation, drug therapy, survival rates, and mastectomy—boiled to the surface in a confused jumble. My body started to shake involuntarily as the tears came faster and harder. I couldn't keep them back.

"What am I going to do? What? I'm thousands of miles away from home. I've got nothing. I've got no one. Why is this happening to me! Just when things were finally starting to go right. I can't have cancer! Not now!"

I covered my face with my hands and gave myself up to despair, sobbing until I was dry. Long moments passed, and I finally raised my head to look at the three strangers standing witness to my collapse.

Abigail was silent, her face still and unreadable. What little color there was in Liza's cheeks had completely drained away. Her eyes were full of tears but empty of answers. Only Margot moved toward me, reaching out to wrap her arms around me.

Turning to her, I whispered, "Please. Somebody please tell me. What am I going to do?"

12

Abigail Burgess Wynne

While I was getting dressed that morning, I dropped the cameo brooch, the one Woolley bought for me in London. The fall chipped it. I knew it was not going to be a good day.

Of course, I didn't need a jewelry omen to tell me that. There was nothing about the idea of spending the afternoon sewing a quilt that appealed to me, especially sewing a quilt while Liza sat next to me glaring recriminations. But there was no way to avoid it, so I finished getting dressed and walked across the Green, slowly, to meet Liza.

I was late, though not nearly as late as Liza claimed when she blurted this information out to two strangers. The girl dramatizes everything. Thinking that correcting her would only make things worse, I decided to ignore her, focus completely on the task at hand, and get through the ordeal without becoming engaged in some sort of emotional scene. But at the end of the day, it was unavoidable, though the drama erupted from an unexpected source—not my angry, bitter niece, but the owner of the quilt shop, Evelyn Dixon.

When Evelyn entered the storeroom, where Liza, Margot Matthews, and I were seated, I was surprised by her appearance. Her newspaper photograph had made her appear so elegant and well put together, but today her clothes looked careless and rumpled, almost as if she'd slept in them. Perhaps someone else had supervised her wardrobe selection for the newspaper picture, I thought.

In any case, I was glad to see her. My goal was to make the quilt block as quickly as possible, fulfilling my promise to Liza, and leave Cobbled Court Quilts, never to return. But I was getting frustrated trying to understand the instruction sheet that the frowzy woman with the horrible rhinestone glasses had handed out along with the kits. And Liza and Margot were just as confused as I was.

In spite of Liza's rude and embarrassing outburst, once Evelyn started showing us what to do, there was a definite easing of tension, and I began, if not to enjoy myself, at least to become more interested in what I was doing. In school, I'd enjoyed geometry, and as Evelyn explained the basic construction of a quilt and quilt blocks, I saw that the whole thing was based on geometric theories. After a time, I was so concentrated on my task and trying to make sure that all my angles and points were cut and sewn properly, so as to make a perfect square, I forgot why I was there in the first place. It was a pleasant distraction from tensions of the day. Time passed quickly, and, while focusing on the quilt block, it was easy to avoid making eye contact with Liza.

By the time Evelyn began to demonstrate the appliqué technique, I'd started to think that the day might not turn out as badly as I'd feared and that, at least in terms of blackmail payments, I'd gotten off fairly cheaply after all. All it cost me was a half a day spent sewing a quilt block that was actually turning out rather nicely, and allowing Liza to repaint the walls of her bedroom, not black, but in shades of blue, gray, and green with a technique that made the walls look like Italian marble. It wasn't a look I'd have chosen for myself, but she'd made a good job of it. If I had paid a decorator to do it, I'm sure it would have cost a fortune.

All in all, I said to myself, *this is a small price to pay to preserve*

*your niece's neck in its current pristine state, free of a family mono-
gram.*

But I spoke too soon. Without warning, Evelyn Dixon's calm veneer cracked. She pricked her finger with a needle, producing a few
drops of blood, a veil of tears, and the shocking revelation that she
had been diagnosed with breast cancer on the day before she was
hosting a fundraiser to fight the same disease.

Naturally, I felt badly for her. Who wouldn't? However, it really
was her personal business, not mine. Though the irony of the situation was not lost on me, any more than I'd missed the fact that her
sobbed confession occurred in front of my eyes, and my niece's, on
the same day my own sister succumbed to her fight with cancer.
Clearly, the world was full of ironies. Either that, or God had a cruel
sense of humor. Or was there something else to all this?

I didn't have time to wonder further. The next thing I knew,
Margot Matthews had taken charge and was ordering me about.
Was there to be no end to the humiliations of this day?

"Abigail, run get a glass of water, would you please? Better yet,
make some tea," she commanded. "Evelyn, do you have a teapot or
a microwave around here somewhere?"

Tears streamed through Evelyn's closed eyelids. "Upstairs. In my
apartment." She sniffed loudly, making a sound I'd rather not describe.

"You live upstairs? Even better. Let's just take you home." As if
she were an invalid, Margot placed her forearm under Evelyn's
elbow and helped her to her feet, supporting her as she walked
wearily toward the stairs. "Liza, would you turn off the lights and
make sure the CLOSED sign is out on the door?"

I stood there for a moment, uncertain of what I should do. I didn't
know Evelyn Dixon; none of us did. Did Margot expect me to follow her up the stairs into Evelyn's home and actually make tea for
her? Liza, having completed her assignment, hurried for the stairs,
brushing past without looking at me, not even bothering to give me

her customary glare. It felt silly, standing alone in the now-darkened shop, so I followed the others.

Upstairs, in the small, neatly arranged apartment, Evelyn reclined on a narrow green sofa. Liza was tucking a quilt around her legs, and, though her eyes were red, she was actually smiling. In the time she'd been living with me, I'd rarely seen Liza smile. She was really quite pretty when she did.

Margot emerged from another room carrying a box of tissues and handed some to Evelyn. I went into the kitchen, a galley affair separated from the living and dining area by a counter and stools, and started boiling water for tea. It felt odd, rooting around in a stranger's cupboards and drawers, but I found the cabinet where Evelyn kept her teabags and sugar. There were some crackers as well. It occurred to me that, what with her shop being overrun by customers and the distress of her diagnosis, Evelyn might not have eaten. Clearly, she had bigger problems than an empty stomach, but hunger and fatigue certainly didn't help the situation.

I'm not much of a cook, but anyone can slice cheese. I found a block of cheddar and some grapes in the refrigerator and arranged them on a platter along with the crackers.

"Here we are," I said cheerily as I carried a tray with the food and four steaming cups of tea into the living area. "I couldn't find any lemon, but there's milk and sugar for the tea and a few things to munch on. Evelyn, may I fix you a plate?"

"No, thank you. I'm not hungry." Her eyes were dry now, but still rimmed in red, and I thought that it wouldn't take much to bring on a fresh wave of weeping.

"Why don't you just have a little something," Margot urged and, without waiting for an answer, put some cheese and crackers on a plate and handed it to Evelyn. "I bet you haven't eaten all day, have you?" Evelyn shook her head. "On top of that, you're probably exhausted. You can't think clearly on no sleep and an empty stomach. You've got to come up with some sort of plan about how you're going to live your life and manage your business while you beat this thing. And we're going to help you."

We were?

Margot Matthews was awfully free with her use of personal pronouns. Certainly, I admired her capability, her calm reaction in a difficult circumstance. In fact, I couldn't help but wonder why any company would have let her go and why someone else hadn't snapped her up, but she was going a little overboard. I've nothing against being a Good Samaritan; my involvement in local charity was certainly a testament to that, but hadn't we all done our good deed for the day? After all, until this afternoon none of us had laid eyes on Evelyn Dixon.

Evelyn swallowed the bite of the cracker she'd been dutifully chewing. "You are? But you barely know me. You never even met me before today."

My point exactly.

"What difference does that make? God put us on this earth to help one another, didn't He?"

Oh no. She was one of those. A moderate amount of religious feeling never hurt anyone, but people who wear their faith on their sleeves are off-putting. Margot, I decided, was one of those people. Suddenly her long stretch of unemployment made sense. Perhaps her religiosity made her coworkers uncomfortable. Spying the silver crucifix she was wearing around her neck, I was certain that was what had happened.

Margot smiled brightly and looked around at the rest of us, as if waiting for an actual answer to what I'd felt was a rhetorical question. Liza shot me a look, not her usual evil glare but a pointed gaze that elicited a sudden rush of heat to my face, and said, "Absolutely. No one should go through this alone."

I shifted my eyes away from Liza's. "Yes. Of course," I said. "Anything I can do to help."

Margot turned back to Evelyn. "You see? The three of us coming into the shop so late and sitting together, getting hidden away in the back room so you'd find us after everyone was gone—none of that was a coincidence. I've got a feeling we were all handpicked to be here today. You might feel like you're alone in this, Evelyn, but it isn't true. God knows you need some friends to help you through this. Well, here we are! You'll see. We're all in this together."

And, as suddenly as Margot the Cheerleader made this pronouncement, we all were in it—whether we wanted to be or not.

Margot pulled a notepad out of her purse and started conducting a series of probing, fact-finding interviews. First, she began quizzing Evelyn, asking about her conversation with the doctor and what she knew about the details of her diagnosis, which wasn't much. Apparently, the poor thing had lapsed into something of a state of shock upon hearing the news and either didn't hear or didn't comprehend much of what her doctor had said after giving her the bad news.

Then Margot began asking questions about the quilt shop, some of them rather personal, relating to the financial stability of the business, which seemed tenuous, but more about the day-to-day running of the store and any kinds of special projects that might be coming up in the immediate future.

Finally, she asked Evelyn about her family and any friends she had in New Bern. There wasn't much on either count. She'd moved from Texas after an unpleasant divorce, so there was no husband on the scene. Her only son lived in Seattle, too far away to be much help. Having recently arrived in New Bern, she had a number of acquaintances, customers mostly, like the women who had volunteered to help her with Quilt Pink day, but didn't seem to have many friends. However, she did seem to have a fairly close relationship with Charlie Donnelly, and that surprised me.

I adore Charlie. He has an almost famously gruff manner that some people find intimidating but I rather enjoy. Over time, I'd discovered that his rough exterior hid a personality of rare charm and quick wit that was well worth the effort it took to unearth them. Still, even after all these years, I couldn't say we were close. As far as I knew, he had very few close friends. Interesting that he and Evelyn had hit it off so quickly.

Next Margot turned her investigatory skills on the rest of us, quizzing first Liza and then me about our interests, experiences, and contacts before filling us in on her own background in business, specifically in marketing and public relations, which was considerable. It was all very interesting, this whole getting-to-know-you session, but I was having a hard time seeing where it would lead. Besides, it was already eight o'clock. Florence Pearl was hosting a surprise birthday party for her husband, Stephen. Truthfully, I don't like Stephen, who owns an insurance agency and is forever bothering me about "adequate coverage," but Florence was nice enough, and I had promised her I'd drop by. I considered saying something about being late for the party, but when I looked across the room at Liza, who was sitting on a plum-colored ottoman with her body turned toward Margot but her eyes continually stealing back to Evelyn, I kept silent. The party would go on for a couple of hours yet. I would just have to be late, which wasn't such a terrible prospect.

With any luck, I thought, *I'll be in and out in thirty minutes, fulfilling my social obligations without being subjected to any conversation with Stephen beyond "Happy Birthday."*

"So, that's about it for me," Margot said. I'd been lost in my own thoughts and missed the last part of what she'd been saying.

"Evelyn, I think we've got a pretty good idea of what you need, at least for the next few days." Margot chewed on the end of her pen as she scanned the notes she'd taken. "The way I see it, your biggest priority right now is trying to understand exactly what you're up against—what your diagnosis means and what your best treatment options are."

Evelyn, who was much calmer now, nodded. "Yes. That's right. Dr. Thayer is a good doctor. I'm sure he tried to explain all that to me, but I was too stunned to take any of it in."

"That's all right," Liza said quietly, reaching out to pat the quilt that covered Evelyn's legs. "It's a perfectly normal reaction." She hesitated for a moment, and her eyes darted away from Evelyn's. "At least . . . I suppose it is."

"And anyway," Margot continued practically, "even though Dr. Thayer is a good doctor, you're going to need a specialist, probably more than one. It's always good to have a second opinion. That's where Abigail will come in."

I'd been sipping the last dregs of lukewarm tea from my cup. When Margot said my name, I choked on it. "I will?" I sputtered. "How? I don't know anything about breast cancer."

"No, but you know the people who do know, or at least you know the people who know the people who do." I looked at Margot blankly, and she smiled. "Abigail, you're on the library and hospital boards, right?"

I nodded.

"Tomorrow I'd like you to go to the library and ask the librarians to help you find out all the latest information on breast cancer—causes, treatment options, clinical trials—anything you can find. Then I'd like you to call up the hospital administrator and the head of oncology and ask them for the names of the three best breast-cancer specialists in the area, not just at the New Bern hospital or even in the state, but the three best in New England. Ask them to get appointments for Evelyn as soon as possible. By the end of next week at the latest."

At this, Evelyn sat up a little straighter, brightening visibly. "Can you really do that?"

"Well, of course I can," I said, a little insulted by the question. "Ted Nichols is the administrator at New Bern Memorial. We've known each other for years. And the Wynne Foundation just purchased a new CAT scan for the hospital. Of course Ted will help us. If he doesn't, I'd certainly like to know the reason why."

"That's the spirit!" Margot cheered.

"But," Evelyn said, doubt overshadowing the expression of hope that had so briefly crossed her face, "how am I supposed to pay for some famous specialist? I've got insurance, but not much. With all the expenses of opening the shop, I got the cheapest policy I could manage, with a huge deductible. And I'm sure they won't cover visits to any out-of-state doctors."

"We're not going to think about that right now," Margot said. "At the moment, our job is to help you understand what you're up against and get you the best advice available. We'll cross the money bridge when we have to. However, that will be a lot easier to do if Cobbled Court Quilts is actually making a profit. That's where Liza and I come in."

Margot flipped to a new page in her notebook and laid it on the coffee table. Everyone leaned forward to watch as she drew a line to divide the page into two columns, labeling one "Projects" and the other "Assigned To." She wrote my name next to the first two projects, "Information Gathering" and "Specialist Appointments."

"All right," she said, looking up while still holding the pencil. "Evelyn, you mentioned you're way behind on checking your inventory and accounting?"

"Yes. I've been so busy getting ready for today that I've really fallen behind. I don't know what's selling, what's lagging, or what needs to be reordered. And I still haven't settled my books from last month, so I don't know if I'm bankrupt or merely teetering on the edge of it." She smiled a little, joking even in the midst of her tragedy. In spite of her earlier meltdown, I admired her strength. She was tougher than I'd thought.

Margot laughed, emitting a girlish giggle that was at odds, though pleasantly so, with her businesslike command of the situation. "Well, that's probably information worth knowing." She wrote down "Inventory" on her project list.

"Liza, you and I are both between jobs, so we've got time on our hands. You said that you'd worked in a music store in high school and helped with inventory. Would you like to take charge of that?"

"Sure. I'm not doing anything. I can start tomorrow if you want."

"Tomorrow's Sunday, so let's wait until the next day. I think we could all use some rest, but I'll help you." Margot wrote her name and Liza's next to the task before going on. "And, Evelyn, I'm no accountant, but I'm pretty handy with the computer. I'm going to see about installing an accounting program that will update your inventory, profits, and losses at the point of sale. It'll save you a lot of time going forward. Also, do you have a Web site?"

Evelyn shook her head. "No. I've thought about getting one, but I haven't had time, and besides, I really didn't know where to begin."

Margot nodded as she wrote down "Web site" and put her name next to it. "I'll get you set up with one right away. We can just use a template for right now. It won't be fancy, but they aren't expensive and at least it will give you a presence on the Web. It's great PR. Come to think of it," she mused, "I'm going to call the paper and see if we can't rework the story they ran about you—update the information and then see if we can get other papers in the area to run it. Something like that could bring a lot of new business in the door." She quickly scribbled "Newspaper Article" onto her list and assigned herself this responsibility.

"So that just leaves one thing for the moment, and that's the day-to-day running of the shop. How long has it been since you had a day off, Evelyn?"

Evelyn laughed. "A day off? What's that? I'm always here. Even when the shop is closed I'm still working, trying to catch up on all the things I couldn't get to during the day. I'm planning on hiring some help, but I can't do that until the shop starts to show a profit."

"That's terrible!" I exclaimed. "You can't keep working at that kind of pace! No wonder you were feeling so overwhelmed today. You must have been on the edge of exhaustion even before your doctor gave you the news. You're going to have to take it a little easier, especially once you begin whatever treatment your doctor recommends. You've got to get some help!"

"She's right," Margot agreed. "Fortunately, you've already got experienced help right in this room. Liza and I have both worked in retail. We can definitely give you a hand during business hours. What about you, Abigail? Do you have any retail experience?"

Before I could say anything, Liza interrupted. "Oh, I'll say she does," she said in a voice dripping sarcasm. "My aunt's whole life is about retail. Shoes, bags, jewelry, furniture, artwork—you name it, she's bought it." She turned toward me. The angry glare was back.

"And what about you?" I asked. "Shall we tell them about your experiences in some of New Bern's finer retail establishments?" I looked at the other two women. "She once got hold of a cashmere sweater for a price you wouldn't believe. Really. It was a crime!" I smiled sweetly at my niece. She stared at me with daggers in her eyes, but her mouth was shut. Mission accomplished.

"Well, that's it, then!" Margot clapped her hands in a "let's wrap this up" gesture. "Evelyn, I think we've got you covered. At least for the immediate future, though we should get together soon to see what kind of progress we're making and update our assignments. How about Friday night, right after closing? Would that work for everyone?"

I thought about my calendar. Yes, I was free Friday at five. After all, it would only be this once. I'd show up, give my report on breast cancer and the best doctors to treat it, wish Evelyn Dixon well, and that would be that. I nodded along with the others.

"Great! Evelyn, I'll be here at ten on Monday. If you need anything in the meantime, even just someone to talk to, here's my phone number. I live just a couple of blocks away." Margot scribbled a number on the notepad, handed it to Evelyn, and then got up from her chair.

Tears welled in Evelyn's eyes as she took the notepad. For a moment I was worried that she was going to fall apart again and I'd never get to the Pearls' party, but instead of breaking down she smiled.

"I don't know how to thank you all. I'm just so grateful." She sniffed and laughed through her tears. "Thank you. But I still don't quite understand how all this is happening and why you're putting yourselves out so much for a stranger."

That made two of us.

"It's like I said before," Margot replied, giving her a quick squeeze. "God knew you needed us today. We're put on earth to help each other."

❧ 13 ❧

Abigail Burgess Wynne

By the time we were finished, I didn't have time to go home and change for the party. Liza went back home, and I walked in the opposite direction, to the Pearls' house on Elm Street.

When I got there, Florence greeted me at the door. She said she'd been worried that something had happened to me and asked what had held me up, but didn't wait for an answer before turning around to the assembled guests, who seemed to be having a fine time without me, and calling out gaily, "Now the party can really start! Abigail's here!"

Someone took my coat. Someone else got me a drink. I worked my way into the living room and stood near the fireplace, listening to Grace Kahn tell the story about the time we were playing tennis and she accidentally hit our last ball into the upper branches of a nearby beech tree, dropping it right into an abandoned bird nest.

"And before you can say Jack Robinson, Abbie drops her racket, shimmies up the tree trunk, and plucks the ball out of the nest!" Everyone in the room, the same group of people I've been socializing with for as long as I can remember, laughed uproariously, though they must have heard this story a dozen times. "And then she shimmies right back down and beats me forty-fifteen!"

The crowd of listeners, who'd had quite a bit to drink by that time, howled with laughter. I chuckled and excused myself, saying I needed to freshen my drink. No one seemed to notice that my glass was still full.

Franklin stood near the bar, filling a glass with his customary mineral water and lime. "Finally," I said as I approached, "a sober party guest."

"Oh," he said. "Are you speaking to me? Last time I saw you, you weren't."

"Don't be silly. I have to speak to you. You're my lawyer."

"Yes, so you reminded me when we parted. Right before you told me to mind my own business and butt out of your life." He took a sip of his drink. "Or words to that effect." He smiled, and I knew that all was forgiven.

"Franklin, let me ask you something. Is everyone we know as dull as I think they are? Seems like I've been to this same party fifty times in my life."

He raised his eyebrows, amused by my observation. "Well, it's a small town, Abigail, and your circle of acquaintances has always been a tight one."

"Don't be silly. I know everyone."

"No, you know everyone you think is worth knowing. And that is a very short and exclusive list. By the way, how was your little quilting bee? I don't know that I've ever seen you with a needle and thread in your hand. Checkbook and pen, yes, but—"

I interrupted him before he could have any more fun at my expense. "Obviously, you've been talking to Liza again. Really, Franklin, I don't know what you see in that girl."

"So," he said, wisely refusing to engage in battle, "did you enjoy yourself?"

"It was . . . interesting."

"Interesting? Really? Well, that's something. A far more positive reaction than I'd supposed you'd have. You must have found something appealing about it."

"Hmm." I shrugged noncommittally and put my glass on the bar. "It's been a long day, Franklin. I'm going to tell Stephen happy birthday and go home."

"Abigail, are you all right? You don't seem quite yourself tonight—you're introspective. Don't do it, Abbie. Introspection can become habit forming."

"I'm fine. Just tired. I've got a lot on my mind."

"See? What did I tell you." When I failed to respond to his teasing, Franklin's normally merry eyes grew serious. "Is it Liza again? Do you want to talk about it? I know my advice wasn't especially well received last time, but if you ever want to talk, you know I'm always ready to listen."

"Of course you are," I said lightly. "You lawyers are always ready to listen—in billable quarter hours."

"Abigail, you have me on retainer. Whether I listen to you or not, you still pay me just as if I did, so you might as well take advantage of what you've already shelled out good money for." He smiled. "Seriously, are you sure you're all right? Can I give you a lift home?"

"It's kind of you to offer, but no. Thank you. It's a nice night. The walk will do me good. Good night, Franklin." I leaned in and gave him a quick peck on the cheek.

"Good night, Abigail."

I had been telling the truth. There was a lot on my mind. Trying to sort out the events of the day was confusing—and distracting. It was only after I left the party and began walking home in the crisp fall air, shuffling through the first spent leaves of the season, moving down the sidewalk from one tight circle of lamplight into the next, like an actor trying to find the spotlight, that I realized I'd actually agreed to let Stephen Pearl drop by the house to give me "an insurance checkup."

I must have been more distracted than even I'd realized. I decided to call Franklin the next day and have him deal with it. Though perhaps I should tell him to throw some sort of business Stephen's way. Maybe a life-insurance policy. I could name Liza as the beneficiary. After all, she was my only living relative.

My only living relative. I stopped, standing still in the darkness, immobile and silent, suspended between one circle of light and the next. My only living relative. Two years ago today, my sister died.

I raised my hand to cover my mouth. Somewhere in the distance, an owl hooted, calling out to other owls, but none answered. Through the lattice of my open fingers, I whispered a name into the night.

The house was dark when I came in. Liza had turned off the lights before retiring. I hung up my coat, left my purse on the sideboard, and climbed the stairs toward my bedroom, treading lightly on the creaky fifth step so as not to wake Liza. But as I crept down the dim hallway past the guest-room door, I thought I heard a noise coming from inside. I leaned my ear close to the door and heard the sound of muffled crying.

I raised my hand as if to knock on the door, but my arm froze in midair. I couldn't bring myself to do it. Instead, I leaned in, resting my cheek on the door, and whispered.

"Liza?" There was no answer. I raised my voice a little. "Liza? Are you all right?"

Inside, the sound of crying abruptly ceased. I heard a shuffling noise, as if she were moving under the blankets, and then nothing. I waited for a long moment, then walked up the hall to my room and got into bed, where I lay looking out the window, wondering if Liza had fallen asleep, listening to the sound of owls hooting as they searched the darkness for others of their kind.

14

Evelyn Dixon

When Abigail received her assignment that night, I had the impression that she was less than thrilled at being suddenly drafted into Margot's army. Part of me wondered if I'd ever see her again. But she was as good as her word, and her influence in the community of New Bern was unquestionable.

When Abigail Burgess Wynne showed up at the public library seeking information on breast cancer the next day, the research librarians must have clicked their heels and saluted. By midafternoon she returned to the shop with reams of information, all neatly cataloged with particularly important sections highlighted in yellow marker. I read it all. Nothing in what I read changed my situation, there was no magical cancer cure in those pages, but just having that information made me feel a little less powerless. I used what I'd read to formulate a list of questions to ask when I interviewed the breast surgeons who, again thanks to Abigail's influence, all agreed to see me within two weeks' time, an impressive response considering that the surgeon Dr. Thayer referred me to couldn't fit me in for at least six weeks.

* * *

Ten days later, I was sitting in the waiting room of Dr. Deanna Finney, the third and last of the doctors on Abigail's list. Liza was keeping an eye on the shop, and Margot had come along to drive. I told Margot it wasn't necessary, but she insisted, claiming she wanted to visit an antique shop that was right around the corner from the doctor's office.

Having interviewed two other surgeons, both highly recommended and obviously very skilled, I was now familiar with the drill—the nervous minutes pretending to read magazines until the receptionist showed you into a chrome and white and cold exam room, silence and more nerves waiting for the harried and brilliant surgeon to appear, going through my list of questions and trying to make sense of the doctor's answers, and a quick handshake as the doctor moved on to the next patient.

So I was surprised when the door of the waiting room opened and a petite woman with short, spiky brown hair and a warm smile strode across the room and said, "Evelyn? I'm Dr. Finney." She shook my hand and then Margot's when I introduced her. "It's nice to meet you both. Shall we go into my office and talk? Would you like Margot to join us?"

Sensing that I wanted to speak to the doctor privately, Margot said she was just going to run around the corner and visit the antique shop.

"That's fine. Come back in about forty-five minutes. I think we'll be done by then, though it could be a bit longer. No more than an hour. That's when my next patient arrives."

Again, I was surprised. "You've put aside an hour just to talk to me?"

The doctor smiled. "On a first visit, I like to give a patient plenty of time. I'm sure you have lots of questions."

She showed me into a space that looked more like a cozy sitting room than an office. There was a desk shoved up against one of the walls, but that was the only businesslike piece of furniture in the

place. Most of the room was taken up by four easy chairs uphol-
stered in sage green chenille that circled an antique oak coffee table.
There was an oak sideboard under the window holding a Christmas
cactus just coming into bloom and a white ceramic tea service. After
telling me to make myself at home, the doctor went to the sideboard
and made tea. "All I have is chamomile. I hope that's all right. I'm
trying to cut down on caffeine."

"That's fine. Thank you." I sat down in one of the chairs and noticed that two of the office walls were covered with black-and-white
photographs of women, some smiling, some serious, all beautiful.
"Who are these pictures of? Your patients?"

"Yes," she said and placed two cups of tea on the table. "Those
are my patients. Not all of them, of course. Just the ones who didn't
mind having their picture taken."

Without thinking, I blurted out, "Are they still alive?" And then
blushed at the frankness of my question. But the doctor didn't seem
to be at all fazed.

"Most of them, yes. And there's every reason to believe you will
be too." She smiled, noticing my embarrassment. "It's all right, Evelyn. It's a perfectly fair question. When a woman finds out she has
breast cancer, the first question that enters her mind, and the question she is most afraid to ask, is 'Am I going to die?' When I learned
about my own cancer, that was exactly what I was thinking."

"You had breast cancer?"

She took a sip of her tea and nodded. "I did. I had a mastectomy
to remove my right breast six years ago and reconstruction after.
The plastic surgeon did a great job, don't you think?"

I couldn't help but stare at Dr. Finney's chest. Her breasts were
perfectly even. "I would never have guessed if you hadn't told me.
Is that why you decided to become a breast surgeon?"

"No, I was already in the field, but having cancer myself completely altered the way I run my practice. Up until then, I was confident in my skills. I had excellent training and the survival rate of my

patients was extremely high. As far as I was concerned, that was all that mattered. But when it happened to me, I realized that there is a lot more to this than removing diseased tissue and thereby saving someone's life. Now I treat people, not cancer. When faced with the prospect of losing my own breast, I was shocked by how devastated I felt. I'd never realized how deeply I associated the image of myself as a woman with my breasts."

I understood exactly what she was saying. Sitting across from another woman, a woman who knew what I was going through, who had felt what I was feeling and talked about it while we sipped tea, it felt more like we were just two friends talking over a problem than a doctor telling a patient what she must do. Before she said another word, I knew that this was my doctor.

"Not everyone feels that way, of course. Everyone comes to this with different life experiences and needs. Some of my patients want the breast removed immediately. Some of them want reconstructive surgery after and some don't. Some choose to wear prosthetic breasts and others don't bother. Every woman is different, and every choice is as valid as the others. I try my best to listen to my patients, present all the options, and work with them to find a plan of treatment they can be comfortable with. If a woman wants to conserve her breasts, I try my best to do so. It isn't always possible, of course. In the end, I had to lose my breast to save my life, but I take comfort in the knowledge that I explored all the avenues before deciding on a mastectomy."

"Do you think you can save my breast?" I asked. "The other surgeons I interviewed only talked about mastectomy."

She tilted her head to the side and nodded. "Many excellent surgeons believe in pursuing the most aggressive treatment possible. In many cases, that is the best course of action, and, as I explained before, that's how many women wish to proceed. It's a perfectly reasonable response if that's what you'd prefer. In your case, I think that it may be possible to conserve the breast." She opened the file that contained my charts, medical history, and X-rays and spread them out on the coffee table where I could see everything easily. "Let me show you what I mean," she began.

As Dr. Finney explained, breast cancer comes in many different forms. Previous tests showed that I had DCIS, Ductal Carcinoma In Situ, a non-invasive cancer, which meant that the cancer b-cells had not yet broken through the duct walls—a good thing. In fact, the doctor explained, some people consider DCIS to be a pre-cancerous condition, but I had a high-grade DCIS with markedly abnormal cells and that meant it was much closer to becoming an invasive cancer.

"However, as far as we can tell right now, the cancer appears to be contained," she said, holding up one of the mammography films and pointing out the suspicious area. "Which makes me think you'll be a good candidate for a lumpectomy. That's where we only re-move the cancerous breast tissue, leaving the rest of the breast intact. It can actually be done as a day surgery."

"Really?" This was the first good news I'd had in a long time. "You mean you'll just scoop out the cancer and that's it?"

She smiled. "It's not quite that easy. The surgery will be over with fairly quickly, but you'll need some time to recover. You own a quilt shop, is that right?" she asked, glancing at a sheet of personal information in my chart. "Do you have capable assistants in place to help run the business until you're fully healed? It's crucial that you have a good support system in place and people you can count on to help you through the rough spots. Do you?" Dr. Finney looked up, waiting for an answer.

I bit the inside of my lower lip, thinking. I really wasn't sure how to answer that. "I don't have any family in the area, if that's what you mean. I only moved here a few months ago. And I don't really have any paid assistants in the shop. I can't afford assistants until I start to show a profit, so I've been doing everything myself."

"Really?" the doctor asked incredulously. "You run your entire business yourself? No paid employees?"

I shrugged. "Well, my original business plan called for me to hire some help within the first month, but things haven't gone quite as well as I'd hoped, at least not yet. Sixty hours is a short week for me. There are a few women from my quilting classes who volunteered to help with a big event I had recently, but they all work during the week. There are some others though. Margot, whom you met in the waiting room, has said that she'll help however she can, and there are two others, Liza and Abigail. I only met them recently. They sort of appeared out of nowhere, and they've already done so much for me. I don't know how I'll ever repay them. I'd feel funny asking them for more."

"Don't," the doctor said emphatically. "You simply can't work the kinds of hours you've been working while you're dealing with this. If you've got friends, new or old, who are willing to come alongside you, don't be shy about letting them. I know it can be hard, taking help from strangers, but believe me, there will be ways for you to pay back those kindnesses in the future. But you can't do that unless you get well. Right now that is your first priority." I knew that what she was saying made sense; if I'd been in her shoes, I'd have said exactly the same thing, but still . . .

"Evelyn." She put down her teacup and took my hand. "I hope this will be as easy as going into the breast, removing the cancerous cells, and you going on with your life experiencing nothing more than some postoperative discomfort, but that may not be the case. The diagnostic equipment and tests we have today are excellent, but I won't really know what the situation is until I get in there. After the surgery, we'll do more tests to make sure we've gotten clean margins; that means that there's an area of healthy cells surrounding the place where the cancerous cells were. That's what we're aiming for, but it doesn't always happen. Sometimes we have to do another lumpectomy or follow up with chemotherapy. Sometimes it becomes necessary to take the whole breast."

"Oh." Instinctively, my hand rose to cover my chest. "I see."

Dr. Finney reached for my hand and looked me in the eye. Her gaze was warm and understanding. "Listen, Evelyn, you've just got to take this one day at a time. If I didn't think we could save your breast and get all the cancer, then I wouldn't bother with the lumpectomy. But it is important that you have all the facts and are ready for what *could* come. You need to plan for the long haul, Evelyn. The better prepared you are, the wider your support network, the easier this will be. If God has sent you three ministering angels to see you through this, don't question it. You need all the help you can get right now. Nothing about this is going to be easy."

A month later, I was feeling more in control of my own destiny and actually impatient for the two weeks to pass before my surgery would take place, anxious to get it over with and get back to normal.

In the weeks since I'd met Margot, Liza, and Abigail, fall colors had peaked and passed. The stream of New Bern tourists became a trickle and then slowed to a wholly unpredictable drip as the weather grew colder.

I ate, slept, ran errands, cleaned house, paid bills, went to work, and taught classes, just like before. Cancer or no, life marches on. There were a few times, for minutes and even an hour altogether, when I forgot to remember that I had cancer. But then someone would say something, or not say something, or there would be a momentary calm in the busyness of the day, and I would remember that my own body had betrayed me. Somewhere within my breasts, the breasts whose appearance I had anxiously awaited and proudly welcomed as a girl, that had drawn my husband's eyes and known his caress as a woman, that had suckled and nourished my son as a mother, there was a terrible and slowly growing secret that, left unchecked, would end my life.

Sometimes the truth of this was almost more than I could bear. If it had not been for Margot, Liza, and Abigail, it would have been. Where did they come from? Why did they appear when they did? Maybe it was like Dr. Finney had said, that God had sent me three angels. I didn't know for sure, but it seemed possible. What would I have done without those three? I don't want to imagine it.

Which is not to say that everything was hunky-dory since those three angels entered my life, far from it, but without them I would certainly have lost my business and possibly my sanity.

In Margot's case, the title of angel seemed perfectly apt. She was darling; endlessly optimistic and giving. On top of that, she was a marketing genius. Not only had she streamlined my accounting and inventory process, her plan to get more papers to run the article and set up a Web site had indeed brought in new business. And while she didn't wear her religion on her sleeve, I knew her faith was an integral part of her being and that she prayed for me, which I found comforting. Yes, the words angelic and Margot just seemed to go together.

But oh! How Abigail would have balked at hearing herself described as an angel! There was nothing of harps and gossamer wings about Abigail! Still, I considered her one, and, for that matter, Liza too. They might have been angels in very unlikely disguises, but the effect was the same. They appeared when I was sorely in need of a message of hope. They had abilities that I lacked and used them to help me.

Liza was quiet and hardly spoke to me at first. I was surprised to realize that, in spite of her tough-girl gothic fashions, she was really very shy and lacked confidence. But my other instincts about her had been correct; she had a deep appreciation for the power of color and an innate artistic sensibility. She knew exactly how to arrange colors and textures for maximum impact. On that first Monday when she came in to help with the inventory, she timidly asked my permission to rearrange some of the displays. Her initial efforts, moving my collection of batiks toward the front of the store and displaying them against a collection of sea-grass matting and big plastic glasses filled with rolls of brightly colored batik fabrics, electric blue straws, and paper umbrellas reminded me of a picnic on a tropical isle. It was darling! Not only that, the new point-of-sale inventory system that Margot installed told me that sales of batiks, which were some of the most expensive fabrics in the shop, were up by 46 percent. When I asked Liza if she had any ideas for other displays, her face lit up.

"Really? You like what I did?"

"Are you kidding? I love it! And so do the customers. You've got a real eye, Liza. You're an artist."

She laughed derisively. "Funny. That's not what the teachers at art school thought. I did pretty well in my sculpture classes; guess I like working with things that have texture. I tried adding different found objects to some of my paint canvasses, but my teachers didn't like it—said I hadn't followed the project guidelines. I failed oil painting. Got a D in watercolor. Abigail thinks I flunked out, but that's not quite true. I would have before long, so I figured, why stick around and wait for them to throw me out? At least this way I got to leave while it was still my own idea, you know?"

I didn't know, but this was the longest conversation I'd ever had with her and the first time she'd ever confided in me. I didn't want to interrupt. She needed to be heard. I'd already come to realize that communication between Liza and her aunt was more than a little strained.

Liza bit her lower lip and then shrugged. "I don't know who I was kidding anyway. Thinking I could be an artist. It was just a silly dream."

Hearing that, I couldn't keep silent any longer. "It's not silly!

Dreams may be the only things on earth that aren't! I don't care what your teachers said, Liza, you are an artist. Maybe you're not a conventional sort of artist, but who cares? You're in very good company. Throughout history the real artists, the innovators, were never appreciated initially. Did you know that Vincent van Gogh only sold one painting in his lifetime?"

Liza laughed, and this time she meant it. "Yeah, and he died insane, lovesick, and minus an ear. Is that supposed to make me feel better? Seriously, Evelyn, you're not actually trying to compare me to Van Gogh, are you?"

"Well, I don't know. I haven't seen any of your paintings yet, but you certainly have a unique eye for color, and you're very creative. What you did with the batik display was so inventive! If you have any other ideas for displays, just say the word. You have my permission to display the stock in any way you see fit."

"You really mean it, don't you?" I nodded, and she beamed.

"Well, I was thinking about arranging the whole shop into seasons—fall, winter, spring, and summer groupings. I just think it would be a lot more interesting than the standard color-wheel system."

"Have at it," I said. "Do whatever you want. Also, I've got some quilting books I'd like to show you. This idea you had, of trying to add objects within a piece to create texture and interest? Quilters have been doing that for years; it's called embellishing." I pulled a couple of the more innovative art quilt books off a nearby shelf. "Take a look at this and see what you think. It might give you a few ideas. And feel free to take anything you need in the way of fabric or notions if you want to give it a try."

"Really?" She looked around the shop eagerly, and I could practically see the wheels turning in her mind. Her eyes were full of ideas. "Anything?"

"Absolutely," I assured her. "I'd love to see what you come up with."

"Well," she continued shyly, "to tell the truth, I was wanting to start working on a quilt, but I'm not sure how to get started. I made a sketch and was hoping I could show it to you at our regular Friday night business meeting. That is, if you don't mind."

Mind? Of course not. In fact, I was thrilled! "Liza, that's a great idea! I should have thought of it myself, but I've been so wrapped up in myself that I never . . . But I should have. Oh well. No time like the present. Starting this week, Friday night business meetings are a thing of the past!"

Liza looked a little confused, not realizing that she had inadvertently hit upon the thing I'd most desired—a way for me to give something back to my three angels. "What are you talking about?"

"We're going to start a quilting circle, that's what I'm talking about! Just you, me, Margot, and Abigail. Come Friday night, instead of all of you helping me, I'm going to do something for you— help each of you start making a quilt that's all your own! But don't say anything to the others. I want it to be a surprise!"

❦ 15 ❦

Abigail Burgess Wynne

"Aren't you ready yet?" Liza's frowning visage unexpectedly appeared in my dressing-room mirror, giving me a start.

"Obviously not." I pulled the edges of my silk blouse together to cover myself. There were three shirts lying on top of the dresser. I was having trouble deciding between them. "Didn't anyone ever teach you to knock?"

She ignored the question. "Evelyn said to be on time. We have a lot to do tonight."

"Oh, she did, did she?" I groused. "You see? That's what you get for going out of your way to help strangers. You do one or two things for them and suddenly they think they're entitled. No one ever asked if I wanted to spend every Friday evening of my life sitting around Evelyn Dixon's apartment discussing how much she should charge for thread. I've got better things to do with my time."

"Like what?" Liza glared at my reflection, waiting for a response to her question, which I refused to dignify with an answer.

Finally, she sighed and said, "Hurry up, would you? It's too cold for a blouse anyway. Why don't you wear that turquoise sweater you had on last week. You looked really good in it."

Was that a compliment? From Liza? I was surprised and, judging by the look on her face, she was too.

"Just hurry," she said, resuming her usual impatient tone. "I'll see you over there."

She left, and I returned to the problem of getting dressed, finally deciding to take Liza's advice. The sweater did look good, and it was comfortable. After spending the whole day in a suit and heels at the Women's Shelter board meeting, listening to Ted Carney drone on endlessly about the need for more stringent intake guidelines, a cozy sweater was a welcome change.

Liza was so judgmental, I thought as I stepped out of my heels and slipped into a pair of soft leather driving moccasins. "Like what?" she'd said, mocking how I spent my time. What did she know about it anyway?

The shelter was an important resource for all sorts of families in crisis. Someone had to provide the funds to keep it running. Someone had to sit through the silly board meetings. Of course, I sometimes wondered if the board didn't overcomplicate the mission. No, that wasn't quite true. I didn't wonder. I knew. Today was a perfect example.

Ted Carney was such a pompous blowhard. All during the meeting, I'd sat drumming my pen on the conference table and wishing someone would pipe up and tell Ted he was ridiculous. We didn't need more stringent intake guidelines! If anything, we needed to make the intake process easier. Then we needed to raise more money so we could help more people.

Just the week before, I'd taken a tour of the shelter. Until then I'd only seen the facility during the construction phase, before there were any people actually living there. Now that the building was finished, every inch of space was filled. The director told me that the waiting list of new applicants was months long. And there were so many children! Of course, I'd seen the facts and figures regarding the demographics of the people served by the shelter. However, it's one thing to read a report and note that X percentage of our residents were under eighteen and quite another to meet a six-year-old girl named Bethany with mismatched bows in her pigtails, one blue and one green, who, until she'd moved into the shelter, had been living in a car. I'd had no idea. The shelter apartment she shared with her mother and baby brother was tiny, just one room with a kitchenette and bath. There were no curtains on the windows, just white blinds, no pictures on the walls except a crayon drawing that the girl made at school and proudly hung on the refrigerator. Even so, she was eager to show me her new home.

It was, to say the least, a disturbing visit. I didn't sleep well afterward.

What did Ted Carney think? That families were lining up to live in a shelter because it was such an appealing prospect? That they crowded in the tiny studio apartments we could provide because they were trying to save money on rent?

People came to us because they were desperate. What the board should do with its time was figure out how to raise more money and to build more apartments to help more people in need, not create more red tape to keep them from getting that help. Why hadn't someone told him that?

It had been a long day. I reached up and massaged the sore muscles in my neck. The last thing I wanted to do right now was go to yet another meeting, but I was resigned to my fate. If I didn't show up, Liza would glare daggers at me for a least a week. Wearily, I pulled myself to my feet. At least with Margot running the agenda, there would be no time wasted on long speeches and speculation. Margot was all about action items and assigned responsibilities—far too many of them directed at me.

Once again, I wondered how I'd gotten roped into all this. A year before, my life was fine—my dance card full of tennis, luncheon dates, cocktail parties, a few board meetings, and charity galas. I was happy.

Now I was too busy for tennis and lunch, questioning the value of my various community commitments, and unable to sleep at night. I was tired and troubled. On top of that, I was living with a teenager whose very presence in my home was an ongoing accusation, who displayed her despise for me with every glance, and I was on the verge of offending some of the most influential people in New Bern by standing up in public and announcing that they were full of hot air.

What in the world was going on? When was I going to get my old life back? When would I just be able to relax and enjoy myself again?

I arrived at the shop at five-fifteen. The CLOSED sign was out, but I went inside, knowing that Evelyn would have left the door unlocked for me.

As I climbed up the back stairs to Evelyn's apartment, I was surprised to meet Charlie Donnelly coming down. I was even more surprised to see him grinning broadly and whistling a tune. I'd known Charlie for years and never once had I known him to whistle or seen him with such a lighthearted expression on his face. It made me wonder if there was more to Evelyn's "friendship" with Charlie than she was letting on, but of course Evelyn's private business was certainly no concern of mine.

That's one of the problems with letting yourself get too close to other women; they are always butting their noses into each other's private affairs and then reporting their findings or speculations to anyone within earshot. There's nothing worse than a gossip. That's why I keep my own confidences.

"Hullo, Abigail. You're late," Charlie announced with his customary tact.

I gave him a look. "Hello, Charlie," I said, stopping in the stairwell and leaning forward to accept a peck on my right cheek. "Shouldn't you be at work?"

"That's where I'm headed right now. I had a bit of a catering job to see to first," he said, tipping his head toward the door of Evelyn's apartment.

"A catering job? Here?"

"You'd best get up there. The food is getting cold." He pushed past me without answering my question and continued down the stairs, whistling all the way.

Being brushed aside like that was irritating, but something did smell wonderful. I suddenly remembered that I hadn't eaten since breakfast. Evelyn answered the door, looking cheerful and well put together in a flattering black knit dress worn over black leather boots with an exotic hemp belt with silver accents circling her waist. Stylish. Perhaps I should have worn the silk blouse after all.

"You're here!" she exclaimed, as if genuinely pleased to see me. "Come in!"

The dining table was set with a white cloth and a bright bouquet of Gerbera daisies. Candles gave off a warm yellow glow and a faint scent of vanilla that wasn't quite overcome by the enticing smell of roast fowl. Evelyn's apartment, which I'd always felt she'd decorated in simple good taste, letting her many beautiful quilted wall hangings take center stage on the exposed brick walls, looked quite elegant in the candle glow. Margot walked over and handed me a glass of cabernet.

"Here you go. Charlie said you only drink red."

"Charlie is right," I said, taking a moment to appreciate the scent of oak and newly turned earth that emanated from the glass before taking a sip. "Very nice. What is going on? I thought we were having a meeting." Margot shrugged, obviously no better informed than I.

"We are," Evelyn confirmed. "Just a different sort of meeting. But first we're going to have a lovely dinner. After everything you three have done for me, I wanted to do a little something for you." She took a sip from her own wineglass. "And I wanted to give us a chance to talk about something besides my cancer or the shop, so we could get to know each other a little. We've spent every Friday night of the fall together, but I really don't know any of you."

It was everything I could do to keep from rolling my eyes. The idea of dinner was nice, a lovely gesture, but the last thing I wanted to get involved in was some touchy-feely female tell-all session. I'd already been dragooned into helping Evelyn through her illness. Wasn't that enough? Did she have to become my new best friend? Evelyn was right; she didn't know me. If she had, she'd have realized that I didn't have a best friend, nor was I looking for one.

Evelyn picked up a pair of hot pads and began pulling platters of food out of the oven. "Margot, would you mind getting the salad out of the refrigerator?"

Liza emerged from the bathroom. She looked at me. "Oh good. You're here." The word "finally" hung in the air unspoken, but I paid no attention. She turned to Evelyn. "Did you tell them yet?"

"Tell us what? What's the big secret?" Margot asked.

"Later," Evelyn insisted. "After dinner."

It was a delicious meal. After the salad, Evelyn served the Grill's signature roast chicken with clear, pan-juice gravy, garlic mashed potatoes, and sautéed greens. It was heavier than my usual evening fare, but the perfect menu for a chilly winter night. My resistance broken down by the pressures of the day and two glasses of good wine, I decided to forget about my diet, at least for one night.

But good food and pleasant surroundings aside, I still didn't like the idea of this forced camaraderie. The others could bare their souls if they liked; all I was going to do was listen.

It was interesting, however, learning a bit more about the others. Evelyn told an amusing story about her hiding in the towel department of a J. C. Penney when she was a little girl because she was so entranced by the rainbow of colors on the wall.

I learned that Margot had graduated from Hamilton College, my late husband Woolley's alma mater, but I didn't bother to ask if they knew any of the same people. She had been there decades after

Woolley graduated. Margot asked me a few questions about Woolley, how we'd met and fallen in love and all that, but I kept my answers appropriately brief, revealing little beyond saying I'd first met
him at a museum.

So odd, this modern bent for asking personal questions. It wasn't
that way when I was growing up. It's all this television psychology
that's done it. When people go on national television to tell the
world every sordid detail of their pasts, I suppose asking personal
questions at dinner seems perfectly normal. But as far as I'm concerned, it's perfectly rude. And I haven't noticed this trend in com-
munal honesty improving the world; quite the opposite. Seems like
the entire world has enrolled in a collective twelve-step program—
"admitting you have a problem is the first step." Not in my book. As
far as I'm concerned, the first step is deciding that life is hard and
getting on with it. Like Daddy said, "Never complain and never explain." Not a popular piece of philosophy, but it has served me well.
I have no intention of abandoning it now.

Besides, I've discovered that you don't need to ask many questions to get people to reveal everything you'd want to know about
themselves and more. Generally one, delivered with a penetrating,
deeply interested gaze, is sufficient. Then all you have to do is sit
back and listen. Try it sometime. You'll be shocked at what you
hear. It works almost every time, but not on me. As I said, I prefer
to keep my own confidences.

Margot and I cleared the table and rinsed the dishes while Liza
made a pot of decaffeinated coffee and Evelyn served dessert, a tall
chocolate cake with crushed peppermint candies sandwiched between the layers and decorating the top. She'd made it herself. It
looked tempting, but I simply couldn't eat another mouthful; the
waistband of my slacks was already too tight. I sipped a cup of coffee while the others dug into the cake and the conversation continued.

At Evelyn's urging, Liza revealed a bit more about her interest in art and how, when she was nine years old, she'd helped her mother paint a carnival mural on her bedroom wall. She said she'd decided, then and there, that she wanted to be an artist when she grew up. Her artistic bent wasn't surprising, given her parentage. And, of course, Susan had shown an early talent for painting herself. As I recalled, some of her landscapes had been quite good.

There was a lull in the conversation. Margot broke it, saying, "Liza, I hope you don't mind me asking, but what happened to your mother? I know she passed last year, but . . ."

Liza did mind her asking, I knew. When all this business started with Evelyn, she'd told me in no uncertain terms that I was not to mention Susan's breast cancer to Margot or Evelyn. Once news of Susan's illness had become public, all kinds of people had started sharing their cancer stories with her. Usually the stories had been encouraging, but sometimes they had been sad, even frightening. Really! Why don't people think before they speak?

"So don't you dare go telling anyone about Mother," Liza had ordered. As though I'd ever dream of doing something like that! Yet again, I was irritated by Liza's low opinion of me.

Margot's question hung in the air. Liza took a long, slow drink of her coffee, buying time, I thought, trying to figure out a way to answer without answering.

I tried a diversionary tactic.

"Evelyn, you said you have a son. Where does he live?" I smiled, looking directly at our hostess, but out of the corner of my eye I could spy the look of relief on my niece's face.

"Garrett lives in Seattle. He went to Harvey Mudd College and graduated with a degree in computer science. Now he's a programmer for a big company. It's a good job, or at least the pay is good, but it seems like he's always working. I've given up trying to call him at home. He's always at the office, dealing with some emergency or other. I spoke with him last weekend and he joked that he was considering giving up his apartment in favor of a cot in the employee break room and a storage unit. At least I think he was joking." She smiled.

"Well, it's good that you raised such a hard worker. Will he be coming to visit any time soon?"

Evelyn shook her head. "No. He's so busy with his work, and it's only his first year on the job. He doesn't have much in the way of vacation. To tell you the truth," she admitted sheepishly, "I haven't told him about the cancer."

"Evelyn!" Margot exclaimed. "You haven't told him!"

"How can you keep something like that from your own son," Liza added, using the disapproving tone I thought she reserved exclusively for me. "He has a right to know. If he did, I'm sure he'd want to help you."

Evelyn reached up and rubbed the side of her neck with her hand, a gesture I'd noticed she employed when under stress. "I know. I know. I will tell him, but in a few weeks. After all this is over." Liza glowered at her, and Evelyn sighed.

"Liza, you're right. Garrett is a wonderful son. If he knew about this, he'd insist on coming out to help, and he just can't afford to do that right now. Not when he's just starting out with a new job. Claremont Solutions is one of the most important firms in the industry. This is a great opportunity for him. Garrett was up against fifty well-qualified applicants for this position. If he took time off to come help me now, the people at Claremont would only have to whistle to find someone to take his place. I won't have him jeopardizing his future just because I've got some silly little lump that's going to be removed and forgotten in just a couple of weeks," she said with finality.

Margot was about to say something, but I beat her to the punch.

"Very sensible, Evelyn. You're quite right. In another couple of weeks you'll be through the worst of this. There's no point in endangering your son's career over a little surgery, is there?" I looked pointedly at Margot.

"Well," she said slowly, and I could see she was wrestling with a response, "I'm not sure it's fair, keeping this from him. But you know your son, Evelyn. Maybe it isn't a good idea to tell him until after the operation. He shouldn't jeopardize a good job. They can be hard to find these days. I know from experience. Besides, we're here to give you all the help you need until you're well."

In the candlelight, I could see the sheen in Evelyn's eyes. "You've all been so wonderful to me, truly. If I'd been born with three sisters instead of as an only child, I couldn't have asked for three sweeter, more giving women to help me through this. There just aren't words to thank you."

Oh dear. Defying my expectations, this had been a pleasant evening. At least so far. The last thing we needed to do was spoil it with some emotional scene. I jumped in.

"Well, you've certainly done a lovely job of thanking us tonight," I said expansively. "It was just delightful. Such a treat at the end of a long, tiring week."

Evelyn smiled, and I was relieved to notice that she swallowed back her tears. "It really was my pleasure. I've been wracking my brain thinking of what I could do for the three of you, and then I figured it out."

"You didn't have to do anything for us," Margot said. "It's been no hardship helping you. Actually, I've enjoyed it. It's certainly more fun working at Cobbled Court than sending out endless resumes and cover letters for jobs I don't get." Margot's usually smiling face grew serious. It was the first time I'd seen a cloud on her normally sunny disposition. Clearly, the months of unemployment had been harder on her than she'd let on.

"I know the economy is in a slump, but I never imagined that I'd have such a hard time finding a new job. I was really beginning to doubt myself and my skills, but, Evelyn, working with you has reminded me that I actually am good at what I do—even if corporate America doesn't seem to need my services. I can't speak for the others, but I suspect that, even though you think we're helping you, you're helping each of us just as much. I know everyone might not feel the same way," Margot said, looking at me as if anticipating my discomfort with her assertion, "but I think God has brought us together for a reason. In some way or other, we need each other. So, really, you don't need to thank us."

"Maybe not, but I do. And this," Evelyn said, sweeping her hand over the table, "was just the appetizer. The best part is yet to come."

Pushing back her chair, she got to her feet. "Ladies, grab your coffee cups and follow me downstairs. There's something I want to show you."

❦ 16 ❦

Evelyn Dixon

"There!" I snapped on the light in the dark workroom. "That's better."

I'd set four rolling chairs around the sides of the cutting table and positioned a sewing machine behind each chair so everyone could easily move from the table to the machines and back. Additionally, I'd set up two ironing boards in the corners of the room. In the center of the table, I'd placed a basket with rulers, markers, template plastic, seam rippers, and scissors. Each spot was supplied with a new rotary cutter and mat, a box of silk pins, a project bag, and a stack of pattern books that I'd felt might appeal to each of the three women.

Abigail and Margot looked a little confused, but Liza, already in on the surprise, was grinning from ear to ear. "Don't you get it? We're starting a quilting circle. Evelyn is going to help us make quilts."

"That's right," I confirmed. "Now, instead of going over the books on Friday nights, we can relax and enjoy each other's company while we work on our quilting projects. Of course, tonight's dinner was a little more elaborate than I can manage on a weekly basis, but I'm sure we'll be able to rustle up something in the way of provisions."

Margot looked pleased, but a little concerned too. "Evelyn, this is sweet of you, but do you think you really have time for this? Even without the surgery coming up, you've got a lot on your plate. And you're teaching three nights a week as it is. Now you want to take on yet another class? Besides," she protested, "what will we do about our Friday night business meetings?"

"But this isn't a class. I'll be here to help and advise, but I'll be working on a project of my own just like the rest of you. It'll be as much fun for me as for you. And believe me, I could use a little fun right now." I laughed, but Margot's brow remained furrowed.

"Margot, at first we needed those weekly meetings, but now you know everything there is about running Cobbled Court Quilts. You can probably do it better than I can." She started to deny this, but I interrupted. "Besides, you and I see each other practically every day anyway. We can discuss the business during business hours. There's no point in boring poor Abigail with all this. She's on so many other boards and committees in town, doing things that can affect the lives of hundreds of people, not just mine. I appreciate all her help, but she's done her part. She has other commitments, important ones. She can't be involved in the day-to-day of operating a quilt shop."

Abigail didn't say anything one way or the other, as was her style, but I read a flash of appreciation in her eyes. I meant what I said. During one of our morning coffee dates, Charlie told me about the extent of Abigail's charity work. Her contributions, monetary and otherwise, clearly had a huge impact on the community. Of course, some of that may have been for appearance's sake, writing the right checks to the right organizations, showing up at the right parties. But I couldn't believe anyone, even someone as wealthy as Charlie said Abigail was, would be so generous with her money and time unless she really wanted to help people. I wanted Abigail to know that I truly appreciated her generosity, and not just to me. She deserved my gratitude and my respect. It was too bad her niece didn't share my feelings.

I knew that Liza didn't get much affirmation from her aunt, but clearly that was a two-way street. They were so much alike, those two. The physical resemblance was striking, of course. They had the same high cheekbones, the same piercing gaze and beautiful complexions, and the same graceful, loping gait, leading from the hips like off-duty runway models, but there was so much more they shared. They were both intelligent and talented, though in very different ways. It was impossible not to be drawn to them, curious to know what made them tick, but they each put up walls to keep others from getting too close.

Liza's, constructed from an off-putting combination of goth clothing, ripped jeans, and stony stares, with a thick coating of hard-edged attitude to fill in any chinks, was easy to spot. Hers was the armor angry, hurting teenage girls had been donning for generations. As I recall, I'd adopted a similar stance myself for a time but thankfully, as most girls do, had thrown it off in adulthood. Someday, I hoped Liza would do the same.

Abigail was different. Her personal barrier was harder to identify and to penetrate, an irresistible but blinding beam of light that drew people close but kept them from getting too close. Abigail's wall was composed of equal parts unquestionable generosity, impeccable manners, and an astounding gift for getting information from others without giving away any herself. She was incredibly skilled at this; I'd seen her in action. But I wasn't convinced that she actually wanted most of what people so readily handed her; she was just out to charm them, to dazzle them into believing that she was deeply interested in them and so could add them to her extensive collection of admirers, trinkets for her charm bracelet.

I know this makes Abigail sound cold and calculating, her alluring veneer just a cover for a manipulative personality, but it was more complicated than that. If she had been merely manipulative, people would have seen through her ruse years before. It's impossible to hide something like that for long, especially in a small town, and Abigail had lived in New Bern most of her life. I felt certain that a genuinely kind, compassionate person was trapped behind Abigail's magnetic but impenetrable wall, fighting to get out. The same was true of Liza.

They were so similar. So scarred. And so alone. Yet they were family. They lived in the same house. What was it that kept them from acknowledging what was good in the other? From comforting each other? I wondered if the death of Liza's mother had something to do with it. I knew Susan had passed little more than a year before. It seemed to me that whatever was keeping them apart had been in place for many years, but there was no way of knowing for sure. Liza's hesitancy to respond to Margot's question about her mom and Abigail's rapid and deft repositioning of the conversation said it all. Liza and Abigail didn't agree on much, but in this they were united: the Burgess family secrets would stay secret.

"Thank you, Evelyn. You're right. My calendar is full of commitments at the moment, and the shelter may have a new capital campaign in the offing that will require more of my attention, so I hope you'll understand why I need to bow out of your little quilting circle." She looked at her watch.

"Really, I should be going. I didn't realize it was so late. I promised to drop by Alana and Link Burkstead's house. They're hosting a benefit for the New Bern Historic Association."

Already seated and flipping through pattern books, Liza puffed contemptuously. "Yeah. Right. I'm sure they won't be able to hold one more charity auction and boozefest without your direct participation."

"Liza, that's not very nice," Margot chastised her, but gently. I was glad she said something, otherwise I would have, probably far less diplomatically. "Like Evelyn said, Abigail's work is very important and helps all kinds of people. I've really enjoyed getting to spend time with her these last weeks, but if she doesn't have time to be part of our quilt circle . . . well, we should just respect that. Really, Abigail, we understand. But we'll miss you." She walked across the room and gave Abigail a hug that Abigail tolerated, but briefly.

I smiled. Margot was such a dear and such a contradiction in terms. She was a business genius with a heart of gold, brilliant in strategy and execution but utterly kindhearted, looking for the best in everyone. I wondered if that was what was keeping her from finding a job in the city. An interviewer would only have to spend five minutes with her to know that she was completely lacking in killer instinct or guile, commodities that were highly valued in most corporations. I hadn't paid myself in months, but if ever Cobbled Courts could afford to hire an employee, Margot would be my first choice. Not that I could afford to pay her anything like what she was worth—even very successful quilt shops can't compete with corporate pay packages—but if I could, she'd be worth it.

"Margot, Liza, why don't you keep looking through the books. Figure out what projects you might want to start, while I walk Abigail to the door. I'll be right back." I left the workroom and Abigail followed, politely thanking me for a lovely evening and just as politely apologizing for the necessity of her departure.

"Really, Evelyn, it was such a considerate thought on your part, but as I said, I'm really too busy to add yet another obligation to my schedule."

I stopped in the middle of the darkened shop and turned, standing face-to-face with Abigail, sandwiched between rows of fabric bolts. She couldn't move in any direction unless she actually backed away from me, and I knew that her sense of propriety wouldn't permit her to do anything so rude.

"Abigail, is that what you think? That I wanted to saddle you with one more obligation? That's not it at all. I was trying to give you a gift of time, a few hours each week to do something that I think you'd enjoy. I meant what I said in there, the extent of what you do for all kinds of people in this town. . . ." I shook my head in amazement. "Well, I just wouldn't like to think what kind of a place New Bern would be without you. That's why I think this would be good for you. It would give you a much-deserved break after a busy week, something fun and relaxing."

She stood still for a long moment. I couldn't tell what she was thinking, but somehow or other I'd said something that struck a chord.

"That's considerate of you, truly it is, but I don't think I'd be very good at it. My talents are more philanthropic than artistic." She paused for a moment, and her tone softened. "Susan was the creative one."

It was the first time I'd heard Abigail refer to her sister by name.

"Abigail, everyone has a creative side. It's just that most people don't tap into it."

I wasn't sure what to say next, but I sensed a definite wavering in her resistance. What could I say that would change her mind?

"Besides, Abigail, you are such a generous person, and quilts make wonderful gifts. There is really nothing that shows your concern and love the way a quilt does, not flowers, not money, nothing! It doesn't matter if your quilt is perfectly sewn or the colors aren't exactly right. That's not the point. When you give someone a quilt, they know that you care about them even if you can't find the words to say so. Is there someone like that in your life?" I asked, thinking of Liza. "Someone you'd like to encourage?"

She was quiet for a long moment. Then she said, "Well, there is a little girl I met a few days ago, Bethany. She . . . she took my hand, held on to me while she showed me around her house. I didn't ask her to. She just did. She had yarn ribbons in her pigtails, one blue and the other green. Because those were her favorite colors, she said.

"I wonder . . ." I could hear her breathing slowly, trying to keep the catch out of her voice. "I wonder if she might like a quilt. A blue and green one. For her new home."

❧ 17 ❧

Evelyn Dixon

Initially, Abigail wanted to pick a more complicated pattern but with some prodding from me finally chose a simple friendship star as the base block for her quilt. When it is finished, this block looks more like a pinwheel than a star, a pattern certain to appeal to a child. Abigail chose the fabrics all herself, nine brilliant shades of blue from cobalt to turquoise and an equal number of vibrant greens from emerald to lime. I was surprised, considering that Abigail's wardrobe centered on a subdued palette of black, gray, and earth tones, with an occasional accent of red or burgundy in the fall, that she would pick such bright colors, but her choices were right on the mark. By the time she'd sewn the first couple of blocks it was obvious that the quilt would be darling when it was finished, like a garden of gaily colored pinwheels planted in a field of white, spinning on the breath of an invisible wind. It had the potential to be such a happy quilt.

Too bad that Abigail couldn't manage to relax and be happy with it.

It was the day before Thanksgiving and four days after my lumpectomy. Even though I'd protested that I was feeling much

better, Margot insisted that someone sit with me during the day
"just in case you need anything."

If I needed anything, all I had to do was holler down the stairs
where either she or Liza was busy tending to customers, but that
didn't seem to matter to Margot. I knew that Dr. Finney said I
should accept all offers of help that came my way, but right now I
just wanted to be alone. Margot meant well, and I was so very, very
grateful for everything she'd done for me, but sometimes I felt as if
I had suddenly regressed to childhood and a pretty, thirty-something,
blond marketing manager had become my mother, supervising my
care and feeding with all the attention and intensity she'd have given
to running a Fortune 500 corporation. Sometimes her solicitousness
got on my nerves.

It didn't help that I was still sore and tired from the surgery and
on tenterhooks waiting for Dr. Finney to call with the postsurgical
test results. Why did it have to take so long? Every time the phone
rang, I jumped. And every time it turned out to be someone other
than the doctor, I became more and more irritable.

I'd have never imagined I'd be saying this, but I was grateful that
it was Abigail on babysitting duty that day. Margot was sweet, but
her constant hovering and strained attempts at cheery conversation
were tiring. And Liza became distant after the operation, sitting
quietly in a chair and barely speaking to me, as if she was afraid of
saying something wrong. Charlie came over on the days when the
restaurant was closed, but he was nervous without anything to do,
so, after a few minutes, ended up in the kitchen clanging pots and
chopping things and making elaborate meals I was too tired to con-
sume.

Abigail alone seemed to realize that I was sick of people talking
about me, or my cancer, or even worse pretending *not* to talk about
those things. Either that, or she truly was absorbed in her quilting
project. Whatever the reason, she brought her quilting along and
started working on it. I did the same, appliquéing holly leaves on a

Christmas tree skirt I hoped to finish before the holidays. It was a relief just to sit in silence and stitch, focusing on something other than the cancer, if only for a few minutes. But before long, I was just too sore and tired to sew. I put the half-finished skirt on the table next to the sofa where I was reclining and closed my eyes. Abigail looked up from her work.

"Does it hurt? Do you want a pain pill?"

"No," I said with my eyes still closed. "It's not time yet. I'm just taking a break."

I opened my eyes and saw Abigail, bent over her work again, ripping the seam out of a block she'd just finished. I noticed that the edge of the fabric was frayed.

"Abigail, why are you ripping that seam? It looks fine."

She pursed her lips, displeased, and kept on ripping. "No. I measured it, and this side is an eighth of an inch narrower than the other. This point doesn't look anything like the rest."

I scooted back on the sofa, shifting myself so I sat up straighter on the mound of pillows wedged behind my back, and peered at the half-disassembled quilt block. Honestly, I couldn't see what she was talking about.

"How many times have you taken that block apart and put it back together?"

"This will be four," she said, pursing her lips but still not looking up.

"Well, no wonder your seams are off. Look how the edge is all frayed. Taking a seam out once is fine if there really is a problem, but if you do it over and over you stretch the fabric out of shape and it just gets worse."

Abigail sighed. "Well, then I guess I'll just have to cut out a whole new block and start over." She tossed the block aside with a disgusted look on her face. "I thought you said quilting was supposed to be relaxing."

"It is," I said and added silently, *at least if you're not quite so anal, it is.*

"Let me see that." I reached over, picked up the discarded block, and examined it carefully.

"Abigail, this is fine. You'd have to put your face right next to it to see the difference between the two sides. Just sew the seam back up and start on the next block."

She shook her head firmly. "No. I'll cut out another one. I want it to be perfect."

"What do you mean, you want it to be perfect? Perfect as in every single block is like every other? Perfect as in a machine could have done it? If you're trying for that, you've missed the whole point of quilting, especially hand quilting. You don't want it to be sloppy or carelessly made, but you do want this quilt to express your personality, to be authentic, to show that a real human being made it with real human hands. Otherwise, what's the point? You could just buy her something in a store ready-made, for heaven's sake!" I was on a roll. This was one of my pet peeves, when people took something as beautiful and creative, as *human*, as quilting and tried to turn it into yet one more modern expression of faux perfection.

"Evelyn—"

"No," I said irritably, "let me talk. Do you know that some of the most prized quilts, priceless quilts that are hanging in museums today, are full of wobbly seams and mismatched fabrics? And they are beautiful! Not because they are perfectly constructed, but because—"

Abigail got up from the wing chair she'd been sitting in and walked into the kitchen. "Evelyn, the phone is ringing." She picked it up and, after listening for a moment, said, "Yes. She's here. Just a moment, please."

"Dr. Finney," she mouthed silently as she handed me the phone and then, without my asking, walked quietly to the apartment door and down the stairs into the shop, giving me my privacy.

"Hello. This is Evelyn."

"Hi, Evelyn. This is Dr. Finney. I've got your reports back. Would you like to come in to the office and discuss them?"

My stomach knotted and my heart beat faster. When the news is good they don't ask you to come into the office and talk about it. I knew that by now. "No. It's bad, isn't it. I want to know now. I don't want to wait."

"All right, I understand. Evelyn, we didn't get clean margins," she said flatly. "There is still cancer in the breast."

"Oh God," I whispered and closed my eyes. "God."

"I know, Evelyn. I'm sorry," she said and then took a breath. "And I'm afraid there's more. The MRIs we took right before your surgery showed some suspicious-looking lesions in the other breast too. We're going to have to do a biopsy. It may be nothing, but there's no way of knowing for sure until we do the testing."

"I don't understand. Why didn't this show up before?"

"The equipment we have at the hospital is more advanced. That's why I ordered the test. I know this all comes as a shock, but it's a good thing that we caught this now."

"Yes. I see." I wanted to cry but couldn't. The disbelief, the disappointment, the fear was a building pressure at the back of my brain and eyes. It hurt to speak or to think, but I had to. "What now?"

"I'd like to see you as soon as possible, to perform the biopsy and just to talk things over. I can see you tomorrow morning if you'd like."

"Tomorrow? But tomorrow is Thanksgiving. Is it that bad? What aren't you telling me?"

"Oh no! It's nothing like that," she assured me. "Truly. As I told you before, this is a fairly slow-growing cancer. There's no rush. I just didn't want you to have to wait. I know how nerve-wracking that can be. Maybe you'll be able to enjoy your holiday if you had a chance to talk this out and get the ball rolling on the biopsy. If it would help, I'd be happy to see you tomorrow."

And I knew she meant it. She was so kind. "But all the labs will be closed tomorrow, won't they? Unless you can perform the biopsy, run the lab tests, and write the report yourself before the turkey comes out of the oven, I don't think there's much point. It's fine, Deanna. Really. Have dinner with your family, and I can see you on Friday."

"All right. If you're sure. But, Evelyn, if you change your mind or have any other questions, you just give me a call. I already gave you my home number and my cell phone, didn't I?"

"Yes. I wrote them down in my address book."

"Good. Don't be shy about using them. I'll see you on Friday at nine. Will that work for you?"

"Friday at nine. I'll be there." Normally I wrote down all my appointments, but I didn't have a pen handy; besides, there was no chance I'd forget. The next forty hours would just be a countdown to Friday at nine.

"See you on Friday, Evelyn. Happy Thanksgiving."

I hung up.

"Happy Thanksgiving," I said to the empty air and sat holding the phone to my chest and staring out the window.

After a few minutes I heard movement behind me. The door opened a crack.

"May I come in?" Abigail asked. When I didn't answer, she opened the door and came to stand beside me.

"What did she say?" Lines of genuine concern creased a spot in the center of her brow. Abigail's face always had such a capable expression, but there was no trace of that now. Just like me, she didn't seem to know what to do next. "Is anything wrong? Shall I call Margot?"

"No," I said. "Nothing's wrong." The pain from the incision made me wince a little as I got to my feet.

"What are you doing?" she asked nervously. "What do you need? Tell me and I'll get it for you."

I walked slowly into the kitchen. "I'm fine. It's Wednesday. I just remembered. I want to make a turkey."

"You want to what?" she gasped, following close behind as I shuffled my way to the refrigerator.

"I want to make a turkey," I repeated. "And a pumpkin pie. What are you doing for Thanksgiving, Abigail?"

∾ 18 ∾

Abigail Burgess Wynne

"You had Thanksgiving dinner at the shelter?" The incredulous look on Franklin's face was more than a little insulting.

"Yes," I snapped. "Is that so surprising?"

"Yes," he said, grinning widely. "It is."

"Oh, stop it, Franklin! I don't know why I ever tell you anything. No matter what I do, you find a way to make fun of it."

Not without effort, Franklin wiped the smile from his face. "I apologize, Abigail. I wasn't mocking you. Quite the opposite. It's just hard to picture you standing behind a steam table doling out plates of mashed potatoes and gravy. Tell me"—he leaned across the desk, making the rusty springs of his leather barrister chair squeak—"did they make you wear one of those hair nets?"

"Shut up, Franklin," I said irritably. "And get your chair oiled. It sounds like nails on a chalkboard. Better yet, buy a new one. Surely I pay you enough so you don't have to keep using that same broken-down desk chair you've had since you passed the bar."

"You do, but I like this chair. Took me ten years just to get it broken in, and I have no intention of replacing it. However, if it makes you happy, I'll get the springs oiled. Now, is there anything else I can do for you today, Abigail, or did you just come in to offer me decorating advice?" He smiled, and his eyes twinkled mischievously.

He was always so terribly pleased with himself, I thought. He was even older than I was, but at that moment he looked positively boyish, like the illustration of Puck that I'd seen in a volume of Mr. Shakespeare's *A Midsummer Night's Dream*.

I scowled at him, but not wholeheartedly. "Of course I wanted something. I was trying to tell you that when you interrupted. Do you think I've nothing better to do with my time than hang about your office?"

Franklin nodded. "It's true. I've tried to call you several times recently, but you're never home. Hilda said you've been spending a lot of time helping out at the shelter, is that right?"

"Hilda," I sighed. Hilda has been my housekeeper for twenty years, and no matter how many times I tell her to just take a message and tell people I'll get back to them but not to tell them where I've gone, she doesn't listen. "I guess you just can't teach an old dog new tricks. No matter. Yes, I've been spending more time at the shelter recently. That's what I've come to see you about." I cleared my throat and sat up straighter in my chair before beginning.

"I've been thinking recently. About my money. And how I spend it." Franklin leaned back in his chair, frowned and, making a tent of his clasped hands and two raised index fingers, rested his fingertips against his lips. It was the thinking pose he struck whenever he was nervous about what I was going to say next. "I have about ninety million dollars, is that correct?"

"Yes," Franklin said, his fingers partially blocking his mouth. "If you're discussing fairly liquid assets, that's about right. Of course, if you count your various property holdings, the figure is substantially higher." He paused, waiting to hear what I would say next.

"And currently we give away about eight million annually to various charities, is that right?" Franklin nodded again. "Very good.

Well, I'd like to increase our level of giving. Substantially. And I'd like to become more involved in deciding where the money will go and what will be done with it."

"I see," said Franklin, lowering his hands. "That's fine. What did you have in mind? What organizations are you interested in? And how much would you like to donate?" He pulled a yellow legal pad toward him and took up a pen so he could take notes.

"All of it."

Franklin was silent.

"Don't look so stunned. I haven't lost my mind. I don't mean you have to give it away immediately, but I've been thinking long and hard about this. By the time I die, I'd like to make sure that almost all of my assets have been donated to worthy causes. Things that can do some real good. And I want to be involved in those decisions, not just sign the checks."

"You mean you'd like to join some more boards? Yes, that can be arranged, Abbie. But your schedule is already awfully busy. I don't see how you'd—"

"No! Not more boards! Heavens, no! I'm on too many as it is. In fact, right after Christmas I'm going to make up a list of the boards I'm currently on and cut the number by half. I'm going to rotate off the ones that I've joined for social reasons or whose missions I'm not as passionate about, also those whose board members seem more committed to hearing the sounds of their own voices than actually doing good work. Though," I said, thinking of Ted Carney, "in cases where the cause is good but the board is weak, I'm planning on organizing a few purges, trying to fill up the vacancies with fresh, eager talent that wants to make a difference. Hopefully, after a while, the dead wood will either begin to sprout new life or resign."

By this time, Franklin was leaning over the legal pad, scribbling furiously while I talked. "So you want to be on fewer boards but be more active in the remaining organizations. Is that right?"

"Yes!" I confirmed, pleased that he understood what I was reaching for. "I'll continue to support the arts, the various libraries, and community organizations at the same levels I always have, but I'd like to increase my focus on charities that deal with poverty, especially those that help children. With the right kind of emphasis, I believe we can really make a difference, a lasting difference, in the lives of children all over the state!" I continued excitedly. "And I want to make actual visits to the programs and organizations I'm supporting. Since I began volunteering at the shelter, really meeting the people and learning about their needs and problems, I've realized that you have to get in the trenches if you want to win the war. You're an old military man, Franklin. You know that."

"Six years in the National Guard; it's how I paid for law school. Never saw action though. I flew a desk." He looked up briefly, his pen poised over the pad of yellow paper. "Go on."

"Well, as I said, I want to get more personally involved. There is just no reason, in a community as well off as ours, that so many poor people should be suffering. I think it's because people who are well off just don't want to acknowledge the problems that are all around them. It's disgraceful! You know, when the rich finally meet the poor face-to-face, then poverty will cease to exist!" I said and thumped the top of Franklin's desk to emphasize my point before going on.

"Now, we'll need to plan it out so I can live comfortably—not lavishly, just comfortably—to the end of my life, but if my last dollar goes to pay for my headstone and there's nothing left after, then I'd say we've done our jobs properly." All this talking was making my throat dry. I poured myself some water from the pitcher on Franklin's desk and took a sip before going on.

"Except for whatever bequests I leave in my will, of course. Speaking of which, don't you think it's time to update the will? I'll want to leave something for Liza and for any heirs she might have someday. Nothing outrageous, but enough for a nice home and then some kind of educational trust. How much do you think that would take? Franklin? Why have you stopped writing?"

Franklin put down his pen and looked at me, actually stared at me is more accurate, as if I were someone he knew he'd met before but whose name he couldn't quite recall. I shifted uncomfortably in my chair. The pointed nature of his gaze was disconcerting.

"What?" I asked, unable to stand the silence.

"Abigail, what's happened to you? The holidays are just a week off; have you had some sort of Ebenezer Scrooge epiphany? Have you been going on midnight romps with the spirits of Christmas?"

I made a face. "Ha. Very funny, Franklin."

He took off his glasses and wiped the lenses with his pocket-handkerchief. "I'm serious, Abigail. You've changed. For the better, I think, and markedly. 'When the rich finally meet the poor face-to-face, then poverty will cease to exist.' You took that from Reverend Tucker's sermon two Sundays ago. I was in the back pew and you were in the fourth. You always sit in the back, Abigail. And you never attend except on the big holidays. Is that what's going on here? Have you found God?"

"Don't be stupid, Franklin," I snapped. "I've always believed in God. And I've always gone to church. It's just that now . . . Well, I've just started attending more often, that's all!"

His amazement in the face of my generosity was insulting. As if I hadn't been giving away millions for years. Now, just because I wanted to give a bit more than I had been, he made it sound like I'd been hoarding my money for my own pleasure. "Really, Franklin! You make me sound just awful."

"I'm sorry, Abbie." He sounded sincere. "I wasn't trying to offend you. I'm just trying to understand what has brought about this sudden change. You want to give away all your money? You want to remember Liza in your will? You're going to church and not only listening to the sermons but actually quoting the minister? I watched you at service last Easter, Abbie. You fell asleep in the pew and were startled awake when the Williams boy played the 'Gloria Patri' on the trumpet."

I remembered that. It was a terrible service. Why did they have to bring in trumpets just because it was Easter, when we had a perfectly good organ? Besides, the Williams boy has a tin ear. The whole thing was off-key.

"Next," Franklin said, "you start volunteering at the shelter? Working in the kitchen, getting your hands dirty 'in the trenches'? And cooking and serving Thanksgiving dinner? Abigail, you don't cook."

"That's not so. I helped Evelyn Dixon make a turkey and pie just a few weeks ago."

It had turned out rather well too. I wasn't there for dinner, of course. I hadn't told them where I was going, just that I had a previous invitation, but Evelyn saved me a piece of the pie. And Liza had said the turkey was very moist.

"And that's another thing. I called on Friday to see if you wanted to have dinner at the Grill, and Hilda said you were at the quilt shop." Hilda again! When would she learn to keep a confidence? "At your quilt circle. Quilt circle? Abbie, you don't quilt. At least, you never did before. Now you're spending every Friday night at Cobbled Court, baking cookies with Evelyn Dixon or making quilts with Liza and that other woman, what's her name?"

"Margot Matthews."

He nodded. "Margot. Abbie, you haven't made a new friend in thirty years! You barely tolerate your old friends! And now this? What is going on?"

I slapped my hands against the arms of the chair in exasperation, then got to my feet, gathering up my purse and my Cobbled Court project bag, and headed to the door.

"All right! I've changed! So what? I admit it. I've changed! I don't know why, and frankly, Franklin, I don't care. But whatever the reason, I like it!" I was practically shouting. "I feel better than I have in a long time. Is that all right with you?"

Franklin got to his feet. The puckish smile returned to his face. "Yes, Abigail. Perfectly all right."

"Hooray!" I said, raising my hands heavenward as if addressing an invisible balcony of witnesses. "We can all rest at ease. Franklin Spaulding approves! What a relief! Now if you'll excuse me, I have to go. I'm late for an open house."

I shut the door behind me, nodding at Franklin's receptionist before heading down the stairs and onto Commerce Street. Outside, the sun was shining but the air was cold. The sidewalk was dusted white, like it had been sprinkled with powdered sugar, evidence of a recent snow flurry. Clutches of holiday shoppers scurried along, carrying bags and leaving stencil-sharp footprints in the snow as they walked. I turned to the left, in the direction of Cobbled Court Quilts.

When I looked up, I could see Franklin watching me from the window of his second-story office and smiling.

❦ 19 ❧

Evelyn Dixon

It was a week until Christmas. I'd finished the appliquéd tree skirt just in time. But that night, sitting on the floor of the apartment and sorting through the box of ornaments I hauled out of the storage closet, I suddenly didn't feel like putting up the tree anymore.

We'd held our "Holiday Open House and Quilt-In" that day. Invitations had gone out to all our customers, inviting them to drop by for cocoa and cookies and to bring along any last-minute projects they wanted to work on before the holidays. Probably a hundred people showed up, though—thank heaven, not all at once. The flow of guests was steady but manageable.

We ran some in-store specials, but by the time we paid for invitations, postage, refreshments, and a small gift for everyone—a wrist pincushion—I don't think we made any money. But that wasn't the point. I just wanted to do something to thank my regulars. It was a nice party.

Margot, who knew that our improved sales still hadn't caught up with expenses, scolded me a little. The extra sales generated at the Quilt Pink day were an unexpected boon, but it wasn't enough. No matter what we did to advertise, Cobbled Court's tucked-away location made it hard for people to find us. With Christmas fast approaching, the streets of New Bern were packed with shoppers, but only a fraction of them wandered into our courtyard. Margot was worried. "If we had the new class listings ready we could probably have registered twenty or thirty new students today. You said you'd have it ready a week ago."

"I know. I'm just having a hard time deciding what classes to offer. I'll get to it as soon as I can. I've just been a little overwhelmed, what with the holiday traffic and all."

It was an excuse. Business had been better since Thanksgiving, especially on the weekends, but it was far from overwhelming. Most days, I'd manned the store myself with a little help from Liza, who had put together the most darling display in the bowfront window. Using rolls of quilt batting for their bodies, she'd constructed a fluffy snow family "warming" themselves around an icicle-festooned fireplace with a mound of snowballs where the logs should have been. In the corner she'd tucked a little snow-flocked Christmas tree hung with clear white and blue and silver balls strung on white ribbons. She spent hours on that display. I think she really enjoyed doing it, and it certainly drew a lot of attention. In fact, the newspaper used a picture of it to accompany a story, "New Bern Merchants Deck the Halls," and credited Liza as creator of "one of the village's most charming holiday windows." And they were right.

Liza's display and the resulting story had brought some extra customers our way, but not in the numbers that would have kept me too busy to plan for next year's classes. Margot knew that as well as I did.

"I'm sorry," Margot said and put an arm around me. "I'm sure you're still not feeling one hundred percent after the surgery. I don't mean to nag, but I hate to see you lose potential business."

"Don't apologize. You're right. I should have had it done by now. I'll get to it just as soon as I can. Really," I said and then changed the subject. "Do you know if we have any more of those chocolate macaroons in the back? They really went through them. No wonder people gain weight during the holidays."

"I'll check to see what we've got left." Margot went into the break room, taking an empty cookie tray with her. I rang up a sale, assuring the disappointed customer that the new class schedule would be ready soon.

Customers came and went all afternoon. Margot and Liza helped work the counter when things got busy, but we all had a chance to sit down with the rest of the customers and chat while we worked on our various projects. It was nice. Even Abigail dropped by to show me her nearly finished pinwheel quilt. The only thing she had left to do was sew one side of the binding so it would be ready to give to Bethany at the Women's Shelter Christmas party the next day.

When she spread it out on the worktable, everyone put their projects aside and gathered around to see what Abigail had done. I think she was uncomfortable at first, finding herself at the center of a crowd of strangers, but quilters are never strangers for long. Once she'd relaxed and quit tearing out the blocks over and over, the quilt had come together fairly quickly, and while it wasn't perfectly sewn, it really was a lovely quilt.

"I can't believe this is your first quilt. It's just gorgeous!" Wendy Perkins exclaimed, pushing her rhinestone glasses higher on the bridge of her nose and leaning down for a closer look. "I love the colors you picked. All those blues and greens. It's cheerful but soothing at the same time. Wish I had your eye."

Another woman, who'd taken my Mariner's Compass class, crowded in to have a look. "Look how well her points match! It's hard to believe you're a beginner." The others murmured their agreement. "What's your secret?"

Abigail thanked the woman but assured her she didn't have a secret and turned the conversation around, asking her admirer about her own project. I'd noticed that Abigail always did that, deflected any conversation that centered on herself, so that without their even realizing it, she got the questioner to talk about herself instead. There was no more expert interviewer in the world than Abigail Burgess Wynne. She knew that almost everyone loves to talk about themselves. Not for the first time, I wondered what made her so hesitant to open up to other people. It simply didn't make sense. Recently though, I felt that was changing. The other day, with only minimal prodding from me, she'd gone on for a good ten minutes about her volunteer work at the shelter and Bethany, the little girl she was making the quilt for.

A few minutes later, I looked up from my own work and saw Abigail carrying on a conversation with some of the other quilters and looking, not precisely relaxed, but more comfortable than she had before. Like I said, quilters are never strangers for long.

It had been a long day, but a successful one. When the afternoon light started fading, casting the dull rays of the setting sun through the bowfront window and stretching the shadows of the fat snow people out of shape like pulled taffy, and everyone began collecting their things and heading home, I felt sad. I didn't want the night to come.

Everyone had somewhere to go. Liza was going to the movies with a friend, and Margot had choir practice at the church. Since it looked like she was going to be in New Bern for a while, certainly until after the New Year, when she said companies might start hiring again, she'd decided to join the church. As it was the last Saturday before Christmas, Abigail had a round of parties to attend. I would have liked to call Charlie and see if I could join him for dinner, but I knew he'd be too busy for that.

Business at the Grill was booming. The city dwellers who owned weekend places in New Bern opened them up for the holidays and brought lots of friends along to enjoy the snow-covered hills, the picturesque shops, and the antique homes bedecked in fresh evergreen wreaths and garlands with the poignant glow of a single candle in each window. At the end of a day of antiquing, or shopping, or sledding, or skiing, or just hanging around a cozy fireside, residents and visitors alike flocked to the Grill on the Green. Every table was full every night of the week. Even the regulars had to call in for reservations. And Charlie's catering business was going great guns too. Abigail had a list of six parties she had to attend that evening, and the Grill was catering three of them. I hadn't seen Charlie in weeks, he was so busy. He'd even had to put a temporary moratorium on our morning coffee dates.

I counted up the till, locked the shop door, shut off the lights, went upstairs, and put a plate of leftovers in the microwave. Standing by the counter, waiting for the timer to go off, I sighed and said aloud, "Poor Evelyn. It's Christmas. Everyone has somewhere to go. Everyone but you. Poor you."

The microwave timer dinged cheerily, and I pulled the plate of leftover kung pao chicken out of the oven. "This is ridiculous. Stop being such a baby. This is a perfect way to spend the evening. You've got a warm house on a bitterly cold night, a nice big plate of your favorite Chinese food, and a whole evening to yourself. What's so bad?" I asked myself, and then, echoing one of my mother's favorite admonitions, "Life is what you make it. Quit feeling sorry for yourself."

Thinking I had given myself good advice, I decided to have a little Christmas party of my own. After spending so much time and effort decorating the shop for the holiday, I'd completely neglected my personal surroundings. No wonder I was feeling so blue.

I put a CD in the stereo, a compilation of Christmas music that Garrett had burned for me when he was still in college, and listened to it while I ate. After washing my dishes, I started hauling boxes marked "Xmas Décor" out of the closet. It wasn't long before I realized there was no way that my one-bedroom, seven-hundred-square-foot apartment was going to accommodate all the items that had previously decorated my three-bedroom, three-thousand-square-foot home in Texas. Even if it could, there was no point in putting up so many decorations just a week before Christmas. I decided to limit myself to two: the ceramic Nativity that had belonged to my mother, and a Christmas tree.

I preferred fresh trees, but Rob always insisted on a fake tree because he said real trees were too expensive and dropped too many needles. "Besides," he'd say every year, "you can't tell the difference. The manufactured ones are better anyway. You'd never find a natural tree with a trunk that straight."

He was right. And that was my point exactly. You'd never mistake a fake tree for a real one; they didn't look the same, and they certainly didn't smell the same. As far as I was concerned, the fragrant, resiny scent of pine was half the pleasure of putting up a Christmas tree. Still, even a fake tree was better than none at all. I pulled pieces of evergreen "branches" out of the box and assembled them into a five-foot tree, noting wryly that there were a good many manufactured needles littering the floor before I finished.

After sweeping up the needles, I opened the boxes, unwrapping several layers of tissue-wrapped bulbs and ornaments, including one with a picture of Garrett beaming a toothless, infant grin and the words "Baby's First Christmas!", until I found the strings of lights.

They were tangled, of course. It took forever to unravel them. After I sorted out the mess, I wrapped each branch in lights, put on the ornaments, and then plugged in the tree only to discover that two of the strings of lights didn't work.

I muttered a few choice words under my breath. I should have checked them before putting them on the tree. The last time these lights had been used was two years ago, back when it was Rob's job to untangle the lights and check for burnt-out bulbs while I unwrapped ornaments and Garrett played DJ, making sure the music selection was sufficiently festive. Two years ago. Back when we were a family. When everything seemed safe and certain, and the only change I could have imagined in our holiday traditions was that they would expand to include Garrett's someday wife and someday children, who would make our Christmases grow taller and wider and more splendid each year.

Instead, Christmas was shrinking, from the three of us to just me. And next year?

All day long, I had tried not to think beyond this day, to take Dr. Finney's advice and enjoy the holidays, and not to let my mind wander into the land of what next, worrying about what would happen come January.

Further testing had shown that there was cancer in both breasts. Given this news and the fact that the lumpectomy had failed to achieve clean margins, Dr. Finney now recommended that I undergo a double mastectomy. At her urging, and because I hoped she was wrong, I sought the opinions of two other surgeons; both of them concurred with Dr. Finney's assessment. And so I agreed to the surgery, though not to the doctor's suggestion that I tell my family and friends about it—not until after the holidays at least. I was determined that Christmas should be as merry, and as normal, as possible. Whatever that meant now.

But suddenly, sitting cross-legged on the floor in a nest of tangled tree lights and discarded tissue paper like some lone, sickly bird abandoned by the rest of the flock, I was overcome by sadness, a loneliness that went to the bone. I was so tired. I didn't want to do this alone anymore. I couldn't. I had to talk to someone.

I took one of the crumpled balls of tissue from the floor and used it to dry my eyes and nose before picking up the phone. I started to dial Margot, but then remembered she was at choir practice. Instead, I tried Garrett, first at the office and then on his cell phone, but he didn't answer either call, so I left a message.

"Hi, honey. It's Mom. Hope you're doing well. I sent a box with your presents. It should be there by now but don't open them until Christmas or you'll spoil the surprise." I paused for just a moment. "Um, listen. Honey, give me a call when you can. There's something

I want to talk to you about. Okay? Anyway, I'll hang up now. Hope you're out doing something fun. Miss you. Love you. 'Bye."

When I hung up I felt even worse than before. Now that I'd admitted the need to talk to someone, it was like I couldn't turn it off. I simply had to talk to someone, someone I cared about and who cared about me. At the moment, that was a very short list and everyone on it was unavailable. But suddenly I knew what to do.

What I needed more than anything was to hear that honeyed Texas twang, dark and thick as praline syrup, and the laughter bubbling up like Dr. Pepper fizz poured into a tall glass. I picked up the phone again and dialed Mary Dell.

A man's voice, deep and slow, careful to enunciate his words clearly, was on the other end of the line. "Templeton residence. This is Howard speaking."

"Hey, Howard," I said, unconsciously and immediately falling back into the friendly Texas mode of greeting. "This is Evelyn Dixon. I haven't talked to you in a long time. How are you? Is your mama around?"

"Hello, Evelyn. I'm fine. Mama and I are going to be on television. Here is Mama. It was nice talking to you. Have a good Christmas."

And before I could ask any other questions, he'd put Mary Dell on the phone.

"Baby Girl!" She hooted an enthusiastic greeting. "How are you? Merry Christmas! I've been wanting to call, but we've been so busy with all this book business and everything, you wouldn't believe it. It's funny, not fifteen minutes ago I was telling Howard that I should call you, but I figured you'd be out on a Saturday night so I was going to try tomorrow afternoon. Isn't that something? Your ears must have been burning! How are you?" she repeated enthusiastically. She sounded so happy and it was so good to hear her voice, I couldn't bring myself to launch right into my list of woes.

"Oh, I'm all right. What's this Howard was saying? Something about the two of you being on television?"

She laughed out loud. "Yes! Evelyn, honey! Can you believe it? That's why I haven't had time to call. I'm 'bout as busy as a hound in flea season!" She laughed again, and the sound of her delight rang through the receiver.

"Mary Dell, what are you talking about? I don't understand."

"Oh, I thought Howard told you. Evelyn, hold on to your hat! Somebody at the publishing house called up the folks at the House and Home Network and told 'em about the book! Next thing I knew, some little skinny gal calling herself an assistant producer showed up on the doorstep with a cameraman and sayin' they wanted to shoot some test videos."

"Oh my gosh! Oh, Mary Dell!" I put my hand over my open mouth, my own problems forgotten. I couldn't quite believe what I hoped she was about to tell me.

"Well, I just thought it was some kind of joke or something, so I told 'em to come on, gave 'em some coffee and banana pudding, and let 'em come into the sewing room and film while Howard and I worked on a kaleidoscope quilt. Then they left, and I didn't hear a thing until about a month ago when the little skinny gal—Heather's her name; she's in charge of producing a quilt show, but I swear, I don't think she's ever done so much as thread a needle. Anyway, Heather calls and says they want to put us on television! Our own show! *Quintessential Quilting with Mary Dell and Howard!* Can you believe it? Whoo-whee!"

Mary Dell screamed into the receiver, and I did too. For a moment it was as if we were two high-school girls, giddy with the news that we'd just *both* been elected prom queen. I was thrilled for her!

"Can you believe it! Finding out about the book was exciting enough, but this! Baby Girl, I'm 'bout as happy as a clam at high tide!"

"Mary Dell, this is just amazing! What happens now? When will you be on the air?"

"In the spring. Right now we're working on the concepts for the first six shows, but we'll start doing some actual filming right after the holidays. Evelyn, I'm so nervous! Howard is just taking it all in stride, like he always figured he'd be a TV star someday and was just waiting for somebody to come point him in the direction of the camera. That little Heather just fell in love with him. You know the way he pipes in with some little suggestion about how to place the block or how it'd look nicer with a brighter color? Well, Heather thought that was wonderful. Said she loved the mother-and-son interaction. In fact, they're going to give him his own ninety-second segment every episode, just to talk about color selections. They're going to call it 'Howard's Hint on Hues.' Isn't that wonderful!"

"Well, he always did have a great eye. Oh, Mary Dell, this is just such wonderful news! I couldn't be happier for both of you. Be sure and tell Howard I said so."

"I will. Of course, the only bad part of this is that life has gotten a little crazy. Until Heather called, I'd been planning on hopping in an airplane and coming up your way for a visit, kind of a Christmas surprise. But now, of course . . ."

My euphoria faded. It would have been so wonderful to see her, and I realized that, unconsciously, that was exactly what I'd been hoping she would do, show up on my doorstep with her loud laughter and loud earrings and shake me out of the funk I'd fallen into. I was homesick, not for my old house, or my old life, but for my old friend. Mary Dell was the best. And I knew that, even now, with all she had to do to make this amazing dream of hers come true, if I told her of my troubles, she'd figure out a way to drop everything and come to see me. But that wouldn't do, not when she was on the verge of something so important, at a moment when timing was everything.

"Mary Dell, don't worry about that," I said. "I couldn't be happier for you. Once things calm down we'll get together for a nice long visit. But you've got to tell me when the first show goes on the air. I'm going to have a premiere party and invite everyone I know."

I laughed. "And I've already figured out the perfect menu—buffalo chicken wings, banana pudding, and Dr. Pepper! These New Englanders have never had food like that before. They won't know what hit them. They'll probably have indigestion for a week!"

Mary Dell hooted her pleasure, laughing at the thought of a bunch of Yankees (who she'd once assured me were so straitlaced that they ate pizza with a knife and fork and a napkin tucked into their collars) eating chicken with their fingers and watching her on television. "And barbeque! And cheese straws!" she howled. "Oh, you've got to have cheese straws, Baby Girl!

"Say!" she exclaimed, a new idea suddenly occurring to her. "Why don't you come on down here for the first taping? It'll be in late January sometime. I'd feel so much better if I knew you were in the audience."

Late January. I knew what I'd be doing then, and it didn't include flying to Texas, but I couldn't tell Mary Dell that, not now.

"Oh, honey, I wish I could. But I . . ." I wracked my brain, searching for an excuse. "I just can't. I . . . I'm scheduled to go to Rhode Island for a big quilt show then. I'm presenting some workshops and, well, I just can't back out. It's such a great opportunity— the publicity. You understand."

"Oh sure," she said, trying to convince me that she did indeed understand. The disappointment was evident in her voice. "You can't miss a chance like that, not when you're starting out." I murmured a halfhearted agreement.

"But listen to me going on and on about myself without even asking about you! How are things at the shop? And how are you feeling after your surgery? You must be all healed up if you're going to be teaching a big workshop in Rhode Island."

"Oh yes. Much better. Everything is fine. Couldn't be better."

20

Abigail Burgess Wynne

"She loved it," I replied, answering Evelyn's inquiry. "Absolutely loved it!"

I laid out my purchases, two yards of a novelty fabric covered with grinning pirates climbing the masts of ships with bright red sails that floated on a sea of brilliant blue, plus another yard of a "pieces of eight" companion fabric, and four fat quarters of complimentary accent fabrics in reds and blues. "You should have seen her eyes when she opened the package. Then she threw it around her shoulders like a cape and wouldn't take it off."

"That's wonderful, Abigail. I'm so glad." Evelyn smiled sincerely, but her eyes looked tired. I wondered if she was getting enough sleep. Undoubtedly the final run up to Christmas was wearing her out.

I reached for a spool of blue thread, and added it to the pile for Evelyn to ring up. "So am I. Somehow, I think it made her feel special, and not just Bethany. I had a board meeting at the shelter this morning and saw Bethany's mother, Ivy, in the hall. She thanked me over and over again, said that no one had ever gone to that kind of trouble for her little girl before. Do you know she actually had tears in her eyes? The program director told me Ivy doesn't have any living family. Isn't that sad? Anyway, that made me think I wanted to make another quilt, for Bethany's little brother, Bobby. Can't say I'm too enthused about the pirate theme, but he seems to be crazy about them, and so—a pirate quilt it shall be. You were right, Evelyn; when you give someone a quilt, they know you care."

"I told you." Evelyn smiled as she put everything in one of the red and white checked Cobbled Court Quilts shopping bags. "That will be forty-six dollars and twenty-eight cents."

I opened my wallet and fished out three twenty-dollar bills. The front doorbell jingled cheerfully, signaling the arrival of another customer. Margot came into the shop, and there were tears in her eyes. Before we could ask what was wrong, she launched into a barrage of questions.

"Evelyn, why did you do that? Where did you get the money? What were you thinking? I've seen your books. You can't afford this, and I won't accept it."

"Margot, what are you talking about? Slow down." Evelyn frowned and handed her a tissue from the box she kept behind the counter.

Margot blew her nose. "You know what I'm talking about. Don't try to pretend you don't. The deposit." Evelyn and I both looked at her blankly. "At the bank. I went online to check my balance last night and there was an extra five thousand three hundred and eighty dollars in my account. When I went in today to tell them they'd made some kind of mistake, the teller said there was no mistake, that someone had deposited the money into my account. In cash! So there's no way to say for certain who did it, but I know it was you."

Margot trumpeted into her tissue again. "I told you before, Evelyn. I help you here in the shop because I like doing it. I won't take your money. You can't afford it," she scolded.

Evelyn shook her head. "Margot, look at me. Quit crying and look at me. I didn't put that money in your account. I swear I didn't. I wish I could have, because you certainly deserve it. I will admit, I have written you a check, and one for Liza too, that I'm planning on giving you along with your Christmas present." She held up her hand to silence Margot's tearful protests. "No. Now don't argue with me about it. You're going to take it, and that's that, but don't get too excited. I promise you, there are very few zeros on the check I wrote. I wish there were, but, you're right. I just can't afford it."

"Well, then who made that deposit? I have to give it back. It's too much. I can't accept it."

"Why not?" I asked. "It's Christmas. Are you too old to believe in Santa Claus?"

"Yes!" Margot cried and broke into a fresh wave of tears.

Evelyn came around the counter to put her arm around Margot's shoulders. "Come on now," she soothed. "You haven't worked in months. Heaven knows you must need the money. Maybe that's it. Maybe heaven does know. Maybe you've got an angel walking around the streets of New Bern, just like I do. An angel. Just like you've been to me."

"Oh, Evelyn. It was you! I knew it!" Margot began sobbing.

Her skin became all blotchy, and her face turned a truly unattractive shade of red. You see? That's another reason not to give in to emotional displays. They make you look simply awful.

I shot Evelyn a look and began gathering up my things. This whole drama was making me feel uncomfortable. Evelyn nodded silently, letting me know that it was all right to leave. She knew how I hated this sort of thing.

"Really, Margot. It wasn't me. I swear," Evelyn promised as she patted Margot's heaving shoulders. "Why are you crying? This is good news, isn't it? Why are you so sad."

"I'm not sad!" she wailed. "I'm just so happy. And relieved! I'm exactly four thousand three hundred and eighty dollars behind on my bills. I've just been frantic thinking how I was going to pay them, and now—this! Whoever made that deposit knew exactly how much I needed and gave me an extra thousand dollars besides. How could they have known? If it wasn't you, Evelyn, who was it?" Margot threw her arms around Evelyn's shoulders and simply gave herself up to an absolute tsunami of weeping.

With Margot's back now turned, I rolled my eyes at Evelyn, who shot me a disapproving frown, and waved my farewell. "I'm late for my hairdresser," I said. "Have to run."

"And the quilt circle on Friday?" Evelyn asked, still comforting the weeping Margot. "I know it's Christmas Eve, but you're still coming, aren't you?"

"I'll be there. Better to spend the evening with the whole group than alone with Liza. At least I'll have you to referee."

Evelyn grinned and waved between back pats. She knew that things between Liza and me, while not exactly a picture of familial harmony, had definitely improved. Helping out at the quilt shop seemed to have bettered her mood and attitude considerably. I suppose everyone feels happier when they have somewhere to go and something to do. Her holiday window display really was charming. While I still found some of her artwork to be . . . well, avant-garde would be a kind way of putting it . . . she obviously had talent. Perhaps, after her court-imposed sojourn with me was completed, she should give art school another try. I made a mental note to discuss it with her after the holidays.

Taking my leave of Evelyn and Margot, I made a loop around the counter toward the front door, past the desk where Margot kept file folders, folders for income, expenses, inventory, tax receipts—and one marked "Margot: Personal."

If a person was a nosy snoop, they could have opened that file
and seen exactly how dire Margot's financial situation had become
since she'd lost her job. But on the other hand, they probably
wouldn't have to do that. While meticulous about business, Margot
was sometimes careless about her personal affairs. She had a bad
habit of leaving files open on the desk where just anyone might read
them.

∞ 21 ∞

Evelyn Dixon

Finally, on that awful Saturday night, after being unable to reach Garrett and unable to talk frankly with Mary Dell, I dialed Dr. Finney.

Though she'd urged me to call her anytime, I hated bothering her at home. But I simply had to talk to someone, someone who understood what I was going through.

We spent almost an hour talking through my fears, not just about the cancer but about everything: the future of my business; of what would happen to me if the shop failed, or the surgery failed; of how my body would look after the surgery; of chemotherapy; of how Garrett would react to the news; of living the rest of my life alone; of never being wanted again, or having sex again; of everything—and especially the fear . . . no, make that the certainty . . . that I was no longer in control of my own life.

We talked and listened and cried together and laughed together. And it helped. It didn't change anything, but being able to talk made everything a little less overwhelming.

She said one thing in particular that stuck with me: that while I might not be in control of this disease, I *was* in control of my reaction to it—I could be a victim or a conqueror. It was up to me. "One thing I know from experience," she said, "it's always a lot easier to be a conqueror if you don't try to go it alone. You didn't see Napoleon riding off to battle with just himself and his trusty sword. He brought in some backup."

"Napoleon ended up defeated, imprisoned, and exiled to a tiny island in the Atlantic."

She laughed. "Okay, bad illustration, but you get the idea. Evelyn, you need to talk to your family and friends. I know you wanted to wait until after the holidays, but I think you should tell them now. It's your choice, of course, but think how you would feel if the tables were turned. What if someone you cared about had cancer and kept it a secret from you?"

I saw her point. Margot, Abigail, Liza, and Charlie too—it wasn't fair to keep them in the dark any longer. I would tell them the truth, all at once so I could get it over with, during our regular quilt-circle meeting. I would invite Charlie to be an honorary member for the evening. Sitting at my desk, I wrote a list of every question I thought would come up during our discussion and thought carefully about my answers. I wanted to be prepared, to tell them on my own terms and in my own way, calmly, rationally, and with optimism regarding the outcome. It would be good practice for my conversation with Garrett. That would come next.

I didn't want to give him the news over the telephone. I'd briefly considered flying out to Seattle to see him. But after a quick search on the Internet, I realized there were no airline seats available this close to Christmas, not at a price that I could afford. So I decided to call him as soon as I told the others, that same night. Hopefully I'd catch him at home. I didn't want to tell him while there were other people around.

But it didn't quite work out that way. On Christmas Eve, while I was baking a pan of cranberry cake and preparing a batch of hot spiced cider to serve to my guests later that afternoon, the phone rang.

"Hi, sweetheart!"

"Hi, Mom! Guess where I am? I just landed at Hartford airport, and I'm renting a car. The company handed out bonus checks at the Christmas party; that's where I was when you called. After I heard your message, I decided to spend my bonus on an airline ticket. So you'd better send all your boyfriends home and make up the sofa bed. I'm home for Christmas!"

An hour later, he was in my arms and I was crying, so happy to see him, and all my careful planning went right out the window. I sat him down, then and there, before he'd even had a chance to unpack his things, and told him the truth about everything that had happened since I'd come to New Bern. I had to; the others were due to arrive in less than an hour, and I needed to talk to Garrett alone.

Even without practicing on the quilt circle, I managed to get through my speech without crying. When I first said the word "cancer," his eyes grew wide, but he regained his composure quickly and deliberately, asked good questions, and stayed calm. It was only when he learned about my first surgery that his emotional armor showed a crack.

"And you didn't tell me?" he asked, his voice rising in pitch and volume. "You've been dealing with this since the fall and you never told me? Your business almost fails, you get breast cancer, have a surgery, find out you need another, and you tell a pile of strangers about this and let them help you through it, but I'm left in the dark? Your own son?"

I nodded, conceding his right to be angry. These questions, and his probable reaction, had also been on my list. I'd already thought through what I should say. "I know. I should have told you, but I thought . . . Garrett, you have your new job, your new life. I didn't want to get in the way of that. If the first surgery had turned out the way I'd hoped, I planned to tell you after, so you didn't have to be worried about anything. I guess I was just trying to protect you."

His lips pressed into a flat line of irritation. "Mom, I'm twenty-four years old. You don't have to protect me anymore. I can take care of myself. When the situation calls for it, I can even help take care of you."

"You're right. I should have known better. I'm sorry." I apologized and meant it. "It won't happen again, I promise. From here on out, you'll know everything I do. No more secrets. Ask me anything."

"All right," he said and proceeded to ask the one question I hadn't anticipated. "When were you planning on telling Dad?"

It was past eleven by the time everyone left, and almost midnight when Garrett and I finished washing up the dishes and making up the pull-out sofa in the living room. I tried to get him to take my room, but he wouldn't hear of it.

"I'll be fine here. Last week I put in twenty hours, passed out on the floor of my office for two, then got up and put in another eight. Trust me, I can sleep anywhere."

I had my doubts but recognized that stubborn look on my son's face. "All right. If you're sure. Good night, sweetheart," I said and gave him a squeeze. "I'm so glad you're here."

"Me too, Mom."

I went into my room, sat cross-legged in the middle of the bed, and picked up the phone. It was eleven in Texas. Normally, I'd never dream of calling anyone at that hour, but in all the years I'd been married to Rob, I'd never known him to shut out his lights before midnight. I went to bed around ten while he stayed up to write memos or answer e-mails he hadn't gotten to during the workday, then quietly slipped into bed sometime between twelve and two without ever waking me up.

Gee, I thought to myself, *think that might help explain why we're divorced?*

I started dialing but stopped before I got the last number. I didn't want to call Rob. We hadn't spoken since the divorce. What was I going to say when he answered the phone? Even worse, what was I going to say if *she* answered the phone?

I'd heard from Sharon, one of my old neighbors in Texas, that Tina had moved in with Rob about ten seconds after our divorce was final. Sharon was a terrible gossip, the kind who liked to spread information via her church prayer chain. You know the kind I'm talking about. I was in a neighborhood Bible study with her for a while, and when it came time for us to voice our prayer requests, Sharon's always went something like, "Dear Lord, please help Francine Diamond, who lives in the house with the pink brick on the corner of Lake Mead and Alamo Drive. Her husband, David, lost his job again for looking at pornography on the Internet during office hours, and her daughter, Denise, has just checked into rehab for her bulimia problem. We just ask that you would help this family, Lord. And encourage poor Francine. Help her lean on your strength so she may be a better wife and mother and understand why her family is in a shambles. Amen."

Suffice it to say that when Sharon called to tell me that Tina had moved into Rob's condo and to ask how she might pray for me in my hour of need, I declined the offer.

Sharon was terribly disappointed by my reaction. "Well, if you change your mind and want me to pray for you, don't hesitate to call. I know how you must be suffering," she sighed sympathetically.

"Actually, Sharon, I'm not suffering at all. I'm happy in my new life and so busy with my business that I rarely have time to think about Rob," I said, and it was the truth. Then I said, "But I appreciate your concern," which was a lie.

Until now, I hadn't thought much about Tina, except to wonder how she'd lasted as long as she had. I'd only seen her once—about twenty-eight, skinny, big blue eyes, big blond hair, big . . . well, you get the idea. She worked as a receptionist at the gym. If you'd called central casting for someone to play "the other woman" opposite a midlevel manager in a midlife crisis, the talent agent would have sent Tina. That was part of what made our divorce so awful. I mean, not that I'd have been any happier if my husband had left me for a rocket scientist or a Pulitzer Prize winner, but at least it might have made some kind of sense.

At first I'd really believed Rob would wake up and realize that he'd sacrificed his home, his family, in fact everything that mattered, just so he could move into Barbie's Dream House, but he never did. It was sad and still a little hard to believe. I'd always credited him with more sense.

An irritating recorded message was telling me, over and over, to "Please hang up and dial again." I pushed my finger against the receiver, closed my eyes, and groaned. I did not want to call Rob. If Garrett hadn't insisted, if he hadn't played on the guilt I felt over not telling him and made me promise . . . But I had promised. There was no getting around it.

The phone rang several times before Rob (not Tina!) answered. "Hello."

"Hi. It's me." There was a brief pause. For a moment I wondered if he'd forgotten my name and was about to remind him, but he broke in. His voice was worried.

"Evelyn? What's wrong? Has something happened to Garrett?"

"No. Nothing like that. Everything is fine. Garrett is fine. In fact, he's here. He flew in to spend Christmas with me."

"Oh. That's nice," he said, and I imagined I heard a touch of wistfulness in his voice, remembering what Christmas was like when we were all together, but if he was thinking of those happy times, he didn't say anything. He just waited for me to speak.

Taking a quick breath, I jumped in, trying to keep everything as matter of fact and to the point as possible. "Listen, Rob, I said everything is fine, but that isn't quite right. I have breast cancer."

"Oh my God!" he gasped. "Evelyn, I'm so—"

"I first found out a few months ago and had an operation," I interrupted, plowing on. The last thing I wanted right now was for him to start voicing some guilt-ridden apology or insincere expressions of concern. "They weren't able to get everything on the first go-round. I'll be going in for a double mastectomy at the end of January."

"A double . . . Oh my God," he repeated. "Evie . . . I just . . . I can't believe it. Is there anything I can do?"

His use of my old nickname annoyed me. "I wouldn't have bothered you about it, but Garrett wanted me to."

"I'm glad you did. Yeah. I . . . I'm just in shock, I guess. Can I help you with anything? Do you have good insurance? Do you need money?"

I shook my head. Typical, I thought. Rob always was a quick draw with his wallet. So much easier than actually doing anything that might encroach on his work schedule or, heaven forbid, his emotions.

"No," I snapped. "I didn't call to beg you for money. At the moment, that is the least of my worries."

"Hey. Evie, that's not fair. Don't be like that. I know you must be upset and worried, and I was just trying to—"

"You know, Rob, I really don't care what you were trying to do. Seems like half the conversations in our marriage were you trying to explain your way out of something. I don't want to hear it anymore. Since we're not married anymore, I don't have to. And don't call me Evie. I didn't call to ask for your help, or your money, or your sympathy. I did it for Garrett. Our son made me promise to call and tell you that I have cancer. And now I have. There."

I banged the receiver down without saying good-night, telling myself it felt good to be able to slam the door in his face for once and wondering if the satisfaction of revenge was supposed to make people cry.

~ 22 ~

Abigail Burgess Wynne

We bid Evelyn and her son, Garrett, good-night and walked out into the darkened courtyard. A gentle fall of snow floated down from the night sky at a leisurely pace, like that soapflake snow they use on holiday television specials. Everyone was quiet. I think we were all still in shock. Charlie was the first to speak, and he was angry.

"How could she have waited so long to say anything? I know I'm not family, but surely after all these months she has a clue about how I . . ."

His voice trailed off, and he left the rest of the sentence unspoken, but it didn't take any special insight to know what he'd intended to say. For some time, I'd suspected that Charlie's feelings for Evelyn went beyond friendship. The signs were all there—the lilt in his step as he whistled his way down the street, the special meals he'd made during her recovery, their morning meetings at the coffee shop. He was happier than I'd ever seen him. He'd even taken to complimenting his waiters, a hereto unheard of development. Charlie wasn't the kind of person who made new friends easily. The life of a restaurateur was much too busy to allow for relationships with people who weren't also in the business, but somehow or other he found time for Evelyn. It was obvious that he cared about her deeply. In my mind, I finished the question for him: after all these months, how could Evelyn have failed to notice Charlie was in love with her?

I waited for a moment, thinking that Margot would jump in and say something to comfort poor Charlie (she was good at that sort of thing), but she seemed to be lost in her own thoughts.

Awkwardly, I reached over and patted Charlie on the arm. "She has so many worries right now, Charlie. I don't think she was trying to exclude you from her life. You heard what she said; she didn't want to worry any of us, especially with the holidays coming."

"Well, what difference does that make?" His voice was raised, and I shushed him, concerned that Evelyn might hear him through the windows of her apartment. She was only one floor up from the courtyard. "What difference does it make?" he repeated, whispering but still angry. "I *am* worried. The number of the day on the calendar doesn't make me less so."

Margot, as always the soul of sensitivity, spoke. "It doesn't make much sense to me either, but I've never had to face what Evelyn is facing right now. None of us has. Who knows how we would react in a similar situation? Maybe she really was trying to be protective of us, or maybe she was just trying to avoid dealing with reality. Who knows?"

"Well, I can understand her reluctance," I said. "It's her private business. Why should she have to share every detail of her personal life with us? After all, it's not like we're family."

Without saying anything, Liza turned to face me. I heard the heel of her boot crunch down into the snow. In the dim half-light cast by the bulb of a single spotlight in the far corner of the courtyard, I could just make out the expression on her face: a look of intense disgust, bordering on hatred; a look she hadn't cast in my direction with quite as much vehemence since her early weeks in New Bern. What in the world had I done wrong now?

"No," Margot continued, "but she needs us as if we were. I'm glad her son is here now. He seems like a nice man. But Evelyn said he'll have to go back to Seattle on Monday. Even if he could stay, she'll still need our support. This is going to be much tougher than the last operation."

"It is," I concurred. "I've known several people who've been through a mastectomy. It won't be like before, when she was out of commission for just a few days. We'll all have to pitch in to help run the shop while she's recovering. I don't know much about retail, but if I can help . . ." Next to me, Liza coughed a few times, interrupting my train of thought.

Margot looked at her. "Are you all right?"

"Fine," she answered hoarsely. "Getting a cold."

"Well," Charlie growled and pulled his coat collar up, "Evelyn can count on me. She always could. She only had to ask. That's all I'm saying. It wasn't fair to leave me . . . I mean . . . us in the dark for this long."

Margot nodded. "I know, but she wasn't trying to be hurtful or uncaring."

"If anything, it was the opposite," I interjected. "She didn't say anything until now because she does care."

"That's right!" Margot beamed, happy to have my support in her efforts to restore Charlie's spirits. "And after all, she did apologize. That's why she decided to tell us tonight; because she realized her mistake."

"Mmmm. I suppose." Charlie twisted his lips thoughtfully. "We're supposed to spend Christmas Day together, Evelyn and I. Do you suppose she'll still want me to come? I mean, what with Garrett here and all? I was going to make my duck confit, but maybe she'd rather have dinner with just the two of them."

"I'm sure she'd have said something if her plans had changed," I said, and Margot nodded agreement.

"In that case," Charlie said, puffing out a big white cloud of breath that seemed to dissipate the last vapors of his anger, "I'd better get back to the restaurant and see to my duck. And my customers. You'd think that people would want to be around hearth and home on Christmas Eve, but the Dillards have decided to throw a party for their friends in my restaurant. Aren't you one of the guests, Abigail? We'd better get over there. Karen Dillard hates it when people show up late."

"I'd almost forgotten about the party. Thank you for the reminder, Charlie. I'll be over directly."

"All right. I'll see you soon. Good-night, ladies. Merry Christmas." He waved over his shoulder as he walked down the alley and disappeared around the corner.

Margot and I responded to his farewell, but Liza said nothing. I could still feel her eyes on me. Her gaze was making me feel very uncomfortable, which was exactly her intention, but I didn't look at her. I wouldn't give her the satisfaction.

"I guess I should be going too," Margot said. "I have to get up early tomorrow."

"Are you still going to go to your sister's in Buffalo for Christmas? Maybe you should cancel and have dinner with us instead," I said hopefully. At the moment, the prospect of spending Christmas alone with Liza was far from appealing. She was obviously in one of her moods. Thank heaven I already had plans for the evening, but tomorrow it would be just the two of us. Margot would be the perfect buffer. I had hoped Franklin might join us, but he was going into Manhattan to spend Christmas with his daughters.

"I hate to think of you driving all that way in this terrible weather."

Margot laughed her musical giggle, looked up at the lazily drifting snowflakes, and held her arms out wide. "You mean this little flurry? Abigail, I thought you were a native New Englander. You can't think a little snow is going to keep me from getting where I need to go."

"No," I fumbled. "I suppose not, but you never can tell. They get terrible storms around Buffalo this time of year."

"Believe me, I know all about it. I grew up there," she said. "I'll be fine, but you're sweet to worry about me. I'd love an excuse to spend the holidays with you and Liza, but if I don't show up, I'll never hear the end of it. It'd be one more thing for my sister to resent about me," she sighed.

"You don't get along with your sister?" Liza asked, clearly surprised. Margot shook her head. "Why not? I can't imagine anyone not liking you."

Margot smiled. "That's sweet of you to say, Liza, but nobody gets along with everyone. And it really isn't that we don't get along, it's just that . . . Well, I don't know what it is, really. It just seems like my sister has never approved of anything about me. Not since we were kids. Still, she's my sister, and I love her." Margot shrugged. "I might not always like her, but I love her. That's just the way it works in families."

Liza paused a moment before responding. "So I've heard," she said flatly. "But I really wouldn't know. Not from personal experience."

She shot me a final cold stare before turning on her heel and walking away. Her shoulders were hunched as she tramped angrily down the alley. She was trying to make a dramatic exit, but the snow muffled the intended intensity of her stomped footsteps, turning what should have been a drumbeat of departure into a soft "flumph, flumph" of waffled rubber treading on snowflakes. Still, the message came through loud and clear. The sound of her steps grew fainter as she moved farther off; they were an accusation just the same. Reluctantly, I said good-night to Margot, wished her a Merry Christmas, and followed Liza.

At the end of the alley, Liza crossed the street in the direction of the house without speaking to me, still stomping her disapproval. When I exited the alley, I paused on the sidewalk for a moment, considering my options. Perhaps I should go after her, follow her to the house, and try to get her to tell me what was bothering her so we could clear the air and enjoy a nice Christmas together.

It had been years since I'd spent Christmas with family. Not since Woolley died. Of course, I always had my pick of invitations to Christmas dinner. Sometimes I accepted, but more often than not I just stayed home. It was always such a bother—having to buy gifts for a crowd of people you really didn't know and fussing over what to wear. It always felt so much more like putting on a costume to perform your part in a play about Christmas than partaking of the actual celebration. Christmas should be about walking to church in the snow, attending midnight services with the sanctuary bathed in candlelight, waking up early the next morning and going downstairs in your robe to open gifts from and to people you care about, wandering in and out of the kitchen trying to steal a bite of whatever it was that smelled so delicious, then playing board games in front of the fire, or singing around the piano, or doing whatever you wanted to do until dinner was ready and everyone sat down together to bless the food, talking and laughing and eating too much, tucked up warm and safe together while the snow drifted past the window and the shadows of evening began to fall.

That's what Christmas should be, I thought bitterly, *but somehow it never has been. Not even when Woolley was alive. Not since I was a girl, spending Christmas with Mother, and Father, and Susan. . . .*

A sudden gust of wind blew down the street, whipping the snow into a furious cloud that stung my face and made me close my eyes against the pain. Liza marched across the Green toward the house.

I shivered, looked at my watch, then took a left turn and hurried down the street in the direction of the restaurant.

Karen Dillard hated for her guests to arrive late.

23

Evelyn Dixon

Though Garrett's arrival was a surprise, I managed to pull together some semblance of a family Christmas. Of course, it helped that I owned a quilt shop. Downstairs I found two samples from the "Crazy Quilted Christmas Stocking" class to hang by our hearth. We took turns playing Santa and filled them with gifts.

Our offerings were improvised but very creative. The next morning, we laughed as we sat on the floor next to the tree and emptied our stockings.

I'd scoured the apartment for gifts and found an orange, a pack of chewing gum, a box of matches from the Grill, some soap and a plastic-wrapped toothbrush they'd given me at the hospital, and a mostly unused book of crossword puzzles that Margot had given me during my recovery. The rest of the presents came from the shop. After I added a spool of thread, a package of needles, another of safety pins, an official pink "Cobbled Court Quilts" tape measure, and a pair of embroidery scissors, the stocking fairly bulged with bounty.

"Mom," Garrett grinned as he held up the measuring tape by one end, letting it dangle from his fingers like some sort of pink and black striped snake, "I know you always hoped I'd be a girl, but get over it already, will you? I'm never going to take up quilting."

"Very funny. I just thought it would be nice for you to have some kind of sewing kit. You probably have a closet full of shirts with loose buttons that need repairing."

Garrett nodded. "Actually, I do. I brought them all with me in my suitcase. Along with my dirty laundry. Thought you wouldn't mind taking care of that for me."

"Not a chance, darling. But I'll be more than happy to teach you how to thread a needle."

"Hmmm. Somehow I thought you'd say that. Well, it was worth a try."

He leaned over and gave me a hug. "Thanks for the presents, Mom. They're just what I needed. Now go on. Open yours."

Garrett seemed to have done his shopping at the Seattle airport and en route to Hartford. In addition to a pound of coffee beans and a mug, a Seattle Mariners baseball cap, and a tiny Seattle ferry tree ornament, I received a package of pretzels, a pair of plastic headphones, an eye mask, and a thin blue blanket still sealed in a plastic bag, all from the same airline.

By the time I finished going through the stocking, I was laughing so hard there were tears in my eyes. "What did you do? Make friends with the flight attendants or just wait until their backs were turned and steal this stuff?"

"Oh, very nice," Garrett said with mock indignation. "Here I go to all the trouble of getting you some presents, and you accuse me of theft. Listen, this took some doing. This isn't the cheap junk they gave me and the other poor saps riding back in steerage. This Christmas stocking is First Class. Of course I made friends with the flight attendants! I had to! Back where I was riding, they don't even give you pretzels. Getting all this took a lot of sweet-talking on my part."

He stretched his arms out wide as though yawning and then flexed them in a bodybuilder pose. "Of course," he said in his best "surfer dude" impression, the one he'd perfected in high school, "I always have been lucky with the ladies. One look at these guns, and they're putty in my hands."

"That right? Last I heard you were still dateless in Seattle. Are you trying to tell me something?" I asked hopefully. It worried me that Garrett never seemed to have any dates, let alone a steady girl-friend. He was a good-looking young man and so much fun to be with. In college he'd gone out with a number of very nice girls.

"Nope. Sorry, Mom. No news to report on the girlfriend front. I don't have time to look for one; I'm working seventy-plus hours a week. By the time the weekend comes, and by weekend I mean Saturday after dark, I'm too exhausted to go out. I just go home and sleep until it's time to go to work on Monday."

"Well, what about at work? There must be some girls at the office."

He shook his head. "There's not a woman in my entire department. The only female I see during the day is Antoinette, our fifty-six-year-old, married cleaning woman with varicose veins and a bad attitude. And I gotta tell you, she's starting to look pretty good to me." He laughed, and I joined in, but not wholeheartedly. In typical Garrett fashion, always trying to put the best face on things, he was making light of his troubles, but I knew he must be lonely.

"But what about you?" he said, changing the subject. "Are you seeing anyone? Looks to me like that Charlie fellow has a thing for you."

I got up from the floor and went into the kitchen to start making breakfast. "Charlie? We're just friends."

Garrett followed me, opened the silverware drawer, and started setting the table. That had always been his job when he was growing up. We'd had so many good conversations, me fixing dinner while he put out the cutlery. I smiled to myself, thinking how wonderful it was to have him here and how easily we settled into our old routines. I was glad he'd come.

"Didn't look like that to me," he said. "Haven't you noticed how he looks at you? Even when he's talking to somebody else, he's got one eye on you. The man is completely gone on you."

I felt myself blushing as I cracked eggs into a mixing bowl. "Don't be silly. I told you. We're friends. We have a lot in common, since we both own our own business, that's all." Charlie had been kind to me, a wonderful friend in every way, but I couldn't imagine that he would want to be more than that. Truth to tell, I couldn't imagine anyone feeling that way about me. Especially not now.

"Really, Garrett, it's just a friendship."

Garrett shrugged. "Have it your way." He put down two knives and set spoons next to them. "But I don't know why you're so surprised. You're beautiful, Mom." He grinned. "I mean, for a woman your age and all."

"Oh, thanks very much." I tossed a red Christmas napkin across the kitchen island, hoping to hit him playfully in the face, but it landed on the table instead. "You're not so bad yourself, for a computer nerd and all."

Garrett finished setting the table, and I brought the dishes over. It wasn't a fancy meal, just scrambled eggs, grapefruit sections and red grapes garnished with mint, plus orange juice, coffee, and some banana muffins, not nearly as splendid as the Christmas breakfasts I'd prepared when Garrett was little. But I knew Charlie was bringing his fabulous duck confit for dinner, and I was providing the side dishes as well as two desserts, my chocolate peppermint layer cake and a pecan pie, so I wanted to make sure we had room for later. Still, with an evergreen and holly centerpiece and my best dishes and cloth napkins, the table looked very pretty.

"Mom, this looks great!" Garrett exclaimed as I put down a

platter of eggs. "Oh, wait a minute! I almost forgot!" He ran back into my bedroom, where he'd stowed his bags, and emerged with a half bottle of champagne.

"Here we go." He peeled the foil wrapper off the neck of the bottle and started trying to uncork it. "It's warm, but we can mix it with the cold orange juice for mimosas."

I laughed. "Well, this is a surprise! When did you have time to buy champagne?"

"I told you, Mom, the ladies love me. Katherine, the head flight attendant, slipped this into my briefcase."

"She did? Wow! Was she cute? Did you get her phone number?" I'd have rather Garrett found a girlfriend who didn't travel all the time, but the way things were going, I was willing to compromise; besides, she must be a smart, ambitious young woman to have been made head flight attendant.

"Cute? Definitely. Gray hair swept up in a bun, swell reading glasses." He let out a wolf whistle and then laughed. "Mom, she was about sixty and has a son older than me. I was hanging out in the galley to stretch my legs. When she heard I was flying home to surprise my mother for Christmas, she gave me this."

"Oh," I said, a little disappointed. "That was sweet of her."

After some struggle and a flurry of excitement when the bubbles foamed up and spilled from the bottle, Garrett poured a little of the champagne into each of our orange-juice glasses, and we sat down to eat.

"This looks like a pretty skimpy breakfast compared to the old days, but I didn't want you to fill up too much before dinner. Charlie's duck is out of this world," I said and put a scoop of eggs onto Garrett's plate. "I hope you don't mind that Charlie's joining us for dinner. I'd already invited him before I knew you were coming."

Garrett shook his head and picked up a fork. "No. He seems like a great guy. You've got to respect a guy who knows how to cook a duck. My cooking skills haven't progressed much beyond ramen noodles and toaster strudel."

"Looking at you, I can believe it. You're too thin," I scolded, watching him devouring his breakfast and wondering if I shouldn't have scrambled more eggs. "I'm worried about you. You work twelve- and fourteen-hour days. You're too tired to even take a girl on a date, and you don't eat. I know you're making good money at your job, but I wonder if you're at the right company. Life is short, honey. Too short to spend it working for nothing more than a paycheck. I know you like your job, but—"

"Actually," he said through a mouthful of scrambled eggs, "I hate my job. Don't get me wrong. I love working with computers, but I trained to be a designer. My dream was to work with clients to create new sites, new programs, and solve problems. Instead, I sit in front of a screen all day long and stare at long rows of code. I can go days without talking to another human being in person." He put down his fork and took a deep breath. "That's why I quit."

"You did? When did you decide to do that?"

"Last night, actually. So I guess you could say I'm going to quit. First thing Monday morning. I'm going to fly back to Seattle, give my two weeks' notice, and then fly back here for a while to figure out my next move. That sleeper sofa of yours is more comfortable than it looks." He grinned and bit into a muffin.

"Garrett, you just decided this last night?" I was worried about the hours he was keeping, but this seemed like an awfully rash, and suspicious, decision. "This wouldn't have anything to do with finding out that I had cancer, would it? Because I told you, Garrett, I'm going to be fine. I can handle this. I won't have you jeopardizing your future because of me. . . ."

His mouth was still full of muffin, so he held up both his hands, cutting off my protests until he could speak. When he did, the light-hearted tone was gone. He was dead serious, calm, and undeterred.

For the first time, I saw not my son, full of boyish charm and mischief, but a competent and determined man. No wonder so many company recruiters had courted him when he graduated from college.

"Okay," he said, swallowing the last of the muffin, "first of all, I'm not jeopardizing my future. Not even close. If I want another corporate job I can have one tomorrow, but I don't want another corporate job. I want to do what I was trained to do: design. The only way to do that is go out on my own." I tried to jump in, but he cut me off. "And before you even bring it up, I can completely afford this. The upside of working for Claremont Solutions is the money. They give you lots of it and keep you so busy that you don't actually have time to spend any money. It's all sitting there in my bank account.

"And yes, even though you say you don't need my help, I want to hang around until you're back to your old self." He said the next part so firmly that I wondered if he was as confident about my recovery as he sounded. "You're going to get well, and I want to be there to help you do it. Is that such a terrible thing for a son to want to do? Help his mother, who has spent her whole life helping him?"

"No," I said quietly. "Of course not, but I don't want you sacrificing your future just because of me. You've got your whole life in front of you."

He nodded in agreement. "Yes, but as you said, life is short. Too short to spend another ten years, or five, or one doing a job I hate. I'd have figured it out myself before too long, but talking to you last night and seeing how happy you are here"—he tilted his head toward the door that led downstairs to the shop—"what great friends you have and how you're finally getting to do what you always wanted . . . It's just helped clarify some thoughts that have been floating around my brain for months."

He smiled, reached across the table, and grabbed my hand.

"Mom. I want to do this. It's the right decision at the right time in my life. And if it helps you too, that's even better. Trust me. I'm a grown man. I know what I'm doing."

I was quiet for a moment. Garrett's eyes searched my face, waiting for me to speak.

"All right." I nodded slowly. "Good. It'll be good to have you around for a while, but Garrett, if you change your mind, or if you get an offer for a job you think you'd like, don't feel like you have to come back here to New Bern. Don't worry about me. I can—"

"I know. I know. You can take care of yourself. Tell me about it." He reached for the champagne bottle, topped off our mimosas, and raised his glass in a toast. "To living our dreams!"

"To living our dreams!" I echoed and lifted my glass and touched the rim against his.

∽ 24 ∽

Abigail Burgess Wynne

I stood in front of the open refrigerator, surveying the contents and wondering if I should heat up a bowl of leftover vegetable soup before going to Margot's. She would undoubtedly have something delicious to serve, but that was the problem. The holiday revelries had left me four and a half pounds heavier.

When I'd sat down at my desk the day before to write down my New Year's resolutions, I'd vowed to lose the holiday weight plus another three and a half pounds besides. At my age, it is important not to let extra weight creep up on you. If a stray pound settles in around your middle for more than a week or two, it can take months to get it back off.

I took the soup pot out of the refrigerator and put it on the stove to warm.

Liza, dressed in a parka and those big, clunky boots I detested, brushed past me and headed toward the back door. "Where are you going?"

"Out."

"I can see that, but you're early. We're not due at Margot's for another thirty minutes."

She fished her gloves out of her pocket, not even bothering to look at me. "I'm not going to Margot's."

"Not going?" I sighed, exasperated. "Don't you remember? I told you that Margot called right after Christmas. We're going to get together at her house today to work on a new quilt, a present for Evelyn. It's to be a surprise."

She said nothing, just zipped up her jacket and pulled on her gloves, getting ready to leave as if she hadn't heard a word I'd said.

I was absolutely at the end of my rope with the girl. How much longer was she planning on acting like this?

As I'd suspected, Christmas with Liza had been simply awful. I'd gotten up early, made coffee and some hot cider, and heated up the breakfast casserole Hilda had left for us in the refrigerator. I'd waited nearly an hour for Liza to come downstairs, thinking the delicious aromas coming from the kitchen would surely rouse her, but they didn't. Finally, I knocked on her door and told her breakfast was ready. She said she was coming, but another hour passed before she finally deigned to grace the dining room with her presence. The casserole was completely dried out.

Still, I tried to put a pleasant face on things, ignore her rude behavior, and enjoy the day as best I might. After breakfast, I invited her into the living room and gave her the gifts I'd wrapped and hidden under the tree for her. I hadn't put up a tree in years but had decided to do so for Liza's sake. I had to admit I had enjoyed it. It wasn't a large tree, but it looked so pretty and festive standing next to the fireplace. Just looking at it cheered me. And much to my surprise, I'd also enjoyed shopping for Liza's gifts.

Originally, I'd thought about getting her a cashmere sweater from Kaplan's Clothes Closet, but recalling her sullen mood of late felt she might not appreciate my attempts at humor. Instead, I went to Pam's Boutique and bought a heavy black knit shawl—really it was more of a cape, very warm and very elegant—and a pair of knee-high leather boots with decorative crisscrossed lacing and black fur edging the tops. They would look simply wonderful on Liza's tall, willowy frame: simple but dramatic, in line with her personal style and, of course, they were her favorite color—black. I was sure she'd love them. On top of that, I purchased one of those tiny music recorder-downloader things, the ones all the young people had. I got the very latest model, and the most expensive, also in black.

Surely, I told myself, once she saw her beautiful presents she'd cheer up, but I was wrong. After opening the gifts she'd just mumbled a thank-you and returned to her room. So irritating! And what's more, she hadn't even gotten me so much as a Christmas card, let alone a Christmas gift. Not that there was anything I particularly needed or wanted, but you'd have thought she'd have gotten me something! Just some tiny token to thank me for all I'd done for her. After all, if not for me she might have spent her Christmas behind bars.

Sitting alone by the fireplace, listening to a recording of "The Holly and the Ivy" by a boy's choir and surrounded by wrapping paper and ribbon debris while Liza was up in her room brooding, I felt hurt and a little lonely. I had thought we might go to the Christmas Day services at church, but now I realized there was no point in asking her to come, and I didn't want to go alone. After tidying up the living room, rinsing the dishes, and leaving the dirty casserole dish in the sink for Hilda to clean when she came in the next morning, I decided to call the shelter to make sure everything was going well with their Christmas celebration. It was a good thing I did. There was a virus going around, and several of the people who'd volunteered to serve dinner had called in sick. I told them I'd come right over to help. For a moment, I considered inviting Liza to join me, but then thought better of it. Instead, I left her a note on the counter and hurried over to the shelter.

Cutting and serving pieces of pie and whipped cream for the children and parents at the shelter took my mind off my own problems. Bethany came through the line with her mother and little brother.

They had a present for me; a small lavender sachet and a card that Bethany had made herself. It wasn't an elaborate gift, but I was touched. After all, it's the thought that counts.

The next day, Hilda came into my room holding the music player, the one I'd given to Liza. She said she'd found it in the trash and wondered if I'd accidentally thrown it away. Well! As you can imagine, I was incensed! But I decided not to confront Liza about it. Instead, I told Hilda to take it home to her fourteen-year-old grandson. She, at least, had the courtesy to thank me properly. Liza might be a Burgess, but Hilda could have given her a few lessons in manners. Heaven knew someone needed to—apparently me.

Now, as she deliberately ignored me, still wearing those dreadful, clunky hiking boots that she knew I hated instead of the expensive new stylish ones I'd bought precisely because she knew it would annoy me, I decided the time had come to take the bull by the horns. I was not going to tolerate this rudeness for one more moment.

"Liza! Did you hear me? We're supposed to go to Margot's and work on a quilt for Evelyn."

Silence.

"Don't you stand there and pretend you don't hear me! And close that door! We have to go to Margot's!"

"I told you before, I'm not going."

"Why not? Do you have some more pressing engagement that I don't know about? Are you scheduled to perform brain surgery or something?" She mumbled something. "What was that? Speak up."

"I said," she shouted, "that it isn't any of your damned business where I'm going or why! I'm going out, and that's all you need to know." She opened the door, but I crossed the kitchen in three huge steps and slammed it shut again.

"Listen here, young lady! I've put up with enough of this. You are going to Margot's with me, and for once in your miserable, ungrateful, selfish little life you are going to be pleasant! You're the one that got me into this in the first place. I was perfectly happy with my life, but you blackmailed me into going to that Quilt Pink event, and helping Evelyn through her cancer, joining the quilt circle, and all the rest. None of this was my idea! But now that we're in it, we're obligated to see it through. You are going with me today, and we are going to work on a quilt to cheer up poor Evelyn. Good heavens! Isn't that the least you can do? For all you know, this cancer will prove fatal! Had you even considered that? Honestly! I never met such a rude, inconsiderate, self-absorbed person in all my life! I—"

"Self-absorbed?" Her expression, purposely flat and enigmatic a moment before, suddenly transformed into one of seething anger and loathing beamed directly at me. Her eyes sparked like firecrackers. "Are you ******* kidding me?" she asked, using an expletive I prefer not to transcribe. "Do you actually have the audacity to stand there and call *me* self-absorbed? Well, **** you!" She tried to push her way past me, but I blocked her. I was determined to finally have this thing out.

"Don't you dare use that kind of language with me! Not in my home! I simply will not tolerate it, not after all I've done for you!"

Liza let out one sharp bark of a laugh. "All you've done for me? What have you ever done for me that the judge didn't make you do? Don't try that one with me. Don't play Our Lady of Mercy and Philanthropy with me, Abigail. I see right through it. The only reason I'm here is because you couldn't figure out a way to get rid of me without making the papers and thus besmirching the precious name of Burgess Wynne. If not for that, you'd have left me to rot in jail!"

"That is not fair and it's not true! I was just trying to help you!"

"Oh come on! You don't actually believe that, do you? You didn't want to help me. You never want to help anyone unless there's something for you in it." She laughed again, longer this time, but there was no mirth in it, a laugh so infused with hatred that it frightened me a little. I took a step backward.

"You are so completely clueless," she spat and moved toward me. "But you're right about one thing. I dragged you to the quilt store, blackmailed you into going, because I wanted you to have to acknowledge the fact that my mother, your own sister, died of breast cancer and you never, ever did a single thing to help her! You never visited her, you never called her, you never even sent her a ******* get-well card!"

She was screaming now, and tears started to fall from her eyes, but there was no hoarseness in her voice, no sound of choked-back sobs, just tears seeping slowly from the corners of her eyes and running down her cheeks, crystalline and bright, catching the light from the kitchen window, as if something frozen behind the brown orbits of her eyes were melting.

"I was so happy to see how miserable you were that day! To see you finally forced out of your perfect little world with your perfect friends, and perfect clothes, and perfect house. Actually having to mix with real people with real problems. And then, when we met Evelyn and you started helping her, I thought that maybe, finally, you were starting to face what you'd done. That you were feeling sad about deserting Mom, and me, when we needed you most and were looking for some way to make amends for it. I thought maybe you'd changed." Finally, her fury seemed to subside, at least a little. When she said this last there was a sad, almost mournful tenor to her voice.

"I have," I said quietly. "I have changed."

She kept on talking as if I hadn't said anything. "And then, that night when Evelyn told us that they hadn't gotten all the cancer and you were suddenly so solicitous, so anxious to help, I saw that it wasn't true. You hadn't changed. You'd just put on another costume, one more layer of veneer to hide what you really are inside— whatever that is." She barked out a bitter laugh. "I've lived in your house for months, and I'm still not sure who you are. But one thing I do know, you're not sorry about what you did to my mother. Not one bit. You just like the idea of this new part you're playing—Abigail Burgess Wynne, Compassionate Caregiver to the Ordinary and Downtrodden. Helping poor quilt-shop owners with cancer, taking in ungrateful nieces with criminal records, making quilts for little kids you barely know, serving Christmas dinner to the homeless."

She lifted her face and looked at me. The angry spark was rekindled. "It'll all look good in your obituary, won't it?"

"Liza! That's awful! What a hateful thing to say!"

"Is it? Good! Because I do hate you! I hate everything about you! Your house, your clothes, the sound of your voice. And I hate, I absolutely despise, the fact that every time I look at you, I see my mother. You look just like her; did you know that? Like she would have looked if she'd gotten to live to be your age. When I see you, I remember that she's gone and you're still here. She was good and kind and loved me and she's dead. You're cold and self-centered and you only put up with me because you have to, but you're still alive. Why is that?"

She hates me? How could she? After all I've done . . . My usual refrain, the one I always played in my mind when working myself into indignation over Liza's behavior and attitude. But then, for an instant, just a breath, everything seemed to freeze. The voice in my head was silenced, and I looked at Liza, truly looked at her, as if I were seeing her for the first time. I looked beyond the angry eyes, the hard-edged clothes and makeup, and the sullen attitude, and saw grief, despair, and wrenching loneliness. And I finally realized the truth—at least some of her anguish had been caused by me.

All this time, I had been congratulating myself on everything I'd done for Liza, moaning like a martyr about all I'd given her. But what had I given her, really? Everything but what she needed. My indignant inner monologue, briefly interrupted, began again, but something had happened, the tirade twisted and turned in my head and became something entirely new, a realization that forbid indignation, pulled me up short, and filled me with shame. . . . *After*

202 • *Marie Bostwick*

what I've done. And what I've never done. She hates me. How could she not?

Tentatively, awkwardly, I took a step toward my niece, my sister's only child, the only person on earth who shared my name, my history, the only human being whose birth and past were connected to mine. I lifted my hand, thinking I should touch her shoulder, but she shrank back from me and wrapped her arms across her heart like a shield. She looked so young.

"Liza . . . I . . . I'm so sorry for . . ." I didn't know what to say, how to begin to apologize. It had been so long since I'd made an apology to anyone—for anything. Never complain, never explain. It was the rule I lived my life by. Finally, at a loss, I simply said, "You must miss her terribly."

Liza's jaw tightened. She swallowed hard. I could see the muscles twitch under the pale parchment of her long neck. "When I went into the quilt shop that day, I only went for one reason. To see you squirm. I didn't care about quilting, or even raising money for breast cancer, but then I met Evelyn and Margot, and they were so nice to me, and the quilting part was fun. For a little while, I forgot to think about hating you. Then, when Evelyn fell apart . . ." Her voice trailed off for a moment, remembering that night.

"For a second, when Evelyn started crying so hard, I was really scared. It was like watching it happen to Mom all over again. But then Margot jumped up and took charge. Next thing I knew, everyone was helping her—even you. And it felt good. You know? It wasn't like it was with Mom, when I was the only one she could count on. Everyone was pitching in, and Evelyn was getting better, and it felt so good! Like I was saying, 'Screw you, cancer! You're not going to win this time!' And I believed it was true. I really did.

"You know, Evelyn is a lot like Mom was," she said in a voice hushed with remembering. "Not the way she looks, but the way she talks and acts and everything, encouraging. She likes my artwork. She just let me have that whole window to do whatever I wanted with. Never told me what to do, she just told me to go for it," she said, shrugging her shoulders ever so slightly, quietly amazed by this vote of confidence in her talent. And she was talented. I could see it. How hard would it have been to tell her that?

"You did a good job," I said.

Her tears came faster now, streaming down her cheeks, drawing a transparent line from her lashes to the ledge of her jaw and falling, one after another after another, onto her jacket, turning the black fabric even blacker, blooming into an inky, indelible blossom of grief.

"When we went to the quilt circle that night and she told us the cancer was back, that she was going to have more surgery . . . I just—"

She covered her eyes with her hands. "I can't . . . I can't do this again. I can't be around her. It hurts too much. I can't be around her. Or you. I can't," she repeated and lowered her hands to look at me. Her tears fell like rain as she finally gave up her hopeless attempts at self-control.

"Who are you?" she sobbed. "All of a sudden, you can't do enough to help Evelyn, or everyone else for that matter. When Mom needed you, you were nowhere to be seen. You never tried to help her! You never pulled strings to get *my* mother the best doctors in New England—the doctors that might have known how to save her life! Did you ever stop to think about that? You didn't lift a finger to help your own flesh and blood, but when it comes to the needs of strangers, you suddenly can't do enough! How did it happen? This amazing transformation? A magician waves his wand, the old Abigail disappears, and poof! Everyone gasps as the new Abigail, looking exactly the same but dressed in an entirely new ensemble, steps out. The audience is dazzled and bursts into applause." She was looking at me again, staring right through me as if I were a ghostly presence, composed of nothing more substantial than vapor and suspect intention.

"You don't fool me, Auntie. Not me. Not anymore. You haven't changed anything but your tactics. You've just found a new way to impress everyone." Her voice was thick with loathing.

"You don't care about Evelyn," she said. "You just want every-one to like you, preferably to adore you, without ever letting them get close enough to actually touch you. And the sick part is, they do! Your fancy friends around town, the elegant people who go to the right parties and sit on the right boards, are crazy about you be-cause you've got what they want most of all—style. And just having you around makes them feel more clever and important than they really are. But when I forced you to step out of the boundaries of your little club, the crowd of sycophantic disciples who worship you, and into a world where people aren't impressed by cocktail banter, or the number of zeros in your checking account, you didn't know what to do. How would you make them like you? You must have wracked your brain trying to puzzle out that one, didn't you, Abigail?"

She was wrong. I did care about Evelyn. Maybe not at first, but I did now.

Liza kept on without giving me a chance to defend myself. "But you're no dummy," she said. "Once you figured out what mattered in the new club, things like kindness and generosity, you adapted right away. Overnight you became kind and generous, because that's what they wanted. You even started going to church. You're such a hypocrite! You think you're so special, but you're nothing! You don't care about anyone but yourself, not even your dying sis-ter!"

"That's not true. It's not!" I insisted. "Things aren't as simple and clear-cut as you've made them out to be. When you're older you'll understand."

A sneer. A voice like ice. "Then I pray to God I never live to be that old."

Her cutting remarks did just that, cut me to the heart, wounded me. But I realized that she was hurting too, far more than I. If I could only get her to calm down, to see how unreasonable she was being. I took a deep breath and tried again. "Maybe you're right about some of what you've said. I've made my share of mistakes, but—"

She shook her head and said hoarsely, "Be quiet. I don't want to hear it. If I didn't hate you so much, I might almost feel sorry for you. You can't even see how pathetic you are. God! How did you get this way?"

"Liza—"

"I ask myself that question all the time now. When I look in the mirror I see my face, I see you, how you must have looked forty years ago. Everyone says we look just alike."

It was true. I had noticed.

"You were like me once. You couldn't have been born this way. Something must have happened to you, but I don't know what. I look at myself and wonder if it's happening to me too. I'm so afraid. . . ."

She hadn't said as much to me in the previous seven months as she had in those few minutes. I didn't know if she truly believed everything she'd said, but the last part was the absolute truth. She was afraid. She had been for a long time.

Liza was only sixteen when she'd found out about Susan's cancer and eighteen when she'd died, far too young to have to known such loss. She'd had to face it all alone, with no more support or care from me than the cold comfort of a check. The things that had happened before, the events that had opened the terrible gulf between my sister and me, had swallowed up Liza too, the only innocent person in the whole awful scenario. No wonder she was so hard and mistrustful of me—and everyone else. She'd learned the hard way that even the people who should love you sometimes don't, and even those who do love you will sometimes leave you. The poor child.

And now, just when she'd begun to open up, to trust a little, she was facing it all again. How could I not have realized? How could I not have said anything?

"Liza. Oh, Liza, come here. You don't understand." I reached out for her, opened my arms.

"Don't!" She jumped back as if burned by my touch. "I told you. I can't do this again. I hate you! I hate you!" she repeated, once for me and once for herself.

"I can't stay here anymore!" She turned away from me, opened the door, and ran down the steps and across the back yard, leaving a cratered trail of footsteps through the deep drifts of snow.

I followed her to the door. "Liza, wait! Where are you going? Come back and we'll talk about it. Come back! I need to explain some things to you!"

I was yelling as loud as I could, my words ringing through the thin, cold air, my mouth exhaling a frozen fog, but she didn't stop. The snow was at least two feet deep, and I was in my stocking feet. I ran upstairs, pulled on the first pair of boots I could find and a warm jacket and gloves, then ran back downstairs and out the back door. But she was gone.

I followed her trail of footsteps around the side of the house, down the driveway, and onto the sidewalk. I'd come as quickly as I could, but she was nowhere to be seen, and the sidewalks had been shoveled, leaving only a thin dusting of new snow. The print of Liza's boot mixed in with the prints of dozens of others who had walked down the street that day. There was no way to distinguish hers from anyone else's or to tell which direction she'd taken. I ran to the corner, hoping to catch a glimpse of her, twice slipping and falling on the icy walkway and then scrambling back to my feet to continue the hunt, but it was no use. She'd disappeared.

I ran back to the house, laboriously making my way through the drifted snow. My heart was pounding in my chest as I climbed the back steps, realizing that I'd left the door wide open. I stood at the doorway, panting from exertion, and laid my hand over my pounding heart. Where could she have gone?

A voice in my head told me not to worry, that she was just being dramatic, manipulating the situation, trying once again to blackmail me with emotion. But I knew it wasn't true. Not this time. I was worried, afraid of what she might do in such a state. What should I do?

Barely pausing to kick the snow off my boots, I walked into the kitchen, trailing snowy, melting footprints across Hilda's clean floor, picked up the telephone, and dialed.

"Margot? It's Abigail. No, we're not coming now. Can you come over here? Right away? Please. It's about Liza. I need your help."

25

Evelyn Dixon

Margot's yellow Volkswagen, parked in Abigail's driveway, appeared trifling and incongruous next to the patrician grandeur of the enormous colonial mansion with its three stories of white clapboard siding, four chimneys, and symmetrical rows of windows blinking in the winter sunlight like unseeing eyes. Someone had told me that Abigail's house had once been an academy for young women from rich families. It was certainly big enough. Hard to believe that Abigail and Liza lived here all alone.

I parked my car behind Margot's and went to the front door. Margot answered.

"Hi," she said and gave me a welcoming hug. "Thanks for coming. Abigail is in the kitchen. I made her a cup of tea. She's terribly upset."

I followed Margot through a series of cavernous rooms filled with expensive antique furniture, rugs, and paintings. But I was so surprised by Margot's assertion that I barely took note of the elegant surroundings.

Abigail was upset? That was hard for me to imagine. She always seemed so in control of every situation. I'd never even seen her flus-

tered, let alone upset. But Margot was right. The woman sitting at
the table sipping tea with the red-rimmed eyes, disheveled hair, and
wearing no trace of makeup or lipstick was Abigail. And she was
more than upset; she was absolutely distraught.

"Margot?" Abigail called. "Was that Liza? Is she back?" She
looked up hopefully when Margot entered the room, but her face
fell when she realized I was the only person following behind. "Oh.
It's you, Evelyn. What are you doing here?"

"I called her," Margot said.

Abigail shook her head. "You shouldn't have bothered Evelyn.
She's got enough problems without having to deal with the ones I've
created."

I pulled up a chair and sat down. "Don't be silly. I'm glad Margot called. Now, what happened? Liza's missing?"

Abigail dabbed her eyes with an already damp tissue. "We had a
terrible argument. I knew she was upset about something, but I just
kept trying to ignore it. This had been brewing for a long time, years
really—even before she came to live with me."

Abigail's face crumpled, and she started weeping softly. I was
amazed. In all the time I'd known her, I'd never seen her give way to
any emotion stronger than carefully controlled disapproval. Now
she was sitting here letting the tears flow freely. I barely recognized
her. Whatever had happened between Liza and Abigail, it must
have been something big. Otherwise, she would never have allowed
herself to be so vulnerable.

Margot, normally so capable, was standing near the table, seem-
ing as much at a loss as I was. I looked a question at her, but she just
shrugged.

"Abigail," I said, "you know that Liza's an emotional girl. Whatever happened between the two of you is probably just a passing
cloud. I'm sure she'll come back after she blows off a little steam.
Don't worry."

"No," Abigail insisted, sniffing. "This wasn't just some little spat. She was furious. We've had our moments, but I've never seen her like this. She walked out that door, and I know she's not planning on coming back."

Frankly, I didn't know what to do. Perhaps what Abigail was saying was true and perhaps it wasn't, but even if she had walked out the door with the intention of never returning, I didn't see what any of us could do about it. Liza was a grown woman. If she didn't want to live with her aunt anymore, then that was her decision.

"I can see how hard this is for you," I said, "but Liza is of age. I'm sure she'll come back once she cools off and thinks things over, but if she doesn't, then that really is her choice. It's difficult to let a child leave the nest, but sometimes that's what we have to do."

"You don't understand," Abigail protested. "Liza can't leave my home. Not without the judge's permission. If she does, she could end up in jail."

Margot's eye grew wide. "Jail? You mean Liza's on parole? I didn't know that." Neither did I.

Abigail bit her lower lip. I could see she was struggling inside herself, wondering how much she should tell us and regretting what she'd already blurted out. Finally, she said slowly, "No. She's not quite on parole. It's just that . . . well . . . a few months after her mother died, she made a terrible mistake. And I said I'd be responsible for her. That is, the judge said I had to be responsible for her. I didn't want to at first. I'd barely laid eyes on her before I saw her in Judge Gulden's chambers that day. If I could have figured out a way to get out of it, I would have, but now . . . everything's changed. Do you see?"

Margot and I looked at each other. We didn't see. Margot pulled up a chair and sat down. "Maybe you'd better start from the beginning," she said gently.

Abigail swallowed hard before speaking. I could see how hard this was for her. Abigail was used to relying on her own resources and, until this moment, had been more than equal to the challenge.

There was so much to admire about Abigail. She was so competent—intelligent, well-read, well-dressed, socially capable, and quick to find the most direct solution to any number of problems. And in the last months I'd seen her grow in ways I would never have imagined. She was more giving, more sensitive to the needs of others, and, it seemed to me, happier because of it. But for all this, she was still lacking one important skill: the ability to trust. It obviously did not come easily to her. What had happened to make her so wary of others? Why, whenever I made even the most innocent inquiries about her past, did she so quickly and deftly change the subject? Even after all these months of working together and quilting side by side every week, she was obviously hesitant to open up to Margot or me.

Normally she was able to keep her feelings carefully concealed, but today her emotions were battling inside her. Could she trust us? Should she? She still wasn't sure.

I leaned closer and took her hands in mine. "It's all right," I said softly. "You can tell us. After all, we're friends. Aren't we?"

Her eyes shifted and locked with mine. For one long moment, she searched my face, and then, after taking a breath, she began. "Yes," she said tentatively and then with more conviction. "Yes. I believe we are."

Winter days in northern Connecticut are short, and by the time Abigail finished talking, the shadows of evening were beginning to fall.

When she'd started speaking, I had determined to show as little emotional reaction as possible so Abigail would feel safe in opening up, but it hadn't been easy. Though she refrained from explaining what caused the rift between them, she told us about her estranged relationship with her deceased sister and, by extension, with Liza. No wonder Liza was so hostile toward her aunt. Then she went on to share the truth about Susan's death from breast cancer. It had been hard to hear, frightening. As soon as she'd said the words, Abigail looked at me anxiously, concerned about my reaction to this revelation. With effort, I urged her to continue. After all, I told my-self, this wasn't about me. Not that day. It was about Liza and Abi-gail.

In a strange way, this realization was something of a relief. For so many weeks and months, everyone had been trying to help me, wor-rying about *my* needs, *my* health, *my* fears, that it felt . . . well, not exactly good, but right somehow to be worrying about someone else. "Go on," I said in response to Abigail's worried glance. "It's all right. Then what happened?"

She told us about how Liza had come to be remanded into her custody, about the tension that had been building between them ever since the day I'd told them about my upcoming mastectomy, and finally about the fight they'd had. Awful. Actually, awful didn't even begin to describe it. It broke my heart to hear the hurtful things Liza had said to her aunt.

Liza wasn't always pleasant to be around—in fact, she could be a real pain—but she wasn't an intentionally cruel person. I'd always known that the death of her mother had been a terrible blow, but I'd had no understanding of the depth of her suffering. How hard it must have been for her, knowing that I was facing the same disease that had so recently claimed her own mother. A lot of people having been through what she had would have immediately backed away, but Liza hadn't. She'd tried to help me in every way she knew how, but it couldn't have been easy. Especially when Abigail had used her influence to help me get access to the kind of medical care Liza felt might have saved her mother. Abigail shared that Susan hadn't found out about the cancer until the disease was in its latter stages and had progressed beyond the reach of medical intervention. But you couldn't blame Liza for clutching at straws, looking for a mira-cle that could have saved her mother, and someone to blame when that miracle hadn't come. Abigail made for an easy target.

Poor girl. She was so much kinder than I'd ever imagined and so much stronger. Still, even a strong person can only shoulder the secret burden of tragedy for so long. When she'd learned that my first treatment hadn't been successful, that cancer was threatening to take someone else close to her, it had unearthed the grief and anguish she was trying so hard to keep buried. God alone knew the depths of pain Liza was going through.

Abigail wasn't faring much better. As I said, there was a lot I admired about Abigail, but I wasn't blind to her faults. Or at least, I hadn't thought I was. Listening to her story, the broken relationship with her sister, the tearful admission that she'd never come to her aid, not even after she'd learned about Susan's breast cancer, I was in shock. Of course, she had taken care of Susan's medical bills, had kept tabs on Susan and Liza via the reports she received from her attorney, Franklin Spaulding, and taken financial and, eventually, physical responsibility for Liza, but still!

For someone like Abigail, writing a check was the easiest thing in the world, the equivalent of the average person tossing a quarter to a homeless person without ever bothering to look them in the eye, done more to assuage their own guilt than as an act of any real compassion. How could she have been so completely clueless when it came to the emotional needs of her own niece? How could she, knowing Liza's background, have been so cold?

Part of me wanted to reach across the table and slap her. But when I saw her crying openly, bowed down by shame and remorse as she did what was, for her, the most difficult thing in the world, admit her faults to others, my anger subsided. It was true. The Abigail Burgess Wynne who had been dragged into my shop so many months ago wasn't the same woman who was sitting next to me now. Somewhere along the way, she'd changed. Or at least she'd begun to. I'd always thought that somewhere, trapped underneath that hard, proud shell, there was a finer Abigail trying to get out. It seemed she had. As painful as it was, maybe this crisis with Liza and being forced to hear how much grief she had caused was the only hammer strong enough to break that shell and finally set Abigail, and Liza, free. Only time would tell.

"I ran as fast as I could," Abigail sniffed plaintively, "but she was gone. That's when I decided to call Margot, but I didn't mean to bother you, Evelyn. You've got so much on your plate already."

Margot broke in and said what I was already thinking. "Well, of course, I had to call Evelyn. She cares about you just as much as I do. And we all care about Liza."

"I know," Abigail nodded her head and whispered. "I do. I haven't been very good to her up until now, but I do care. If she'll only come home, I know I can figure out a way to make her believe it."

I was pleased to hear a little of Abigail's old determination return to her voice. If Abigail decided to do something, then she'd do it. Of course, that didn't solve our immediate problem, as Abigail knew full well.

"But what if she doesn't come home? I'm so worried about her. If Judge Gulden calls to check on her, or if she does something crazy again and the police pick her up, she'll end up in jail. I was able to pull some strings to help her last time, but I don't think the judge would be lenient if it happened again. It's getting dark outside, and it's so cold. She ran off so fast, she didn't even take her pocketbook with her. I'm sure she doesn't have any money." Abigail buried her head in her hands.

"This is all my fault," she said for the tenth time that afternoon. "I've behaved despicably. If only I'd taken the time to try to talk to her, to explain things. When she ran out of here, she was completely overwrought. I'm afraid for her. What if she does something crazy?" Abigail asked, and I knew she wasn't talking about something as relatively innocuous as shoplifting a sweater in an unconscious cry for help. Abigail was worried that Liza might give in to her despair in a much more dangerous and permanent way. "What if she tries to—"

"No," I insisted, pushing back my chair and getting to my feet. "Liza would never do something like that. Never."

I grabbed my pocketbook and car keys off the counter where I'd left them. "Come on. Let's go."

"Where?" Abigail asked. Her eyes grew wide as she watched me put on my jacket. "Evelyn, we can't go to the police and tell them Liza is gone! I told you, she'll go to jail if they find out."

"I know that," I said. "We're going to have to find her ourselves. She was on foot, and she didn't have any money. She can't have gone far."

I zipped up my jacket and started giving instructions. "Margot, you and Abigail go together. Start on the east side of town. I'll take the west. We'll cover more ground if we split up."

❦ 26 ❦

Abigail Burgess Wynne

As Evelyn suggested, Margot and I started on the east side of town. Her Volkswagen was cramped, but I was glad Margot was driving. As I've gotten older, I've found it hard to drive at dusk. Also, distressed as I was, I really wasn't sure I'd be able to focus on driving. It was probably for the best. Margot hadn't lived in New Bern for long and needed me to navigate. Together, we made a good team.

Margot was very encouraging, echoing Evelyn's assertion that since Liza had run off so quickly with no car, no money, and probably no plan, we'd surely find her very soon. After all, only a few hours had passed since she'd bolted. The cold weather and the blanket of snow covering the ground would have made it difficult to walk very quickly. Chances were she was still within a five-mile radius of New Bern. I sat up straight and peered out the window, eagerly searching the sidewalks and roadsides for any glimpse of Liza, giving Margot directions when she needed them, and keeping one ear tuned for the ring of Margot's cellular telephone. Evelyn and Margot had agreed to call each other the minute they spotted Liza.

But as minutes and then an hour passed and dusk became night without any sign of her, or any message from Evelyn, my despair deepened.

"It's so dark. She was wearing that black jacket she likes and, of course, her black jeans and those awful black boots. We could be driving right past her and still not see her."

"We'd see her in the headlights," Margot assured me. "With all this drifted snow, she'll have to stay close to the road. Come on, Abigail. You've got to think positively. We're going to find her. Soon. And if we don't, Evelyn will. You'll see."

Margot was saying all the right words, but I wasn't convinced she entirely believed them. We drove in silence for a long time. My stomach rumbled. It was well past dinnertime, and I remembered now that I hadn't had any lunch, but I didn't say anything about being hungry. The only thing I cared about now was finding Liza. I looked at my watch. It was nearly nine o'clock.

"Where can she be? Oh, Margot. This is my fault. Everything. We're not going to find her. And even if we do, I know she'll never, ever be able to forgive me."

Margot glanced away from the road briefly, quickly turning her head to look at me. Her eyes were full of compassion, and somehow that only made me feel worse. I didn't deserve her pity.

"Abigail, don't say that. Yes, it's true. You've made some terrible mistakes, but you're only human. If you tell Liza how truly sorry you are and try to explain why you've acted the way you have, she'll forgive you."

"How could she? I abandoned her, and, what's worse, I abandoned Susan. My own sister." I sighed. "How can I expect Liza to forgive me? I was never able to forgive her mother. Susan hurt me so badly, and I was never, ever able to forgive her for what she'd done.

"Margot, you go to church a lot, don't you? Since you were a little girl?" She nodded. "I've always been a church member, written checks and showed up at services every once in a while, but I never attended regularly. Not until recently. A couple of weeks ago, the minister was preaching on the Lord's Prayer, the part about asking God to forgive our sins as we forgive those who sin against us." I paused, waiting for Margot to say something, to give some verse or judgment on the subject, but she just kept her eyes on the road and listened.

"When you hear something like that, that you can only be forgiven if you've been willing to forgive. . . ." I didn't have a handkerchief or tissue with me, so I wiped my eyes on the edge of my sleeve as I thought of Susan on that day when I told her that I could never forgive her and I never wanted to see her again.

"It's too late now," I whispered to myself. "She's gone. It's too late."

"No, it's not," Margot said. "It's never too late to forgive someone else, just as it's never too late to ask for forgiveness."

I looked at her skeptically. Margot was sweet and well-intentioned, and I'd come to admire the genuineness of her faith. In fact, the strength of her faith was part of why I'd gone back to church. She seemed so happy and at peace even when things weren't going well. I hoped that a little of what she'd found there would rub off on me. But I was beginning to think she'd spent too much time watching those Sunday morning television programs hosted by those preachers with the blow-dried hair and southern accents. My problems couldn't be solved by repeating the Lord's Prayer and promising to try harder next time.

"Margot, that's easy to say, but you don't understand. What went on between my sister and me was just so incredibly awful. It was beyond awful. What Susan did to me was unforgivable. And I gave it right back to her, kept my promise never to have anything to do with her, not even after I knew she was dying of cancer. And that was worse than unforgivable."

"Abigail, my mother always said that there is no pit so deep that the love and forgiveness of God is not deeper still."

Margot was trying to help, but inwardly I was rolling my eyes at this platitude. Sure, it was easy for someone like Margot or her mother, people who'd probably thought of jaywalking as a form of civil rebellion. They couldn't possibly understand what I was dealing with, years and years of selfishness, betrayal, and deceit—and I wasn't just talking about me. Lies and duplicity were part of the Burgess family legacy. By comparison, Margot's family probably looked like the Brady Bunch. I sighed, and as if reading my unspoken thoughts, Margot went on.

"Abigail, I don't know all the details of what happened between you and your sister. I don't need to. Sure. Maybe if I knew the whole story, I would feel that both of you were beyond the possibility of pardon, but fortunately I'm not in charge of forgiving anyone anything. This is between you and God. Not you and me, and not even you and Susan. When we sin against someone else, yes, we are wronging them, but we are also wronging God, and that's even worse. Susan may have deserved some of your anger, but God never did."

She pulled up at a four-way stop and looked both ways before crossing through the intersection. Her eyes were still on the road as she continued talking.

"The thing is, we're all in the pit at some point in our lives. Some people are able to climb out and some never do. The ones who climb out are the ones who recognize their need for help, have the humility to grab hold of the rope, and faith to believe that rope is strong enough to lift them up."

I was quiet for a moment, thinking. When I'd first met Margot, she was so happy and smiling all the time that I'd honestly thought she wasn't all that bright. I'm embarrassed to admit it, but it's true. Most smart people I knew, the intellectuals, were brooding and miserable and forever bemoaning the deplorable state of the world and the dumbing-down of our national standards in everything from political discourse to musical theater. They had all kinds of opinions on all kinds of subjects, but I'd very rarely seen any of them *do* anything besides complain. As far as they were concerned, the world was bad and getting worse, and anyone who thought there was anything to be done about it was a fool.

Margot, on the other hand, was the kind of person who, once she recognized a problem, immediately started searching for solutions. And I'd noticed that, very often, she found them. Sweet temper and girlish giggles notwithstanding, Margot was clearly a very intelligent woman. My brooding philosopher friends, that Greek chorus of hopelessness, would have scoffed at the simplicity of her illustration, but I also knew if I'd asked them how to get out of the pit, they'd have nothing more to offer than conferring nods and the brilliant observation that it was certainly a complicated issue. Margot was an intelligent woman, and it was clear that, somehow or other, she'd found a peace I hadn't. But still. It *was* a complicated issue.

"Margot, I know you mean well, but you make it sound easy, and it's not. This whole thing started before Liza was born, even before you were born. There's been so much water under the bridge. So much went wrong. At this point, I wouldn't even know how to begin to make it right."

"Sure you do, Abigail. Your minister told you exactly how to begin—with forgiveness. Even though she is gone, you can choose to forgive Susan. Once you have done that, you can ask God to forgive you." She turned her eyes away from the darkened road to give me a quick smile. "And He will, Abigail."

"And Liza?" I asked. "Will she forgive me too?"

"Well, that's the one thing in all this that isn't your choice," Margot said, squinting a little as a car with its brights on approached and she flashed her high beams at it. "Maybe she will and maybe she won't. Deep down, in spite of all that she's been through, Liza has a good heart, but there are no guarantees. One thing I do know for sure, she never will if you don't ask."

I was tired. I let my head drop back against the headrest and closed my eyes for a moment. Margot had given me a lot to think about. At my age, was it possible to change, to make things right again? Maybe. But none of that would matter if we couldn't find Liza. Where could she be?

With my eyes still closed, I said a silent prayer.

God, I know there really isn't any reason for you to listen to me tonight. I haven't done a very good job of listening to you these past sixty-two years, so a part of me feels kind of hypocritical coming to you after all this time. I wouldn't blame you a bit if you ignored me, but I pray you won't. Margot says I have to forgive Susan so that you can forgive me, and I want to. I'm just not sure I can, not unless you help me. Please, dear Lord, please help me. I've always thought of myself as so strong, but I'm not strong enough for this. I just can't do it alone anymore, and I don't want to. Help me.

And God, about Liza. I'm so worried about her, and I can't find her. I don't know much about you, God, but I do know that you know where she is. Please help me find her. Help her to come home. And to forgive me. Amen.

Just as the "amen" was forming in my mind, I heard the tinny, computerized chirp of Margot's cell phone. My eyes flew open, and I turned in my seat to face Margot as she flipped her phone open and held it to her ear.

It's Evelyn! God heard my prayer and helped her find Liza!

And it was Evelyn. When I raised my eyebrows, silently questioning Margot as to the identity of the caller and mutely mouthed "Evelyn?", Margot responded with a grin and a quick nod.

"Evelyn! Hi! Where are you? Did you find her?" The expectant smile on Margot's face faded. "Oh. No, we haven't either. No, not a sign." She was quiet for a moment, listening. "Me too. It's so cold out there. I'm worried. We really don't have a choice." Another moment of silence. A quick glance in my direction.

"She's sitting right here. All right. Wait just a minute." Margot took the telephone away from her ear and gave it to me.

"Here. She wants to ask you something."

27

Evelyn Dixon

After a couple of hours driving up and down every street in town, looking for Liza in every likely spot, I decided it was time to change tactics and look in the unlikely spots. That's when I decided to call Margot and Abigail.

It was painful ground to cover, but when Abigail got on the line, I asked her several questions about Susan and Liza, their life together, and the circumstances surrounding Susan's death. It occurred to me that perhaps Liza had headed to the house she shared with her mother, or some other place that reminded her of her old life. It was just a hunch, but I had to try something and soon.

We didn't speak of it to Abigail, but Margot was in agreement with me. If we couldn't find Liza by morning, we would have to convince Abigail to file a missing person's report. Neither of us wanted to see Liza end up in front of a judge, but with the temperatures so bitter and Liza having disappeared with no money, it seemed we had no choice.

After we talked, Abigail put Margot back on the line.

"Margot? I'm going to head over to Stamford. Maybe Liza is trying to get back home. It's too far for her to have walked, but maybe she had some extra cash in her pocket Abigail didn't know about and caught a train. She might even have tried to hitchhike."

"Oh! I hope not! You never know who might have—" Probably remembering that Abigail was sitting right next to her, and not wanting to alarm her, Margot didn't finish the sentence. "Anyway, that sounds like a good idea. Now, what do you want us to do?"

"I guess you'd just better keep driving around town. Maybe she's still there and we just missed her. You should probably go back to Abigail's and check there. Maybe she calmed down and came home on her own."

"All right. Did you go by the shop? Maybe she went there."

"Good point. You have a key, don't you? Could you drive by and see if she's there? I'm going to start driving south."

"No problem. Abigail and I will head over there right now. I'll leave my phone on. Call if you find her."

"I will. You do the same. Thanks, Margot."

It had started snowing again, and the roads were terrible. It was well past midnight when I got to the address Abigail had given me, the townhouse that Liza had shared with her mother. I had been praying during the entire drive, asking God to let Liza be sitting on the doorstep of her old home, but she wasn't. Next I drove around the neighborhood, through the downtown area, past Liza's old school, and, finally, past the hospital where Abigail said Susan had died, but there was no sign of Liza.

Finally I checked in with the others and we decided to call it a night. Margot was going to drive back to Abigail's house and sleep there; we were all still hoping that Liza would turn up on her own. I was going to head back to my place, grab a couple of hours' sleep, and be back at Abigail's by seven-thirty. If Liza hadn't come home by then, we would have to consider calling the police.

Snow was falling even harder as I headed back to New Bern. Fat flakes drove toward my windshield with a constant, monotonous force that gave me the feeling of being trapped on a conveyor belt and surrounded by a continually rotating image of snowfall, running as fast as I could but getting nowhere. I was tired. It took all my concentration to focus on driving through the whirling snow. About ten miles from home, the storm subsided and I started thinking about Liza again. Where could she be?

I went over it all again in my mind, trying to think of every possible place she might have gone, but nothing new came to mind. Logically, I knew I'd done everything I could, and my exhausted body craved the comfort of my bed and a few hours' rest, but my mind was still uneasy.

It's just so frustrating, I thought. *I've spent half the night looking for Liza, driven across the whole state, and I've still reached a dead end.*

A dead end.

That was it! The New Bern exit was coming up on my right, but I stepped on the gas and flew past it, heading farther north toward Winthrop, a sleepy village just a few miles from the Massachusetts border. I'd never been there before, but if I could find Winthrop, I'd find Liza. I was sure of it.

The gates were open, but the wind had pillowed the snow into drifts. I didn't want to risk getting stuck on the unplowed road, so I pulled my car up in front of the cemetery and parked.

Getting out of the car, I saw that the snow wasn't quite as pristine as it had appeared on first glance. Someone had tromped a trail through the front gates of the cemetery and down the road, past the ancient, crumbling headstones so battered by wind, weather, and time that it was impossible anymore to know who was buried beneath them, only that those who lay sleeping there had once been "Beloved" of someone.

I followed the footsteps, first through a grove of evergreen trees shrouded with an icy blanket of snow that glittered in the first light of morning, into the newer sections of the cemetery, where those who had known this life in the nineteenth and twentieth centuries rested awaiting the clarion call to a new world, and finally to a small plot set apart, surrounded by a short wrought-iron fence, to a gray marble crypt that bore the name of Burgess.

Liza, dressed all in black, stood in front of the crypt with her head bowed. The snow muffled my steps. She hadn't heard me coming.

"Liza?" The fence gate squeaked as I opened it and stepped into the Burgess family plot.

Liza turned around. Her eyes were red from crying, and there were dark circles under them. She didn't ask how I'd found her.

"Sweetie, are you all right? You must be freezing. We were all so worried about you, especially Abigail."

"I'm sure." Her voice lacked the smug sarcasm Liza so often used when referring to her aunt, but there was a flatness, a hopelessness, to her tone that was even more disturbing. I came up alongside her and read the inscription on the stone.

SUSAN KATHERINE BURGESS
BORN—JUNE 26, 1950
DIED—SEPTEMBER 20, 2005

Susan's tomb did not declare that she was a beloved mother, but she was. It was written in her daughter's eyes. How she missed her. I put my arm around Liza's waist. Her eyes were fixed on the crypt, but I could feel her body relax a little as she leaned into me.

"Tell me about her."

"She was my mother," Liza said simply. "She took care of me. She made sure I did my homework and cleaned my room. She told me she loved me all the time, and sometimes, when I messed up, she yelled at me. Usually I deserved it, so I didn't mind that much. She worked really hard because I don't have a dad. I mean . . . I have a dad but he bailed out before I was born." Liza shrugged. "I don't even know who he is. Mom had to pay the bills all by herself, and sometimes she was really tired, but every Sunday was our day together. She always got up and made a big breakfast, pancakes or waffles or something, and then we'd do something together, something inexpensive like go to the park, or window shopping, or to some free concert she'd read about."

Liza smiled a little as she remembered. "Some of those concerts were pretty awful. Once, in February, when it was cold and miserable and there was just nothing to do, the only thing she found in the paper was an accordion recital at the Moose Lodge. Have you ever been to an accordion recital?" I shook my head. "Well, you aren't missing anything. And it just went on and on! Mom kept making this goofy face at me and kind of bouncing in her seat, you know, like she was about to break out and start doing the polka or something. I just about choked trying not to bust out laughing. That was Mom. She could make anything fun."

"She sounds like a wonderful mother. You were lucky."

"Yeah," Liza whispered. "I was lucky. For a while I was. She was the only person I could always count on. At least, I thought I could, and then . . ." A tear seeped from the corner of her eye as she stared at the tomb. "Now I've got nobody."

"Nobody like your mother. There will never be anyone like her, but you're not as alone as you think, Liza. There are a lot of people who care about you. Margot and I. And your Aunt Abigail. She cares about you, Liza, much more than you realize."

Liza's lips flattened into a thin line of disgust. "She doesn't care about me. She puts on a good show, but she doesn't care about anyone but herself."

"That's not true. And it's not fair." Finally looking up at me, Liza's eyes flashed, and she started to protest, but I wouldn't let her interrupt. "Listen to me. I know she hasn't always been the easiest person to live with, but she's changed. And the way she treated you and your mother was . . . well, it was despicable. I know that because she told me all about it and that's the word she used to describe her behavior."

Liza furrowed her brow, listening but not able to completely believe what I was saying. "She told you about Mom? And me? About why I'm living with her?"

I nodded. "She told me everything." A flush of color rose in Liza's cheeks. I suppose she was embarrassed that I knew about her run-in with the law.

"Liza, don't worry about that. I don't think any less of you. What you did wasn't right, but sometimes, when people are laboring under the weight of a terrible grief, when they're suffering and in pain, they do things they normally wouldn't. That doesn't mean they are bad people. Even if, sometimes, they act like they are." I paused for a moment before going on.

"You may not believe it, but Abigail really has changed. Truly. She realizes what she's done, and she's sorry. She wants another chance. She wants to make things right between you. She wants you to come home."

"She does? How nice for her!" Liza let out one bitter laugh. "Isn't that just her all over? Abigail wants another chance. Abigail wants me to come home. Abigail! Abigail! It's always about her! Abigail wants something, and everyone is supposed to run to get it for her. Not this time. Abigail's sorry? Well, *I'm* sorry, but I really don't give a damn what she wants! And I'm not going back!" She pulled away from me, turned, and started to walk toward the gate that separated the Burgess family plot from the others. I reached out and grabbed her arm.

"Liza! Wait a minute! This isn't about Abigail. It's about you. She's your only living relative, your only surviving link with your mother. Whether you know it or not, whether you like it or not, you need Abigail."

"No, I don't!" Liza shouted as she spun around to face me again.

Angry tears filled her eyes. "I don't need anybody. You can't trust people! They always let you down! They always leave!"

I nodded. "I know all about that. It's true, Liza. Sometimes the people who are supposed to love you most let you down. My husband left me. After twenty-eight years, he decided he didn't love me anymore. And it hurt, Liza. It hurt so badly that I wanted to close myself up in a box and hide. I didn't want to risk being hurt again. For months and months, I just cut myself off from everyone. I sat at my kitchen table and cried and felt sorry for myself. I stayed there for a long, long time, but eventually I realized I had to get up and move on. I had to! Even if it meant that I'd fail or get hurt again. Liza, everything that makes life worth living—finding love, finding our dreams, trying to make them come true—is risky, but we can't do any of those things alone. It took me a long time to realize that, but it's true." Liza's breath was coming out in short, frozen bursts, and her chest rose and fell heavily as she tried to calm herself. I took a step nearer.

"I think that's what Abigail is realizing. You might not believe it, but I think you should come home and find out for yourself. You and your Aunt Abigail are very much alike. And you're about to fall into the same pit that she's been trapped in for all these years. You're going to cut yourself off from everything that matters—from family, friends, and any possibility of finding love or happiness—all because you're afraid of getting hurt again. You say you hate Abigail, but you're about to make all the same mistakes she has. Come back with me, Liza. Listen to what Abigail has to say, not for her sake, but for your own."

"I don't know if I can," Liza whispered. "It hurts so much." She lifted her head and looked around the frozen graveyard at the rows and rows of stone markers surrounding us. "Sometimes I just want it to be over."

Her eyes were so weary, so sad. Eyes too old for such a young face. My heart broke for her.

"I know," I said. "There are times when I've felt that way too, like I just wanted to give up, but I'm glad I didn't. If I had, I'd never have met you. And that's something I wouldn't have wanted to miss. We're not meant to live alone, Liza. Everyone needs someone to care about and someone who cares about them. We need someone to share with, to laugh with, someone who'll yell at us when we mess up." I smiled and reached up to wipe a tear from Liza's frozen cheek. "We need someone to go to accordion concerts with."

Liza sniffed and tried to smile, but couldn't quite manage it. Her face folded in on itself, crumpled into an expression of despair. She turned her head and covered her face with one hand. "Evelyn, you're so nice to me. You're just like . . . You remind me so much of Mom."

"Thank you, Liza. That's probably about the nicest thing anyone has ever said to me."

"I don't know. Maybe you're right. Maybe I should go back and at least hear what Abigail has to say, but if I do, will you promise me something?" She turned back to look at me, her eyes earnestly examining my face for a pledge of honesty.

"I will if I can," I answered.

"Don't die, Evelyn. Don't! I like you so much. Really! I know I haven't been very nice to you the last few weeks. Ever since you told us about your surgery. I know it's not your fault, but sometimes I just can't stop myself. I get so mad at you. At Abigail. At everyone, I guess. I'm sorry, Evelyn. I'm so sorry."

"I know you are. I understand. We all do."

Liza swallowed hard and nodded, relieved. "Good," she said. "That's good. Okay." She squared her shoulders and took a step away, as if she was ready to go.

"Liza, I can't do it," I said. "I can't promise you I won't die. That's the kind of promise that children make. Promises that are really just wishes. You're not a child anymore, Liza. You know there are some things that no amount of wishing will prevent. This is one of them."

Liza's shoulders sagged again. She looked at me, then back to her mother's grave marker. "I know."

I reached out and took her hand. Even through the fabric of her black gloves, Liza's fingers felt like ice. I cupped my two hands around hers, trying to warm them. "Liza, I don't want to die. Your mother didn't want to die either. I'm sure that, more than anything in the world, she wanted to live so she could see what an amazing young woman you're turning out to be. But by the time she found out she was sick, it was just too late. It's not fair, but that's what happened. It wasn't anyone's fault. Sometimes bad things happen and there's just nothing we can do about it."

"I know," she repeated sadly, her voice and face registering a weary resignation. "I just don't understand why life is so unfair sometimes."

"Yeah. You and everyone else on the planet." I smiled. "But I can promise you one thing. I am going to try absolutely everything I can to beat the stupid cancer and live a long, full life. If I've got any say about it, I'm going to be around to make quilts to celebrate your wedding, and the births of your babies, and of your babies' babies. So don't you dare give up on me yet, Liza. I'm feisty!"

The corners of her mouth twitched into a small smile. "I believe it."

"Well, you'd better, because I mean it! I'm coming at this cancer with both barrels, or both boobs, or whatever it takes." Liza rolled her eyes at my terrible joke, but that was all right with me. At least she was smiling. "And I'll need all the help I can get. You know what I'm saying? I'm expecting you to be right there beside me the whole way."

"I will," she said and squeezed my hand.

"Promise?"

"Promise."

*   *   *

Back in the car, Liza turned the heater on full blast, then stripped off her gloves and held her frozen fingers directly in front of the heat vents. "That feels so good!"

"Here," I said, nodding toward her feet. "Pull off your boots too. I've got a stadium blanket in the back seat. Bring it up here, and you can wrap it around your feet." Liza complied and started pulling off her boots and then her socks. Her feet were bright pink with cold.

"Oh!" I clucked. "Will you look at that? You're lucky you didn't get frostbite. How did you get all the way up to Winthrop anyway? Please tell me you didn't walk all night through the snow. It has to be at least twenty miles."

Liza shook her head. "No. When I took off, I walked into town. I didn't really have a plan, but next thing I knew I was standing in front of the library. I went inside to get out of the cold and stayed until closing time. Then I decided I wanted to come up here, so I hitched a ride. A guy with a pickup truck stopped right away and gave me a ride."

Of course he did. Liza was gorgeous. Even dressed in her clunky boots and winter jacket, she had a face and figure that could stop traffic and obviously had. "Liza," I scolded. "You just got in some stranger's car? What were you thinking?"

She shrugged and said a little sheepishly, "I wasn't, I guess. It probably wasn't the brightest thing I ever did. The guy seemed real nice at first, gave me a ride as far as Brighton. Then said he was hungry and would I mind if we stopped at the diner to get something to eat, and I said sure. He wanted to buy my food, but I wouldn't let him. I had six dollars in my pocket."

"That was smart. You didn't want him to get any ideas. My mother always used to say there's no such thing as a free lunch, if you know what I mean." I gave Liza a sideways glance.

"Funny," Liza said and raised her eyebrows, "my mom used to say that same thing."

"Well, there you go. Great minds."

"Yeah, well, this jerk apparently hadn't heard about that particular rule. When we got back in the car, he started trying to get funny with me."

"Oh, Liza! He didn't! Are you all right?" She nodded. There was a trace of a smile on her lips. "What did you do?"

"Nothing much. Just picked his hand up off my thigh very slowly, held it real close to my lips, and then bit it as hard as I could. Of course, he dumped me out by the side of the road and I had to walk the last six miles, but it was worth it. You should have seen the look on his face." She was grinning from ear to ear. "Served him right, the big creep."

I put my hand over my mouth, trying not to laugh. I knew I should lecture her about the terrible chance she'd taken getting into that car. But instead, I replayed the picture in my mind, Liza sitting in the cab of the pickup, gently lifting the hand of that masher, giving him a sultry glance, and then ever so slowly and sensually taking his fingers and moving them toward her lips while the eyes of that pervert darted from the road to Liza's luscious lips, certain that this was his lucky day, and then—crunch! Liza was right. I'd have walked six miles through the snow to see the look on that guy's face.

I couldn't help myself. I started laughing, and Liza joined in.

She's going to be all right, I thought. *It won't be easy, but she's going to get through this thing.*

Just like her aunt, Liza Burgess was one tough cookie. And I loved her for it.

✑ 28 ✑

Abigail Burgess Wynne

Liza hardly looked at me when Evelyn brought her home. Not that I'd expected her face to suddenly light up at the sight of mine, but her muttered one-word responses to my questions about how she was, and where she'd gone, and how sorry I was, were not encouraging. I was glad she was home and safe, but what good would it do to have her back if we were just going to fall into the same old patterns of resentment and recrimination?

Completely ignoring me, she turned to Evelyn and said she was exhausted and was going to sleep for a while. Then she gave Evelyn a quick squeeze and trudged up the stairs.

It had been a long night for everyone. I walked Margot and Evelyn to the door and thanked them both for all they'd done. And I really meant it. If not for them . . . Well, I didn't even want to imagine how badly things could have turned out without their help. Of course, it still wasn't over. Liza was home, but the situation between us was far from resolved.

"Good-bye!" I stood at the door and waved to Margot as she climbed into her little car and drove off. "Thank you again!"

Evelyn was in the foyer, putting on her hat and gloves. "Good-bye, Abigail, and don't look so worried. Everything is going to turn out just fine."

"How do you know that?" I asked. "Did you see the look in her eyes when she came in here? She hates me."

"Give her some time, Abigail. She's cold and tired."

Certainly that was true, but I noticed that Evelyn hadn't made any attempt to deny my assertion. "It's no use," I said. "The girl simply hates me. That's all. There's no point in trying to make up with her. She's never going to forgive me. I know. She's a Burgess, and if there's one thing a Burgess knows how to do, it's hold a grudge."

"Yes, I've noticed that." Evelyn yawned. "Abigail, calm down. Really. Liza is exhausted. She needs some rest, and so do you. Go lie down for a while, and then, after you've both had some sleep and can think more clearly, you can talk to her."

Panic filled my breast. "Talk to her. But how? What am I supposed to say?"

Evelyn sighed and tipped her head to one side, her eyes weary. She put a gloved hand on my shoulder. "The truth, Abigail. Just tell her the truth. It's the only thing that ever works anyway."

I tried to take Evelyn's advice and take a nap, but two hours later I was still sleepless under the blue and yellow Grandmother's Fan quilt Evelyn had given me for Christmas. Tell the truth, Evelyn had said, but what was the truth? I had spent so many years of my life, decades, trying not to think about the past, that I wasn't even sure how to explain it to myself anymore, let alone to Liza. Liza—the collateral damage in a war between two sisters who, once upon a time, had been inseparable. When I had been Liza's age, more than forty years ago, I could never have imagined that anything in the world could have come between my sister and me. Where had it all begun? With Susan? With David? No. It started before that. Long before.

For the first six years of my life, I was an only child, a situation that suited me perfectly at the time.

But on a summer day in 1950, my father pulled up in front of my grandmother Alice's house in Winthrop, jumped out of the Packard and ran around the passenger side to open the door for Mother, and then took the pink flannel bundle from her arms, and my world changed forever. I ran down the walkway toward my beloved father, thrilled to see him, thinking only of him. But as I ran near, pigtails flying and arms open wide, Father got down on one knee and pulled back a corner of the pink flannel.

"Hey, Kitten! Look here! This is your new baby sister. Susan. What do you think?"

I thought she was the most beautiful baby in the whole world, and from that day forward, I'd have come to blows with anyone who said differently. Not that anyone would have said such a thing. Susan was, in fact, a beautiful child, and she grew into a beautiful woman. I adored her. We adored each other. Everyone in Winthrop used to comment about it, telling my mother they'd never seen more devoted sisters. And it was true. No big sister could have been more committed to her baby sister than I was. I'd have done anything to protect her, and did. But as we got older, that job became harder.

My father was a handsome man, witty, charming, and something of a dandy. Even at home, I never saw him dressed in anything less formal than a three-piece suit and tie. He'd met my mother, who was just seventeen at the time, at a dance. Four weeks later, they were married. Father was a broker on Wall Street, but he insisted that Manhattan was no place to raise a family, so, as soon as Mother became pregnant, Father moved her out to Winthrop to live in his family home with Grandmother Alice. Father kept a little apartment in the city and came out to see his young family on weekends. That was how we grew up, and, when I was younger, I thought nothing of it. While I adored my father and would have loved having him at home during the week, I was very proud of the glamorous life he led in New York.

My friend's fathers only worked at boring jobs in boring Winthrop. They and their families lived in poky little houses and drove even pokier old cars, but every two years Father drove up in a brand-new Packard, and, even though Mother complained about having to share it with Grandmother Alice, we lived in the biggest, most beautiful house in town. My friends' fathers came home every night cranky and tired from the long workday. But every Friday night, my father would drive up from New York, bearing smiles and presents and eager to hear every little thing that had happened to us while he'd been gone. It was like Christmas every weekend. Some of my friends' parents barely spoke to each other. Their parents were about the same age as mine, but somehow they seemed decades older. Mother and Father were the handsomest couple you'd ever hope to see. Father took Mother out to supper every Saturday night. Susan and I didn't like having to stay home with Grandmother Alice on those nights, but when mother floated downstairs, smelling of White Shoulders cologne and wearing a new dress Father had bought for her at Bergdorf's, and took Father's arm as he escorted her out the door, I was entranced. When I grew up, I planned on marrying a man just like my father. We were the happiest family in town.

I believed that for a long time.

I can't remember when I first heard the embarrassing rumors about my father and what he did all week in town, or the angry, hissed conversations between Mother and Father that abruptly stopped whenever I'd enter the room, or began noticing the red rims around Mother's eyes on those increasingly frequent Friday afternoons when Father would telephone to say he was swamped with work and couldn't come out that weekend. The only thing I know for certain is that, as the years passed, my beautiful and bright princess of a mother became a bitter and complaining nag. The second Father came in the door, she would start in, quizzing him about what he'd done all week, complaining about how he neglected us, demanding an explanation of how he spent the hours away from her. After a few minutes, Father would start to shout at her, saying that nothing he ever did was enough and he didn't know why he'd bothered to come home at all. Sometimes he would become so angry that he would get in the car, drive to the city, and not return to Winthrop for weeks at a time.

I blamed my mother. It was her complaining and criticism that was keeping Father away. That's what I believed, and that's what I told Susan, that Father was a good man, a wonderful man, and that, if we wanted him to come home, we had to be very good too and never complain. Father worked very hard all week on Wall Street, I told her. When he did come home, we mustn't make him feel badly or ask him why he hadn't come sooner. We mustn't bother him by asking questions about the nasty things other children whispered at school. None of it was true. Those other children were just jealous of our fine house and our pretty cars and our handsome parents. We shouldn't bother Father with such things; if we did, he might turn around and leave again.

"No one wants to be around someone who is sad or complaining, Susan. People like to be around people who are happy," I instructed my six-year-old sister. "Even if you feel sad inside, just smile and tell Father how happy you are to see him. Then he will want to stay here with us." I learned at a very young age to keep my true thoughts and feelings to myself.

When I was fifteen and Susan was nine, Father had a heart attack and died. In the aftermath of his death and the financial ruin that followed, I finally had to face the truth about our family. My father had been leading a double life for years, keeping his family tucked up in a corner of rural Connecticut, playing happy family on the weekends, while, during the week in Manhattan, he led the life of a playboy bachelor, carrying on with a number of women, spending lavishly in pursuit of them, and, when he ran out of his own money, borrowing more to maintain his sumptuous lifestyle. He died penniless and in debt. For the first time in her life, Mother had to work outside our home. She got a receptionist position that paid enough to cover our basic expenses, but barely. Thank heaven our home in Winthrop was owned by Grandmother Alice. She died shortly after Father and left the house to Mother. If not for that, we'd probably have been put out on the street.

Truthfully, I don't know when Father's dalliances began; perhaps my parents' marriage had been a sham from the very first. But, at the time, I continued to lay the blame for the disintegration of our family at Mother's feet. No matter what he had done, Father was my hero. I was certain that, in the beginning at least, we were that perfect family of my memory and that my mother's suspicious and complaining nature was the cause of all our problems. Maybe it was. Maybe it wasn't. I don't know. But one thing I do know for sure, after Father died and left us penniless and everyone in town knew why, Mother's negative nature became worse and she lived the rest of her life as an embittered, angry woman. I hated being around her, and I promised myself that, no matter what, I would never be like my mother.

Eventually, I just couldn't bear living at home anymore, enduring Mother's daily barrage of acrimony and resentment. I applied to New York University, was admitted on a scholarship, and escaped to the city. I felt guilty about leaving Susan, but came home to see her nearly every weekend, neatly stepping into Father's old schedule.

Manhattan was like a breath of fresh air after life in Winthrop. I felt so alive and independent in the city, so completely free. It was the early sixties, and a good part of the nation, especially the younger part, was likewise throwing off the perceived shackles of their parents' expectations. Freedom was the mantra of the decade—free speech, free living, free love. To a young girl recently arrived from rural New England, it was an exhilarating time to be alive.

Not too long after moving into the tiny apartment I shared with three other girls, I met David Collier. David was six years my senior, a sculptor. I fell in love with him almost immediately. With his deep brown eyes and broad shoulders, David looked a lot like my father, but he wasn't quite like anyone I'd ever met. He was free-spirited, expressive, and always so happy and carefree. I adored him. When he asked if I wanted to move in with him, I threw my arms around him and nearly smothered him with kisses.

"Whoa!" he said with a laugh. "I guess that must be a yes."

"Oh yes! Yes, David! Can we bring my things over tonight?"

He nodded. "Sure. If that's what you want, Abbie. But listen," he said, his laughing eyes growing serious for a moment, "you need to understand something. I love you, Abbie. You make me so happy. There is no one I'd rather be with than you, but I don't plan on ever getting married. I don't believe in it. Marriage is just a lot of bull invented by society and religions, just one more way they try to control us. A piece of paper couldn't make me love you any more than I do right now. Besides, it wouldn't be fair to ask you to be pinned down to just one man." The smile returned to his face. "I mean, you might wake up one day and decide you couldn't stand me anymore."

"Oh, no, David! That would never, ever happen! I'll love you till the day I die."

David nodded. "I feel the same way, Abbie. But still, you have to understand, I'm never going to get married."

"Yes, David. I understand," I said and kissed him again.

But deep in my heart, I didn't suppose he really meant it. I was sure that once he saw how much I loved him, how happy I made him, he'd surely change his mind. It might take a while, but that was all right. All that mattered to me at that moment was David. I needed him and would have agreed to anything he proposed just to keep him near.

For almost four years, we lived together in David's artist's loft, behaving as man and wife in every sense except legally. I went to class during the day while David worked in his studio, and then scurried home in the evenings to make our dinner. At night we'd go to poetry readings in the Village, or take walks in the park, or meet up with some of David's artist friends. On Friday nights, we'd drive David's beat-up station wagon to Connecticut and spend the weekend with Mother and Susan. Susan was crazy about David. She used to watch at the window, waiting for our arrival, just like I had waited for Father when I was a little girl. Then she'd run out the front door to greet us. Mother liked him too. Even when she was in one of her moods, David was always able to get a smile out of her.

Of course, I never told Mother that David and I were living together, but I'm sure she suspected. One Sunday morning, while David and Susan were out in the garden picking strawberries for our breakfast, Mother, clearly embarrassed, tried to talk to me about "the facts of life." I laughed and assured her that it wasn't necessary, that I knew all I needed to know in that regard. Mother looked relieved, and that was the end of that.

But perhaps I should have let her give me that talk after all. Near the end of my senior year at NYU, I discovered that I was pregnant. I was terrified. When I finally worked up the courage to tell David, I dissolved into tears and begged him not to leave me. At first, he looked stunned, but he quickly recovered and crossed the room to take me into his arms.

"It's all right, Abbie. Don't worry, baby. Everything will be all right."

I began sobbing even harder, this time with relief. Everything was going to be all right. David wasn't angry. I was pregnant, and he was telling me it was all right! For a moment, the terror in my breast gave way to elation. I was going to have David's baby!

But my joy was short-lived.

"Don't worry," David whispered into my hair as he held me. "It will be all right. I've got a friend who knows a doctor who can take care of it. No one will ever have to know. Everything will be fine. I'll be right beside you the whole time."

And I did it. Even though I wanted my baby. Even though I knew it was wrong. I did what David wanted because I couldn't bear the idea of living without David and I knew that if I had the baby, he would leave me. So I did it. Late at night, after business hours, David drove me to the doctor's office, and I walked up the stairs to a cold, white examining room and had an illegal abortion.

I have never told anyone about this before. Don't ask me why I did it. I have no good answer for that. I will not try to make excuses for what I did, because it was inexcusable. Only know that however harshly you may judge me, it cannot be as harshly as I judge myself. I have regretted it every day of my life.

That night, David supported me as, weak and in terrible pain, I slowly climbed back down the stairs. He helped me into the station wagon and took me home. The doctor said I would be fine in a day or two, but it took much longer for my body to heal. I was never again able to get pregnant. Healing my spirits took even longer. For weeks that stretched into months, I felt sad and depressed. Sometimes I would start to cry for no reason at all. But, of course, I hid all this from David. As I knew only too well, there were two things he would not tolerate, self-pity and commitment, so I made sure not to bother him with either. After all that had happened, I still couldn't bear the thought of losing him.

But in the end, none of that mattered.

One day, David came home and said he'd received a grant to study sculpture in Rome. At first I was excited, thinking he meant to bring me with him, but before long I realized that he was going alone. He said that the grant was a small one, not enough to support us both, and that Rome was expensive. The place he was going to live, he said, was small and filthy, and I would hate it. I told him I didn't care, that I would get a job to help with expenses, but he wouldn't be swayed. He was going to Rome alone.

"It's just for a year, baby. Then I'll be back. Why don't you move out to Connecticut with your mother and Susan for a while? You know how much Susan misses you. Think how great it would be for you to be able to spend some time with her. Especially now. She'll be off to college soon, and you'll never have another chance like this." He leaned over and kissed me on the forehead.

"It'll be great. A year will fly by so fast you won't believe it. This is my big break. This will make my reputation, and I'll finally be able to make a decent living as an artist! When I get back, I'll come out to Connecticut, and we can talk about our future."

And because I wanted to believe him and knew that if I complained he'd never come back, I did what he wanted me to.

Three weeks later, we loaded the station wagon with the last of my things from our now-empty loft, and David drove me to Winthrop. He left the car for me, so, after we unpacked it, I drove him to the train station so he could go back to New York and catch a cab to the airport. Traffic was terrible. When we arrived at the station, the train was getting ready to leave. David had to run and left without kissing me good-bye.

It would be two years before I saw him again.

Other than the pleasure of being reunited with my little sister, living at home was just as bad as I'd thought it would be. Mother was as impossible as ever, disapproving of everything and everyone. She was particularly vocal in her criticism of me, frequently decrying my stupidity at letting David leave the country without extracting a ring from him and making a lot of speeches about not buying cows when milk was free.

"How could you be so foolish, letting him just dump you off on my doorstep and then breezing off to Europe? And what are you supposed to do now? You're a beautiful girl, Abigail, but you're nearly twenty-three years old! Beauty is fleeting. Believe me, I know what I'm talking about," she said bitterly. "The second the flower begins to fade, they're off to greener pastures. I don't care what these women's libbers say, it's still a man's world. Marriage is the only protection a woman has. What if he doesn't come back—"

"He *is* coming back! I've told you that a thousand times."

Mother smirked. "So you say, but what if he doesn't? I hope you don't expect me to support you, because I can't do it. Slaving away day after day in that office for a measly three hundred and twenty dollars a month," she muttered. "When I think about your father and all the thousands he frittered away on cheap floozies, leaving us all with a single—"

"Stop it, Mother. I don't want to hear it anymore. And I don't expect you to support me. I'm going to get a job."

And I did. I had graduated from NYU with a BA in Humanities and a minor in Art History, which was perfect for the life I'd planned on living in Manhattan, running a gallery filled with David's sculptures. However, in Winthrop, the job market for someone with my education was nonexistent, not that it was much better anywhere in Connecticut. Still, I decided to try my luck in New Bern, and, that day at least, I was lucky.

Resume in hand and wearing the darling Mary Quant dress—a black sleeveless bodice with white pleated skirt and stand-up collar, that David bought me as a going-away present (or perhaps it was intended as more of a consolation prize)—I marched into the New Bern Art Museum to ask for a job. As luck would have it, there was a board of trustees meeting going on that day. Forty-three-year-old Wolcott Wynne III was on the board. He saw me come in, pulled the museum director aside, and, next thing I knew, I had a new job . . . and a new admirer.

Woolley asked me out to dinner that day, and when I refused, he came back to the museum every day for nearly three weeks to make the same invitation. Eventually, I relented. Woolley was a nice man, if a little arrogant, good looking, athletic, and very persistent. He took me to expensive dinners, the theater, sent flowers, brought me gifts, and almost from the first made his intentions very clear: he wanted to make me his wife. I liked Woolley. He was fun to be with, and I was happy to have him squire me about, but I knew I could never love him. My heart still belonged to David. I told Woolley so, but that didn't seem to discourage him. Every time I told him that David was coming back, he'd just nod slowly and make this "We'll see" face. It was very irritating.

David wrote, regularly at first, then with less frequency. Sometimes, when weeks had gone by with no word from him, I'd get angry and tell myself that I was going to end it and move on with my life. But about the time I did, a letter would arrive full of apologies, explanations, and the endearments I longed to hear, and I would forgive him yet again.

As the end of his year of study approached, David wrote and told me that he had been asked to stay on at the studio for a second year and that it was too good an opportunity to pass up. I tore up his letter and sat down to write one of my own, telling David exactly what I thought of him and his broken promises, but I lost my nerve. I threw the letter away and wrote another, saying that I was happy for him and not to worry about me. For spite, I threw in a couple of lines about my new friend, Woolley, and what a good time we'd had when he'd taken me into the city to see George Feyer at the Café Carlyle. I hoped that hearing about my adventures with Woolley, a wealthy, powerful man who took me to elegant places David could never dream of affording, would make him jealous and he would change his mind and come home, but it didn't work. He just wrote back, saying that he was glad I wasn't too lonely.

And as all this was going on, Woolley kept pursuing me. One

Saturday morning just a couple of weeks before David was to return, Woolley showed up on our doorstep with three dozen yellow roses and a three-carat diamond engagement ring. Right in front of Mother and Susan, he got on his knees and proposed again, and, again, I turned him down. I was really angry with him for pulling that particular stunt. He knew that the minute he left, Mother would be all over me, pressuring me to reconsider.

"Abigail, have you lost your mind!" she screamed. "You're going to give up the chance of a lifetime, on the barest hope that this time David won't run off and leave you whenever he gets a whim? You can't trust that man, Abbie! I know what I'm talking about. You can't trust anyone in this world. Even the people who say they love you will let you down. But security? Social position? Money in the bank? Those are things no one can take from you."

"Mother, I don't love Woolley Wynne, and I'm not going to marry him!"

"Love," she snarled. "What did that ever get anyone besides a broken heart? You must be the stupidest, most selfish girl on the face of God's earth. Have you ever considered what it would mean to me or to your sister if you accepted Woolley? Forget me and the fact that I've been working my fingers to the bone to support this family for years; think what this could mean for Susan! She could go to a good college, have a chance at life! But no, all you can think of is yourself and that good-for-nothing David." She threw up her hands in disgust. "Listen to me, Abigail, and save yourself some heartache. David doesn't love you. If he did, he'd have asked you to marry him a long time ago."

That might have been one of the only intelligent things my mother ever said to me, but it didn't matter. All I cared about was that David was coming home, and somehow, when he did, I was sure everything would be all right. And for a while, it was.

David returned to the States in June, just in time to attend Susan's high-school graduation. He didn't have a dime left of his grant money, so I begged Mother to let him stay with us for a while, until I could save up enough money at my museum job so we could get an apartment in the city. Mother agreed, but reluctantly. Though in the old days, before she'd turned on him, Mother had been happy to let David stay in the guest room, she now insisted that he had to sleep in the garden shed.

"I won't have you two cavorting around the house doing God knows what in front of your sister," Mother said. "I don't want Susan getting any crazy ideas in her head. Not like you did," she said, giving me a look meant to convey her complete disappointment in me.

I was ready to lash into her, but David cut in before I could say anything. He thanked her profusely and proposed that he spend the summer painting the house for her, by way of repaying Mother for her kindness. Mother accepted his offer—the house was in desperate need of painting—but I could see she wasn't won over.

One day in July, a thunderstorm blew out the power at the museum and we closed early. I went right home, thinking it would be nice to have dinner ready when Mother got home from work, hoping that would put her in a better mood. I ran into the house, dripping wet from the rain, and called for Susan, but she didn't answer. I supposed she'd gone to a friend's house. Thinking what luck it was that David and I were home alone a good three hours before Mother was due, I grabbed a bottle of wine and two glasses from the refrigerator and ran out to the garden shed to find David.

He was already undressed, lying in the narrow iron bedstead that he and I had found in the attic and repainted. Susan was with him.

There were tears, and scenes, and dramas that I don't care to replay anymore. What's the point? At the end of it, I drove away in David's decrepit station wagon, found Woolley at his office, and told him that I did not love him and didn't expect I ever would, but that if he still wanted me, I would marry him.

Two weeks later, I did. Woolley wanted a church wedding, but at my insistence we eloped to Reno. I wanted to be married in private, without my family.

I never slept another night at our house in Winthrop. When I saw my mother, I would meet her somewhere else because I didn't want to be reminded of what had happened there.

Over my mother's protests, Susan moved in with David, just as I had. I suppose she loved him, just as I had. Poor thing. She deserved my pity far more than my wrath, but I couldn't see that at the time.

I didn't see or speak to Susan for the next seventeen years, not until Mother died. David, thank heaven, had had the good taste to stay away from the funeral, but Susan came. It was awkward, but we were civil to one another. And oddly, in spite of all that had gone on before, it was almost a relief to see her again. But I was worried about her. She was only thirty-four, but she looked old and tired. I kept thinking about her.

A month later, I worked up the nerve to call her on the telephone, with the excuse of telling her that mother had left her a small bequest and asking where I should have the money wired. In truth, there was no bequest. At the funeral, I had noticed Susan's worn-out shoes and threadbare coat. I guessed that David wasn't doing any better job of providing for my sister than he had for me. When I called to tell her about the check, her tearful reaction of gratitude confirmed my suspicions; Susan was desperately in need of money. I wasn't entirely ready to forgive her, but I couldn't bear the idea of her being hungry or out on the street because she didn't have enough to pay the rent.

After that, Susan and I talked on the telephone on three occasions, and each time it was a little less awkward. I believe that, given time, we would have eventually reconciled, but then something happened. . . .

Susan and David lived together for seventeen years. Then, just as I had, Susan became pregnant. But unlike me, she refused to abort her baby, and when she refused, David walked out.

And after that, I never spoke to her again. You see, in the end it wasn't a man or her betrayal that came between us. It was me—my shame, my pride, and my terrible envy. Eventually, I would have forgiven her for taking David from me, but I could never forgive her for finding the courage that I lacked and, in doing so, getting the one thing I so longed for, the thing that all of Woolley Wynne's millions could not buy for me—real love.

"And that was what you were to her," I whispered, trying to keep my voice steady and failing. "You were the love of her life. I envied her so. It seemed that everything I had wanted in life, Susan had taken from me. I see now that it wasn't true. I made my own choices, if only by refusing to choose or to stand up and say no when I had the chance. There is so much I'd do differently. If only . . ." I tried to stop and steady myself, but it was no good. I could not stem the tide of tears.

"If only I had realized it sooner. Everything could have been so different for all of us. I'm sorry. Dear God. Liza, I'm so, so sorry. It's my fault. I know you can never forgive me. It's all my fault."

While I had talked, Liza sat silent and small in one of the big wingback chairs that flanked the library fireplace. As she listened, she seemed to shrink into herself, drawing her arms closer into her body, curving her back into the chair cushions as if trying to put as much physical distance between us as possible. Silent tears streamed down her cheeks as she heard, for the first time, the sad and secret tale of her own ancestry.

Now she got up from the chair and walked across the room to the sofa where I was sitting, weeping. I felt a tentative touch on my shoulder and heard Liza's hoarse voice.

"I have to, Aunt Abigail. I don't want to forgive any of you, not you, or Mom, or that lying scuzzball that fathered me either, but somehow I have to. We already know how things will turn out if I don't. This has been going on for too long, through too many generations of this family. I don't want to live like this anymore. I've got to forgive you, Aunt Abigail. I do. You forgive me too, okay? We're all we have left."

✤ 29 ✤

Evelyn Dixon

"Mom?" Garrett's face looked anxious as he leaned over me. "Mom? How are you feeling?"

"Great."

It was a lie. Everything hurt: my head, my arms, and the flattened expanse on my chest, the place where my breasts used to be.

"Honey, could you get me some water? I'm so thirsty."

"Sure." He took the plastic cup from the nightstand and went to the sink to fill it.

"Your lips are all chapped." Blinking, I opened my eyes and saw Margot, flanked by Abigail, Liza, and Charlie. Margot dug into her handbag, pulled out a tube of lip balm, and used a finger to rub the balm on my cracked lips.

"There. I bet that feels better."

I nodded and then took a sip from the straw Garrett held to my lips. The water tasted good.

"The doctor was here a little while ago," Garrett said, "but you were still asleep. She said everything went fine. She has to wait for the final lab reports, but she thinks they got everything this time."

I looked down at my flat chest. "Well, that's good. If she has to go in again, I'll be the only woman I know who has to buy bras size triple A inverted." I tried to smile, but it wasn't easy.

As much as I had tried to prepare myself for this moment, for waking up and seeing myself without breasts for the first time, it was still a shock. I felt like I had fallen asleep and woken up to find myself inhabiting a different body. My shape, my weight, the very mass and volume of my being had changed. I didn't recognize myself anymore. I was trying my best to put up a brave front, but it was too hard. Everything was too painful. A tear rolled down my cheek.

"Look at me," I whispered. "What did they do to me?"

Garrett swallowed hard and squeezed my hand. He didn't know how to answer me. Abigail came to his rescue.

She moved to the side of the bed and leaned down toward me. "It's all right, Evelyn. Everything is going to be all right soon. You're tired, dear, and you're hurting. It's all right to cry."

Liza nodded, and her eyes were solemn. "Yeah. Abigail's right. You can cry if you want to." She took my other hand and held it tenderly. "Just remember that it's going to be worth it. You're going to get well. After all," she said. "We've got a deal."

"We do," I said and swallowed back my tears. "I'll try my best to keep up my end of the bargain."

Liza smiled at me, then looked up and smiled at Garrett, who was standing on the opposite side of the bed, still holding my other hand.

"Well, in that case," Charlie said, trying hard to sound cheery, which was what we were all trying to do, trying to sound pleasant and ordinary, as if we were actors carefully repeating lines in an overrehearsed, overwritten script. It wasn't their fault. This is what people do when they are faced with an awkward situation; they try to pretend that everything is perfectly, wonderfully normal, which, of course, makes everything more awkward and abnormal than it was in the first place. "I think it's time for the presents, don't you?"

Everyone murmured agreement. Charlie went over to the windowsill, opened up a giant shopping bag that was sitting on the ledge, and pulled out a white bakery box.

"These are my famous butterscotch macadamia-nut cookies. I made a double batch so you'll have some for yourself and some for visitors."

"What do you think I'm going to be doing while I'm in here, having tea parties?"

He made a face. "No, of course not. But you're going to have guests. You should have something to serve. I left off another box at the nurses' station—a bit of a bribe," he said with a wink. "Just to make sure they take proper care of you. I know what a difficult patient you can be."

"Thank you, Charlie. That was sweet of you."

He bobbed his head, uncomfortable as always in the face of praise. "And I'll be bringing in your meals too, while you're here. I brought a chicken soup for your lunch, and I'll be back with poached salmon for dinner. Unless you'd rather have the lamb?"

"Charlie, you don't have to do that. Really. Besides, if I eat your food for every meal, they'll have to cart me out of here in a wheelbarrow. I'm fat enough as it is."

"Don't be silly," he said. "You look beautiful. If anything, you're too thin. We Irish prefer women with a little meat on their bones. Oh!" he exclaimed before I could protest further. "And one more thing. I almost forgot."

He reached into the bottom of the shopping bag and pulled out another brown paper bag with a piece of red string tied around the neck in a bow. "Didn't have time to wrap it properly," he apologized. "But here. Go ahead and open it."

I pulled on the red string, reached inside the bag, and pulled out an enormous box of crayons. "One hundred and twenty! I didn't even know they came in boxes that big! I love it. How'd you know?"

Charlie grinned broadly. "And I brought you a big pad of graph paper to go with it. Thought maybe you'd want to work on a few quilt designs while you're laid up."

I smiled, and this time it was genuine. "Thanks, Charlie. This is perfect. You're perfect. You cook. You bake. And you know exactly the right present to bring. You're the best friend a girl could hope to have," I said.

Still smiling, Charlie nodded again, but there was a flash in his eyes, a look of disappointment that I didn't quite understand, but, then again, it was so brief I might have imagined it.

"And I brought you those," Garrett said, indicating the vase of bright Gerbera daisies that was sitting on the nightstand. "Thought they'd brighten up the place a little."

"Thank you, sweetheart. They do." He leaned down and gave me a peck on the cheek.

"And this," Margot said, holding out a box wrapped in violet-covered paper with a sage green bow, "is from the three of us."

"It's heavy. What is it?"

"Open it and find out."

Usually, I'm careful about how I open gifts, not because I save the paper, but when someone goes to the trouble to wrap a package, it seems to me that you ought to treat it with respect. But I was so weak, and my arms were so sore, that I couldn't keep my hands from shaking. I accidentally ripped the edge of the paper.

"That's all right," Liza said. "Just open it. Do you want some help?"

I nodded, and together we tore the paper off the box. Liza pulled off the lid. When she did, my hand instinctively rose to my mouth to cover my surprise. "Oh!" I breathed. "It's lovely! Oh, girls! I don't know what to say. It's just the most beautiful quilt I've ever seen in my life. And you made it? The three of you?"

All three were beaming, but Abigail spoke first. "It was Margot's idea, but we all worked on it together. We had a few secret circle meetings without you, but we didn't think you'd mind."

"No," I said. "Not at all."

It was a beautiful quilt. Knowing how I love strong colors, they'd chosen a palette of bright greens and vibrant pinks with surprising accents of a white and black fabric that enhanced the depth and richness of the colors. Such happy colors. The design was bold, using a traditional theme—hearts—but giving it a fresh, modern interpretation. The theme blocks were patchworked hearts, strippieced in varying shades and patterns of pink and then outlined, first in spring green and then again in the black fabric. There were eight complete hearts in all, scattered over the pieced green backing in an unpredictable pattern. Most interesting of all, there were several half-heart blocks, again sprinkled around the backing at irregular intervals, some isolated and lonely, floating in a field of green, others set near but not quite next to another half-heart, slightly off center, as if the broken halves were moving toward each other in varying stages of becoming whole again.

I traced the stitching on one of the hearts with my finger. "It's just so incredibly beautiful. Where did you find the pattern? I don't think I've ever seen it before."

"You haven't," Margot confirmed. "Liza was the designer. Isn't it gorgeous!"

Liza ducked her head modestly. "It's just something I drew up one day," she said. "You can't call me a designer; more of a doodler."

"Well, of course you can," Abigail said a little impatiently. "You sat down, thought of a theme, then took up your pencil and created a design that expressed what you were trying to say. That's what a designer does. Don't be so silly. There's nothing that irritates me as much as false humility."

Liza turned slightly and made a face. "Whatever," she said with a shrug.

"Anyway, I was thinking about us, you know, about our quilting circle and what it is that we all have in common. That's how I came up with the idea. In one way or another, we've all had our hearts broken. But at the same time, we've helped each other get through it. It's not like everything is better yet. We've still got problems to work through, but slowly we're helping each other heal. You know what I mean?"

"Yeah," I said quietly. "I know what you mean."

Realizing that everyone in the room, including Garrett, had been listening as she described the inspiration behind her design, Liza blushed. "Well. That was the idea anyway. I decided to call it Broken Hearts Mending."

"I love it," I said sincerely, looking at all three of my friends. "Besides your friendship, this is absolutely the nicest gift I've ever received. Thank you all so much."

There was a warm, almost a burning feeling in my chest, but it wasn't caused by my incision; it was the warmth of gratitude. Liza had hit the nail on the head. We'd all had our hearts broken, but together, with each other's help and support, we were on the road to recovery, each in our own way and at our own pace. I felt truly blessed to have found such friends at the time in life when I most needed them.

My poor, ravaged body was too sore for hugs, so I reached out and clasped my friends' hands. "You're the best," I said.

The door to my room swung open, and a nurse came in carrying the biggest, most ostentatious, and, quite frankly, ugliest bouquet of flowers I had ever seen in my life—there were three shades of pink carnations, at least a dozen blood red roses, grouped with some enormous orange lilies, all topped off with one large, garish bird of paradise. The moment I saw them, I knew who'd sent them.

I turned to Garrett. "How did Mary Dell find out I was in the hospital? I told you I didn't want to worry her, not when she's getting ready to shoot her first television show."

"Don't blame me," he said, holding up his hands in surrender.

"She called and started asking all these questions, and, well . . . it just sort of slipped out. Sorry." The nurse put the bouquet on the windowsill. It was so big that it blocked out the light. "Wow. Until this minute, I never realized flowers could be ugly."

I sighed and shook my head. "Howard must have been too busy to go to the florist with her," I said. "She definitely picked these out herself."

The nurse stood back from the flowers with her hands on her hips. "Well, I've never seen anything quite like them, that's for sure." She turned to look at me. "How are you feeling? Do you want some more pain medication?"

With everyone standing there, I didn't like admitting how much I hurt, but I definitely needed something to ease it. "Maybe that would be a good idea."

"As soon as I take your vitals and check the dressings, I'll get you another pill. Then you can get some sleep, all right?" I nodded gratefully. I was so tired.

The nurse smiled sympathetically and then addressed the group. "Folks, I'm afraid I'm going to shoo you out of here for a while. Ms. Dixon needs to rest right now."

Charlie clapped his hands together like a teacher trying to get the attention of a group of unruly fourth graders. "All right, gang. You heard Nurse Ratched. Clear out." The nurse shot him a look, but he gave her a wink. "Now, don't be like that. I'm the one who baked those delicious cookies and left them at the nurses' station."

"Trying to bribe the hospital staff?" she asked.

"Absolutely."

"It's working," she deadpanned. "Now take your own advice. Clear out and let this lady get some rest."

She turned to me again. "Is he always like this?"

"Yes."

"Gee, that's too bad. At least he can bake."

Charlie grinned and started shooing everyone out the door. They all filed by the bed to say a quick good-bye. "Come on. Let's go. Come on over to the Grill, and I'll buy you all lunch."

Garrett was the last to leave. " 'Bye, Mom. I'll come back tonight. Think you'll feel up to having a visitor by then? You look a little tired."

"I'm sure I'll be fine after I get a few hours of rest," I assured him. "It was so good to have everybody here, especially you, sweetheart. But I really do need to get some sleep now. I didn't realize having visitors could be so exhausting."

"It's all right, Mom. Don't worry. Just rest and I'll be back later. I love you."

"I love you too, Garrett."

Garrett walked toward the door while the nurse put a blood-pressure cuff on my arm. I closed my eyes, suddenly feeling completely drained.

I heard the door swing open as Garrett started to leave and then the whisper of a familiar but unexpected voice.

"Hey, Garrett. How's your mom? Is she asleep?"

"Dad? What are you doing here?"

My eyes flew open. Rob stood at the foot of my bed holding a dozen red roses.

30

Abigail Burgess Wynne

Though Evelyn was still in the hospital, we decided to hold the quilt-circle meeting as usual on Friday night. We had quite a bit of work to do. The three quilts that Cobbled Court was contributing to the Quilt Pink project had to be bound so they could be sent off to the auction by the deadline.

The three of us had worked in the shop all day, Margot and I waiting on customers while Liza and Garrett took inventory. At closing time, Garrett took his laptop computer and went upstairs to Evelyn's apartment. Liza said he was working on some new ideas for the Web site. It's not every young man that would leave a lucrative career on the other side of the country to come home and take care of his ailing mother. I liked Garrett. Too bad his father was such a louse.

After we locked up, we reconciled the register. Unfortunately, that didn't take long. With Evelyn in the hospital and unable to teach any classes, sales had been very weak. Once everything was in order, Margot went into the break room and took a tray of sandwiches she'd made out of the refrigerator, while I sliced up a plate of oranges and Liza popped a bag of popcorn in the microwave and poured some diet cola into three glasses. That was dinner.

We carried everything into the classroom and sat down to sew the quilt bindings, using the blind stitch that Evelyn had taught us so that, when the quilts were completed, it would be all but impossible to see the threads that joined the binding to the quilt edge. We arranged our chairs in a circle so we could talk while we worked. There was certainly a lot to talk about.

"Honestly," I said. "I don't know how he found the nerve. Waltzing into Evelyn's hospital room with flowers in hand after he's taken up with another woman and then divorced poor Evelyn. I never heard of such bad taste. The man is utterly déclassé."

Liza frowned at me and then bent back over her sewing. "Abigail, not so loud. He's staying right upstairs in the apartment. He might hear you."

"Oh please! As if I care. Besides, I doubt he knows what déclassé means. He doesn't look like the sort of fellow who has studied a great deal of French." Liza glanced up quickly from her work, unable to suppress a little smile.

"Well, the cowboy boots are kind of interesting," she commented. "I can see them in Texas, but you'd think he would have thought to switch to snow boots or loafers once he hit the Connecticut border. Not that I want to dictate anybody's fashion choices, but they aren't very practical around here. I was looking out the window yesterday and saw him walking through the courtyard and next thing I knew, bam! He slipped and fell on the ice." Liza paused a moment to put the end of a piece of thread into her mouth to wet it, then slipped the pointed end through the eye of a needle before continuing.

"And I mean, he's from Wisconsin originally! You'd think he'd know that snow and cowboy boots don't go together."

I shifted my reading glasses down the end of my nose so I could see my seams better. I hated those glasses. They made me look old. I'd never have been caught dead wearing them in public, but they were a necessity when I was quilting, especially after dark; besides, Margot and Liza didn't care how I looked.

"That's exactly my point," I added. "Everything about that man is affected. I don't like him, and I don't trust him. What's he doing here anyway?"

Margot, who eschewed what she called gossip and I called a simple exchange of viewpoints, had been listening quietly and working diligently during this whole exchange. Now she finally broke in. "It does seem a little strange," she admitted. "Him coming here after the surgery and then just moving in to Evelyn's apartment even though they're divorced. She didn't ask him to come, did she?"

Liza shook her head. "No. Definitely not. Garrett told me that Evelyn had called him a few weeks ago, told Rob about her cancer, and that they'd had an argument. Evelyn hung up on him. The apartment is so small that Garrett overheard the whole thing. He wouldn't say so, of course, but I think that even Garrett is wondering what his dad is doing here. It must be a little awkward for him."

"Exactly! And it'll be a lot more awkward when Evelyn is discharged from the hospital tomorrow." I lowered my voice to a whisper. In spite of what I'd said to Liza, I really didn't want Rob Dixon to overhear our conversation. "Evelyn only has one bedroom, which, I assume, Rob is using right now. Garrett is sleeping on the sofa." I peered meaningfully at the others over the tops of my reading glasses. "Where do you suppose Rob is planning on sleeping after Evelyn gets home?"

"Abigail, stop that," Margot clucked with a disapproving wag of her head. "Evelyn and I already decided that she's going to stay with me for a while. That way she won't have to climb the stairs and will be able to rest better without all the noise from the shop. Rob can stay on in the apartment if he likes." Margot took the pair of snips that she had hanging on a ribbon around her neck and cut the end of a thread.

"Of course, I'm sure he'll be leaving soon," she continued. "His presence seems a little strange to us, but, after all, he was married to Evelyn for close to thirty years and they still have a son together. I'm sure he must have some kind of feelings for her. Maybe he just felt like he ought to show up to support her. No matter what happened between them, I think he genuinely wants to help. Yesterday he gave me a hand carrying and shelving the new spring fabric bolts. That was nice of him, don't you think?"

Liza just shrugged in response. I decided to keep my thoughts to myself as well. I supposed Margot could be right, but I really didn't think so. Margot was an innocent, always trying to see the best in everyone, so much so that at first I'd doubted her sincerity. I mean really, how could anyone be that sweet? But Margot was. I had to admit, she'd grown on me. And sometimes, I'd discovered, she was right. There were people in the world who truly did operate from good intentions, with Margot leading the pack. I just didn't happen to believe that Rob Dixon was one of them. In her heart, I could tell that Margot didn't think so either. Margot might be an innocent, but that didn't make her a fool.

Margot picked up the now-finished quilt she'd been working on and took it to the ironing board for a final press. "Still," she said, tipping her head to one side as if trying to see the situation from a different angle, "you'd think he'd have gone home by now. Why hasn't he?"

Liza gave voice to the exact thought that was going through my mind. "Because he wants something, that's why." I lowered my head over my quilt and smiled to myself. It was good to know that my niece had inherited some of the Burgess common sense.

"Well," I said, "one thing is for sure. If he left right now, it wouldn't be a second too soon for Charlie. Did you see the look on his face when Rob breezed past him in the hospital corridor and barged into Evelyn's room? He didn't introduce himself, but the cowboy boots were a dead giveaway. I thought Charlie was going to chase him down, rip those roses out of his hand, and shove them down Rob's throat."

Liza grinned. "I like Charlie."

"So do I," echoed Margot. "At first I thought he was a little gruff, but he really is so sweet."

"I've known Charlie for almost twenty years, ever since he moved to New Bern and opened the Grill. You won't find a kinder, more tenderhearted man on the face of the earth than Charlie Donnelly. I think that's why he puts on that brusque businessman act. He's afraid that if people knew what a softhearted soul he really was, they'd run ragged over him. Which, of course, might be true."

"Did you see that box of crayons?" Margot laughed. "What man goes to the trouble of finding such a perfect gift? He's obviously crazy about Evelyn, but she doesn't seem to get it."

"Or maybe she's just not interested," I posited. "Just because he's in love with her doesn't necessarily mean that she's in love with him. Maybe she just wants to keep their relationship platonic."

Margot sighed as she set the hot iron in its holder and folded the now-finished quilt. "Well, I can't think why. If a man showed up at my doorstep with presents and jokes, and brought meals to my bedside so I wouldn't have to eat hospital food, I'd fall in love with him that quick!" She snapped her fingers. "Why can't I find someone like Charlie? For that matter, why can't I find anyone at all?"

"What about Tom, the guy who works at the post office?" Liza asked. "When we went to pick up the mail, he gave you a big smile, then held up the line for at least three minutes chatting you up. The people behind us in line were getting really ticked off."

"Engaged," Margot said in a flat voice. "Men like me. I have all kinds of men friends, but they're all either married or about to get married. Even when I meet a single guy that I think I could go for, they always start telling me their problems with women and I give them advice, which they follow, and next thing you know, they're engaged too!" Margot let out such a disgusted growl that I couldn't keep from chuckling.

"I'm not kidding," she said. "That's happened to me three times! Men like me, but they never seem to fall in love with me. I'm like everybody's favorite kid sister. Why is that? Why can't somebody fall in love with me?" she wailed.

Looking at the shapeless jumper and scuffed flats Margot was wearing, her colorless lips and eyelashes that had never known the touch of a mascara brush, I had some opinions. Margot was a genuinely pretty woman with an intelligent mind and an endearing personality, but she could definitely use some lessons in the art of female allure. I was about to make a few suggestions, but Liza spoke before I could say anything.

"Don't be silly," she said. "You just haven't found the right man yet. You will." Liza looked to me for support. "Isn't that right, Abigail?"

"Yes," I said quickly. "Of course. It's just a matter of time."

Margot looked doubtful. "Well, I hope you're right. I'm going to be thirty-six years old in a few months. I'd always figured that, by now, I'd already be married and have children, preferably two or three."

"You've still got plenty of time," I said. "Besides, better to wait for the right man to come along than marry in haste and repent at leisure."

"Trust her," Liza chimed in. "She knows what she's talking about. And by the way, speaking of waiting for the right man, I haven't seen Franklin around lately. Are you mad at him again?" Liza winked at Margot, and I suddenly had the feeling that I was the punch line of a joke whose point I'd missed.

"Franklin? No, I haven't seen him recently. I've been too busy with all this Evelyn business and my work at the shelter. I imagine we'll get together for our monthly business meeting in a couple of weeks. Why do you ask?"

"No reason," Liza said and began folding up her project and putting away her sewing notions. "Just wondering."

≈ 31 ≈

Evelyn Dixon

Iheard the front door open and close, footsteps, and Margot's voice calling my name. I didn't answer, hoping that maybe she'd think I was sleeping and go away, but she didn't.

The bedroom door opened, and Margot peeked in. "Oh, there you are. Didn't you hear me call you?" I just shook my head, a lie.

She held up a disposable aluminum dish with a white cardboard top. "I've got your lunch—Charlie's special chicken pot pie. I hope that's all right. Charlie said he called over here to ask what you wanted for lunch but nobody answered."

"That's fine," I said. "I'll have it later. I'm not very hungry right now."

"Oh." She sounded a little disappointed. "Well, all right. I'll just put it in the refrigerator." She turned to go into the kitchen but then paused at the door just a moment and tilted her chin up and breathed in, as if she was sniffing the air for scent of a coming storm.

"Evelyn, is there anything I can do to help you? You barely touched your breakfast or your dinner last night. Maybe we should call Dr. Finney. I'm worried about you. Are you in pain?"

I was. But there is pain and then there is pain, the kind that seeps in through your pores and joints and nostrils and refuses to be banished by something as simple as a couple of white tablets you take every three to four hours as needed. It's the "as needed" part that gets you in trouble. There is no end to it.

I looked into Margot's sweet, troubled face. I felt bad for worrying her, but then there were so many things I felt bad about. Where to begin? How to explain? I'd gone to sleep in the white-hot light of a sterile operating room and woken up in a fog that had become a black and ever-thickening miasma of despair. It had seeped into my mind and heart, blocking out every ray of light, filling my throat and nostrils so that with every breath I took, I inhaled hopelessness. I couldn't explain it, couldn't control it, and couldn't make it stop.

Margot, with her thick fringe of brown lashes ringing caring eyes, had no experience with this kind of pain. I hoped she never would. I didn't even want her to know that such desolation existed, so I just told her what she wanted to hear.

"I'm fine, just tired and sore. That's all. I'll eat later. Promise." I tried to smile, but my lips felt like they were lined with sandpaper, scraping across my teeth into a grimace.

"All right," Margot said doubtfully. "I'll just put this away and then run back to the shop. Things are going well. All the customers are asking about you."

"That's nice."

"Oh, and did I tell you? Rob installed the new display case. Then he fixed the copier and the tension on that broken sewing machine. You never told me he was so handy." She waited a moment for me to say something. "He keeps asking if he can come over and see you. Charlie too. He—"

"No!" I interjected before she could say more. Margot's eyebrows shot up, and I took a deep breath, told myself to calm down. "I mean, not yet. I'm still so tired. Visitors wear me out. But tell them both I said thank you. All right?"

She nodded her agreement. "You're going to take a nap? That's good. You just need a lot of rest, Evelyn. You'll be back to your old self soon." She smiled, and I wondered if she was trying to convince herself or me. "I'll bring you some soup for dinner. Call the shop if you need anything at all."

"I will." I lay down on the bed and rolled onto my side, my face turned toward the wall. Margot went into the kitchen and puttered around for a few minutes, but before she left, she came back into the guest bedroom.

Feigning sleep, I kept my eyes closed. Margot tiptoed up to the edge of the bed and pulled the broken-heart quilt up over my shoulders. She stood at the edge of the bed for a long moment, not moving, standing over me the way a mother stands over the sickbed of her child. Finally, she bent down, brushed her fingertips lightly over my hair, and whispered, "It'll be all right. Just rest now. I'm praying for you, sweetie. We all are. It's going to get better. It will. Soon."

Margot crept out of the room and closed the door quietly behind her. The center of my chest throbbed in a place deeper than the cut of the surgeon's knife. For a moment, a silent, desolate groan—half prayer, half flag of surrender—rose from the black like an arm reaching out from the deep, fingers opening and closing on empty air, blind, desperate, grasping for a lifeline.

Help me. Please. I can't do this alone.

There was no gentle creeping, no whispered worried voices afraid of saying or doing the wrong thing and making things worse than they already were. I heard the sound of heavy feet treading on wooden floorboards and a decisive turn of the knob before the door flew open, banging against the wall like it been blown by a hard wind. She didn't have to say anything; I knew who it was. Mary Dell had come to town.

"Evelyn, get up!" she commanded. Before I could consider a response, she threw back the bedclothes. The room was chilly without the protection of the broken-heart quilt. I shivered in my nightgown. "Get up," she repeated. "You've been lying here for almost two weeks. That's long enough. Now get up."

Her tone was impatient; it didn't occur to me to argue. I sat up and hung my bare feet over the side of the tall, antique bed, my toes barely brushing the cold wooden floor. I wrapped my arms over my flat chest protectively and looked up. Mary Dell towered over me. Her face was stern.

"You're supposed to be filming your show," I said. "What are you doing here?"

"Came to ask the same question." She turned around, and for the first time I noticed Margot clinging to the doorjamb, half in the room and half out of it, as if she wasn't quite sure what to do next.

"Would you excuse us for a minute? I've got to smack some sense into my friend here, and I'd just as soon do it without any witnesses."

Margot's eyes grew wide, not quite sure what to make of this, and gave me a questioning look.

I nodded. "It's okay, Margot."

She bit her lip, not sure of the wisdom of leaving me alone with Mary Dell, but after a moment she took a step back. "I'll be in the kitchen if you need anything," she said and shut the door.

Mary Dell waited to hear the sound of receding footsteps and then turned to face me again. "What is the matter with you? Since you refused to take my phone calls, I finally called Garrett to see how you were doing and he told me that you were depressed, feeling so sorry for yourself that you wouldn't see anybody, wouldn't even get up out of bed.

"When he told me that, I didn't believe him. 'That can't be right,' I said. 'No way is my friend Evelyn Dixon lying around having a pity party for herself for two weeks. It is simply not possible that Evelyn, the woman who rose up like a phoenix from the ashes of divorce, found the guts to pick up and move to a new state, build a new life, pick up her old dreams where she'd let them lie, and open a quilt shop in spite of the protests and predictions of the naysayers—there is just no way that a woman with that kind of backbone is going to let her spirit be crushed by cancer. I just refuse to believe it!'"

She shook her head as if, even looking around and seeing the evidence of my withdrawal into depression, the blinds drawn to keep out the daylight, the litter of crumpled, damp tissues that filled the wastebasket, and the curling edges of the cheese sandwich that was supposed to be my lunch but sat untouched on the nightstand, she still couldn't quite believe her eyes.

"But Garrett assured me that was the case. I wanted to get myself a second opinion, so I talked to those new friends of yours: Margot, and Liza, and that Abigail. She's different, isn't she? Not exactly the soul of warmth, but she sure is fond of you. I even talked to that scum-sucking scab of an ex-husband of yours. What's he doing here anyway?"

I started to say something, but Mary Dell didn't give me a chance.

"Never mind. We can talk about that later. Anyway," she said, taking a big breath as she returned to the subject at hand, "when they all told me that, I just had to come up here and see for myself, because I was sure they were wrong. I told the television producer that everything was going to have to wait for a couple of days, that the whole film crew was just going to have to cool their jets while I flew up to Yankeeland to correct these malicious rumors that were flying around about one of my dearest friends. But look at you!"

She moved her head slowly from side to side, murmuring the classic Southern mantra for disbelief and disappointment. "Mmm. Mmm. Mmm. What happened? Here you are, looking like something the cat dragged in, lying about in this musty old room that smells like the windows haven't been opened in about a year, letting everybody else do your work for you while you lay here feeling sorry for yourself and worrying everybody half to death. Evelyn, I want a straight answer. What's the matter with you?"

I wanted to start crying again, but curiously, finally, I was out of tears. The burning sensation behind my eyes migrated to my throat, erupting into a belch of angry words.

"Don't, Mary Dell," I warned. "Don't start with me. You don't know what it's like. So don't you stand there and tell me that I'm feeling sorry for myself. Nobody has hacked off pieces of you. You're not going to have to live the rest of your life wondering if they really did get it all, if the cancer is going to come back to finish you off. You don't know what I'm going through."

She put her hands on her hips and opened her mouth as if she was about to begin lecturing me again but then thought better of it and pressed her lips into a tight line. She walked across the room to the window. "You're right," she said and turned to pull the cord on the window blind. "I don't know what you're going through. So tell me. Talk to me."

Bright light streamed though the glass directly into my eyes. I turned my head and screwed my eyelids shut. "I didn't know . . . I wasn't prepared," I stuttered, struggling to find words. "My doctor and I had talked through this whole thing, discussed exactly what would happen during the operation, and what my options would be for reconstruction, the possibility of followup with chemotherapy or radiation, and we even discussed the mental side of this. She warned me to expect a roller-coaster ride of emotions and I . . . I thought I understood. I thought I had a handle on it, but I didn't. Not even close."

Mary Dell leaned back, resting her weight against the window-sill. Listening intently, she tipped her head to the side, making it easier to look her in the eye, damming the late afternoon sunbeams until they pooled behind her and spilled sunlight through frizzed tendrils of hair, making each gray-blond strand glow pink and gold, glinting against the myriad crystal beads of her dangly earrings so that illumined shadow phantoms spun around her head, giving her the aura of some angelic, benevolent being.

"Before the operation, I'd worked it all out in my mind logically, like I was talking about someone else, you understand?" I don't know if she did or not, but she nodded.

"Of course, I was going through with it; it was the sensible course of action! My breasts or my life? There was no choice! But why is that? Why didn't I get a choice? Why did this happen to me? What did I ever do to deserve this?" I pushed myself off the bed and stood in front of my friend. My voice and my hands clenched in anger.

"Why?" I demanded. "Tell me why!"

"I don't know. No one does."

"Do you have any idea what it's like? Can you imagine? Everyone keeps saying how lucky I was to have caught it in time, and isn't it wonderful what they can do with reconstructive surgery these days. If one more person says that to me, I swear I'm going to slap them! What do I have to feel lucky about?" I barked out an incredulous laugh and covered my flattened chest with both hands.

"Do you know what the reconstruction surgeon calls them? Mounds. Not breasts—mounds. After I'm healed, they will put implants in my chest and then tattoo on something that is supposed to represent nipples. There will be a swelling where my breasts used to be, but they won't be breasts; they will be mounds."

My anger wasn't spent, but I was. Drained and exhausted, I covered my eyes with one hand. "I'm alive. I know I should be grateful for that, but I don't feel grateful. I feel cheated. For the last few years, everything I knew myself to be is being subtracted piece by piece. I keep losing parts of myself—my marriage, my family, my home, and now even my womanhood. Who am I supposed to be now?"

I opened my eyes, looking for answers in Mary Dell's patient gaze. "If this is it, if I'm going to be subtracted bit by bit until there is just nothing left, then why doesn't God just get it over with? It's easy to say I should get up and move on with my life. Sometimes I even say it to myself, but what kind of life will it be? Will I ever know love again? Will any man ever find me desirable again? And even if he did, will I be able to respond? Yesterday I took off my clothes and looked in the mirror. I look like some worn-out rag doll, all jagged tears and mismatched patches. Who could ever want me? And what will I lose next? My business? It's the one good thing that happened to me during these last awful years, and I'm inches from losing that too, and what was left of my life savings with it. What am I supposed to do if that happens? I'm fifty years old. Too old for second chances—make that third chances. I can't face the idea of losing anything else, Mary Dell. I can't."

Shifting her weight forward, she stood up and walked toward me, moving out of the glow of celestial radiance into the ordinary light of day so I could see that she wasn't an angel at all, just Mary Dell. Just an old friend who'd known pains and fears of her own and was willing to drop everything and fly across the country to listen to mine. Just Mary Dell. Just what I needed, just when I most needed it.

She crossed the room. For a moment, I thought she was going to put her arms around me and tell me it would be all right, but instead she pushed past me and started making up the bed, straightening the sheets and tucking them in so tightly I'd have had to pry them loose to get back into bed.

"Before I had Howard, I miscarried six times. I wanted a baby so bad. So did my husband, Donny. We kept trying, but every time I'd get about five months along, far enough so everybody'd know I was pregnant and start congratulating us, I'd lose the baby. The first couple of times, people would even send presents and cards. By the third time, they'd just stop me in the store or at church with this concerned look on their faces and say they were praying for us. I knew they meant well, but I wanted to slap them just the same." She picked up the broken-heart quilt by the edges and gave it a couple of good shakes, sending a luminous flutter of dust motes into the sun-drenched room before laying it on top of the bed. She didn't look at me as she worked, methodically smoothing out the wrinkles on the quilt.

"After the sixth time, the doctors said we should give up, that there was no hope and these continued miscarriages weren't good for my health. Donny and I talked it over and decided to listen to the doctors, to try adopting instead, but every time we'd get close to getting a baby, something would happen and we'd get our hearts broken again. Donny wanted a son so badly. One day I came home and found him in the back bedroom crying his eyes out, holding a letter saying that the adoptive mother had changed her mind and decided to keep the baby we'd thought was going to be ours. I was thirty-six years old, but we decided to try having a baby on our own one more time."

"Howard," I said.

She nodded and began fluffing up the bed pillows. "Howard. Other than Donny and the doctors, I didn't tell anyone I was pregnant. I started wearing big clothes right off and griping about my weight, so people would think I was just putting on a few pounds. But when we passed that six-month mark and I realized that, this time, we really were going to have a baby, I was so excited! Donny too. We had all kinds of plans for him. I decided he was going to play the piano, design bridges, find the cure for cancer, and then be president of the United States, just as a sideline. Donny wanted him to play quarterback for the Cowboys." She smiled briefly as she gave the pillowcase a final pat, then straightened up and put her hands on her hips as she looked over her work, her expression serious and appraising.

"Then Howard was born, and the doctors said he had Down's syndrome. In a way, it was like miscarrying all over again. We'd lost the child we'd been expecting, the boy who was supposed to build bridges, and call plays in the Super Bowl, and fly in Air Force One. That child had never existed, except in our imaginations, but we grieved his loss just the same. I sat in the rocking chair in the nursery and sobbed myself dry, and Donny went out for a quart of milk and never came back.

"Inside of a week, I lost my husband, my marriage, and my dream child. I had no money, no job, and no idea how I was going to raise a child with special needs all by myself. I'd lost so much, so fast, and was feeling so sorry and so confused about what I'd done to bring this on myself, that I couldn't see what I had left. For the longest time, I just sat in that rocking chair and cried. But the thing about Howard is that when he was a baby, he could cry louder than I could. He wasn't at all worried about the answers to the meaning of life, or how unfair everything was, he just wanted something to eat and a clean diaper, and he wasn't taking no for an answer. So I got up out of the chair. I had to."

"Howard is great," I whispered.

"He is. When he was born, the doctor told me he'd never be able to read or tie his own shoes, and now here he is, on the threshold of becoming a television star—and me along with him. And you know that could never have happened if I didn't have Howard. If Howard wasn't picking out the colors and fabrics, I'd have spent my life sewing the best-constructed and ugliest quilts in Texas."

She grinned. "And the best part is, Howard doesn't seem to be fazed by any of it. It's like he always knew this was bound to happen eventually and was just waiting for the rest of us to wake up and smell the coffee." Mary Dell laughed, and I did too. The sound coming from my throat was raspy, and I realized how long it had been since I'd laughed.

"You know, it might have been nice, having a president for a son, the perfect family, a husband by my side as our child grew up and I grew old." She shrugged. "Well, it worked out that way for plenty of folks; some of them seem pretty happy and others don't. I used to wonder about that a lot, but after a while I gave up wondering. There's never an answer to those kinds of questions."

She walked to the closed door, where a white terry-cloth robe was hanging, and took it off the hook. "If you or I were running things, we'd arrange life so it came with a money-back guarantee, but we're not. And probably that's for the best. Maybe I didn't get the life I'd planned on, but I can tell you now, and mean it, that if I had the chance to take the life I have and trade it in for what I thought was best for me then, I'd pass. But I'd never have found that out if I'd have kept my butt glued to that rocker."

She walked behind me and held open the robe so I could put my arms in the sleeves, then came around front to tighten the belt around my waist. The job done, she looked up and smiled that wide Mary Dell smile, big white teeth ringed with bright red lipstick. "Like my old granny used to say, 'When your dreams turn to dust, maybe it's time to vacuum.' "

With tears in my eyes, I laughed and put an arm around my friend's waist as, together, we walked through the bedroom door.

❧ 32 ❧

Abigail Burgess Wynne

Standing in my dressing room, trying to figure out which of my jackets, the camel or the houndstooth, made me look more like a solid citizen, I paused to marvel that so much could happen in the course of a year.

Thirteen months had passed since the day Judge Gulden's ruling saddled me with my unwelcome and unwilling houseguest. How much had changed since that day, for me and for Liza. We were neither of us the same people. As if to prove my point, Liza walked into my dressing room wearing a navy blue wrap dress with a chunky cobalt and silver bead necklace, high heels with narrow ankle straps tied in a bow and, most astonishing of all, stockings.

"How do I look?" she asked and twirled in a circle, making the skirt of the dress flare. "Reformed? Rehabilitated? Ready to be released into society?"

I stood for a moment, speechless in the face of this transformation. I remembered another day, so long ago, the tap-tap of a pair of heels clamoring down the stairs, Susan's breathless excitement and shining eyes as she spun in a circle, showing off her first party dress, a face and voice so like Liza's, wanting to know how she looked.

"You look beautiful," I said. She was.

Liza smiled. "I found it in that new boutique that opened around the corner from the Grill. I thought I should dress up a little for Judge Gulden."

"Good idea."

"It's the newest style," Liza reported, running her hands down her sides to smooth the jersey fabric of the skirt. "Just simple and comfortable and modern."

"Wonderful," I murmured, deciding there wasn't any point in telling her that's what Diane von Furstenburg had said too, when she introduced the wrap dress to the fashion world in 1973. "Blue is a good color for you. It sets off your eyes." It was true, but frankly, I'd have said the same thing if she'd waltzed into my room wearing bright red, pumpkin, seafoam green, or puce—anything but black.

"The necklace is nice too. Where did you get it?"

"I made it."

"Really? Well, it's very pretty."

"Thanks. The lady who owns the boutique liked it too. She said if I could make some more, she'd buy them for the shop."

That was an interesting idea, I mused. Starting a jewelry business might be a good way for Liza to use her talents. Working in the quilt store was fine for now, but Liza needed to expand her horizons. With a little encouragement, financial backing from me, and introductions to the right people—also courtesy of me—who knew? Before long, Liza Burgess originals might be available in the jewelry departments of Barney's in Manhattan, Neiman-Marcus in Dallas, and Harrod's in London—a worldwide jewelry empire! And the whole thing headquartered right here in New Bern, Liza's home, where she lived with me. Of course, when she decided to marry and perhaps have a family—which might happen sooner than later; I'd noticed how Garrett Dixon had been looking at her lately—then the whole family, Liza, Garrett, and their children (girls, I decided, two of them), could live right here on Proctor Street. The Hudsons had been grumbling about the Connecticut winters for years, always swearing that this year they were selling and moving to Florida. I wondered if they were serious. Their house would be perfect! The gardens were large, perfect for children, though the kitchen needed updating badly, and we'd have to build some kind of office so Liza could run the business out of the house and still spend time with the children. Maybe we'd have to add a nanny or housekeeper suite as well. If the business really took off, Liza would need some extra help around the house. Hmmm. Maybe I should hire an architect? No, I decided, better just to call Dominic D'Rosa, the contractor who'd remodeled my bedroom suite three years before. He did good work and would understand exactly what I wanted. Yes! That would be perfect! After the hearing, I'd ask Franklin to call the Hudsons and see if they were willing to sell. Of course, if I came to them first they'd probably be stubborn about price, but what did that matter? Money was nothing compared to family. All that mattered was that Liza was happy.

"Abigail?"

I shook myself out of my reverie and saw Liza staring at me with a quizzical look on her face.

"Are you all right?"

"Oh. Yes. I was just thinking." I grabbed the camel jacket from off the hanger. "Are you ready?"

"Yes," she said slowly, narrowing her eyes. "What were you thinking about?"

"Nothing important. I'll tell you about it later." I patted her on the arm and smiled. "Let's go."

Harry Gulden was pleased.

Liza, Franklin, Mr. Corey, and I—the same cast of characters who had stood in the judge's chambers a year before—sat quietly as

Judge Gulden flipped through the sheaf of papers that made up Liza's file, peering through the reading glasses that were perched on the end of his nose and nodding approvingly.

"Good," he murmured. "Very good. No arrests; not so much as a parking ticket. It says here that you've been participating in a grief-recovery workshop at the church. Has that helped you?"

"Yes, Your Honor. A lot."

"Good. I'm glad to hear it. And you're still working at the quilt-shop part time?" Liza nodded. "Well, this character reference from the owner, Ms. Dixon, is excellent. She says you're a hard worker and have matured greatly in the last year. Looking over your file, I'd have to agree. Good for you, Liza."

Liza blushed a little. "Thank you, Your Honor."

The judge cleared his throat, gathered up the papers, and tapped them on his desk to straighten them.

"Mr. Corey," he said, peering over the tops of his glasses at the young attorney. "I take it that, given Miss Burgess's excellent record during the last year, the district attorney's office will agree whole-heartedly that she can be released to her own recognizance and that any record of this unfortunate incident can be safely expunged? It is always so much better to resolve these little problems without resorting to unnecessary and unneeded bureaucracy, don't you agree?"

It was a statement phrased as a question; the judge had clearly made up his mind. But Mr. Corey still seemed slightly begrudging in his assent.

"Yes, Your Honor."

"Excellent!" The judge beamed. "Very sensible of you."

"In that case . . ." He picked up his gavel ceremoniously and banged it down once. "Miss Burgess, you are free to go. Congratulations."

"Thank you, Your Honor."

"You're welcome. Now that you're out from under your aunt's

benevolent and watchful eye, do you know what do you plan to do with your life?" Harry winked at me.

I took a step forward, ready to explain the exciting plans I'd made for Liza's future, but Liza spoke first.

"Yes, sir. I've decided to go back to school."

She had? When? She'd never discussed it with me.

"But," I protested, so surprised by this revelation that I didn't stop to think out what I was saying, "the administration asked you to leave. You can't be thinking of going back to that place!"

Liza drew her brows together and shot me a look, clearly irritated by my interruption and my impolitic reminder of her past academic failure. "No," she hissed, her cheeks flushing, "I'm not going back to Rhode Island, but there are other art schools, you know. During the last year I've come to realize how much I really love being an artist; it's my calling.

"And," she continued, straightening her shoulders, "I've also come to realize that, no matter what my old professors said, I do have talent. But I need to develop it. I just need to find the right school. Probably in New York. I've been talking with Evelyn, and she says—"

"Evelyn!" I shouted, ignoring the elbow that Franklin shoved into my ribs. "What does Evelyn have to do with it? Why would you be discussing this with her?"

Liza tilted her head and looked at me curiously, as if she didn't quite understand the question. "Because Evelyn's my friend, that's why. She knows me, and cares about me, and wants me to be happy. Just like you do, Abigail."

It was raining. The three of us, Liza, Franklin, and I, stood clumped together under the overhanging eve of the courthouse in a fruitless attempt at staying dry.

"Well, of course I understood that you couldn't live at my house forever," I said, thinking about the Hudson place down the block.

"I just don't see why you're in such a rush to go. You could go to school and still live in New Bern. The community college has art classes."

Liza rolled her eyes, and Franklin grinned. Even I knew that wasn't a real option. Liza's talents were far too advanced for some beginner's watercolor classes taught by some part-time associate professor, but I was grasping at straws.

It had been a long time in coming, and the road had been rough—make that cratered with sinkholes big enough to swallow a Buick—but over the course of the previous year I had come to care about Liza. I liked having her around, liked coming home and hearing her clattering around in the kitchen, or walking into a room and discovering she'd decided to rearrange all the furniture without asking, then arguing with her about it. Before Liza came into my life, I hadn't realized how lonely I was. I didn't want to go back to being that way again.

"Abbie," Franklin said as rainwater dripped from the edge of his hat and onto his shoes, "there comes a time when every fledgling has to leave the nest. You've done a good job helping her through a hard time, and I'm sure she appreciates it." Liza nodded earnestly. "But it's time for her to go out and try her wings."

Now it was my turn to roll my eyes. "What a beautiful illustration, Franklin. So original. Did you think that up just now?"

Franklin laughed, and Liza smiled. "Franklin is right. Clichéd, but right. I love New Bern, and, though I never thought I would have said it, I love living with you. But it's time for me to leave. At least for a while. Who knows? When I've finished school, maybe I'll come back."

"But," I protested, "what about Garrett? You two have been seeing quite a lot of each other. How does he feel about your leaving?"

"He's fine with it because he knows this is what will make me happy. Sure, we care about each other, a lot. But it isn't like he's asked me to marry him. Even if he had, I'd still want to go to finish my education. It's like Evelyn says, falling in love shouldn't mean letting your dreams fall by the wayside. Any man who truly loves you won't just love who you are; he'll love who you're capable of being."

Evelyn again, I thought. She was certainly generous in doling out pearls of wisdom. The trouble was, she happened to be right.

I exhaled a deep breath of resignation. "All right. I see your point." Liza smiled and put out her arms to embrace me, but I held out a hand to stop her.

"Wait! You've got to promise me two things. First, that you will work hard, have confidence in your talent, and won't ever let anyone talk you out of being everything you can be."

"Done."

"Second, that you'll come back home during school vacations."

She frowned. "Well, I don't know. There are these cool spring-break parties in Aruba I was looking forward to," she said, and then, before I could start to tell her exactly what I thought of that plan, her face split into a grin. "Just kidding, Abigail. Of course I'll come back for vacations. Where else would I go? This is my home."

My conditions being met, I submitted to Liza's embrace, reaching carefully around her shoulder to dab at my eyes before she released me.

"Glad that's all settled," Franklin said. "I saw Charlie on my way here, and he said they've got a halibut special that is out of this world. So come on, you two. Lunch is on me."

Liza wrinkled her nose, remembering something. "Sorry, but I can't. Garrett and I are driving to Massachusetts to check out the new art exhibit at Williams College."

This was news to me. "That far? You won't be back in time for Evelyn's surprise party tonight. Besides, I thought Garrett was going to take Evelyn to her doctor's appointment and then lure her back to the shop for the party."

"Change of plans. Rob volunteered to do it instead, and Margot said she'd handle everything else."

"Well," I said, "I still don't think this is the best time for you two to be running off to Williamstown. Don't forget, the party starts at seven and everyone has to be in hiding before she gets there. Otherwise it'll ruin the whole thing."

"I know. That's why I need to leave right now. Don't worry," Liza said. "We'll be back in time. Garrett is a really fast driver." She turned around and dashed down the street in the direction of the quilt shop, leaping over puddles as she went.

"Liza!" I called after her. "That's not funny! You tell Garrett to drive responsibly!" She didn't turn around, just raised her hand up over her shoulder and wiggled her fingers in farewell. I couldn't see her face, but I knew she was smiling.

"Well, I guess that just leaves you and me," Franklin said, hooking his arm into mine. "Come on, Mother Hen. I'll take you out to lunch."

"Actually, Franklin, I've got to run too. There's so much to do before tonight. I can't leave it all to Margot. It wouldn't be fair. "

"But I was hoping to get a chance to talk with you. I've got some . . . some business I wanted to discuss with you."

"Tonight," I promised. "After the party. Are you still going to the Grill? Ask Charlie if he could send over a tray of the spring rolls. And some of the nori salmon rolls too." Following Liza's lead, I turned around and headed toward the quilt shop, trying to run between raindrops.

"But, Abbie, you've got to eat something. Just let me buy you a quick lunch. We were supposed to be celebrating."

"We are celebrating," I called over my shoulder. "We're celebrating Evelyn's recovery. Oh, I almost forgot! Tell Charlie I'll need a half case of his best champagne as well. He can put everything on my tab. See you tonight, Franklin. Don't be late."

❧ 33 ❧

Evelyn Dixon

It was seven o'clock on a rainy Wednesday in late winter, too late for Christmas shoppers and too early for tourists. All the downtown shops, including mine, had shut out their lights and locked their doors.

Rob had left his keys and his cell phone inside the locked shop. I was tired and just wanted to get back to Margot's and told Rob he could drop me off and then borrow my keys, but he absolutely insisted that we retrieve his phone before he took me to Margot's. The whole thing was ridiculous, but he'd already had a rotten day. I didn't want to make it worse by arguing.

Walking in the dim light while groping in my purse for the shop key, I tripped on a loose cobble and stumbled. Rob reached out in time to keep me from falling.

"Careful!"

"Thanks," I mumbled and pulled away. In light of our conversation between the doctor's office and the shop, it felt awkward to have him touch me.

I hadn't asked or wanted Rob to come to New Bern, but even I had to admit he'd been a big help: stocking shelves, installing the new display cabinets, fixing broken machines, and running errands, like offering to take me to the doctor's appointment today. Still, he'd been around for weeks. It was time for him to go home.

I was feeling better, so much so that in the morning I was going to start working half days in the shop, building up my schedule until I was working full-time again, and not a minute too soon. I was anxious to get back to work and into my apartment. Stairs were no problem now. I'd have moved out of Margot's guest room and back home a week before, but Rob was still there. Leave of absence or no, wasn't it time he went back to work? And what about Tina? Wasn't she wondering why he was in New Bern with his ex-wife instead of back in Texas with her?

It was a strange situation. I had considered asking Garrett to inquire when Rob was planning on leaving, but I didn't want to put him in the middle. I knew I'd have to talk to Rob myself.

And so, as we drove back from Dr. Finney's office, I finally broached the subject. It wasn't an easy conversation. Almost as soon as I hinted that it might be time for him to go, Rob started crying! I didn't know what to think! My big, former football player, wannabe cowboy of an ex-husband was crying so hard that he had to pull the car over to the side of the road while he sobbed out the whole story.

It turned out that, right after I'd called to tell him about my cancer, Tina decided to move out. She told him she was in love with someone else, someone younger and more "fun." And then the next week, he'd lost his job.

A few months before, I'd have danced a jig to hear Rob's tale of misfortune and woe, but I didn't feel that way anymore. I wasn't interested in exacting revenge or placing blame. Mary Dell had reminded me that, even in the midst of tragedy, it is possible to find unexpected blessings. Mine had been exactly this, a newfound ability to let go of the past and the bitterness I'd harbored toward Rob.

Life was just too short to spend it nursing old wounds. It was true; I didn't love Rob anymore, but neither did I hate him.

We sat there by the side of the road with the engine idling and the windshield wipers going full blast while Rob told me how miserable he was. He'd managed to find a new job, and was supposed to start at the first of the month, but it was in an industry he didn't know much about. "I still can't believe that they just let me go after all these years. I gave my heart and soul to that company!"

And he had. I could certainly attest to that, but it wasn't worth mentioning now. "Are you worried about money?"

"No. The salary is fine, actually a little more than what I was making before; it's not that."

"Well, then what is it?"

He paused, thinking for a moment. "I'm scared. Evie, for the first time in my life, I'm really scared. I can't believe that, at my age, I've got to start all over again. I'm not sure I've got it in me. And worse than that, I just feel . . ." He clutched the steering wheel tight and dropped his head while he searched for the right word. "Adrift, I guess. That's it. It's like I woke up to find myself sitting in a boat in the middle of the ocean. I've got no sail, no oars, and no idea where I am. I don't know who I'm supposed to be now."

"And so you decided to come back to what was familiar—to a time when you knew who you were?"

He nodded. "Evie, it was a mistake. The divorce, I mean. I'm sorry. I'm so sorry. I understand now what I put you through. And I'm just so sorry. When you called that night and I thought about how I would feel if anything happened to you . . . I think that's when I really started to realize what I'd done."

He shifted in the seat, turning so he could look at me fully. "I was planning on coming up here anyway, at least for the surgery. I honestly wanted to make sure you were going to be okay, but when all this other stuff started piling on . . . Yes, I came hoping we could get back together. I'd like things to be the way they were before."

We talked for a long time. I told him the truth; that everything had changed. I had changed, and so had he. We would always be linked by our child and our memories, but we could never go back to the way things were. And though I didn't say so to Rob, I realized I didn't want to go back.

Rob stared vacantly out the front windshield though it was impossible to see anything through the rain and fog that clouded the glass. "I guess I can't blame you, Evie. I'll pack my stuff and go in the morning. But I just want you to know I meant what I said. I'm sorry for everything. I don't expect you to forgive me."

And to my surprise I said quietly, "Rob, I do forgive you. This isn't just your fault, you know. There were things we both could have done differently. I'm sorry too."

"Well, maybe, but when the going got tough, I was the one who called a lawyer, not you." I didn't say anything to that.

"I just wish there was some way I could make it up to you." He pushed his fingers up through his hair in a gesture of fatigue and futility. "That's crazy, I know. Some things you can never make up for, but Evie, if you ever need anything, anything at all, I want you to know that you can call me. I mean it. I know we can't go back to what we were before, but maybe we can try something new. Maybe we can be friends?"

Standing in the dark courtyard and finally finding the key to the shop, I wondered if Rob and I could be friends. After all, that's how we'd started out in the first place. Poor Rob. In spite of all that had happened, I didn't like seeing him hurting. He looked so pitiful standing there in the rain. Of course, I probably didn't look any better, but still. I sighed as I slid the key into the lock.

"Are you all right?" Rob asked and put his hand on my sleeve, his voice concerned. "Do you need to sit down?"

"No. I'm fine, just a little tired. That's all."

The safety bolt clicked over as I turned the key. I pushed open the door of the darkened shop and jumped, shocked to my toes when a score of shadowy figures leaped from behind counters and cabinets and bolts of cloth, shouting.

"SURPRISE!"

And it was—a complete and utterly lovely surprise. Nearly everyone I knew was there, and it was astounding to realize how many people I'd met and made friends with in less than two years. Besides Garrett, Rob, Abigail, Margot, Liza, and Franklin Spaulding, at least a dozen of my best customers had shown up, plus most of the other business owners in New Bern, and several people I'd met at church, including the pastor and his wife, whom I'd gotten to know better when they'd come to visit me in the hospital. And Charlie, who was standing at the buffet table on the other side of the room. He looked at me and smiled when I came in, then turned his attention to arranging spring rolls on a tray.

It took me a good fifteen minutes to work my way through the crowd of congratulants, thanking everyone for coming and assuring them over and over that I had been well and truly surprised, until I finally got over to the table where Charlie was fussing over the food with a stormy look on his face.

Charlie put as much care into his food as I did into my quilts. He insisted that every dish be plated just so, every ingredient the absolutely freshest available, and every recipe prepared with minute attention to detail. If it wasn't, he was not a happy camper and utterly unable to conceal it, his discontent clearly visible on his face, like now.

I picked up a spring roll and dunked it into a sauce that was pungent with the aroma of soy, sesame, and ginger and put it in my mouth. The delicate, golden crust of the spring roll crunched as I took a bite.

"Mmmm. Delicious as always."

He grunted but didn't look up as he took a service napkin and carefully wiped off the edge of the tray where someone, probably me, had carelessly dripped some of the sauce.

"Charlie," I said, reaching out to stay his hand and smiling. "Lighten up. Everything looks wonderful. Why don't you leave it for now and join the party? Garrett said something about opening a bottle of champagne. Let me get you a glass. Tonight you're a guest, not the caterer."

With his eyes still down, Charlie gave his head a quick shake, like he was twitching away some annoying insect. "You're wrong. Abigail is paying for this."

"Oh. Well, still. Everything looks and tastes fabulous. Leave it. Relax and let me buy you a drink."

"No. Can't stay. Just came over to do my job, see that everything is set out properly, and then I've got to get back to the restaurant. I've a business to run." He frowned as he put grilled shrimp onto stripped rosemary skewers and then shoved the skewers into a styrofoam cone covered with more rosemary to make it look like an herbal topiary.

"Oh, come on," I scoffed, wondering what was bothering him. This was more than just Charlie's usual obsession with serving perfect food. He stabbed the shrimp on their skewers with a violence that, had they been alive, would have constituted cruelty to animals. "It's a Wednesday night in the deadest part of winter. Half your regulars are at this party. I'd be shocked if you have more than six customers at the Grill. Stay for a little while, Charlie. You look like you could use a night off," I teased, hoping to jolly him out of his bad mood.

He stuck the last skewers in the rosemary tree. "I can't." He wiped his hand on a towel, stuck it out for me to shake, and said formally, "Good night, Evelyn."

"Charlie, you can't leave! The party is just starting, and we've got so much to celebrate! I saw the doctor today and guess what? No chemo for me! Isn't that great news?"

For the first time that evening, he looked at me. His expression softened, and his eyes were kind, but sad. "That's great, Evelyn. Really. I'm happy for you. So happy that you're well, but I really do have to go." He gave my hand a quick squeeze and then turned to leave, disappearing in the throng of partygoers.

"Hey!" I called after him. "I'm coming back to work tomorrow. Do you want to meet at the Bean for coffee first?"

He didn't answer. I saw him turn up his coat collar and open the door to leave, the jingle of the front doorbell blending in with the laughter of guests.

Abigail approached the table, took a salmon roll off a tray, and nibbled at it delicately. She was smiling, relaxed, and just a tiny bit loud. Garrett must have started pouring the champagne.

"Did you try one of these? They're my favorite. Charlie is a genius."

"He is. Difficult, but a genius."

"Well then, that makes him just our kind of people, doesn't it?" Abigail laughed at her own joke, but when I didn't join in her brows drew together in a line of concern.

"What's the matter? Aren't you having a good time? Maybe this is too much for you. Would you like to go lie down somewhere?"

"No. I'm fine. It's a wonderful party, Abigail. Thank you so much for going to all this trouble. I'm having a lovely time. It's just that I'm worried about Charlie. Something's bothering him, but he won't tell me what it is."

Abigail waved her hand dismissively. "Oh, don't worry about it. Charlie's probably just in one of his moods. Maybe his sous-chef decided to quit, or his supplier raised the price of free-range chicken." She shrugged. "Who knows? He'll be fine by tomorrow."

"I don't know. I've seen how he gets when things aren't going well at the restaurant, but this wasn't like that. He seemed sad. A little depressed even."

Abigail's head tipped to the side. "Evelyn, I've known Charlie for twenty years. You've known him for one. He's fine. He's just a little complicated, that's all. Trust me."

I murmured noncommittally.

"If you're so worried, why don't you go see him tomorrow? In the meantime, come and join the party."

Someone walked by with a tray of champagne glasses. Abigail took two and handed one to me. "To your health," she said, raising her glass.

I smiled and touched the rim of my glass to her. "To my health."

Most of the revelers left by ten, but a few stayed to help clean up. Rob, more helpful than he'd ever been during our marriage, carried the leftover food upstairs to the apartment and was in the kitchen with Wendy Perkins and Franklin, doing dishes and wrapping up the leftovers. I could hear them above us, Franklin's shuffling footsteps, Wendy's muffled snort-snort as she laughed at her own jokes, and the decisive clunk of Rob's cowboy boots as he walked over my head.

Garrett, Margot, Liza, Abigail, and I stayed downstairs to clean up, wiping down the tables, throwing away used plates and napkins, and rounding up the stray champagne glasses that seemed to have been abandoned on nearly every flat surface. Someone had even left one on top of the crown molding that encased the bowfront window. It must have been a good party. How had thirty-five party guests managed to go through ninety champagne glasses?

The place was a mess, but many hands made light work and soon everything was tidy again. I turned in a circle to look at the shop, my shop, and hugged myself.

"Thank you!" I said. "Thank you all so much. I can't imagine how I could ever repay you, but I want you to know that if I ever have the chance, I'll try."

"It was a nice party, wasn't it?" Margot said with a smile, her eyes sparkling. "Everyone had a good time."

"Yes, but I'm not just talking about the party. I'm talking about everything." I spread my arms wide. "I'm talking about this! Cobbled Court Quilts. My dream come true!

"Back when I first opened, Charlie told me I needed to think out of the box, to dream about what I truly wanted the shop to be, and this—this is exactly what I imagined. Something more than a quilt shop. A community, a neighborhood, where people would come together to quilt, and create, and learn, and heal, and take risks. This is what I wanted!"

I laughed with pleasure, so delighted with everything I saw around me that unexpected tears started in my eyes. "And none of it would have happened without all of you. I wanted to open a quilt shop that would help others find all those wonderful things, but I never realized that I'd find them for myself as well. Thank you," I repeated, looking into the faces of my precious son and three dear friends.

The sparkle in Margot's eyes faded, and I saw her bite her lower lip the way she always did when she was trying to figure out how to say something she didn't want to say. I held up my hand to stop her.

"Margot, it's all right. I've seen the cash-flow statements. I know. I'm going to have to close the shop."

Ever since I'd asked Margot to bring the books over to her house so I could look at them three days before, I'd known it was over. This was just the first time I'd actually said it out loud, to myself or anyone else. I took a deep breath, composing myself.

"But it's okay. I want you all to know that. Of course, I wanted the shop to succeed, and, in every way but financially, it did.

"In a few months, this place will be empty. With two failed businesses to its credit, this wonderful, improbable old building in this terrible, beautiful location will probably be abandoned forever. Cobwebs will gather in the corners, the paint on the windowsills will chip, and the plumbing will spring leaks. Maybe someone will knock it down to make way for something newer and more practical, a parking lot or a stack of office cubicles. That would be sad, but even if that happens, all of us and everyone who walked through those doors will remember that, for a little while at least, there was a remarkable little community of people who found something simple and genuine here, and it gave their lives a little bit more joy." I blinked back the tears. I wanted to get through it, wanted them to hear me out.

"If you think about it, that's a pretty good day's work: more than most people accomplish in a lifetime. And you were all part of it. Even knowing how it was going to turn out, I'd do it all over again in a heartbeat. But only if I got to do it with all of you by my side."

Now the tears began to flow in earnest for everyone except Abigail and Garrett, who had his arm around the shoulders of a sniffling Liza and was trying to comfort her.

"It's not fair!" Liza said. "You've been up against so much and you worked so hard. We all did. It isn't as if people don't like the shop. Yesterday I waited on a lady who was buying fabric to make a quilt for her daughter's wedding, and she was so excited. She said she'd never have had the courage to try it if she hadn't taken your class. Your customers love Cobbled Court Quilts—and you."

Margot pulled a tissue out of the pocket of her skirt and used it to wipe her nose. "And we were making progress on the financial side too. Every month was a little better than the last, and every month we added to our customer base. If we'd had another year, two at the outside, I think we could have made it. Liza's right. It isn't fair."

I patted Margot's arm. "I know. After Quilt Pink, I thought we might make it to the tourist season. Maybe, if I hadn't gotten sick and could have taught more classes over the winter, we'd have been able to squeak by. Who knows? But it just didn't work out that way. It's no one's fault. There are some things we just don't have control over."

Abigail, who had been listening to this exchange with dry eyes and furrowed brow, spoke up. "Do you really believe that?"

"What? That there are things we don't have control over? Of course I do."

"I don't," she said flatly. "I mean, of course you don't have control over things like flood, fire, famine, or breast cancer—things like that. But this *isn't* like that. If you close the shop now, it'll be because you gave up."

In the face of this pronouncement, Margot looked shocked and Liza looked insulted—and me? I guess I was a little of each.

"Abigail! How can you say that? After all that we've done? There isn't a promotion or project we haven't tried! We worked our fingers to the bone and did everything we knew how to do to increase our customer base."

"I know," Abigail said, "and it was working. Margot just said it was. So, given that, I just don't understand why you're going to throw in the towel and walk away."

"Because I'm out of money, time, and ideas—that's why!"

Abigail made a face. "Ridiculous! Preposterous! Money is one of the few commodities that, in a sense, is nearly infinite; you may not always *have* more, but you can always *get* more. Money is easy. Time is tougher. I'll admit, we don't always have control over how much time we've got, but, now that you're recovered from your surgery, it looks like there's every reason to believe that you have plenty of years ahead of you. And as far as ideas," she said brightly, looking around at the assemblage, "has anybody got one?"

For a moment everyone looked at everyone else, waiting to see if someone was going to speak. Finally Garrett raised his hand, slowly and cautiously, like a schoolboy asking for permission to go to the restroom in the middle of a math test. "Actually, I have been playing around with an idea."

"Well, go on," Abigail said. "Let's hear it."

Garrett cleared his throat. "All right. I've been looking over the books too, and I'd noticed that, even with the very basic kind of Web site that Margot put together—no offense, Margot."

"None taken."

"Even with a simple site and no real marketing to promote it, Web sales are the most rapidly growing segment of our business. And do you know what our best-selling items are? The charm packs and fabric medleys that Liza created, especially that chocolate brown and turquoise collection. Customers just love the way she puts colors together."

Liza beamed at the compliment, and Garrett winked at her before going on. "The problem is this: New Bern is a great little town, but it's a *little* town. Even if you could turn every woman and some of the men in town into avid quilters, you still wouldn't generate enough in-store sales to make more than a small profit. The population is just too small to support a really thriving quilt store."

I nodded. It was true. I'd known that from the first, but somehow I'd hoped to attract just enough customers from the surrounding area to keep my head above water. I'd never been looking to get rich, just to survive financially while making my vision of a quilting community a reality.

"We've got to think big," Garrett said, his voice growing stronger now that he realized everyone was tracking with him. "There are lots of quilters who don't have access to a local quilt store. If we had a truly first-class Web site, with an extensive online catalog, an inventory that is second to none, where people from all over the country and even the world would be able to find any kind of fabric, pattern, kit, or notion they could possibly imagine and have it sent to them quickly, plus unique features that would make our site stand out, I think we could make it. In fact, I think we could do better than that. I think we could make Cobbled Court Quilts into the biggest, most recognized name in quilting."

He said it with such conviction that I wanted to believe him. I think everyone did, but I still had a lot of questions. "But all that would take money and staff . . ."

"And space," Garrett confirmed. "We'd need warehouse space to house the additional inventory and to give us a place to coordinate order fulfillment."

"Well, where are we supposed to get all that?"

"Mom, I've got money saved. A lot—sixty thousand dollars."

My jaw dropped. "Sixty thousand? I . . . I had no idea."

Garrett grinned. "I told you, I was way overpaid at Claremont Solutions as well as way overworked. I never had a chance to get out of the office and buy anything, so it all went into the bank. I've been looking for a good investment, and I think this is it."

"Garrett," I protested, "you're the best son on earth, but what if you're wrong? What if you lose everything you've saved?"

"I'm young." He shrugged. "If I lose it, I've got time to make more. Like Abigail says, you can always make more. Besides, experienced computer programmers are always in demand. If I had to, I could get another cubicle job tomorrow, probably making more than I was before. But I'd rather work for you at a vastly reduced salary doing something much more exciting, something I really believe in."

"Me too!" Margot piped in. "You're going to need a marketing manager for all this. I happen to be available, and if I don't have to live in a ridiculously overpriced apartment in New York, which I'd rather not anyway, I can work cheap. But, of course, we'll need entry-level people to help with stocking, and mailing, and waiting on customers."

"There are at least a dozen women—smart, capable women who've never been given a chance—at the shelter right now who'd jump at the chance to work here," Abigail announced. "All I have to do is make a few calls and you'd have all the workers you need."

I laughed and held up my hands. As much as I wanted it to be true, I was finding it hard to keep up with everything I was hearing. "Slow down! We've got to sit down and think this through. Everything is happening so fast. I can't believe this is as easy as you're making it sound."

Garrett shook his head. "Oh no. Don't get me wrong. There's nothing easy about this. I've crunched the numbers, and, in addition to my sixty, we'll need another fifty thousand dollars just to get started. Seventy would be better. And we still need warehouse space. If we can't find an inexpensive space, that would mean we'd need even more capital. I'm not sure where we can find that kind of money."

Abigail stepped forward, about to speak, but a voice from the stairs interrupted her. I turned and saw Rob, Franklin, and Wendy standing on the stairs, listening. I wasn't sure how long they'd been there.

"I've got some money put away," Rob said quietly. "In my retirement fund. Fifty thousand dollars. If you need it, Evie, it's yours. I'd like to help you."

I didn't know what to say to that. Before I could speak, Abigail put in her two cents. "And I'm sure we can find you some cheap warehouse space. Franklin, who do we know that owns warehouses in New Bern?"

"You do. Several. You've got a big, vacant space less than three blocks from here."

Abigail looked surprised. "I do? I knew we'd bought some real estate, but I thought it was all in Florida. Shopping malls or something."

"Abigail," Franklin sighed with exasperation, "I don't know why you even bother coming to our monthly business meetings. Every month we go out, we have lunch, and I talk while you pick at your food and chat with everyone who drops by the table. Why should I waste my time trying to keep you informed about your affairs? You never pay the slightest attention."

Abigail smiled, clearly enjoying getting under Franklin's skin. "Franklin. Darling," she purred. "You do such a good job managing everything that I don't have to pay attention. I only show up at those meetings to make sure you get out of the office now and then."

Franklin growled a little and went on. "Yes, Abigail, you do own property in Florida, but you also own a good bit of the commercial real estate in New Bern. As a matter of fact, you own this building."

"I do? Evelyn is paying me rent? How much?" Uncomfortable about revealing this information publicly, Franklin crossed the room and whispered into Abigail's ear.

"That much? For this old wreck? My, Franklin, you *are* good at managing my affairs! No one but you would have dared to ask that kind of rent for this building and then gotten it. But I've got a better idea. I'd like to rent this space and the warehouse you'd mentioned to Evelyn for a more reasonable rent. Let's say ten dollars a month for both properties."

"Abigail!" I gasped. "That's too much!"

"Too much? Well, all right then. You drive a hard bargain. Five dollars a month. "

"No! You know I didn't mean it was too expensive. I mean it's too generous! You're too generous. I can't let you do it."

"Don't be silly," she scoffed. "I've got more money than I can spend in a lifetime—in two lifetimes. I don't need a few more dollars in rent money, but I do need friends. If Cobbled Court closes, what will happen to our quilt circle? It'll break up, that's what. And then what will I do with myself? Go back to attending dull cocktail parties and even duller board meetings for a bunch of organizations I never really cared about to begin with? No, thank you. Believe me; this isn't generosity on my part, Evelyn. It's self-preservation."

I shook my head. It was too much to accept, and I was not going to be swayed by glib argument. "No, Abigail. I won't let you do it. If my business is going to occupy property that you own, then I'm going to have to pay a fair price. Just like anyone else."

"Lord, you're stubborn! All right. Fine. You want to pay me? Then let's do it the old-fashioned way. Let's barter. You can pay your rent in goods and services instead of money."

"I don't understand. What could I possibly have that you'd want?"

"Your time. I'd like you to go over to the shelter every other week and give free quilting classes to the residents."

"Every week," I countered.

Abigail gave a quick nod to indicate her acceptance of my terms. "And the Wynne Foundation will pay for all the fabrics and materials for your classes," she rejoined.

"Which Cobbled Court will supply at cost."

Abigail scowled. For a woman who claimed not to have a head for business, she was a tough negotiator, but so was I. And I wasn't going to budge.

"I mean it, Abigail. Either you let me supply the materials at cost or I won't do it. Have we got a deal?"

She hesitated a moment and, seeing my resolve, sighed before clasping my outstretched hand. "We do."

〜 34 〜

Abigail Burgess Wynne

I'd forgotten my umbrella at home. Thankfully, the rain was now a steady drizzle instead of the downpour of earlier in the evening.

And though I'd assured him that there was very little chance of my getting lost or being accosted in the five blocks that lay between the quilt shop and my house, Franklin insisted on walking me home. He was in a talkative mood.

"It was a nice party," he said. "And Evelyn looked well. It's wonderful that she's not going to need any chemotherapy."

"Yes," I said and pulled the collar of my jacket up.

"And Garrett's idea for expanding the business—if it works out the way he envisions, it could change New Bern for the better, bring in all kinds of new jobs. He's a very bright young man. Between Evelyn's creativity and understanding of quilting, Garrett's vision and knowledge of e-commerce, and Margot's marketing savvy, I think they just might pull this off. Amazing that all the right people would be in the right place at the right time." Franklin coughed and glanced at me from under the brim of his gray felt hat. "And, of course, it helps that they have a fairy godmother who happens to have an interest in real estate, wouldn't you say?"

"Hmmm? Oh yes. I guess it is kind of an amazing coincidence."

"Nothing coincidental about it. Some things are meant to be."

I didn't say anything.

"What's wrong, Abbie? Are you still worried about Evelyn?"

I bit my lip, thinking how selfish I would sound if I told him the truth, but I just couldn't keep it to myself anymore. I had to talk to someone. I stopped on the sidewalk and turned to face Franklin.

"It's Liza," I admitted. "I know it's the right thing, her going back to school. I want her to be happy, but the thought of returning to my old, lonely life is awful beyond imagining. I'm going to miss her so much that it hurts even to think about it. What am I going to do?"

Franklin paused for a long moment before speaking, and when he did, his voice sounded strange, soft and oddly hesitant.

"Yes. Well. I've got some ideas on that subject," he said. He didn't look at me, just kept his eyes focused down at the pavement. He cleared his throat. "The thing is, Abbie, that . . . well, you and I have been friends for a long time. At least, that's how I've always thought of us. . . ."

I nodded. "Until this year, I don't think I had any friends other than you, Franklin. But you're still my best friend. I guess you always have been. I just didn't realize it until recently."

"Well, I'm glad to hear it. I feel the same. As you know, over the years, I've overseen the creation of scores of successful business partnerships, as well as the dissolution of scores of unsuccessful ones. And in my opinion, the best partnerships, the ones that last, are always founded on a basis of mutual admiration and respect." He looked at me, as if waiting for me to add something, but I wasn't sure what he expected me to say.

"Yes. I suppose you're right."

He smiled broadly, apparently relieved that I agreed with his point—whatever his point was. "Good! Right! That's why I've been thinking that you and I . . . well . . . We respect and admire each other, and, in the last year, I have to say I've come to admire you more than ever before." He reached out, took the hem of my sleeve and held it gently between his thumb and forefinger and didn't let go, a soft-mouthed retriever intent on carrying home his quarry without leaving a mark.

"I've always . . . admired you, but you were so determined not to let anyone get close. You're different now. This business with Liza, and with your friends, Margot and Evelyn, has changed you, and for the better.

"Tonight, when you told Evelyn you were going to let her have the shop and the warehouse practically rent-free—and then topped it off by figuring out a way she could save face while doing something that would benefit the women at the shelter?" He laughed. "I've always admired you, Abbie, but never quite as much as tonight. You were always generous with your checkbook, but only because it enhanced your public image while keeping you at a safe distance from any real human suffering. Now there are no caveats, no buts, no conditions. You're generous. End of story. Not only that, you're more open with your feelings, more willing to take risks."

I shrugged, not sure what to say to all this. But he was right, something had changed me. Or somebody. Uninvited and unwanted, Liza, Evelyn, and Margot had barged into my life and turned it upside down. Thank God.

"And that," Franklin continued, resuming his normal tone of voice, "is another requirement for a successful partnership, an openness to risk on the part of the parties involved. And I, for my part, am open to the possibility of risk. Therefore . . . I was wondering if you . . ."

He paused, shifting from one foot to another as if he had a pebble in his shoe. He coughed, and I saw some color rising in his cheeks. I looked at him, wondering if he wasn't coming down with a cold and thinking that standing here in the rain couldn't be good for him if he was, but then his meaning began to dawn on me. I was astounded.

"Franklin!" I exclaimed. "Is this a proposal?"

His eyes flew open wide, and he swallowed hard. "Why? Does it sound like one?"

"Well. Sort of. Not quite." The more I said, the sillier I felt. His shocked response to my question made me think I'd been mistaken, but at the risk of making a complete fool of myself, I decided I'd better make my position clear.

"Franklin, I can only assume that in some obtuse, lawyerly way, you're trying to say that you think we might want to, as the young people would say, 'take our relationship to the next level.' Is that right?"

Franklin nodded mutely.

"I see. Well. If you were asking me to marry you, I guess I'd say that, even though we've known each other for thirty years, this all seems a bit sudden. But if you weren't proposing, then I'm wondering what you did have in mind. Maybe it's old-fashioned, but I've learned the hard way that rushing into . . ." I waited for him to fill in the blank, but he just looked at me. I pressed on, embarrassed by what I was about to say and slightly irritated at Franklin for forcing me to say it. "Rushing into any kind of . . . intimate relationship . . . before cementing that relationship in law is a mistake. So if that's what you were thinking, you can just put it out of your mind right now!"

If possible, Franklin's eyes grew even wider. "Lord, no! I wasn't talking about anything like that, Abbie! I care for you too much to compromise you or your feelings in any way." He blushed right to the edges of his receding hairline. In thirty years I'd never seen Franklin blush. I didn't know he could.

"The last thing I had in mind was any kind of indecent proposal, I assure you!"

This information should have been a relief to me, and in a way it was, but it was also somewhat insulting. However, I decided to sort that out later. What *did* he want? It was dark and cold and my feet were wet. I was in no mood for a mystery.

"Franklin, what are you trying to say? For once in your life, quit talking like a lawyer and speak English."

"All right. I will. Abbie . . . I . . . I care about you. In fact, I love you. I have for years. And what I want to know is this . . ." He cleared his throat again. "Would you like to go steady?"

He stood there, wet, cold, and pathetic. I'd never seen him looking so handsome. A voice that I was surprised to realize was mine said, "Yes, Franklin. I believe I would."

He laughed aloud and lunged toward me, arms outstretched, but then remembered his manners. He took a step backward.

"Abbie, would it be all right if I kissed you?"

I frowned. "Frankin, how long is it that you think you've been in love with me?"

"Probably from the beginning, I guess."

"Are you telling me that you've loved me for thirty years but this is the first time you'd ever thought to ask if you could kiss me?" I asked incredulously.

"Oh, I thought about it, all right. Plenty of times. I just never worked up the nerve to actually say it before. I was afraid you might smack me in the mouth or something." Franklin's eyes crinkled just a little at the corners. A whisper of a smiled tugged at his mouth.

"Hmmph! I still might. In fact, I probably should. But that'd probably scare you off for another thirty years. How old would that make us by then? Let me see. . . ."

"Abigail, shut up," he said and opened his arms.

I did, stepping into his embrace and lifting my lips to meet with his while the rain fell, the fat, heavy drops hitting the brim of Franklin's hat in an insistent staccato, like an approving round of applause.

∽ 35 ∽

Evelyn Dixon

It was still drizzling the next morning, but, in spite of the cloudy skies, I woke up feeling better than I had in a long time. I actually whistled as I went into the bathroom, turned on the faucet to get the hot water going, which, on the second floor of an antique building with antique plumbing to match, could take several minutes, and started brushing my teeth.

As I rolled up the tube, trying to coax the last bit of toothpaste out, I thought about the previous night.

Who could have imagined it? Just a few weeks ago I was so downhearted and depressed that I couldn't face the idea of even getting out of bed, and now, here I was whistling, cancer free, and about to embark on the expansion of my business, a business that until a few hours before had been teetering on the edge of bankruptcy. Now it seemed possible that Cobbled Court Quilts was poised to become what I'd always dreamed it would be, not just a successful quilt shop but an important asset to the community and a community unto itself, where quilters of all ages and backgrounds would gather together for companionship, self-expression, and even healing.

I bared my teeth in a genuine grin as I began brushing. Abigail didn't have to ask me to teach classes at the shelter in lieu of rent; I'd have gladly done it for free. But she knew that. It was just her way of helping me save face while at the same time bringing some good into the lives of the women at the shelter, women whom I could see she genuinely cared about. And it would do them good. I knew it would. Just like it had Abigail, Margot, and Liza. These novice quilters from the shelter—many of them abused, debased; women who had been told over and over again that they were worthless—would find confidence and their own artistic voice as they sat side by side, stitching together something surprising and beautiful out of cast-off scraps of fabric that anyone besides a quilter would think were too insignificant to be of any use.

Yes! I decided as I spat a white stream into the sink and filled the cup with water to rinse my mouth. That was it! My beginners class project at the shelter would be a scrap quilt, something that would help them realize that even the most torn and ragged lives could be remade into something to be treasured for generations to come. No doubt about it; this class was going to change lives. I wondered how long it would take to order the machines and get them delivered to the shelter. I couldn't wait to get started!

Lifting my legs high and humming "Zip-a-Dee-Doo-Dah," a tune I'd forgotten I even remembered, I kicked off my slippers one by one, like a chorus girl in a kick line, and reached behind the shower curtain to test the water. Almost hot enough. Another minute should do it.

Best of all, I thought while I pulled a stack of fresh towels out of the closet and put the old ones in the laundry hamper, I was going to be working with some of the people I loved most in the world: Abigail, Margot, and Garrett. I smiled, thinking how wonderful it would be to have Garrett in New Bern permanently. Of course, he'd want to get a place of his own. Living with your mother for a few weeks while you were helping her through a health crisis was one thing, but a young man needed a place of his own—somewhere he could leave dirty dishes in the sink, play video games until two in the morning, and have friends over.

The steam coming over the top of the plastic curtain told me the shower was hot enough.

And one of those friends, I thought as I took off my robe and carried the last towel to the bar near the shower, was certain to be Liza. During her school breaks, I was sure she'd be visiting Garrett often. That was fine with me. Liza was still very young and maybe a little rough around the edges, but she was a smart, lovely, giving young woman. Garrett could do a lot worse, and besides, you didn't need a mother's intuition to notice the spark between them. The way he looked at her when he thought no one else was looking was like thirst gazing on water.

It was the same look that, for just a moment last night, I thought I'd seen on Charlie's face when his eyes seemed to pierce the crowd, searching for my face the same way I was searching for his. Among the shouted chorus of congratulations, Charlie's was the voice my ears were straining to hear, his face the face my eyes hunted for among the throng of well-wishers.

I stood still on the center of the bath mat, clutching a towel close to my body, staring at nothing, my eyes focused on the tiny bathroom window that framed the dull, gray sky.

Yes, for a moment last night, Charlie's eyes had searched for me just as mine were searching for him. At least, that's what I'd thought. And when he'd found me, for a second, I thought his face was going to split into a grin and he was going to come to me, parting the crowd like an ancient sea as he pushed his way to be at my side. But then, in a breath, his eyes changed, flitted up over my head, the spark in them suddenly extinguished, and he turned his back on me. The spark was extinguished. Or had I imagined it? Was it ever there to begin with?

A fist pounded on the bathroom door, interrupting my train of thought. "Mom! How long are you going to be in there? I want to get to the bank as soon as it opens."

"Not long. Five minutes."

"Save a little hot water for me too," he called good-naturedly. "We've got to look like solid citizens today. Good investments."

"Will do, partner," I said brightly, forcing my voice to match the cheery optimism in my son's, an optimism that had been mine until, startled by the sound of Garrett's voice, I'd dropped the towel and, turning to answer him, saw the blurred reflection of my naked body in the steam-clouded mirror, the pink, half-healed scars that traced my ravaged torso. I closed my eyes and turned away.

Stop it, Evelyn. There's no point in thinking about what might have been. And there's no point in feeling sorry for yourself. You're alive. You don't have to get chemo. You've got a new chance at life, a wonderful son, and some of the most amazing friends on the face of the earth—and Charlie is one of them. Don't mess that up. You're lucky. Friendship should be enough for you. It must be.

By the time the meeting wrapped up, lunch hour had come and gone. Garrett headed back to the apartment, saying he'd eat some of the party leftovers before relieving Margot in the shop. I said I'd see him later, after I ran a few errands.

The rain had finally let up. I hopped across a few puddles as I walked to the Grill.

Inside, a single pair of diners lingered over coffee and dessert. The waitstaff had all gone home. Charlie stood behind the bar with his back turned and a clipboard in his hand.

"Table for one?" I asked.

"It's past three. The kitchen is closed." He turned. "Oh. Hi, Evelyn. I didn't realize it was you. Kitchen really is closed though. If you're hungry, I could get you a bowl of soup, but that's the best I can do right now."

I shook my head. "I was just coming over to see you. I was at the Bean this morning. Did I miss you?"

"No. Came in early today. Trying to figure out why we're running low on scotch. Either one of my waiters is taking a wee nip or five when he thinks no one is looking, or they're giving free drinks to their friends when I'm out of the restaurant, or they're just pouring heavy." He shrugged. "One way or another, it's costing me money. I've got to put a stop to it."

"It's probably the latter, Charlie. Your waiters aren't dishonest, just generous. It's to be expected," I teased. "They're taking their cues from the owner."

Charlie didn't so much as crack a smile. "I've got to finish this, Evelyn. Then I've got to go to the market and pick up something before the kitchen opens for dinner. I really don't have time to visit today."

Clearly, Abigail had been wrong and I had been right. Something was bothering Charlie. He was obviously trying to put me off, just like he had at the party, but I was determined to get to the bottom of this.

"Charlie, you've got nearly three hours until dinner. What I've got to say won't take five minutes."

He put down the clipboard and crossed his arms over his chest. "All right. What is it?"

"What's the matter? Why are you mad at me?"

"I don't know what you're talking about."

I stared at him, refusing to be brushed aside. "Pardon me. I take back what I said before. What I have to say should take five minutes, but if you insist on having me pull it out of you like an impacted molar it's going to take five hours. And be just as painful."

"Evelyn," he said, "other than my becoming more behind schedule the longer you stand here blathering, there is nothing the matter with me. I am not angry with you. I am not anything with you. If I seem upset, it's because I'm low on scotch and irritated with my staff. Nothing more."

He opened his hands, a magician showing there was nothing up his sleeve, and tried to smooth the hard edge in his voice. I wasn't buying.

"You're always irritated with your staff, Charlie. This is more than that," I insisted. "Now fess up. What's bothering you? You can tell me. We're friends."

Charlie's bushy eyebrows shot up. "Friends? Is that what we are? Ah. I wondered."

"What's that supposed to mean? Aren't we?"

"If you say so, Evelyn. Friends. Fine. That's wonderful. Now, if you don't mind, friend"—he scowled and started to come out from behind the bar—"I've got work to do."

I walked to the end of the counter and blocked his exit. "Actually, I do mind. For heaven's sake, Charlie. What's got into you? You're always a little grumpy. Oddly enough, its part of your charm, but today you're just plain obnoxious. Now tell me what's up or I'm going to take one of those half-empty scotch bottles and knock some sense into you!" The last remaining diners turned and craned their necks to see what was going on.

"Pipe down!" Charlie hissed. "I've got customers!"

I planted my feet and crossed my arms over my chest. "I don't care. Either you talk to me," I insisted in a somewhat lower tone, "or I'm going to make a scene that'll make your hair curl. Your customers too!"

Whether because they were actually finished with their lunch or, hearing Charlie and me spit at each other like a couple of cats, they decided it was time to leave, the diners got to their feet and headed for the door. Charlie pasted a smile on his face and waved as they passed by the bar. "Thanks for coming in, folks. Hope to see you again soon."

"You will," the man responded as he opened the door for his lady. "It was delicious."

Charlie kept grinning until the door closed behind them and then turned to face me. With the restaurant empty, he didn't bother keeping his voice down.

"Evelyn, I've had enough of this. I don't have the time, patience, or inclination to participate in your little charade. You want to play games—fine! Nobody's stopping you. But you're not going to play them with me. I've got more important things to do with my time."

"Games? What games? What are you talking about?"

He barked out a bitter, derisive laugh and smacked his hand against the bar. "Oh, don't play the innocent with me! It's been a long time since I've had any kind of relationship with a woman, and now I remember why. You're untrustworthy—the whole lot of you. As my mother used to say, 'Beauty won't make the pot boil.' I should have thought of that before last night, but there's nothing to be done about it now. Better late than never."

Charlie was normally a man of few words, but now I held up my hands in an effort to dam this torrent of accusation. "What's that supposed to mean? Charlie, hold on a minute! Will you just take a breath and try to make me understand what you're saying? Try speaking English this time, will you?"

"Oh, you're a coy one, aren't you? Don't try that on me, Evelyn. It took some time, but at least give me credit for having enough sense to see through you at last."

"What!"

"You used me." He shrugged. "Fine! I can accept that. But now that you've got what you wanted from the first, don't come around with any of this 'Oh, Charlie, dear. Let's be friends' nonsense." He batted his eyelashes and raised the pitch of his voice in an imitation of female coquettishness that, if I hadn't been so confused and angry, would have made me laugh.

"You fooled me once, Evelyn. That's my own stupid fault. But damned if I'll let you do it again."

"I used you? That's what you're saying?" I asked incredulously. I could feel the heat of color rising in my face as I began to understand what he was accusing me of. Charlie gave his head one sharp, definitive nod. "I see. That's interesting. Just how did I do this?"

He narrowed his eyes. "As if you didn't know," he scoffed. "You used our relationship to make your ex-husband jealous, lure him up here, and get him to come back to you. And you even got him to bankroll your business in the process! Well, good for you! You wanted the big lout back, and now you've got him. Cowboy boots and all. I'm sure he'll bring you just as much happiness as he always did," Charlie sneered. "But now that you've gotten what you wanted, I'll thank you to leave me out of it!"

I couldn't believe my ears. And I was so angry I didn't know what to say. But my ire had to boil over into something, and it did—my arm. I took a step forward and slapped him hard. It caught him by surprise. Me too.

"Ouch!" he cried and stepped behind the bar again, looking to put something solid between us.

"Have you lost your mind?" I cried. "I'm not interested in winning back Rob. In fact, last night, before we got to the party, he asked me to take him back and I said no!" Charlie's eyebrows shot up and an expression of doubt crossed his face.

"You did?"

"Rob's on his way back to Texas right now. He left this morning."

"But what about the money? Abigail was in here and said Rob was going to give you fifty thousand dollars so you could expand the business. Why would he do that if he wasn't planning on you two getting back together? After all, there's no such thing as a free lunch." He gave me a knowing look, as if this homey wisdom trumped all facts.

"Who told you that? Your mother, I suppose."

"No," he deadpanned. "José Luis Garza. Headwaiter at the Hampton House, where I bussed tables for a year after I got off the boat from Ireland. Taught me everything I know. He was a greedy so-and-so." Charlie smiled a little, trying to coax me into doing the same, but I wasn't buying. "So Rob's not investing in Cobbled Court?" he asked quietly.

"No. He offered, which was kind of him, but I turned him down . . . and for exactly the reason your waiter friend gave. There is no such thing as a free lunch. I think Rob truly wanted to help me out, to make amends somehow, but to avoid any confusion I declined his offer and decided to see about getting another bank loan. Garrett and I went over there this morning. With Abigail's backing and my newly reduced rent, it looks like they're willing to do it."

"Good. Good for you." He nodded. There was an awkward silence as each of us waited for the other to speak. Finally, I took the plunge.

"Charlie Donnelly, you are the biggest fool on God's green earth. Did anyone ever tell you that?"

"Frequently."

"I don't know what you could have thought was going on between Rob and me. No such thing as a free lunch," I muttered. "Anybody would think you were jealous or something. That you and I were . . . You know what I've been through. The operations and all. I mean, after all that, it's not very likely that . . . Well, you know what I mean."

A quizzical look crossed his face. "No. I don't."

I sighed, exasperated. "Charlie, don't make me spell it out. After the mastectomies, I can't imagine there's much in the way of romance on my horizon. No one is going to find me attractive. Not that way."

"What are you talking about? Why wouldn't they? I certainly do."

The weight of this statement and the silence that followed pressed me on all sides, filling the room like water in a swimmer's ear, making it hard to know for sure the meaning and truth of the words that were being said in the dry world above. Charlie spoke first.

"Evelyn—"

"Don't," I said, drawing back. "Don't patronize me, Charlie. You don't have to do that. I'm not asking for more. Your friendship means worlds to me. Don't feel that you have to pretend."

"Pretend? Is that what you think I've been doing all these months? Pretending we're friends? And then pretending to fall in love with you?"

I bit my lip. Not daring to respond. He couldn't mean what he was saying. It wasn't possible.

"I wish to heaven I had been pretending," he puffed. "It wouldn't have been half so painful—coming to admire you, then care for you, then love you and having to watch you suffer so these last months and not being able to do a thing to stop it. I tried to make myself busy at the restaurant, hoping that immersing myself in work would help me forget my feelings for you. It was no good. I couldn't stay away. But you were so sick. The last thing you needed was some lovesick Irishman mooning after you. And I didn't know what to say to you anyway. So every morning, during the hour when I used to meet you at the Bean for coffee, I went to the early mass to pray for you. And after that I went into my kitchen and cooked for you, then brought you what I'd made, hoping you'd know what I was trying to say. The Irish may be a nation of poets, but I'm no Yeats. My kind of poetry is produced in the kitchen; the chicken pot pie that reminds you of your mother's, the dish so perfectly seasoned it brings tears to your eyes, the mousse au chocolate so dense and rich and sinful that it reminds you of your first love." He took a step closer and wrapped his fingers around my wrist like a bracelet.

"Or at least your first lust." He smiled gently. "When you're

316 • *Marie Bostwick*

young it can be hard to tell the difference, but I'm not young anymore, Evelyn. Neither are you. We know what love is. Don't we?"

I nodded, not trusting my voice.

He wrapped his other hand low across my back and pulled me
close. "Then how could you think, Evelyn, that I'd be so stupid, so
shallow, as to let my feelings for you be swayed by your cancer? You
are beautiful. Breasts, no breasts, reconstructed breasts. It makes no
difference to me. I love you. I love your creativity and imagination,
the way you can take little scraps of cloth and turn them into something lovely. I love your kindness, your generosity, how, even in the
middle of the worst crisis of your life, you were looking to take
care of the people who were taking care of you. I love your humor
and bravery, the way you faced the worst that life can dish out and
still came out smiling. I love everything about you. Your spirit, your
mind, your face, and your body. You are beautiful to me, Evelyn.
You always will be."

His lips were soft on mine, but sure, as if he'd known for a long
time exactly how he wanted to kiss me. My head dropped back and
my lips parted ever so slightly, easily, as if I'd known for a long time
that I wanted to be kissed.

Lifting his mouth from mine, he traced a fingertip over the ridge
of my cheekbone and down to my lips. "Sweet girl," he whispered.
"Sweet. Again." He lowered his head again.

"Charlie. Wait."

His eyes, so warm and sparkling an instant before, were suddenly dark and serious.

"Why? What is it?" He paused, searching my face for an answer.
"Do you love me?"

There is no question on earth that leaves a person more exposed,
more vulnerable, than that one. It takes a special kind of courage to
utter it; a courage that I had once known, but which had deserted
me years before, even before the divorce. Charlie's bravery as-

tounded me, touched me, shamed me. Anyone who was willing to risk so much for the sake of love deserved to be loved in kind.

"Tell me the truth, Evelyn. Do you love me?"

"I do. I think I do. But you're right, Charlie. We're neither of us young anymore. We're too old to risk getting our hearts broken for anything less than the genuine article." The wary, belligerent expression came back to his face, and he drew back a little, taking on that defensive stance of his that always reminded me a little of a prizefighter preparing to absorb the next blow.

"Don't look at me like that," I said. "I'm not giving you the brush-off or trying to let you down easy. One thing I've learned from the last year is that life is shorter and more precious than I had imagined—much too short to spend it speaking in code. I've resolved to start saying exactly what I mean. And what I mean is I think I love you and that, probably, I have for a long time. But I was so wrapped up in myself, first in the store and then in getting better, that I was blind to everything else. I couldn't focus on anything else but getting through the next day, let alone think about love or the future. For a while I wasn't convinced there was a future to think about."

"And now?"

I smiled. "Now it's a whole new day. A new life. But that doesn't mean I'm not carrying baggage from the old life with me. What I'm trying to say is, Charlie, that I'm not sure I'm quite ready to believe that anyone can love me. And not just because of the cancer. I've been carrying this with me for a long time."

"But don't you hear what I'm saying to you, Evelyn? I do love you."

"I know. But hearing it and believing it are two different things. Until I work that out in my mind, I'm not sure I'm ready for love. And then," I said, furrowing my brow, "there was the kiss."

Insulted, he reared his head back. "The kiss? And what was wrong with it? I thought it was pretty good."

"It was. Better than good. Spectacular, actually." Charlie grinned, looking very pleased with himself.

"That's the problem. You see, while you say that you love me no matter what, right now the idea of physical intimacy is frightening to me. I'm still getting over the shock of seeing myself naked in the mirror. I'm certainly not ready to let anyone else see me that way."

"Well, it wasn't like I was planning on throwing you to the floor and ravishing you."

"Good thing, because you might as well know right now that my views on love and marriage are very old-fashioned. Not that I'm against the idea of 'ravishment' in general." I smiled. "After all, I have been known to read the occasional Highland romance novel. But there is a proper time and place for everything."

He nodded and reached for my hand again, holding it in his gently. "All right. I can live with that. I can wait. And when the time comes, if it ever does, I can even work on a Scottish accent. If tha' wa' help yeh, lassie."

"Hmmm. A good effort, but no thanks. Besides," I said, "the Irish is starting to grow on me." He laughed, and I did too, amazed to realize that I was actually flirting with a man. I'd forgotten I knew how.

When the sound of our combined merriment faded, Charlie's face became serious again. He took a long, slow breath. "Well, then, where does that leave us? Tell me what you want me to do, Evelyn, and I'll do it. If it's time you need, then I'll give it to you. Anything," he said and then lifted my hand to his lips and kissed my fingertips so softly that it felt like a butterfly had lit upon them. For a moment, I forgot to breathe.

He took my open palm and laid it flat against his chest. Beneath his muscles, I felt the pulse of his heartbeat against my fingers, steady and strong, trustworthy.

"It's taken fifty-four years for me to meet the love of my life. I can be patient a little longer, Evelyn. You're worth the wait."

❧ 36 ❧

Evelyn Dixon

"Evelyn!" Margot shouted over the din of chattering women's voices. "We're out of coffee!"

"Excuse me just a moment," I said to the reporter. "I'll be right back."

Margot stood by the refreshment table holding an empty coffee can. "We're out of coffee!" she repeated. "I had it on my to-do list, but I was so busy assembling extra kits that I forgot. I'm sorry."

"Don't worry about it. Getting those kits put together was more important."

"Maybe I should run to the market now," Margot said uncertainly as she looked around the crowded shop.

I shook my head. "No. We're too busy here. I need you to give Garrett and Wendy a hand at the registers. The customers are lined up six deep. I'll run up to the apartment. Maybe I've got enough to make one more pot."

Ivy, our newest employee, walked by carrying an armload of fabric bolts.

"We were running low on muslin backings," she said. "I thought I'd better bring some down from the stockroom. What's going on?"

"I forgot to buy coffee," Margot mumbled. She really was being too hard on herself.

"Oh, don't worry. I saw we were running low, so I picked some up on the way to work this morning. I should have told you. There's two cans in the cupboard under the sink."

Margot breathed a sigh of relief. "Thanks, Ivy. You're a lifesaver! Do you need help with those bolts?"

"Nope. Got it," she said with a smile and then hurried off with her burden.

"She's fabulous!" Margot exclaimed when Ivy was out of earshot. "Smart, efficient, learns fast, and such a hard worker!"

"She's a find, all right. Still a little unsure of herself, but that will change in time."

Margot nodded. "She must be a great mother too. That little Bethany is such a sweetheart! Of course, after today, I'm not sure Ivy is going to get her daughter back," Margot giggled. "Abigail is practically glued to her!"

I smiled and turned to look at a long table set up by the front window, where Abigail was teaching the running stitch to a group of novice quilters. Bethany sat by her side, her tongue sticking out the side of her mouth as she concentrated on trying to sew straight, even stitches while Abigail, beaming with pride, praised her efforts.

"What about the baby brother, Bobby?" Margot asked. "Where is he today?"

"Franklin's watching him. He's as crazy about Bobby as Abigail is about Bethany. They've sort of become honorary grandparents to the kids."

I laughed. "Remember when Liza dragged Abigail in here a year ago? Could you ever have imagined that under that iceberg exterior there was a quilter, philanthropist, and grandma all waiting to thaw out?"

"Not in a million years," Margot said. "Hey, you'd better get back to your interview. The reporter keeps looking at her watch."

"Oh! I almost forgot. She's got a deadline. You got everything under control here?"

"Well, it's chaos, but it's organized chaos. We're fine. Get back over there and be famous," she teased. "Seems like I can't turn on the TV or open the paper without seeing your face. You're a celebrity!"

"Sure I am. Go make coffee."

"Okay," she giggled, "but be sure to let me know if the paparazzi show up!" She scurried off with the coffee pot.

"Sorry," I murmured to the waiting reporter. "We had a little caffeine crisis. Now, what was your question?"

"I'd just asked how you think this Quilt Pink event compares to last year's." She nodded to the photographer, who turned on the pocket tape recorder and held it close to me, then pulled a lined notebook out of her pocket and started taking notes.

"Oh, that's right. Well, as you can see, it's certainly much larger." I smiled and spread my arms wide to encompass the throng of women. "We've got probably three times as many quilters in attendance as last year. Thankfully, we just opened up a new, much larger workroom on the second floor, and we've used that to accommodate the additional crowds. If we'd had this many people show up last year, I don't know where we'd have put them!"

"Why do you think so many more quilters have chosen to participate this year?"

"That's because of all the media attention. Last month, a producer from *Rise 'N' Shine Connecticut* called to ask if I'd come on the show to talk about Quilt Pink. It was part of their series on breast-cancer awareness. After that, I got calls from all kinds of magazines, newspapers, and radio stations. The press got the word out, and the quilters started coming out of the woodwork!"

The reporter looked up from the notebook. "And were you surprised by the response?"

"Yes and no. Once they heard about it, I wasn't really surprised to see the quilters respond in such numbers. Quilters are some of the most generous, caring, community-minded people you'll ever meet. But I was certainly surprised by all the media attention."

"Well, it's a remarkable story," she commented. "You decide to host your first Quilt Pink event only to be diagnosed with breast cancer yourself. And now, a year later, you're hosting your second Quilt Pink day; this time as a cancer survivor. You don't come across stories like that every day of the week. You've become a symbol of courage to people all over the state."

I couldn't help but grin at this last. "Ha! If you'd seen me this time last year, on this very day, sitting in this shop, overwhelmed, overwrought, and bawling my eyes out—the last thing you could have called me was courageous. I was terrified! But just when I needed them, God sent me three angels—Abigail, Liza, and Margot. Oh! And one more—Mary Dell. I can't forget her! They picked me up, dusted me off, and stayed with me every step of the way. They're the courageous ones. Not me."

The reporter nodded as she scribbled down a few notes. "What advice would you give to others battling breast cancer?"

"The same as I'd give to any woman who is facing any challenge or hardship in her life. Cling to your friends and be a friend to others. The need for friendship is the single thread that we all have running through us. Quilters have always known that. Just look around," I said, scanning the faces of the women as they sewed, talked, laughed, and worked on the individual blocks that, when combined, would become one more piece of ammunition against an enemy they were determined to defeat. There was nothing they couldn't accomplish, no crisis too big for them to overcome, as long as they faced it together.

"See what I mean? They're the real story here. If you want to know about courage and the power of community, go interview them."

"Thanks, Evelyn," the reporter said and closed her notebook. "I'll do that. Any suggestions on who I should start with?"

The bells jingled as the front door opened. Charlie walked in, loaded down with bakery boxes, and gave me a wink before heading back to the kitchen. I smiled and winked back.

"Why don't you talk to Ivy. She was one of the first women who took the beginner's quilting class at the shelter. Now she works here. Or there's Abigail. She's the woman who started the shelter program. Or Carol," I said, pointing to a gray-haired woman who was sitting in a circle of quilters, laughing as she worked a knot out of her thread. "Her husband passed away a few months ago, and she was so depressed she didn't even want to leave the house. Wendy dragged her down here and made her sign up for a quilting class, and look at her now! Really"—I shrugged—"go sit down and talk with anybody. It doesn't matter who. Every woman in this room has a story worth hearing."

"Thanks. I will." She shook my hand. "It was nice talking with you."

"Same to you," I said, walking in the direction of the kitchen. "I've got to get back to work, but let me know if you need anything else."

Charlie had piled the boxes on the counter and was filling an empty tray with my favorite butterscotch macadamia-nut cookies.

"Those look great!" I exclaimed, reaching for a cookie. Charlie smacked the back of my hand lightly.

"Hey! What was that for?"

"Don't touch those," he said. "They're for the customers."

"But I'm starving. I didn't get any breakfast or lunch either."

Unsympathetic, Charlie kept putting cookies on the plate. "That's not my problem," he said. "I was only hired to feed the guests, not the help."

"Yeah, but I'm the one who's paying the catering bill."

"Doesn't matter. Customers first. You can have the leftovers, if there are any. I swear, Evelyn, have you got quilters out there or a plague of locusts? I've never seen women eat so much, so fast!"

"Well, quilting is hard work. They've built up an appetite. Me too. Aw, please," I pleaded and came up behind him, draping my arms over his shoulders and laying my head on his back. "Just one little cookie? Please? For me?"

He turned around, wrapped his arms around the small of my back, and then, using one foot, kicked the door closed.

"Well," he said, pulling me close, nestling my body tight to his and tilting my chin up to meet his lips, "maybe we can work something out."

One minute later, someone was pounding on the door.

"Mom? Are you in there?"

Charlie unlocked his lips from mine and sighed. "She is, Garrett. Come in."

Garrett pushed open the door. "Hi, Charlie. I didn't know you were here. Hey! Those cookies look great!" He grabbed one and took a bite before Charlie could say anything.

Charlie growled and carried the tray out to the refreshment table.

"What do you need, sweetie?"

"Two things. One, where do you keep the extra tape for the cash register?"

"In my office, second file drawer from the bottom."

"Good. Two," he said with a grin, "Liza's here."

"She is! Why didn't you say so! I thought she had a project to finish this weekend!"

Just then, Liza's head popped out from behind the door. "Surprise! You didn't really think I could stay away, did you?" She ducked under Garrett's arm so it was resting on her shoulder. He planted a kiss on the top of her head.

"I told my professor how much you needed me, so she gave me a three-day extension on my project. Now, what can I do to help?"

It was nearly four o'clock. Only one hour until closing. The last few quilters were handing in their blocks and heading home. Thank heaven! I was never so tired in all my life. Tired but very, very happy.

"How'd we do?" I asked Margot.

She held up a hand, demanding silence as she flipped through the stack of finished blocks. "One hundred and seventy-one!" she announced.

"You're kidding! That's more than twice as many as last year," I laughed. "No wonder my feet hurt!"

"Your feet. What about my hands?" Garrett moaned. "My index fingers have gone numb from ringing up sales. I don't know how to tell you this, Mom, but we might actually make a profit this month."

"And that's not even counting the customers who bought kits to make at home," Liza said. "We should be able to make six or seven quilts for this year's auction."

"All of which Abigail will end up buying at a very inflated price," I said.

Abigail entered the room carrying a tray filled with sandwiches and paper cups. "I heard that."

"Abbie, you don't have to buy all the quilts, you know," Margot said. "Someone else might want some."

"Well, then they can just outbid me, can't they? It's all for a good cause; besides, I like quilts. They're art objects. I've decided to collect them and then donate them to the new folk-art exhibit at the museum."

"I didn't know the museum had a folk-art exhibit," Ivy said.

Abigail put the tray of sandwiches on the counter. "They don't, but they will once I donate my quilt collection and money for the new folk-art wing." Abigail tilted her chin and beamed an imperious smile.

"Liza, are you sure you wouldn't like to move back home and work at the museum? They'll be looking for a new curator any day now."

Everybody broke up laughing and grabbed sandwiches from the plate. Charlie came in with an uncorked bottle of champagne.

"Ladies and gentlemen! Your glasses, if you please!" We each took a cup, and Charlie filled them with bubbly.

He put down the bottle and raised his cup. "I propose a toast. To Evelyn!"

"I've got a better one," I said, looking around the circle of faces. "To friends! The old and the new!"

"To friends!" they chanted.

The front door opened, the bell jingling to signal the arrival of another customer. I turned around and saw two women. One was wearing a bright blue headscarf and a smile. It was Vicky. I'd met her while I was in the hospital. I didn't know the other woman.

I went to greet them, giving Vicky a big hug. "How are you? How's the chemo going?" I asked.

"Fantastic! I finished up three weeks ago, and the doctor says everything is looking good. Look!" she said, pulling back the edge of her scarf. "My hair is starting to come back in!"

"Looking good! Hi. I'm Evelyn," I said, extending my hand to the other woman.

"I'm Debbie," she said softly. Her skin was pale, and there were dark circles under her eyes, as if she hadn't been sleeping well.

"Debbie and I met at the cancer support group," Vicky said. "She's just got her diagnosis. DCIS. Just like you." I smiled at Debbie. She tried to smile back.

"I was telling Debbie all about your Quilt Pink event, and I thought it would be nice if Debbie could come to make a quilt block and talk to you." She looked around the almost empty shop. "Are we too late?"

From behind the counter, Abigail piped up. "Not at all! We've plenty of extra kits. Liza, darling, would you clear off that table? The sandwiches are gone, but I think there are some cookies left in the back."

"I'll go get them," Margot said, bustling toward the kitchen. "I'll bring coffee too."

Exhausted a moment before, the whole team now switched into high gear, finding chairs, sewing notions, and fabric for the newcomers. I sat down next to Debbie.

"I've never done this before," she said anxiously as she picked up a needle. "This is all new to me."

"That's all right," I said. "You don't have to be afraid. You're among friends."

I turned the CLOSED sign face out, went out the door, and locked it behind me.

Charlie was hosting dinner at the Grill. Everybody had gone ahead, but I'd lagged behind, promising to join them soon.

The September air was chilly, crisp and clear, just as it had been on that afternoon two years before, when I'd wandered down an uneven, cobbled alley and discovered a different world—a crumbling building, a broken-paned window, a door with peeling paint, a discarded dream.

It had been as easy and unexpected as that. A corner turned. A breath taken. The pendulum swings. Everything changes. As it had and would again, and again, and again.

I always tell students that quilts are made up of straight lines, but that isn't true. Quilts are made of broken lines, just like life. Over and over again, we try to walk a straight path but run into dead ends, sharp corners, and uneven ground that cut us off and forces us to change direction. Sometimes it's painful, other times joyful. But it isn't until you take a moment to stand still, step off the line, and back away that you finally see the truth. Those unexpected turns and startling about-faces, the chaotic path? It wasn't chaotic at all. When you step back to see where you've been, you discover the shape, the reason, the intricately beautiful pattern and vivid colors of a life stitched together from what, at one point, had seemed nothing more than mismatched scraps and broken lines. Stepping back, you see there had been a design all along, and a designer.

At that moment, standing in a shaft of late-day sunlight that bounced beams of light off the sparkling windowpanes, and made the paint on the door glow a brighter shade of red, I was happy. I turned around and looked up into the sky. "Thanks," I said. "For all of it."

I wouldn't always be happy; I knew that. Things would change, whether I wanted them to or not. My line would be broken again and again. But now my line intersected with others. I had companions for the journey, and whatever we faced in the future, we would face together, each a part of a bigger design, bound by a single thread.

I slipped the key into my pocket, then walked across the cobbled courtyard, onto the sidewalk, where stubborn tufts of grass pushed their way through the cracks, and up the street to join the people I love, my friends.

Author's Note

Dear Reading Friend,

Having written three works of historical fiction, the prospect of penning my first full-length contemporary novel was somewhat daunting. My biggest concern was this: could a plot involving ordinary people, living in ordinary times make for compelling reading? Well, it turned out that, for me, the answer is a resounding, "Yes!"

The village of New Bern, Connecticut, and the people who live there have become very real, very interesting, and very dear to me. When I close my eyes, I can picture every shop on Commerce Street, every blade of grass and bench on the Green. As it turned out, my biggest problem in writing A SINGLE THREAD was that I didn't want to see it end. I feel like I could write about this town and these people for years to come. If it turns out you like these characters as much as I do, then perhaps I will.

I hope you'll drop me a note or an e-mail to let me know how you enjoyed A SINGLE THREAD. I'd love to hear from you. My mailing address appears below and my website, *www.mariebostwick.com,* has a contact form for e-mails. While you're there, please check out the special features including my blog, book excerpts and discussion guides, recipes, tips for writers, my "latest crush," photo album, and much more.

Visitors who register as one of my "Reading Friends" have access to special features, can post in the forum, and are automatically entered in my monthly Reader's Contest. Also, Reading Friends get personal invitations for my appearances in their area that may be exchanged for a special gift when we meet.

Oh! And I'm very excited about this special bonus for my Reading Friends who are also quilters! Remember the "Broken Hearts Mending" quilt that Liza, Margot, and Abigail made for Evelyn? Well, a very talented friend of mine, Chris Boersma Smith, has designed a pattern for that quilt. Registered Reading Friends can write me to request a downloadable pattern for free! It's a lot of fun to make. I've sewn one myself and will have a picture of it posted in my online photo album. **But, please remember, this free gift is only available via computer and only to my registered Reading Friends.**

While you're on my website, click the link to Chris Boersma Smith's site or go directly to *www.reapasyousew.com* to find information on spiritually centered quilting retreats hosted by Chris and other talented quilters.

Thank you again for joining me on this visit to New Bern. I hope you enjoyed the journey as much as I did!

Blessings,
Marie Bostwick

Marie Bostwick
PO Box 488
Thomaston, CT 06787
www.mariebostwick.com

A SINGLE THREAD

Marie Bostwick

ABOUT THIS GUIDE

The following questions are intended to
enhance your group's reading of
A SINGLE THREAD.

DISCUSSION QUESTIONS

1. In Marie Bostwick's novel, *A Single Thread*, Evelyn Dixon is a Texas housewife, who in a matter of days must not only vacate her marriage but also her home. If the circumstances of life called for you to leave your home and move quickly, where would you go? How would you cope? What would scare you about the situation? What would excite you?

2. A quilter of more than 25 years, Evelyn likes the exacting precision her hobby requires. But she also revels in the fact that if 100 people were to quilt the same pattern no two of their quilts would be exactly alike. What do we know about Evelyn because she is a quilter? How would you elaborate on her view of quilting as a metaphor for life?

3. After only a few hours in New Bern, Evelyn realizes she feels more at ease in the New England town than she ever did in her planned suburban development. Do you believe certain places can speak to us? Can you recall a place where you immediately felt at home? Do you know why?

4. When Evelyn ventures into the old brick storefront that will become Cobbled Court Quilts, she doesn't really see the grime or the broken windows or the water stains on the walls. Instead, she envisions how the tiny window panes would gleam if washed and how inviting the front door would be with fresh red paint. What allows some people, like Evelyn, to see the possibilities in life—and not be overwhelmed by the negatives? Is there danger in having such a world view? Can you remember one time when you saw potential in something (or

someone) that no one else did? If you took action on your feeling, what happened?

5. Newly divorced, financially fragile, and of an age when some would say she should be sitting on a Florida beach worrying about her grandkids, what possesses Evelyn instead to open a quilting shop—in a new town no less? Is she brave? Foolhardy? Is there something you've always wanted to do or try? Would the people in your life cheer you on? Or brand you delusional? Is it ever too late to pursue your dream?

6. Abigail Burgess-Wynne, the matriarch of New Bern, appears to be popular, pragmatic, and in total control of her life. If she were not a wealthy woman, willing to support many local causes, do you think she would be as popular? Is her popularity only a factor of what she (and her money) can do for others? What could possibly make her so resistant to her niece's cry for help? What do we risk when we pin someone else's sins on another?

7. Why does it take Evelyn so long to realize that Charlie Donnelly is smitten with her? Do you think the challenges to her health had anything to do with her lack of awareness of his feelings? Have you ever been unaware of someone's feelings for you, and what did you do when you finally realized those feelings?

8. When Charlie makes his duck confit and Evelyn hosts her quilting classes, some would say they are just "trying to make a living." But as Charlie tells Evelyn, there are about 200 easier ways to do that. Pushed, Evelyn admits she dreamed that her store would spawn a community of quilters. Where do

you find community in your life? What do we gain through community?

9. Three of the scariest words in the world: You have cancer. After Evelyn hears them, she breaks down not with friends but before three strangers. Why? What is the most unusual situation in your life from which you ultimately made a friend? If you have had cancer or have known someone battling cancer, what did the experience teach you? What would you share about this six-letter word?

10. Abigail may appear chilly, materialistic, and controlling, but Evelyn believes the brittle shell houses a compassionate soul. In fact, she believes the same holds true for the rebellious and prickly Liza Burgess. What would cause Abigail and Liza to hide—even deny—such a positive quality about themselves? Have you ever put up walls in your life, then rued the decision?

11. Too often we believe we are loved for our breasts or our muscles, our looks or our hair, when ideally we all want to be loved for the cocktail of qualities that makes us, well, us. What are your perennial, unchanging qualities—both good and bad, quirky and mundane, silly and serious?

12. Life doesn't promise that we will always be happy, but Evelyn manages to piece together what she needs to face the journey: a group of loyal friends. Name three things that would help you through the ups and downs of life.

Don't miss Marie Bostwick's next "Cobbled Court" novel,
coming from Kensington in Summer 2009!

Read on for a special sneak peek . . .

Prologue

The intake counselor is young, blond and pretty and nervous. I can tell.

She keeps pressing the top of her ballpoint pen with her thumb as she fills in the forms—name, children's names, date of birth, and the rest—tapping the top of her pen several times after she writes down my answer to each question. The clicking sound reminds me of those cheap, plastic toy castanets Bethany had. She used to put the Nutcracker Suite on the stereo, grab her castanets, put her arms over her head, and clack them together, twirling in a circle to the Spanish Dancer song. She loved those things. Now I wish I'd thought to bring them but there wasn't time. So much had to be left behind.

The counselor sees me looking at her hand with the pen in it, laughs, and admits what I'd already suspected. She is new on the job, just finished her training. In fact, I'm her first client, well, the first one she's handling completely on her own. I smile a little, which she takes as encouragement but the truth is, I'm smiling at my own good fortune. Her inexperience will make this easier.

"Congratulations," I say. "It must be exciting to be starting a new job."

She nods. "It is, but it would be more exciting if jobs like mine weren't necessary." She shrugs. "But, anyway, let's get back to you. You're from Pennsylvania? That's a long way. How did you end up in New Bern?"

I take a breath, deep but not too deep, and, keeping my eyes focused evenly on hers, pausing now and again as if to collect my thoughts, not wanting to sound rehearsed, I tell her the story I have prepared in advance, the details I've worked out carefully in my mind, the revised history I quizzed Bethany on before we arrived, reminding her that if she got confused or nervous, she should just say nothing. After all she's been through, silence is a perfectly understandable response for a child. No one will question her reticence.

The counselor bobs her pretty blond head sympathetically, bends over her clipboard now and then, taking notes. She believes me. I can see she does. And I am struck by how easy it is. The lies just slip from my lips like thread from a spool and she believes every word I am saying.

It chills me to think how good I have become at this, at getting people to see only what I want them to see.

But then, why wouldn't I be good at it? I've had so much practice.

And it isn't like my life is a complete fabrication. It's close to the truth, but just not close enough.

I married at eighteen. I have two children I love. Bethany is six. Bobbie is eighteen months. All this is true and the rest of it is almost true.

We were almost a happy family.

But that word is a chasm, an abyss that separates happy families from everybody else. Almost. I wonder if she understands that, this newly minted intake counselor, fresh from training on the care and feeding of women in crisis? She wants to understand, I can see that, genuinely wants to help but something about her, something about the smooth shape of her forehead and the crisp ironed creases of her trouser leg makes me know she is merely an observer, standing on the edge of the chasm and peering into it. She has not been in the valley herself and probably never will. I hope not, for her sake.

That too, makes it easier for her to take my story at face value. She won't investigate it and I have all the paperwork, or enough of it, to prove my claim. I am who I say I am—Ivy Peterman. But what I don't tell her is that I never changed the name on my driver's license and social security card after I married. Maybe I forgot to. Or maybe, deep down, I knew it would come to this one day. But, whatever the reason, I have the documents to prove that I am me.

The rest of the story—the true parts, that my husband abused me for years and that my children and I have been bouncing from emergency shelter to emergency shelter for months now; the almost true parts, that we've got nowhere else to go; and the lies, that my husband was killed in a construction accident—she accepts without question. Even with her training, training that surely included careful admonitions not to buy into the stereotypes of victims of domestic violence as being poor, powerless, and poorly educated—in other words, not like people this woman lives next door to, not people from nice suburban neighborhoods, or even wealthy ones, with neatly trimmed hedges and late-model SUV's in the driveway—part of her still finds it easier to accept my story precisely because it feeds into the stereotype: poor teenage girl marries a boozing, battering, blue-collar boy she thought would be her salvation and didn't realize what she was getting into before it was too late. She finds it easy to believe because it's almost true and because she *wants* to believe it. The whole truth would hit too close to home, send her to the phones and files to verify my background, but this? It doesn't even cross her mind to check my facts. I can tell.

She smiles and gets up from her desk, excuses herself for a moment and promises to be right back.

Maybe, if I wanted to, I could stay here for a while. This seems like a nice town, filled with nice people like the woman who's the intake counselor. She's just a couple of years younger than me. If I lived here, maybe we'd be friends, go to the movies or shopping. Do the things that girlfriends do. It would be nice to have a real friend, someone who wouldn't back away even if they knew the truth about me, to stay here for a long time, to live here, maybe forever.

No, I remind myself. That can't be.

If she knew the true me, she would back away. And we can't stay here. Not forever and not for long. Even if I'm right and the counselor never checks out my story, or if I'm wrong and she eventually does, it doesn't make any difference. We'll be gone before the truth comes out. We have to.

If we stay too long in one place, he's bound to find us. It isn't safe to stand still. But if I'm careful. Then maybe? For a while? I'm so tired of always looking over my shoulder, of carrying my life and my children's lives stuffed into a suitcase constructed of half-truths, and only as large as can be fit into the trunk of my Toyota.

The office has plush carpets and well-oiled hinges on the oak doors. I'm lost in my thoughts and don't hear the counselor when she comes back in the room.

"Mrs. Peterman? Ivy? Are you all right?"

The sound of her voice startles me, jars me back into the moment, into the quiet room with the soothing yellow walls, high ceilings, and thick, dark wooden molding around the window frames. An elegant room. More like the conference room in a fancy hotel than a counseling office in a women's shelter.

"Yes," I smile apologetically. "I just lost my train of thought. Guess I'm tired."

The counselor tips her head to one side, murmurs sympathetically. "I can imagine you are. Don't worry about it. We're almost done here." She puts the clipboard down on her desk and sits down again. "Then we'll get you and the children something to eat and see you settled in for the night."

"You can take us? Tonight?"

My surprise and pleasure is genuine. Most of the shelters we've been to in these last weeks and months have been packed and we had to wait for a day or two or five, living in the car while waiting for a space to open up. I can't quite believe what she's saying.

"You've got a room open in the shelter right now?"

She nods, pleased that I am so pleased. She has gone into this line of work because she wants to help and she beams when she tells me the truly amazing news, like she's handing me a wonderful and unexpected gift, and it's true; she is.

"Even better than that. I just talked to our Assistant Director. We have an opening in the Stanton Center. Not tonight, but soon."

I look questions at her and she goes on to explain. "The Stanton Center is an apartment building for women and children who have been victims of domestic violence, the home of our transitional housing program. You can stay there for up to two years while you're getting back on your feet. Initially, you can live there rent free, but we'll encourage you to find a job as soon as possible and then we'll charge modest rent that's a percentage of your earnings. While you're there, we can offer you vocational, financial, and psychological counseling, and child care." She grins, waiting for me to say something, but it takes me a moment.

"Really? A real apartment?" Tears fill my eyes. I can't stop them.

She nods. "A real apartment. There's a nice community room where we hold special meetings and programs for the residents and a playground with a swing set and slide for the children.

"It's in a secret location, no sign in front, and a good security system so residents feel safe. Of course, since you're a widow, you don't have to worry about that so much, but the other residents have fled violent relationships and we do everything possible to make sure their abusers can't find them. It's like a safe house."

I blink hard, willing back the tears, trying to stay composed, not to let her see the effect those words have on me—safe house. It has been so long since I even dreamed of such things.

"So?" She asks cheerily, already certain of my response. "What do you say? Would you like the apartment?"

"Yes," I whisper. "I would. Thank you."

"Good!" She stands up and nods, indicating that I should follow her. "You're tired. I'll come over and finish the paperwork tomorrow, after you've had a chance to settle in a bit."

She opens the door and leads me through the three right turns of the corridor that will lead us to the playroom that backs up her counseling office, talking as she does. I'm still in shock, able to offer only short responses to her commentary.

"Of course, you're not required to accept any of the counseling services we offer to residents, but I do urge you to take advantage of them as much as possible—even the group counseling sessions. Your abuser can't hurt you anymore, but even so, the effects of domestic violence can stay with you long after the abuse ends. The counseling sessions can help you work though that and I think you'll appreciate the chance to develop relationships with women who've dealt with similar problems."

"Yes. I'm sure you're right," I say, knowing that I'll never go to even one of those group sessions. I'm not going to get close to those women. I'm not going to get close to anyone.

"Good." She looks back over her shoulder, pleased that I agree. She is a good person. I feel bad for deceiving her.

We have arrived at the playroom. She puts her hand on the knob and turns to me before opening the door. "You must be on a lucky streak."

If I am, it would be the first time in a long time.

But, then again, this kind, well-meaning woman just told me she has a place available for us. A safe house. Tonight. Now.

Somewhere in this beautiful little town where there is room for us.

Maybe she is right. Maybe, at last, my luck is changing.